F REIGN AFFAIRS

Simmering sensuality...

Far-away fantasies...

The world's most eligible men!

Dreaming of a foreign affair? Then, look no further!
We've brought together the best and sexiest men the
world has to offer, the most exciting, exotic locations
and the most powerful, passionate stories.

This month, in *Island Pleasures*, we bring back two
best-selling novels – one by spicy Modern Romance™
author Susan Napier and another by Caroline
Anderson who writes compelling, emotional novels
for Medical Romance™ and Tender Romance™. It's
sizzling seduction on an island paradise... And from
now on, every month in **Foreign Affairs** you can be
swept away to a new location – and indulge in a little
passion in the sun!

Be swept into the sands and seduced by a sheikh in
DESERT DESIRES
by Sophie Weston & Barbara McMahon
Out next month!

SUSAN NAPIER

Susan Napier was born on St Valentine's Day, so it's not surprising she has developed an enduring love of romantic stories. She started her writing career as a journalist in Auckland, New Zealand trying her hand at romantic fiction only after she had married her handsome boss! Numerous books later she still lives with her most enduring hero, two future heroes – her sons! – two cats and a computer. When she's not writing she likes to read and cook, often simultaneously!

Look out for more books by Susan Napier in Modern Romance™!

CAROLINE ANDERSON

Caroline Anderson has the mind of a butterfly. She's been a nurse, a secretary, a teacher, run her own soft-furnishing business and now she's settled on writing. She says, 'I was looking for that elusive something. I finally realised it was variety, and now I have it in abundance. Every book brings new horizons and new friends, and in between books I have learned to be a juggler. My teacher husband John and I have two beautiful and talented daughters, Sarah and Hannah, umpteen pets and several acres of Suffolk that nature tries to reclaim every time we turn our backs!' Caroline writes for Medical Romance™ and Tender Romance™.

Don't miss *A Very Single Woman*, Caroline's brand new Medical Romance™, available in June 2002!

island
pleasures

SUSAN NAPIER & CAROLINE ANDERSON

BESIDE THE SPARKLING SEA...

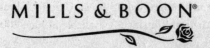

MILLS & BOON®

*MILLS & BOON and MILLS & BOON with the Rose Device
are registered trademarks of the publisher.
Harlequin Mills & Boon Limited,
Eton House, 18-24 Paradise Road, Richmond, Surrey, TW9 1SR*

Island Pleasures © Harlequin Enterprises II B.V., 2002

A Lesson in Seduction and *Captive Heart*
were first published in Great Britain by
Harlequin Mills & Boon Limited in separate, single volumes.

A Lesson in Seduction © Susan Napier 1996
Captive Heart © Caroline Anderson 1998

ISBN 0 263 83186 8

126-0402

*Printed and bound in Spain
by Litografía Rosés S.A., Barcelona*

island pleasures

A LESSON IN SEDUCTION

CAPTIVE HEART

A LESSON IN SEDUCTION

SUSAN NAPIER

CHAPTER ONE

'LEAVE the *country*?'

Rosalind Marlow stopped pacing up and down the hearth-rug in her parents' elegant lounge and stared at her mother in consternation.

'Just for a little while, darling,' Constance Marlow murmured placidly, finishing her cup of tea and settling back on the couch, looking quite unruffled by her daughter's outraged expression. 'Until some of this dreadful fuss dies down.'

'Are you suggesting I *run away*?' Rosalind demanded incredulously, her slender body stiffening in rejection of the idea of such rank cowardice. She and her five siblings had been brought up on the credo that one must always face up to one's responsibilities, no matter how painful or embarrassing. Surely her mother wasn't now suggesting that she compromise her honour for the sake of simple expediency?

Rosalind looked to her father to share her outrage, but he merely gave an expressive shrug, as if to say he was but putty in her mother's hands. Which, of course, he was...but only when it suited him. As a distinguished director with over thirty years' stage experience Michael Marlow was gifted with an unerring ability to control the volatile personalities of the egocentric actors and actresses who cluttered his professional and personal life—his famous wife included.

'Think of it as taking a timely holiday, darling,' her mother murmured in her beautifully articulated drawl. 'You must admit it's absolutely ages since you had a proper one.

And after what you went through on that last job you certainly deserve a relaxing break.'

Rosalind shuddered at the memory of her recent, depressing foray into film. The disaster-plagued production had merely served to confirm her inner conviction that, like her mother, she was born for the stage rather than the screen. She liked to think of herself as versatile enough to tackle anything but she had never really enjoyed the disjointed, repetitive nature of acting for the camera, where everything was done in short snatches and some nameless editor in a booth somewhere controlled your ultimate interpretation of a role.

She should never have allowed herself to be flattered into accepting the female lead in the art-house production but the director, an old drama-school friend, had caught her at a weak moment and persuaded her that it would be 'fun' to work together again.

Some fun. Rosalind had cracked a wrist doing her own stunts and had almost been eaten by sharks!

'That's not the point,' she argued, raking her fingers through her short-cropped red hair, making it stand fierily on end, a vibrant contrast to her pale skin and black rollnecked sweater. 'It's the principle of the thing. Why should I let myself be driven into exile, for goodness' sake? I haven't done anything *wrong*!'

'Of course you haven't, darling,' her mother soothed, looking hurt at the implication that she didn't trust her own daughter.

Rosalind simmered with frustration. She knew that her mother was playing shamelessly on her sense of guilt but she had made a promise and not even for her family's peace of mind was she prepared to break it. However, she couldn't blame those she loved for trying to winkle out the truth.

'Even if you had, you know you'd have our unqualified

support,' commented her father quietly, making her feel even worse.

'I'd tell you if I could,' she burst out. 'You'll just have to accept my word that I haven't done anything to be ashamed of!'

Her eyes avoided the coffee-table, which was strewn with tabloids bearing lurid headlines that variously branded her as a promiscuous sex-kitten, a butch, feminist home-wrecker, a pathetic, mixed-up waif with an insatiable craving for the love denied her by her disapproving family, and a helpless tool of an alien conspiracy to topple the governments of earth!

'I thought we'd already agreed on that,' murmured her eldest brother from the window-seat, turning his broad back on the entertaining sight of his wife trying to keep up with their three aggressively active toddlers in the rambling back garden of the large town house. Hugh pinned Rosalind with his thoughtful gaze. 'But unfortunately the Press aren't quite so trusting. By refusing to answer questions, you've left them free to speculate without the hindrance of having to conform to the known facts.'

Rosalind scowled, her thick, dark-dyed eyebrows drawing sharply together. 'I gave them a statement; that should have been enough. You're a lawyer; can't I take out an injunction or something, to stop them harassing me?'

She slouched with unconscious grace over to the front window and peeked through the curtains. Sure enough, the gaggle of reporters who had been tailing her relentlessly for the last week was still clustered around the gate. Her wide mouth firmed. She was damned if she was going to allow them to hound her into giving them what they wanted.

At least they were no longer knocking on the door and shouting questions through the keyhole, thanks to Hugh's threats to have them arrested for trespass. His hefty size and cold grey stare had added to the deterrent and not for the first time Roz had blessed her parents for having the lucky foresight to adopt a child who had developed into such an impressive specimen of adult masculinity. The natural Marlow offspring were all tall and slender, more accustomed to using charm than muscle to extricate themselves from trouble.

Hugh shrugged his massive shoulders. 'Possibly, although even if successful all a court order would do would keep reporters at a certain physical distance; it wouldn't stop them digging around for information or photographing you in public. In fact it would probably be counter-productive—make the Press even *more* tenacious. They could counter-claim that the public interest in this case transcends your need for personal privacy because of the political implications—'

'But what happened had nothing to *do* with politics!' Roz wailed, infuriated by the unfairness of it all.

'A politician's wife is involved; that makes it political,' Hugh corrected her with his precise, pedantic logic. 'With an important by-election coming up, all sides are going to be quick to try and use the publicity to their advantage, and while I don't doubt that the Government is as keen as you are to see the story die a discreet death it certainly can't be seen to be interfering with the freedom of the Press.'

'Well, I don't see how my running away is going to help,' said Roz, her green eyes sparkling with ire. 'People are sure to think it's because I'm guilty of *some*thing.'

'So what? They think that anyway,' came another unwelcome brotherly opinion. Sprawled full-length on the floor beside the couch, Richard was genially fending off an assault by two miniature versions of himself.

'Look, Roz, take it from one who knows—all this hide-and-seek is merely whetting the Press's appetite and if you won't oblige them with a scandal they'll create their own. You're God's gift to the tabloid industry, you know: a well-known actress with a reputation for wild behaviour and a sexy body that photographs like a dream. All they have to do if the story threatens to lose impetus is to snap another shot of you in a skimpy dress getting in or out of a cab or threatening to deck another reporter and—presto—instant page three! They love chasing you around…you give such good press.'

'Mind your tongue in front of the children, Richard,' his mother chided, rapping him sharply on one up-raised knee.

He grinned irrepressibly, looking much younger than his thirty-one years. He dragged himself up to a sitting position, gently wrestling his sons off his chest. 'Face it, Roz, they're not going to just give up and go away, not while you're dangling yourself tantalisingly under their noses. It's going to get a lot worse before it gets better and the rest of us are bound to suffer along with you.'

His sweeping gesture took in the various members of the Marlow clan who had arrived for what Rosalind had been led to believe was a quiet afternoon tea with her parents. Instead she had found the house bulging with her siblings and their partners and offspring. In fact, the only ones missing from the council of war were her rock-composer brother, Steve, who was currently in Hollywood working on a film score, and her youngest brother, Charlie, who was a mechanic with a race-team on the overseas rally circuit.

For the most part Rosalind was grateful that she came from a close-knit family with a strong interest in each other's well-being, but sometimes their loving interference only complicated matters. Right now she didn't need the extra pressure that they were bringing to bear on her battered self-confidence.

The trouble was that her family still saw her as the over-impulsive, fun-loving and, OK, outright reckless creature that she had been in her teens. Why couldn't they accept her as the mature, capable, staunchly independent twenty-seven-year-old woman she had become? Granted, her basic personality hadn't changed; she was still outgoing and gregarious, throwing herself wholeheartedly into everything she did, and some people might mistake her passionate enjoyment of life for recklessness, but her family should know better.

In the last five years the disciplines and rewards of her profession had become the major focus of her prodigious energies. Because her loyalty, once given, was rarely withdrawn she still had some wild and loose-living friends, but it had been years since she herself had had to be rescued from the consequences of her own folly.

She glanced over to the corner where Olivia sat with her husband, Jordan Pendragon.

Normally she could rely on having her twin firmly on her side, but today Olivia seemed oddly reserved. Like Richard and Steve, Rosalind and Olivia were only fraternal twins, but they had always been closely attuned to each other's emotional wavelength. Olivia's marriage the previous year hadn't seemed to jeopardise their closeness and thus it was disconcerting for Rosalind suddenly to discover herself deprived of the psychic support she had always taken for granted.

Olivia's dreamy, abstracted air was nothing new—as an artist she frequently went around with her head in the clouds—but Rosalind had the feeling that this time the mental aloofness was deliberate, and it hurt. Everything around her seemed to be shifting, changing, veering dangerously out of her control. It was no wonder her nerves were a riot.

'I'm sorry, I had no idea that this was going to turn out to be such a mess,' she sighed, thrusting her hands into the pockets of her skin-tight jeans, her slender shoulders hunching under the thin black sweater. 'The whole thing's been blown up way out of proportion…all because some greedy hotel employee took it into his head to sell his distorted version of events to the highest bidder!' she said bitterly. 'Why can't people mind their own business?'

'People figure that since you make your living in public you *are* their business,' said Richard unsympathetically. 'You're not the only one under siege. My office phone line is tied up handling the constant press calls and I'm fed up with granting interviews that turn out to be a total waste of time...not to mention having to hire security guards to keep reporters away from my cast and crew.'

'I thought you believed that all publicity is good publicity,' said Roz, with a pointed look from Richard to his wife which reminded him of the way he had flagrantly used the gossip columns to manipulate Joanna into accepting his proposal.

'When it's about me, yes,' Richard said deadpan, and with outrageous immodesty, making Joanna put a hand across her mouth to stifle her laughter. 'But they're only gatecrashing my set to ask about *you*...why haven't I cast you in one of my films? Is it because I think you're unstable? Do you have drug/alcohol/attitude problems...what kind of breakfast cereal did you eat as a kid? I tell you, it's driving me nuts! I'm running behind on my shooting schedule as it is; the last thing I need is any more disruptions on the set.

'Do you know we actually filmed five takes of a scene yesterday before I discovered that one of the dead bodies was a reporter from the *Clarion* who had bribed one of the extras to let him take his place? The idiot kept breathing and blinking. Apart from not being able to act, he wasn't even a member of Equity. He could have got me in trouble with the union, for God's sake!'

Of course, she might have known that Richard was more concerned about his precious movie being completed on time than her problems! Rosalind glared at him as he unsuccessfully tried to detach the two red-headed babies from his now woefully stretched woollen jumper.

'Now, Sean, stop sucking Daddy's sweater; you'll get

fur balls,' he scolded. 'You too, David; you don't *have* to do everything your brother does…'

As usual his twin sons ignored his stern command and continued to gum the soggy wool, until their mother gently uttered a word and they began to crawl obediently in her direction. Richard watched them go with a rueful smile that acknowledged a higher domestic authority. He scrambled to his feet, wincing slightly at the pressure on his lame knee, and turned his attention back to Rosalind.

'If you genuinely want to deflect press interest the simple solution is to remove yourself as a potential source of information. Disappear completely for a while…at least until the initial feeding frenzy is over. It's not as if you have to worry about walking out on your job,' he added with cheerful malice, 'since you don't happen to have one at the moment…'

'I'm currently resting between engagements,' Rosalind informed him loftily. It was a point of pride that she had hardly been out of steady work since she had left drama school. 'I'm considering several offers—it's just a matter of deciding which one to accept.'

'But you said yourself that none of them start for a few weeks, darling.' Her mother pounced. 'So why not make the most of your free time until then? Your father and I know the *perfect* place for you to go—peaceful, warm, exotic and—best of all as far as you're concerned—wonderfully remote.'

'It's not an island, is it?' said Rosalind with deep suspicion. 'I think I've had enough of remote islands for one lifetime.'

The film she had just completed was supposedly set in just such an idyllic-sounding location. However, the cast and crew had found themselves virtually camping out on an extremely rugged dot in the South Pacific, in wretchedly primitive conditions and beset by all manner of hardships, including erratic delivery of supplies, a subtropical cyclone and Rosalind's terrifyingly close encounter with a shark while filming the underwater scenes.

Needless to say, the budget had been horrendously over-run, and Rosalind had been relieved to get back to New Zealand with body and soul intact, only to walk slap-bang into a situation of almost equal peril.

'Oh, you'll love this one,' her mother assured her. 'Your father and I had one of our honeymoons there a few years ago. We simply *adored* it. A jewel of a place. Gorgeous scenery, gorgeous weather. A perfect refuge from reality.'

'And exactly where is this perfect jewel?' asked Rosalind morosely, unwillingly tempted.

'Tioman Island!' announced her mother with a vocal flourish that invited applause.

She must have forgotten that geography had always been Rosalind's worst subject at school.

'Is it somewhere around the Great Barrier Reef?' she guessed, thinking that if she *had* wanted to wimp out and hide from her avalanching problems Australia would hardly be far enough!

Joanna, the teacher, looked pained. 'It's in the South China Sea,' she said helpfully.

'Oh, right...' Rosalind closed her eyes as she tried to visualise Asia in her head, but her overtaxed brain refused to co-operate. All she could see against the blackness were wretched images from Room 405 at the Harbour Point Hotel in Wellington...Peggy Staines's anguished, pleading face, her body writhing in pain on the crumpled double bed, the frantic actions of the ambulance crew and the avid cu-riosity of the hotel staff and guests who had seen Rosalind in her bathrobe dazedly gathering up the scattered bank-notes from the floor.

'Off the east coast of Malaysia, north-east of Singapore.' Her father gently reorientated her.

'You *must* have heard of it, darling!' her mother urged. 'It's quite famous. They shot parts of *South Pacific* there.

Remember Bali Ha'i…remember the waterfall? That was filmed on Tioman. Just imagine being able to visit it for yourself…'

Rosalind's eyes flew open. She loved vintage musical movies. She had a good singing voice and had appeared on stage in a number of musical productions, *South Pacific* included. She vividly remembered the waterfall scene from the movie and her interest quickened, much against her will.

'If it's famous then it's probably packed to the gills with tourists,' she said stubbornly. 'I hate tourist traps.'

'Funny how I couldn't drag you away from Disneyland when you came and stayed with me in LA,' murmured Richard, who had lived and worked in the film capital for several years before he'd turned from acting to directing.

Rosalind poked her tongue out at him. 'Disneyland's different.'

'So is Tioman,' her mother said hurriedly, before sibling raillery could subvert the conversation. 'There are a few resorts but the island's still pretty much uncommercialised, and the pace of life is very slow. There's no stress, there's no crime…it's somewhere you can feel wonderfully safe and anonymous. Even a free spirit like you, Roz, wouldn't feel hemmed in. You really need to see it to appreciate it. I think I just happen to have some brochures around here somewhere… Now where did I put them…? Michael, do you see them?'

She looked around vaguely, absently retucking a loose strand of red hair into her elegant French twist. Rosalind watched suspiciously as her father obediently took his cue and 'discovered' the large stack of travel folders conveniently on hand under one of the newspapers on the coffee-table.

Her suspicions were strengthened by the flagrant enthusiasm with which everyone fell on the glossy brochures. Alluring descriptions of virgin rainforest and white coral beaches were read aloud with typical Marlow panache, the delights of scuba-diving in limpid tropical waters and the merits of Malaysian cuisine discussed. Even the babies drooled in ecstasy over the bright, colourful pamphlets that Richard thrust into their pudgy fingers, although that was probably more to do with the fact that they were teething!

'It says here that there are references to Tioman in Arabic literature that date back two thousand years…' murmured Hugh, perusing a hard-back book that had a stamp on the cover indicating that it had come from the library. Something else her mother had just happened to have on hand? Rosalind didn't think so!

'You know, you don't even need a visa to visit Malaysia,' said Olivia, reading the fine print on the back of a brochure. 'Your passport's current, isn't it, Roz?'

'Of course it is. Roz is used to travelling light. She can take off at the drop of a hat, can't you, darling?' her mother encouraged.

Rosalind thought it was time to put her foot down and inject some reality into the situation.

'Even if I *was* thinking about taking a trip, if this place is so wonderful there's no way there'd be vacancies for spur-of-the-moment travellers,' she said firmly. 'And flights up to the East have wait-lists for their wait-lists. Anyway, I haven't budgeted for any extravagances this month…'

Although Rosalind had inherited a considerable trust fund several years ago, she preferred to live mostly off her own earnings. Large amounts of money made her uneasy. She had no head for figures and small amounts slipped far too easily through her fingers for her to trust herself with serious sums.

Besides, the theatre had a strong historical tradition of poverty amongst its acolytes and it went against the grain to flaunt her unearned prosperity when most of her fellow actors were eking out their meagre pay cheques in a noble state of self-sacrifice for their art. So apart from the occasional rush of blood to the head Rosalind lived a life of cheerful self-sufficiency, content in the knowledge that when she was too old and decrepit to tread the boards she would be able to retire in dignity and comfort.

'Credit me with a little forethought, darling,' said her notoriously disorganised mother. 'As soon as I realised you might need a quiet little bolt-hole I got Jordan to use some of his family's muscle. He still has pull in the Pendragon Corporation and he's made all the arrangements for you through their travel section. Of course the economy flights were overbooked but you're going first class all the way, and don't look like that—you don't have to worry about the cost—I booked everything on your father's credit card...even on Tioman you only have to sign for your accommodation and meals.

'Look, here are all your tickets and documentation. All you have to do is turn up at the airport the day after tomorrow and you'll be on your way to three weeks of carefree bliss.'

Rosalind accepted the proffered blue travel folder numbly, opening it as gingerly as if it were a potential bomb. 'You've already *booked* for me to go?' she said shakily, leafing through the evidence, her eyes widening at the sums involved. She didn't know whether to feel pleased or insulted by her parents' generosity. 'What do you expect me to say?'

Her mother smiled warmly and jumped up to give her a hug. 'No need for thanks, darling. We know how determined you are to stand on your own two feet, but at times like this the family should pull together...'

Rosalind struggled free of the fond maternal embrace. 'Pull together?' she snorted, waving the tickets under her mother's elegant nose. 'You're *bribing* me to go thousands of miles away!'

'We thought it would be a nice early birthday present,' her father ventured.

'My birthday isn't for seven months!' Rosalind pointed out sardonically.

'A *very* early birthday present,' Constance Marlow said, giving her husband a repressive look that told him not to deviate from the script.

She shrewdly studied her daughter's sullen expression and abruptly changed her tactics. She threw up her hands in disgust and said crisply, 'Oh, for goodness' sake, Roz. Talk about people blowing things out of proportion! Stop behaving as if you think we're trying to sweep a blot on the family escutcheon under the carpet.'

She ignored the disrespectful snickers of her offspring at the atrociously mixed metaphor and continued with steely emphasis, 'We're very *proud* to have you as our daughter; we just don't want to see you hurt unnecessarily. And it *is* so unnecessary, darling, what you're putting yourself through. Unless you *like* playing the helpless martyr, of course—then I suppose there's nothing more to be said. I might say that most children would be *delighted* if their parents offered to send them on an all-expenses-paid holiday...'

'I know I would,' said Richard with a languishing sigh.

'I see the Met Office predicts a cold front this weekend,' said Michael Marlow, apropos of nothing. 'They say winter is going to arrive with a vengeance.'

'Tioman does look wonderfully lush and Gauguin-ish,' said Olivia traitorously, her soft, rain-washed green eyes wistful, her smile tinged with strain.

It struck Rosalind that it was her twin who looked as if she needed a holiday, and it was on the tip of her tongue to say so. She glanced at Jordan and found him watching his wife with a narrow-eyed concern that stilled the words in her throat. She felt a flutter of inexplicable panic and her fingers tightened on the tickets in her hand.

'You know, you should make the most of your freedom while you can, Roz,' advised Joanna, rescuing a soggy rusk from the carpet. 'Once you have children, taking a holiday is like going on military manoeuvres.'

As if on command, Hugh's three pre-schoolers came thundering into the room, their diminutive blonde mother breathless in their wake.

'Oh, you are going to Tioman, then? Good on you!' Julia panted, seeing the folder in Rosalind's hand. 'I told Hugh you'd do it, even if only to cock a snook at those sneaky reporters. You know, one of those gossip columnists followed us to the supermarket yesterday and tried to chat up Suzie when I left the trolley for a moment in the confectionery aisle. The idiot even offered her a lollipop.' She ruffled the curly brown head leaning against her knee. 'Luckily Suzie blitzed him with her favourite word.'

Suzie blinked up at Rosalind, her blue eyes huge in her doll-like face. *'No!'* she bellowed proudly. 'No! No! No! *No!'*

Julia chuckled. 'She made such a racket that the guy had a hard time convincing everyone he wasn't a child-molester. I bet *that* put a crimp in his column!'

'He's lucky I wasn't there; I would have put a crimp in his face,' growled Hugh, whose gentleness was known to be in direct proportion to his size.

Rosalind smiled weakly, stricken by the thought that her uncompromising stance might have put the trusting innocence of her nephews and nieces in jeopardy. Typically, she had been so swept up in her own problems that she had taken her family's support for granted, without thinking how much it might cost them in terms of their own privacy.

Her certainty that she was doing the right thing by standing her ground dwindled further. Perhaps she *should* just abandon her principles and run for the hills…or rather the South China Sea.

It seemed such a callous thing to do while Peggy Staines still hovered between life and death in the intensive care unit at Wellington Hospital. But it wasn't as if Rosalind could provide any positive help for her recovery. Quite the reverse—knowing that she was around might cause Peggy to have another heart attack.

A brief word of sympathy with a distracted Donald Staines in the hospital waiting room was all that Rosalind had permitted herself. He had asked what had happened but not why, and Rosalind had caught a plane back to Auckland before he or any of the other members of the Staines family had rallied sufficiently from their shock to ask for the details. Until Peggy had recovered enough to carry on a lucid conversation—*if* she recovered—Rosalind was bound by her conscience to remain silent.

Thank goodness the police hadn't become involved, although Rosalind had the sinking feeling that if the publicity continued to escalate either they or someone involved in national security might feel obliged to come sniffing around with some serious questions, and then she might have no choice but to betray her conscience.

'Well, what do you say, darling?' her mother asked eagerly, visibly frustrated by Rosalind's lack of enthusiasm. 'I can't believe you're even hesitating…'

A disturbingly familiar tension began to crawl around the back of her skull as Rosalind looked into the expectant faces around her. A paralysing sense of her own vulnerability swept over her, but she knew she mustn't allow it to dictate her actions. She couldn't let the fear win.

Surprisingly it was Jordan who came to her rescue. Her brother-in-law rose to his feet, dominating the room with his muscled bulk, almost dwarfing Hugh.

'I think we should back off and let Roz make up her own mind in her own time,' he said with the ease of a man confident of his authority. 'She'd probably like to go home and think things over without the rest of us breathing down her neck.'

Rosalind cast him a grateful look and he continued smoothly, strolling over to take her by the elbow, 'Why don't I run you back to your apartment now, Roz, so you can do just that? Here, take these with you.' He scooped up a handful of brochures and thrust them into her free hand, and picked up her embroidered tote bag from a chair, looping it over her shoulder.

'You can leave your own car here as a decoy,' he said. 'The reporters won't bother to follow me if they see me leave alone. You can nip out over the back fence and through the neighbours' gardens and I'll drive around the block and pick you up in the next street.'

'Uh, but I'm going to need my car later,' said Rosalind, disconcerted by the unexpectedness of the offer and the firmness of the grip steering her towards the door. Although Rosalind and Jordan were cordial to each other, she had always been very careful to maintain a cool distance between them that had precluded friendship. Out of the corner of her eye she could see Olivia observing her husband's urgency with a worried crease of suspicion on her smooth brow.

'Richard or one of the others can drop it over to you later.' Jordan brushed aside the feeble protest. 'At least it'll give you a temporary respite from all the unwelcome attention you've been getting.'

The idea of a few hours' respite from the bloodhounds outside was undeniably appealing. 'Well…I suppose…OK, thanks.' She dug her heels in and skewed round to look over her shoulder. 'Uh, are you coming, Olivia?'

'Olivia wants to stay and chat with Connie, don't you, kitten?' Jordan cut in as his wife opened her mouth. 'We're going back to Taupo tonight and with her exhibition coming up she might not get the chance to visit again for a while…'

There was a hasty flurry of startled goodbyes as Rosalind found herself hustled out into the hall.

'For heaven's sake, what's the big rush?' she hissed as

Jordan practically pushed her out the back door. 'Did you see Olivia's face? She looked awfully suspicious…'

'Maybe she thinks you're going to try and seduce me again,' said Jordan sardonically, blocking the doorway as she made a tentative effort to go back inside.

Rosalind, who never blushed, went hot at the reminder of one of the most mortifying encounters of her life. 'That was all a horrible mistake and you know it,' she gritted fiercely. 'I didn't know you two had even met when I pretended to be Livvy…and anyway, nothing happened—'

'Quite. There's zero physical attraction between us. I know it, you know it, and Olivia certainly knows it. After all, even when I thought you were her and *wanted* you to turn me on, you failed miserably.'

'OK, OK, I get the picture,' Rosalind grumbled, jerking her elbow out of his grip. 'But I might point out the failure was completely mutual.'

He grinned, his odd-coloured eyes warming with laughter. 'True. So now we've finally got that out in the open maybe we can relax around each other. Olivia is beginning to worry that we intend to keep up the pussyfooting for ever.'

Rosalind grinned back, relinquishing the last vestige of embarrassment which had constrained her natural, exuberant friendliness. 'Well, I guess if you can accept your total lack of sex appeal, so can I,' she teased with deliberate ambiguity.

'Big of you,' said Jordan, ignoring the overt provocation. 'Do you need a boost over that wall, or can you make it yourself?'

At five feet nine Rosalind wasn't used to men treating her as a wisp of delicate femininity and she reacted with her usual bravado to the implied challenge. Waiting in the quiet cul-de-sac on the other side of the neighbours' property a few minutes later, she brushed off her painfully grazed palms with a rueful acknowledgement that at her age maybe she should start thinking about putting dignity before daring.

Jordan's car turned out to be a macho four-wheel drive, scarcely less attention-grabbing than Rosalind's beloved fluorescent green VW, but, as he had predicted, the journalists outside the Marlows' gate had let him go unhindered when he had forced his way through the gauntlet of their questions.

'So…what's the real reason why you offered me a lift?' asked Rosalind quietly as they cruised towards the city. 'Don't tell me it was just to clear the air between us. You could have done that any time. It's something to do with Livvy, isn't it? Why she was looking so…*pulled* back there at the house…'

She watched Jordan's big hands tighten betrayingly on the wheel, highlighting the nicks and scars that were the legacy of his work as a sculptor.

'She's pregnant,' he said baldly.

The words hit her like a sharp blow. Rosalind's ears rang and she felt a chill across the base of her skull and tasted metal on her tongue.

'Pregnant?' she whispered. She felt a floating sense of utter separation. Olivia. Her sister. Her twin…the other half of herself…was going to have a *baby*…contribute to the growing brood of Marlow grandchildren?

Rosalind was shocked…and more; emotions boiled through her that she didn't dare examine too closely.

'I thought she didn't want a family yet,' she said, when she could get her stiff mouth to work. 'She said she wanted to concentrate on her painting—'

'I know,' Jordan's voice was clipped and slightly grim. 'We agreed we were going to wait a few years…but fate evidently had other plans for us. Olivia found out last week—she's still trying to come to terms with it herself; that's why she doesn't want to tell anyone just yet… No one else in the family knows and she wants to keep it that way for another few weeks. Apart from her own ambivalent feelings, there are one or two early warning signs, like elevated blood pressure, that the doctor is nervous about…'

Rosalind sensed rather than saw the sidelong look that Jordan gave her as he continued carefully, 'It's a little too soon to confirm it, but the doctor suspects from his physical examination that it could be twins…'

Twins. Of course, given their family history, it was only to be expected, but Rosalind's sense of shock deepened. Livvy, the mother of not one child but *two*. The buzzing in her ears increased and she put her hand over her clenching stomach in sudden awareness. 'Livvy's been having dreadful morning sickness, hasn't she?'

'Yes; how did you know?'

Rosalind's mouth twisted. 'I've been a bit nauseous myself every morning for the past couple of weeks. I thought it was just nervous tension, or something I picked up doing that wretched film. The food was quite dreadful…'

Pregnancy was the one thing that she *had* firmly been able to rule out from her self-diagnosis. Oh, God! Her skin prickled with fresh horror. What if she had to suffer these shadow symptoms all through Olivia's pregnancy? What an unspeakable irony that would be…

'Well, Olivia's been as sick as a dog and the doctor's advised as little stress as possible in the next few weeks,' said Jordan bluntly. 'That's why I was hoping that you'd graciously accept Connie's offer. It would mean one less source of emotional turmoil for Olivia. If she thinks you're frolicking happily in some nice, safe tropical haven she might stop beating herself up that she's abandoning you in your time of need…'

'So much for your wonderful idea of whisking me away to make up my own mind in my own time,' said Rosalind, her sarcasm hiding a leap of relief that here was a cast-iron, honourable excuse for running away from her problems. If Livvy had a miscarriage, Rosalind would never forgive herself if there was even the slightest possibility that she was a contributing factor.

Jordan gave a rueful shrug. 'I didn't want to push it too strongly in front of Olivia. She wouldn't thank me for trying to protect her, especially if it compromises her loyalty to you. If you don't go to Tioman, Olivia intends to ask you to come and hole up with us at Taupo, even if it means dragging along your press contingent, not to mention your other little problem…'

Rosalind stiffened, her fingers clutching the seat as he suddenly swung sharply into a parking spot beneath the warehouse that housed her inner-city loft. 'What other problem?'

Jordan switched off the engine. 'You have so many you don't know which one I'm referring to?' he murmured, shaving much too close to the truth for her liking. 'I'm talking about the fan who's been making such a nuisance of himself.'

'Oh.' Aware of his shrewd eyes on her face, Rosalind tried not to reveal any of her turmoil as she probed warily, 'Olivia *told* you about that?'

She couldn't help a trace of outrage creeping into her voice, although, come to think of it, she had only asked that her twin not tell their parents, or their over-protective brothers.

'We *are* married, Roz,' said Jordan drily, effortlessly picking up the nuances. 'That's what marriage is all about—sharing a life, listening to each other's secrets and worries. Olivia said you tried to treat it as a joke but the mere fact that you brought the subject up made her think you were a lot more concerned than you let on, and the tenor of some of the guy's letters disturbed her. She thought they could be interpreted as stalking letters, said that he wrote as if he believed he had a personal relationship with you, one that gave him some sort of a claim on you…'

'I told her I get lots of fans writing to me off and on—'

'But this Peter is very persistent, Olivia said. You told her it had been going on for several years, and that lately he'd escalated from an occasional letter to one or two a week, never with a full name or a return address. He boasts of going to extraordinary lengths to see your performances and even claims to have met you several times at public appearances, though he apparently never identified himself.

'Olivia said she didn't like the obsessive nature of his interest, especially as he knows where you live. She said you had extra locks fitted at your apartment because you were uneasy when he started sending gifts as well as letters. She also thought that one of the reasons you took that film job in such a hurry was because you hoped he might lose interest if you weren't performing live any more…'

'Well, it was better than her idea of involving the police,' Rosalind muttered, shuddering at the thought. 'They probably would have laughed in my face…there was nothing in the letters that was overtly threatening. Anyway, I've thrown most of them away,' she said truthfully, hoping that would put paid to the subject. 'As I told Olivia, the best way to handle these things is to ignore them.'

'Mmm.' Jordan's face was sceptical. Rosalind had the sinking feeling that she had just acquired another over-protective relative.

'Nothing arrived while I was away,' she pointed out. 'Maybe he's finally given up.'

'And another sudden sojourn out of the country might be the perfect way to discourage him even further,' Jordan said smoothly. 'It's either that or the police, Roz—or I could get someone from the Pendragon Corporation's security section to provide you with personal protection while a private investigator tracks this guy down and turns him inside out.'

Rosalind blanched at the implications. 'Me, with a body-guard? God, can you imagine what the Press would make of *that*?' She threw up her hands, hastily conceding defeat.

'You're something of a pirate, aren't you, Jordan? I suppose if I *don't* allow myself to be blackmailed into going I'll find myself shanghaied...'

'There's little I wouldn't do to ensure Olivia's well-being,' he agreed blandly, but with irrefutable honesty.

'Oh, all right!' At least he was allowing her to save face by pretending that she was doing this for her sister's sake, rather than her own. 'If I'm going to be shanghaied, I suppose I may as well make the most of it.' She grinned, her eternal optimism fizzing back to the surface. 'I might even find my own form of protection. Who knows? I might run into my *beau idéal* in paradise, a man ''gentle, strong and valiant'' who'll romance me under the tropical stars and pledge his heart to me for ever! Or, failing that, I'll settle for a gorgeously tanned beach boy who can make me laugh!'

CHAPTER TWO

ROSALIND stood impatiently tapping her scuffed cowboy boot as she watched the man dithering at the check-in counter.

He was tall and thin, his thick, straight, mid-brown hair flopping over his forehead as he bent over to attach the tags to his two suitcases with fumbling fingers. He had a distracted, disorganised air that had Rosalind immediately pegging him as some sort of head-in-the-clouds academic, one of those people who were sheltered by their narrowly focused intellects from the real world—or perhaps he was a computer nerd, she thought as she noted the laptop he was carefully guarding between his feet. The jacket of his dark pin-striped suit fell open as he leaned forward and she saw the pens and folded spectacles tucked into the breast pocket of his white shirt. Ah, *definitely* a nerd!

Whoever he was, he was holding her up. Didn't he realise that first-class passengers didn't expect to have to *queue*? They were supposed to breeze in and out while staring down their noses at the lesser mortals lining up at the parallel desks.

She glanced around the terminal. She was anxious to be out of the public arena and into the relative privacy of the first-class lounge as soon as possible. She had got this far without being spotted, by dressing in androgynous jeans, baggy shirt and denim jacket and shaggy blonde wing *à la* Rod Stewart under a dark fedora.

She had swopped places with Olivia the previous night and knew her regular pursuers were being well and truly led off on the wrong trail, but news organisations often employed stringers or informants at airports. In her boyish guise she hoped that no one would give her a second look, but the longer she stood around, the greater the risk of being accidentally rumbled before she boarded her seventeen-hour flight to Singapore.

The check-in clerk pointed at the weighing machine beside her desk but instead of obeying her polite instruction the man leaned forward to mumble something, patting absently at his pockets.

Rosalind's impatience burst its bounds. Stepping around a polite Japanese couple, she tapped the laggard briskly on the shoulder, lowering her naturally throaty voice an extra notch.

'Hey, mate, she's asking you to put your luggage onto the weighing machine.'

'What?' The man turned his head and his body followed, straightening with an uncoordinated jerk that caused him to almost fall over his laptop. Colour streaked across his high cheekbones as Rosalind snickered.

He was younger than his fussy mannerisms had led her to expect—about her own age, Rosalind guessed. His dark olive skin was unlined, and as he raked back his fine, straight hair with well-kept fingers he revealed an exaggerated widow's peak bisecting a smooth, deep brow. His face was narrow, his steeply slanting dark eyebrows peaking to sharp commas just beyond the outer corners of his eyes, giving his expression a strikingly devilish cast. However, the look in his dark brown eyes was anything but satanic. They were wildly dilated, watching with blank consternation as Rosalind snatched up one of his bags and plonked it onto the platform.

'She can't process you until you weigh your luggage,' Roz told him, her own eyes shooting impatient green sparks at him from under the brim of her hat as he made no attempt to follow her example. He was certainly slow on the uptake. If it hadn't been for that computer she would have thought he was two bricks short of a load. Or maybe he was simply foreign, and didn't understand what was being asked of him.

He cleared his throat. 'Uh…I didn't think weight mattered for first-class passengers…' he murmured vaguely, his mild New Zealand accent immediately shattering her theory.

Rosalind's impatience drained away to be replaced by amused condescension. He was obviously a complete greenhorn.

'The airline still has to know what total weight the plane is carrying,' she pointed out. 'If you're packing elephants with your underwear they might have to shed a few economy passengers to accommodate your eccentricity.'

'Yes, yes, of course,' he muttered, not a glimmer of a smile touching his narrow mouth. She might have known he'd have no sense of humour. He continued to stare at her with the glazed abstraction of a man whose brain was temporarily otherwise engaged. To Rosalind, used to provoking sharp male awareness of her femininity, his lack of reaction was further proof of the effectiveness of her simple disguise. There were quite a few Shakespearian heroines who disguised themselves as boys, and Rosalind had played most of them with great gusto. She knew that gender confusion was largely a matter of body language.

She hooked her thumbs through the belt-loops of her jeans and widened her stance. 'Well?'

He blinked warily at her challenge. His lashes were surprisingly thick, veiling a subtle shift in his expression. 'Well what?' he asked guardedly, his fingers clenching convulsively around the blue travel folder he carried in his left hand.

His white-knuckled tension indicated that he was braced for some sort of scene. Did he think she was angling for a tip? Rosalind rolled her eyes and picked up his other suitcase. It was hefty enough to make her grunt, but her lithe body had the strength demanded by her profession and after staggering slightly she heaved it onto the platform next to the lighter bag.

'It was supposed to be a joke about the elephants,' she commented, panting slightly as she stepped back, tilting her chin to look up at him. 'What have you got in there, anyway?'

'Uh…books,' he said, still in that same thready voice adrift with uncertainty.

It figured. Her gaze swept the empty floor around his immaculately shod feet and a mischievous impulse prompted her to stoop for the case between his polished shoes.

At last she got an unequivocal reaction. 'No! Not my computer!' he exploded, grabbing it up and cradling it protectively against his chest like a baby. 'I'm carrying it on with me.'

So he *could* move faster than snail's pace when he wanted to! Rosalind grinned and tipped him a mocking salute on the brim of her hat.

'So it's just the two cases going through, then, is it, Mr James?' asked the airline employee with marked patience.

He didn't turn his head, seemingly hypnotised by Rosalind's cocky grin. 'Uh, well, I think…'

'He means yes,' Roz supplied firmly. She began to suspect that his air of muddled confusion presaged a man on the verge of panic. Perhaps the poor lamb was afraid of flying and was trying to put off the evil moment.

'Mr James? May I see your passport now, sir?'

'Passport?'

Rosalind decided it would be quicker for everyone if she took charge of the bewildered Mr James.

'You *have* remembered to bring it with you, haven't you?' she demanded, stepping up beside him at the desk. 'Is it in here?'

She plucked the blue folder out of the hand clamping the laptop to his chest and flicked it open to see an impressive wad of US traveller's cheques tucked behind the clear plastic pocket. He made a choked sound of protest and she gave him a chiding look to reassure him that she wasn't a thief. In the other side of the pocket was a slim dark blue cover stamped with the New Zealand coat of arms. She extracted it and, adroitly avoiding his belated attempt to snatch it back, presented it across the desk.

'Do you have any preference for seating?' she asked him, pushing the travel folder back into his hand as the woman leafed through his passport.

'I beg your pardon?' he said, his dark eyes flicking over her face in that irritatingly unfocused way, as if he still couldn't quite believe that she was helping him.

'You know—front seat, back seat, nearest the emergency door...that kind of thing?' she clarified.

'Emergency door?' he echoed, with a swift frown.

The frown had the decidedly odd effect of slanting his wicked eyebrows even more satanically without raising a ruffle on the angelically pure forehead. She wondered idly whether his personality contained as many contradictions as his face. He was actually rather good-looking in a limp-around-the-edges kind of way. At least a woman wouldn't need to fear being dominated by the force of his personality!

'Look, don't you worry about it, chum. Just leave everything to me.' She gave up trying to involve him in the decision-making process and negotiated his boarding pass without further consultation, thrusting his departure card and returned passport at him as the formalities were completed and nudging him away from the desk so that the Japanese couple could take his place.

'Well, go on, then,' she said to him, when he seemed inclined to hover inconveniently. 'You can toddle off to the departure lounge now.'

He didn't appear to recognise a brush-off when he heard one. 'Um, I thought I might wait for you...we could have a drink together—or something…' He trailed off vaguely, flapping his free hand in the air.

Or something? Rosalind studied him with sudden suspicion. Had he guessed that she was a woman, or did he think he was issuing an invitation to a pretty youth? Maybe that little-boy-lost helplessness was a sexual rather than psychological signal. Either way it was up to her to disabuse him.

'I wasn't trying to pick you up,' she said flatly. 'I helped you out because I felt sorry for you, not because I fancied you.'

He sucked in a sharp breath, a rush of blood darkening his skin. 'I wasn't—I didn't mean—'

His outraged stammer almost made her relent. Her initial impression had been right: harmless, prissy, easily embarrassed. But she still needed to get rid of him before she presented her own documentation. Under the country's privacy laws, airline personnel were forbidden to give out information about passengers, but if the woman mentioned her name out loud she didn't want anyone close enough to overhear.

'Good.' She cut him off, pointedly turning her slender back on him. 'Because I'm not interested.'

'I only wanted to thank you for coming to my assistance,' he said rigidly, and she grinned to herself at the hint of grit in his milk-shake voice. Maybe he wasn't such a hopeless wimp after all.

She didn't answer, and after a moment was relieved to hear him moving away. The trouble with helping lame dogs was that they had a lamentable tendency to want to cling to their rescuers.

After she had checked in she headed for the duty-free shop where she spied Jordan browsing amongst the perfumes. He was flying out to Melbourne on a short business trip related to an arts foundation created by Pendragon

Corporation and had conveniently saved Rosalind the taxi fare to the airport.

Their discussion of a couple of days ago having eased her awkwardness in his company, Rosalind gave in to impulse and crept up behind him and whispered menacingly in his ear. 'Poison!'

'Do you think so?' he murmured, withering her with his lack of surprise at her sudden ambush. 'I rather think that Livvy would suit something lighter, fresher...maybe Yves St. Laurent's Paris?'

As usual he was right. Rosalind waited while he bought the perfume and they chatted briefly before Jordan's attention was suddenly riveted elsewhere, his eyes slitting as he gazed intently over her head.

'What's the matter?' asked Rosalind, her overstretched nerves jumping. 'Who is it? A reporter?'

Jordan put a heavily reassuring hand on her shoulder as he shook his head. 'No, no—just someone I know from the old days at the Pendragon Corporation. I'd better go and have a word with him before he comes over and expects to be introduced.' He kissed her absently on the cheek, eyes still focusing beyond her. 'Have a good trip, won't you? And for God's sake try not to attract your usual quota of trouble!'

Rosalind bristled at that, and spun around as he left, intending to send him on his way with a few blistering words of self-defence, but at that moment she caught sight of the James man amongst the swirl of people in the public departure area. He was easily picked out—he looked isolated and alone in the midst of groups hugging and kissing their farewells. She hurriedly turned her back and skulked off to bury herself in a magazine in the relative privacy of the first-class lounge.

Rosalind didn't fully relax until she was on board the plane with the engines powering up. The first-class section was only half-full, which meant that those travelling alone had the added privacy of an empty seat beside them. Rosalind's assigned seat was an aisle one and she had decided to wait until they were airborne before she shifted to the window.

'Excuse me, Miss Marlow, would you like me to store your hat in the overhead compartment?'

'Thanks.' With a straight face Rosalind doffed her wig along with the hat, enjoying the flight attendant's classic double take. They both broke into chuckles and the hostess's mask of impersonal politeness was banished by the relaxed warmth of their shared moment of humour.

Rosalind's natural optimism raised its battered head. She suddenly felt freer than she had in a long, long time. No stresses, no awkward questions, no responsibilities. Maybe this holiday was just what she needed to get her life back on its former smooth-running track.

She sighed with satisfaction as she ruffled her flattened hair into its normal spiky style and accepted the suggestion that she might like a glass of champagne as soon as the flight took off. She stripped off her jacket and rolled up the sleeves of her green shirt, revealing a slender gold bangle on her left wrist.

Glancing at the seats diagonally behind her, she saw the ineffectual Mr James wrenching his seat belt unnecessarily tight, his mouth flat and grim, his precious computer sitting on the empty aisle-seat beside him. He was wearing dark-rimmed spectacles that gave his face a top-heavy look. Maybe it had been myopia rather than mental confusion that had led him to look at her so blankly in the terminal.

He was looking at Rosalind rather than concentrating on his task, and she judged from his frozen expression that he had seen her little performance with the wig and heard her womanly giggle. Evidently he wasn't a theatre-goer, because there was no sign of slack-jawed recognition or avid curiosity in his regard, only cold disapproval, and Rosalind's sense of liberation increased. She gave him a provocative, feminine smile and a flutter of her dark lashes and he scowled, a muscle flickering in his cheek, his skin taking on a betraying colour. She had never known a man whose complexion was such a tell-tale barometer of his emotions.

As the stewardess swished past on the way to strap herself in for take-off, Rosalind attracted her attention and murmured, 'He's probably too embarrassed to mention it but I think Mr James back there might be a first-time flyer with a touch of phobia.'

The stewardess looked discreetly over her shoulder and made a swift professional assessment. 'Hmm, he does look a bit white around the mouth, and that case of his should be stowed away...' Her voice took on an unprofessional lilt of mischief. 'Cute, though. Maybe I'd better sit by him and hold his hand for take-off...'

She suited her action to her words and Rosalind couldn't resist watching the man's disconcerted expression as the attractive young woman stowed his computer and bent over to adjust his lap-belt before slipping into the vacant seat beside him and enveloping his hand in a manicured grasp. She said something to him that made his head jerk up. He pushed his spectacles up his nose and shot an accusing look in Rosalind's direction that was a surprisingly fierce mixture of frustration and annoyance. Rosalind beamed him a plastic smile. Ungrateful nerd!

Dismissing him from her mind, Rosalind settled in to enjoy the flight. She had never flown first class before and intended to take full advantage of the shameless pampering. Some of the pampering involved the liberal distribution of newspapers and magazines and Rosalind almost choked on her champagne when she spied a photograph of herself cavorting on the front cover of a local popular women's magazine. She quickly took it for herself and confiscated several other magazines that she suspected might carry news of her current notoriety in their pictorial gossip columns.

Unfortunately her clumsy attempt at censorship was thwarted by the fact that the other stewardesses were offering an identical selection to other passengers. Taking a furtive peep around the cabin, Rosalind was relieved to note that most of the others were selecting more edifying reading...business reviews and glossy fashion magazines... except for the wretched James man, who received a copy of every single publication and then proceeded to open the very one Rosalind was hoping would be beneath his intellect to notice.

Rosalind muttered to herself as she slid over into the window-seat, out of his sight-line. Maybe he wouldn't make the connection—the cover photo was years out of date, taken when she'd still had long hair. What kind of man picked a women's magazine as his first choice, anyway? And did he *have* to hold it up in such a way that his fingertips appeared to be tucked into an intimate portion of her bikini-clad anatomy?

Thinking she might as well know the worst, Rosalind thumbed open her own copy and read the three-page story, torn between anger and amusement to discover that it comprised euphemistically couched rumours of her bisexuality, supposedly dating from the time that she had 'eagerly' accepted a lesbian role on stage. There was an illustrated list of all the men with whom she had been 'romantically linked', which seemed to consist of every male celebrity with whom she had ever been photographed, and to that list was now added a gaggle of 'gal-pals'.

Turning the page in fascinated awe at the artistry of the inventions, Rosalind learned that she was now on the 'hot list' of a radical gay organisation that focused on outing famous people and that she was on the verge of accepting an offer to appear as the nude centrefold in a famous men's magazine.

Unfortunately this time it wasn't only her own somewhat tarnished reputation at stake. Thanks to the country's strict libel laws, there wasn't one mention of Peggy Staines, but she would obviously be in the mind of any reasonably informed person who read the story.

If only Rosalind hadn't agreed to meet Peggy at that hotel! If only Peggy hadn't insisted on such extremes of secrecy, even down to registering the room in the damning name of Smith. If only Rosalind hadn't been so stunned by the older woman's private revelations that she had ignored the first signs of her distress and then wasted precious time searching Peggy's bag for her medication instead of calling the emergency number straight away.

Rosalind struggled against a renewed flood of guilt. None of it had really been her fault, she reminded herself. She had made a few mistakes in judgement, that was all. She might have been a principal player in the drama, but she hadn't been its author. It was Peggy who had written the original script, and in spite of her sympathy for the woman Rosalind couldn't help resenting the fact that *she* had somehow ended up as the scapegoat in the tangled affair.

She stuffed the offending magazine into the pocket on the seat in front, determined not to brood. Rosalind's philosophy of life was simple: be positive. There was no point in agonising over actions and events that couldn't be changed. Self-pity got you nowhere but in the dumps. You had to keep moving forward, substitute 'if onlys' with 'what ifs' and regard each negative experience as character-building for the future rather than as a destructive barrier to present happiness.

With that firmly in mind Rosalind shucked her boots off in favour of the free airline bootees and prepared to eat and drink and make merry across several thousand kilometres of airspace. If she was going to zonk out on a beach for three weeks she had no need to worry about jet lag!

Her body, however, had other ideas. The stresses of the last couple of weeks and the strain of the past few months caught up with her, and after a superb dinner accompanied by a few more glasses of champagne Rosalind found her eyelids drooping and her mind pleasantly unravelling.

She snuggled under a down-soft blanket and fell asleep watching a movie she had particularly wanted to see, and when she awoke was disorientated to find herself muffled in total darkness. She fought her way free of the blanket covering her face and found that the cabin lights had been dimmed and almost everyone else was asleep. The attendants were murmuring in hushed voices in the curtained galley.

Feeling a pressing need, Rosalind stumbled blearily into the aisle, staggering slightly as the plane hit mild turbulence. Not quite everyone was asleep, she found as she groped her way sleepily towards the toilet. The James man's bent head was burnished by a pool of light, revealing glints of red-gold amongst the nondescript brown strands which had slipped forward to mask his tilted profile. As she passed his seat she saw that his laptop was open on his unfolded table and that in his hand he was holding...

'Are you *crazy*?' Rosalind lurched forward and snatched the object from him. 'Have you been using this?' she whispered, shaking the cellphone accusingly in his startled face.

'I—'

'Didn't you read the safety information? Don't you *know* it's prohibited to use portable phones on board planes?' she hissed.

'Well, I—'

Rosalind glanced around to see if anyone had noticed and crammed herself down into the seat next to him. 'They can play havoc with the plane's electronic systems,' she told him, speaking quietly so as not to disturb the sleeping passengers around them. But even in a whisper her classically trained voice retained its full range of articulation and expression. 'If anyone had reported you, you could be arrested as soon as we land...that's if you don't cause us all to crash first!'

His eyebrows rose above the straight line of his spectacle frames at her fiercely delivered lecture. 'Are you going to report me?' he asked curiously.

She was offended by the suggestion. 'Of course not!' She was still slightly muzzy with sleep but he looked disgustingly bright and alert as he studied her expressive face. For a fleeting moment she thought she glimpsed a smouldering rage in the dark eyes, but when he blinked it was gone and she decided that it must have been a trick of the light.

'There's no "of course" about it,' he said evenly. 'You might have found it amusing to get me into trouble with the authorities—'

Her snort of indignation was genuine. 'You must have a very odd idea of my sense of humour. I don't happen to think it's funny to mock the innocent.'

'Is that what you think I am? An innocent?' His mild voice sounded hollow, incredulous even. No doubt in his own mind he was a witty, sophisticated man of the world... The imagination had wonderful ways of compensating for one's personal inadequacies!

'Well, an innocent abroad, anyway,' she said, humouring him. 'It does rather stick out: you didn't know about not using portable phones...or about the check-in procedures, and you were practically falling to pieces with nerves at the airport—'

'Perhaps I was merely stunned speechless by your beauty.'

His sarcastic retort left her unruffled. She knew she wasn't beautiful in the classical, restrained sense but she had flamboyant good looks that most men found attractive and an innate sense of style. 'You thought I was a boy,' she reminded him smugly.

'Did I?' he murmured quizzically, leaning back in his seat so that his face moved out of the spotlight. Thrown into shadowed relief, his features were stripped of gentleness, imbued now with a brooding strength that seemed vaguely sinister. A man of dark secrets and intriguing mystery...

'You know you did,' she said, admiring the effectiveness of the illusion: comic relief as villain. She had always believed that lighting was more effective than make-up in creating a character and here was the proof.

He said nothing and she frowned, suddenly remembering the magazine he had been leafing through at the beginning of the flight. Her pride bristled. Damn it, if he was toying with her over the matter of her identity...!

'But you obviously know who I am now, right?' she challenged.

His eyes dipped to her breasts, which were barely visible under the loose drape of her shirt, and to the slender curve of her hips, spanned by a wide leather belt which emphasised the narrowness of her waist. His gaze travelled down further, to the cellphone resting on her upper thigh, next to where the snug V of her jeans was pulled flat across her pubic bone.

'Yes...you're obviously a woman.'

The stifled statement was somehow more flattering than a gush of admiring words. To her surprise Rosalind felt her body tingle as if he had physically touched her where his eyes had wandered. Usually perfectly comfortable under the most leering male appraisal, she hurriedly crossed her legs in an unconscious gesture of self-protection.

A woman. If all she was to him was an anonymous female then he hadn't paid much attention to that magazine, she thought with relief. He'd probably just skimmed over the glossy pages of celebrity clones before tossing it aside.

She looked at him through her lashes and received another small shock. Instead of politely averting his gaze, he had allowed it to linger on the deepened V created in her lap by her crossed legs, almost as if he could see the transparent emerald lace bikini briefs she wore beneath the sturdy denim. The muscles along her inner thighs tightened with a feathery ripple and she instinctively sought to shatter her unexpected self-consciousness with flippancy.

'Those aren't X-ray glasses by any chance, are they?' she joked, and his eyes jerked back to hers. 'Or are you going to confess they're just plain glass and you're simply a mild-mannered reporter?'

'I beg your pardon?' His eyes looked like polished jet— or perhaps it was just a coating on his spectacle lenses that made them look so hard.

'You know—like Superman?' He looked at her steadily and she let out a huff of disbelief. 'For goodness' sake, you don't have much of a grasp on popular culture, do you? What do you do for a crust?'

'Crust?'

She rolled her eyes. 'A living? What sort of job do you do?' She leaned sideways to peer at his laptop, to see if it would give her a clue. She glimpsed a busy clutter of characters before, with the swift tap of a single finger, he closed the file he had been working on, leaving the cursor blinking on a blank screen.

'Top secret, huh?' she teased, tilting her head back, the light flaring to fierce brilliance in her short cap of red hair.

'Something like that.'

She shrugged good-naturedly at the rebuff. 'Oh, well, we all have our secrets.'

'Some more dangerous than others.'

The idea that his vague and distracted manner was a cover for a life riddled with dangerous secrets tickled her funny bone. 'Ah, don't tell me…' Her voice dropped to a bare whisper as she rasped behind the back of her hand, 'You're really a spy travelling to the mysterious East on a secret mission of national importance!'

She ruined the blood-curdling effect with a husky chuckle. 'A spy's who's afraid to fly!'

His colour rose. 'I'm *not* afraid of flying.'

'Of course you aren't,' she said, deadpan. 'The stewardess only held your hand for take-off because she thought you looked cute.'

'*You* told her to do that,' he accused through his teeth.

'Oh, for goodness' sake, that was only because I knew you were probably too shy to ask for help. She came up with the "cute" all by herself—'

'Too *shy*?' He looked as if she had hit him over the head. Did he think it didn't show?

'Well, you must admit you don't have a very…um…*assertive* personality, do you?' she said tactfully, patting his arm. It felt surprisingly solid under the dark fabric. Unlike the other men in the cabin he had not removed his suit jacket but merely loosened his tie and a couple of shirt buttons. Through the sagging gap in the crisp white shirt she could see the smooth, surprisingly tanned skin of his chest. No hairy he-man he, she thought with an inner giggle.

'Not that there's anything wrong with being shy,' she continued as he glowered at her. 'A lot of women find that endearing in a man…you know, a nice change from the swaggering macho come-ons. You shouldn't feel embarrassed about asking for help when you need it, though. People respect you more for admitting your weaknesses than for trying to hide them behind a mask of false bravado. It takes courage to let people know that you're vulnerable—'

'I don't *need* anyone's help.' He interrupted her homily with an exasperated snap. 'I don't know where you get your ideas but I can assure you Miss—' He stopped abruptly and sucked in a sharp breath. 'Miss…?'

'Marlow,' Rosalind offered quickly, anxious that his sudden burst of self-assurance should not be undermined by a minor point of etiquette.

'Miss *Marlow*,' he accepted grittily, without a flicker of reaction to the name. 'I can assure you that if I am ever in need of assistance I am perfectly capable of arranging for it by myself!'

'Excuse me!' It was one of the stewardesses, speaking to Rosalind in a sternly admonitory tone. 'That's not a portable telephone you've got, is it?'

Rosalind sensed the man beside her stiffen, as if he expected her to leap at the chance to rat on him. He was probably honest to a fault. Left to himself he would doubtless pour out a full, frank and totally unnecessary confession.

'Yes, but don't worry, I'm not using it,' she said swiftly, with a winsome smile. 'Mr James here has been showing me his state-of-the-art travelling office. I was just holding this while he demonstrated some dazzling technical wizardry on his computer.' She cast him a look of patent awe before switching her attention back to the object of her persuasion. 'Naturally the phone is switched off,' she said, hoping it was. 'We're both well aware of the airline regulations.'

'Hmm, well, just to be on the safe side, perhaps we should remove the batteries to prevent it becoming accidentally operational.' The stewardess smiled, whisking it from her and deftly opening the panel. 'Oh, someone's done it already…'

A masculine arm brushed against Rosalind's breasts as the telephone was firmly retrieved by its owner. 'Yes, *I* did—prior to take-off. As Miss Marlow pointed out, I'm fully aware of the current regulations.'

'You might have told me,' Rosalind protested in chagrin as the stewardess glided away. She scrambled to her feet, acutely conscious that her breasts were humming from his unexpected touch.

'You didn't give me a chance to get a word in edgewise. You were having too much fun jumping to conclusions and patronising my ignorance,' he said sardonically.

Rosalind was tempted to flounce off, except that what he

said was perfectly true. Her green eyes sparkled as her mouth curved self-mockingly. 'I was, wasn't I?'

A twitch of his extraordinary brows showed that her ready confession was unexpected, and evidently unwelcome. 'You also lie extremely well,' he accused unsmilingly.

His chilly disapproval earned him a taunting little bow.

'''If I chance to talk a little wild, forgive me; I had it from my father,''' she said sweetly. The obscure Shakespearian quotation was certainly apt—she had learned much of what she knew about acting at Michael Marlow's knee...including how to make blank verse sound like modern, everyday speech!

He gave her a darkling look, as if he suspected that the lyrical apology was not her own and was frustrated by his inability to challenge her sincerity by quoting its source. She had already guessed that Mr James liked to be safely armoured head to toe in facts before he proceeded into verbal engagements.

Unable to resist rubbing his nose in it, she placed a hand over her heart and flaunted a more recognisable quotation. 'Ah, ''parting is such sweet sorrow'', isn't it, Mr James?' She batted her eyelashes shamelessly at him. 'But now I know that you're such a boringly well-organised individual I suppose I'll have to find someone else to patronise. Enjoy the rest of your trip. Ciao, baby.'

She turned and sauntered on her way, making sure she gave her hips an extra swivel just in case he was still watching.

He was, and it was fortunate for Rosalind's peace of mind that she couldn't see the expression on his face. It was a mask of cold-blooded calculation, the mouth a cruel, hard line of satisfaction, the eyes hot and hungry, seething with an unstable combination of unwilling admiration and reluctant contempt.

The bitter face of a man on a particularly unpleasant mission.

And who was determined to succeed.

CHAPTER THREE

ROSALIND clamped her shoulder bag to her side as she jogged across the shimmering tarmac towards the small, colourful, twin-propellered aircraft. A steamy, swirling Singapore wind whipped her hair into a red halo as she cast an angelic smile of apology at the uniformed airline officer standing beside the lowered steps at the rear of the fuselage. She had been deep in conversation with a young German tourist when she had realised she was going to be late for her connecting flight. She had made it with barely thirty seconds to spare!

The door was pulled smartly shut behind her, shutting out the baking afternoon sun, and Rosalind's smile swept around the narrow, nineteen-seat cabin before zeroing in on the gap halfway up the left-hand side of the aisle. She eased herself between the rows of single seats, scattering apologies as her bag banged protruding elbows, and crammed herself gratefully into her seat. She could see the pilot looking back through the open door of the cockpit and she gave him a cheeky thumbs up.

'You nearly missed the flight.'

Rosalind looked across the aisle into a pair of familiar, dark, disapproving, bespectacled eyes.

Oh, no! The insipid Mr James was a reminder of the country and complications she was trying to escape.

'Don't tell me *you're* going to Tioman too,' she blurted out as the plane began to vibrate with engine noise.

'No, I'll be parachuting out halfway there,' he said drily.

Considering that they were on a non-stop, terminating flight, his sarcasm was justified, but just as Rosalind was appreciating his glimmer of wit he spoiled it by adding

45

ponderously, 'That was rather reckless of you, cutting it so fine. You could have wasted your ticket.'

'Nonsense; I had it timed perfectly to the last second,' she lied airily. 'When you've flown as often as I have you'll realise that there's an art to minimising boring waiting times.'

'Right,' he murmured, eyeing her flushed complexion, slicked with perspiration from her dash to the plane, and the green shirt which clung in interesting patches to her dampened skin.

Rosalind rummaged in her bag and produced a moistened towelette which she used to blot her face, uttering a sensuous sigh of pleasure as the cooling alcohol evaporated on her hot skin. He was still in his suit, she noticed, although he had removed his jacket and tie as a concession to the heat; his ubiquitous laptop was jammed under his feet. Was he going to work all the way across the South China Sea, the way he had across the Pacific?

Curiosity—her besetting sin—got the better of her. If she was stuck with him as a seat companion for the next hour or so she might as well make the best of it.

'What a coincidence we're both going to the same place,' she remarked as the plane taxied down the runway. 'Are you going there on business or pleasure?' she asked, although she thought she knew the answer. Nobody went on holiday wearing a suit!

'You might say a bit of both,' he replied. One corner of his narrow mouth indented briefly, as if he was restraining a smile of grim anticipation. He obviously wasn't expecting to enjoy himself much on either score.

'And what exactly is your business? You never did say…' Rosalind trailed off invitingly.

He hesitated. 'I'm an accountant.'

'Oh…really?' Rosalind managed to keep a straight face but she quickly lowered her eyes, knowing they must be brimming with suppressed laughter. 'I never would have guessed.'

She didn't fool him one bit. His jaw stiffened. 'You find my profession amusing?'

'Of course not; accounting is a very serious, very honourable, highly regarded profession,' she said earnestly.

'Don't overdo it,' he warned her wryly.

She let him see her dancing eyes as she burbled, in a little-girl voice of breathless admiration, 'And so exciting, too. You must get a big thrill whenever you get your accounts to balance.'

His expression was stoical. 'My accounts *always* balance.'

He managed to make his conscientiousness sound like a threat. It was too much for Rosalind's sense of humour.

'So many thrills, so little time!' she giggled. 'No wonder you look so strung up. You have all the hallmarks of a workaholic. I won't ask you what your pleasure is; it probably has something to do with that laptop. I bet you have no idea how to really kick back and relax. Where are you staying on Tioman?'

When he named the resort her first reaction was amused resignation. So much for her flippant 'Ciao, baby'. It seemed that they were fated to run into each other.

'Me too.'

As the words left her mouth a nasty suspicion began to buzz crazily in her head. Ridiculous as it might appear, maybe coincidence had little to do with it...

'Are you following me?' she rapped out.

He looked so alarmed at the prospect that her brief attack of paranoia subsided as abruptly as it had arisen. He was an accountant, for goodness' sake! He wore a *suit*, and an expensively tailored one at that. All the tabloid journalists Rosalind knew—and she knew some of them on a first-name basis by now—dressed for comfort and climbing walls rather than for impressing their quarry with their sartorial elegance.

They didn't travel first class, either, and in the unlikely event of managing to persuade his tight-fisted employer to spring for a ticket no self-respecting hack would have piously waved away the free booze every time it was offered, as she had noticed Mr James do.

'I think you'll find I was the first person to check in for the connection and I was certainly on board this plane first,' he pointed out with the stiffness of outraged innocence. 'How could I possibly be following you?'

Quite. Remembering what her mother had told her about the underdeveloped nature of Tioman, Rosalind conceded that of course anyone who travelled first class would inevitably stay at the island's most luxurious hotel. She tried to smooth his ruffled dignity with a mischievous, melting look.

'Mmm. How indeed? Maybe *I'm* the one following you...'

He blinked rapidly, blurring the expression in his dark eyes. Rosalind noticed a small tick in his left temple and realised that her provocative reply had only made him even more uncomfortable. He jerked his face away from her scrutiny, glancing out of his window just as the nose of the plane lifted, his fingers gripping the armrest as the ground fell sharply away beneath them and they shuddered across the heatwaves rising from the city.

Rosalind looked at the white knuckles. Maybe it wasn't her teasing banter that had made him poker up so suddenly.

'Flown much in small planes, have you?' she asked with studied casualness, determined not to make the same mistake she had on the flight from Auckland.

He wrenched his gaze reluctantly away from the window and gave her a wary, sidelong look as if he still didn't know quite what to make of her. Did he expect her to pounce on him and start ripping his clothes off? Or perhaps he was afraid to admit his vulnerability because he thought she would mock his fears. She smiled kindly, encouragingly, determined to make up for embarrassing him with her absurd suspicions.

His eyes narrowed on her eager, enquiring expression.

'Not a great deal, no,' he admitted slowly, surprising her, for she had half expected a snub.

Rosalind beamed at him and adopted a bracing tone. 'Well, don't worry; the ride'll smooth out when we get up a little higher. And we'll leave the up-draughts behind once we get over the sea. The flight's not much more than an hour long. We'll be there in no time. If your ears start to hurt, suck one of these.' She whipped out a few boiled lollies from the fistful she had pocketed on their previous flight and held them out to him. 'Sorry if they've melted a bit but they're still in their wrapping so you won't get sticky.'

He accepted the peace offering, picking out the paper-sealed toothpick with the airline logo which had been hidden amongst the sweets and gravely handing it back.

'Surely you want to keep your souvenir, Miss Marlow?'

She grinned sheepishly as she dropped the toothpick into the breast pocket of her shirt. 'It's the bargain-hunter in me, I'm afraid. I just can't pass up a free offer. I can never leave a hotel room without making a clean sweep of the teabags and coffee sachets and the soap and little bottles of shampoo. Things like that are built into the room rate, you know, and they can be very handy when you're living on a budget.'

His eyebrows rose steeply. She was beginning to get rather fond of them. They were his most expressive feature.

'A very poorly balanced budget, Miss Marlow, that affords first-class travel but leaves you insufficient funds to buy the small essentials of life.'

She grinned at his professional criticism. 'I didn't say I *couldn't* afford them; it's only that I'd rather spend the money on other things. Actually, this whole trip is a gift. Normally I'm strictly a second-class traveller. And my name is Rosalind by the way. Most people call me Roz.'

No dawn of recognition crossed his expression, no glimmer of licentious speculation intruded into the clear dark gaze.

'Luke James.'

There was a pause, almost as if he expected *her* to recognise *him*. Maybe he was famous in accounting circles.

She prodded him further. 'I'm an actress.'

'I'm afraid I'm not much of a movie-goer,' he began politely.

'I work mostly in the theatre.'

'Or a theatre-goer either.'

'I did have a leading part in a BBC costume drama a few years ago—'

'I don't own a television set,' he said without regret.

'Oh. Well, I've done a number of radio plays—'

'I rarely have the radio on...'

Rosalind was stunned. How could someone of his evident education have no interest in or appreciation of the dramatic arts? Didn't he know that the theatre provided both a window and a mirror to humanity? How could he consider himself a well-rounded personality if he ignored such an influential part of his cultural heritage?

She scowled. Perversely, considering the lengths that she had gone to in the last twenty-four hours to avoid being recognised, she felt slighted by his complete lack of awareness of her talent. She wasn't overly big-headed, but she knew that she had earned every one of her glowing reviews. She worked hard and believed passionately in the importance of her craft. And yet here was a man who didn't even *care* about what she did, let alone how well she did it!

It was on the tip of her tongue to ask whether he read the newspapers, but she wasn't prepared to go *that* far towards betraying herself.

'Well, then, what *do* you do for entertainment?' she asked, hiding her chagrin.

'I don't feel the need for it. My life is very full.'

'It must be,' she said tartly. Full of work, she guessed disparagingly. Parades of dull, unimaginative figures marching across his computer screen. Her generous lower lip pushed out moodily, her green eyes darkening as she contemplated the philistine across the aisle. No wonder he didn't interact very well with people, poor lamb. He lacked the practice in sharing his emotions which was normally imparted by exposure to common cultural experiences. If variety was the spice of life, his must be singularly bland.

'I'm sure you're a very good actress.'

Her trained ear detected the dubious note in the comment that was obviously meant to mollify her.

'How would you know?' she pointed out sarcastically.

'Well...' He lowered his voice, his gaze fixed on her stormy face. 'You *are* very attractive...'

Rosalind bristled like a ginger kitten whose fur had been stroked the wrong way. 'What's that got to do with how well I can act?' she crackled.

'Uh, I...suppose it must make it easier for you to get parts,' he explained.

Did he realise what he was implying? Could those brown eyes really be as innocent and guileless as they seemed? Rosalind bristled even more fiercely. 'You mean sleep my way into them—is that what you're saying?'

Her bluntness had the desired effect. He blinked rapidly. 'Oh, no...I would never suggest such a thing. Uh, I'm sure you're a very respectable, very distinguished actress.'

Rosalind was as quick to forgive as she was to anger. She was aware of the irony, even if he wasn't. Her ire dissolved in a gamine grin.

'Now who's overdoing it? I think you must be confusing me with my mother. Dignity is not exactly my strong point and respectable I ain't! I will, however, concede that my *work* is respected.'

In case her wordplay was too subtle for him she added firmly, 'If I sleep with someone, it's because I want to, not because I have to. As far as I'm concerned, sex is not a marketable commodity.'

Surprisingly he neither blushed nor looked flustered by the raw revelation. One eyebrow flicked up. 'Your mother is also an actress.'

Given his cultural ignorance, Rosalind treated it as a question. Connie would have been mortified that he had had to ask. She had been playing leading roles for nearly four decades. The Marlow name was a byword in the New Zealand theatre. Rosalind felt honour-bound to defend the family pride in its accomplishments.

'Yes. Constance Marlow.'

She half expected him to look blank but instead he dipped his head in acknowledgement.

'You're one of *those* Marlows. Didn't your father receive a knighthood for services to the theatre in the last honours list?'

Where art failed, snobbery succeeded!

'Yes, he did.' The new title had been the source of some mirth as well as pride within the family, since Michael's bark had frequently reduced quavering young newcomers to calling their director 'sir' and Connie had been going under the affectionate theatre nickname of Her Ladyship for years.

'I suppose *your* mother is an accountant?' she teased, basking in the safety of her clan. As 'one of those Marlows' she was shielded from the infamy of her individuality.

Again that slow, assessing look. 'My mother died when I was a child.'

'Oh.' Rosalind's amusement was instantly tempered, her jewel-bright eyes softening sympathetically. 'I'm sorry. What a shock that must have been.'

Her vivid imagination sketched a picture of what he had been like as a child. He would have been a thin, clever, gentle little boy, too shy to attract many friends and, after the loss of his mother, probably even more insecure. She couldn't imagine Luke as the kind of self-confident dare-devil that her brothers had been...or herself, come to that.

Impulsively she spanned the aisle with her slender arm and placed her hand over the one lying on his seat-rest. The back of his hand felt cool and hard against her palm, as if the tanned skin were sheathing cold steel rather than warm muscle and sinew. Rosalind had somehow expected that an accountant would have hands that were soft and pampered. Maybe it was all that exercise on his computer keyboard that made his fingers feel as if they were capable of cracking walnuts!

Even more disconcerting, the hum of the aircraft was transmitted to her via her touch—a prickling vibration which shot from the point of contact right up the length of her arm, raising the fine hairs on her skin as if it were charged with electricity.

Luke looked down at the small, pale, delicate hand cuddled protectively over his.

Absorbed in her imaginative reconstruction of his orphaned boyhood, Rosalind missed the significance of the slight, premeditated pause before he added with stark pathos, 'It was an accident. My father died too.'

Her hand contracted, along with her tender heart, her fingers curling comfortingly between his. The engine hum in her arm increased to a steady tingle that spread up her shoulder and down over her collar-bone. 'You were an orphan? Oh, Luke...how awful for you. Do you have any brothers or sisters?'

He turned his head. She was leaning towards him, her vibrant restlessness momentarily subdued by the desire to comfort, her creamy skin pale with the intensity of her feelings, her beautiful eyes wide with anxiety and muted with sorrow.

All for a virtual stranger.

Where in the hell were her self-protective instincts? wondered Luke James with a savage dissatisfaction. Damn it, she was making this *too* easy...

Or was she? Luke had good reason to know that she wasn't as vulnerable and unsophisticated as her tender expression of compassion invited him to believe. Her apparent openness was an illusion. To an actress of Rosalind Marlow's calibre the lies would come tripping off the tongue. He might admire the act, but he didn't have to believe in it.

'No. No one.'

The tight-lipped answer touched a painful chord inside Rosalind. She couldn't imagine life without her large, loving family. The chord continued to resonate, reaching deep into the secrets of her soul.

She could see the awareness of his loss still there in the back of Luke's eyes, the ghostly reflection of an old bewilderment. And, behind that, an even deeper, colder, darker emotion that she couldn't identify.

'Relatives? Surely you had *someone*...?'

There was a palpable tension in the set of his shoulders. 'I was fortunate to be adopted,' he said tonelessly, sliding his hand abruptly out from under hers and placing it out of reach in his lap.

'I'm glad,' said Rosalind quietly, undismayed by his physical withdrawal. Some people were natural touchers and others weren't. The Marlows were an expressive lot, both physically and verbally.

'Everyone should have a family, don't you think? Even if it's an artificially constructed one,' she continued, her smile tinged with a fleeting wistfulness. 'It's our family that teaches us to expect love and trust and loyalty from those around us, so that when we go out into the world we're not afraid to pass on our trust to others, to admit that we're all interdependent...'

'Ask not for whom the bell tolls...' he murmured.

'Exactly! Although, actually, it's "never send to know for whom the bell tolls; It tolls for thee",' said Rosalind, a stickler for getting her lines right. She was delighted to find out that he had at least a passing acquaintance with poetry. Perhaps he was still redeemable. 'Have you read much John Donne?'

'Enough to misquote him occasionally. The remnants of a classical education.'

'Oh? Where did you go to school?'

He named a private boys' school, famous for its academic excellence and strict code of behaviour—also for the level of its fees. She wondered whether his parents' estate or his adoptive family had paid for his education.

'Were you a boarder?' she contented herself with asking.

'Yes, I was.'

He uttered the words with pride, but Rosalind thought that packing young children off to live in institutions was a barbaric practice and said so. She shuddered delicately. 'All the Marlows went to a state school, thank God, where we were relatively free to express our individuality. I could never have stood boarding-school. All those petty rules and restrictions. I would have rebelled simply on principle.'

'Your parents didn't set restrictions on your behaviour when you were a child? They didn't expect you to adhere to minimum standards of decency and self-control?'

There was a bite to his questions that made her a trifle defensive. The Marlow brand of home discipline might have been liberal but it had never been lax. 'Yes, of course they did, but their rules were tempered with heaps of love and humour and a very broad tolerance, and we weren't threatened with expulsion from the family if we did something wrong!'

'I was never threatened with expulsion either.'

'Probably because you never dared do anything wrong,' dismissed Rosalind knowingly. 'How did you manage in the dorm? Aren't boarding-schools filled with budding little sadists and thugs who lord it over everyone younger and weaker than themselves?' Her voice acquired a pitying husk. 'You must have suffered more than your share of bullying—'

'Must I?' he interrupted crisply. 'Why?'

'Well, you're not exactly built like a rugby player, are you?' she said frankly, giving him the once-over. As her eyes settled back on his face she noticed his heightened colour and the tell-tale rigidity of the muscles in his jaw and— Uh-oh, she must have bruised his masculine sensitivities!

'Actually you're a bit like my brother Richard,' she said hastily. 'He got picked on for being a gawky kid—all elbows and knees and a chest like a chicken—but he wasn't feeble by any means and the older he got, the more he appreciated his natural leanness. Women positively *drooled* over him when he got into the movies—'

'How very reassuring, but your concern for me is quite misplaced,' Luke said, with a cutting precision that rejected her backhanded compliment. 'I was never a particular target for bullying, nor, I'm glad to say, indiscriminate drooling, which sounds equally unpleasant.'

His words had more impact than he could know. Rosalind let her bright head drop back against her seat with a sigh.

'Oh, it is, it is,' she said moodily, thinking of all those salacious tales about her which had floated to the surface over the past week. She had once thought such rumours funny, hadn't minded people entertaining themselves with silly exaggerations about her sex life. But the joke had somewhat lost its savour when it had become coupled with the knowledge that somewhere out there beyond the spotlight was a faceless man who regarded her as his own personal possession, who was obsessively collecting every scrap of knowledge about her, watching, waiting, gradually shaping and fashioning her to fit his private fantasies, turning her from a person into a…a *thing* that he might one day come to claim, perhaps violently…

And because of that life would never be the same for Rosalind. She would never again feel quite as safe, never be quite as carefree and trusting as she once had been. Olivia had been frustrated by her twin's refusal to take Peter seriously, but Rosalind had always handled her fears and doubts by laughing at them, by holding them up to ridicule and contempt, because to do otherwise would be to admit that they had unreasonable power over her.

But this time her tried-and-true remedy had failed her. She had received a harsh lesson in helplessness that she had longed to repudiate. That was why she had gone streaking down to Wellington after that tantalising telephone call.

'We've never met,' the woman had faltered, after introducing herself only as Peggy, 'but I believe we have a mutual…friend—someone who's been writing a lot of letters to you lately—someone I'm worried about.'

Rosalind's heart had accelerated and she'd gripped the receiver hard. 'You're talking about Peter?'

A deep, unsteady breath along the line had signalled her caller's mingled nervousness and relief. 'Yes. You obviously know who I mean. But I…I don't want to get him into trouble…'

'Nor do I,' said Rosalind honestly. 'I haven't made any sort of official complaint yet, if that's what you're asking. I was hoping the situation would resolve itself…'

'Maybe it will. It's just—I saw some of Peter's letters to you, at his flat… I found photos, and things of yours—he has a whole *room* wallpapered with pictures of you; it's almost like a shrine the way it's set out. I think he's more likely to harm himself than anyone else but I— You see… Oh, it's so *complicated*…you can't possibly imagine! I—I thought that you and I might be able to help each other, to help *Peter*, without there being a fuss or any ghastly publicity—'

She broke off with what Rosalind thought sounded like a sob but then continued, her voice choppy with distress. 'It's all so very *awkward* talking like this over the phone. This is terribly *personal*, you see, Miss Marlow. Not even my family knows—they *mustn't* know—'

Rosalind could hear the incipient panic building. Her informant sounded almost at the end of her tether. She might lose her courage any moment and hang up, leaving Rosalind none the wiser as to her, or Peter's, true identity.

'I agree; nobody else has to know. Would it make you more comfortable if we could meet, Peggy, and talk about it face to face?' she interrupted gently, clamping down on the impulse to hammer urgent questions down the line. 'Just the two of us, alone? Trust me, I don't want any unnecessary publicity about this either.'

'Oh, yes, could we do that?' There was a gushing sigh of immense gratitude. 'But it needs to be right away and I live in Wellington...' Her voice swept high again in tense frustration. 'My husband is in the Government, you see, and our comings and goings are sometimes monitored. I don't have any excuse to come to Auckland at short notice and the family is bound to be curious and suspicious if I suddenly take it into my head to insist...'

The woman's ragged dignity and desperation triggered Rosalind's compassion as well as her avid curiosity, especially after hearing that she was the wife of Donald Staines, a conservative pillar of the political establishment and self-appointed watchdog of New Zealand morality.

Reading between the lines, Rosalind guessed that Mr Staines was an authoritarian husband who lived by a set of rigid, old-fashioned standards and expected his wife to be equally upright and unblemished in character. He had no truck with modern, namby-pamby psychology that forgave people their sins because they had been victims themselves, and, whatever Peggy's involvement with Peter, it was obvious she feared she would receive contempt and condemnation rather than help and understanding on the home front.

Rosalind had just got back from location. She had hardly even unpacked, but she didn't hesitate. She threw a few things back into her bag and flew to Wellington that very evening, booking into the agreed meeting place as the ubiquitous 'Miss Smith'. She was eager to shrug off her growing sense of powerlessness by seizing the initiative and taking assertive action instead of passively waiting for events to run their own course.

The hasty trip turned out to be a massive error in judgement. Perhaps if she had been more sensible and less arrogant, and had sought professional advice before rushing off to slay her phantoms, then Peggy Staines would not have had her heart attack, or the accompanying stroke which had complicated her recovery.

Hell!

The burden of guilt now resettled crushingly on Rosalind's shoulders. It all came down to choices and Rosalind knew that in the last few weeks she had made too many of the wrong kind: wrong personal choices, wrong career choices. Just about everything she did these days was turning out *wrong*, she thought, heaving a luxurious, self-pitying sigh.

'Rosalind? Are you feeling ill?'

She blinked and discovered that she had been frowning blankly out of the window of the plane at the vast blue nothingness. The sky was utterly clear, not a wisp of cloud in sight, and as her eyes dropped Rosalind could see the flattened contours of the Malaysian countryside below.

A broad brown river snaked lazily across the blue-green landscape, looping back on itself to almost enclose fat teardrops of lush jungle. Where the jungle gave way to serried ranks of palm trees she could see narrower brown bands—dirt roads running in straight lines for kilometres through the vast palm-oil plantations. From above, the palms looked like clusters of multi-armed starfish, spreading their green limbs across the earth-bed beneath a crystal-clear sea of air.

'Rosalind? Is something wrong? Why are you looking like that?'

The harsh demand shattered her abstraction. She looked around. Luke James had removed his glasses and his naked eyes weren't the least myopic as they drilled into hers. They were razor-sharp with curiosity, and with a jolt of alarm Rosalind recognised a shrewd intelligence at work. She hoped he wasn't as perceptive as he was evidently observant.

'Sorry...what was it we were talking about?' she said, instinctively brandishing the shield of charming vagueness that had served her so well in the past. 'I'm afraid my thoughts wandered off on a tangent. I tend to do that sometimes—my imagination is pretty wild...'

He refused to be diverted. 'Not very pleasant thoughts, whatever they were. From your expression, I thought the wing must be on fire at least!'

That explained his uncomfortably dissecting look. She must have given him a scare! Her mouth relaxed into a teasing curve.

'Believe me, if anything was wrong with the plane you'd be getting a far more extroverted performance than a dreamy stare out of the window! I'm a stage actress, remember? I'm trained to dramatise events and exaggerate emotions. You can't judge me by ordinary standards of behaviour...'

He frowned, replacing his spectacles. Rosalind could see disagreement seeping into his expression and another question forming on his stern lips. For goodness' sake, couldn't he take the hint and lighten up? She wasn't in the mood for serious conversation. She was having a holiday from deep and meaningful discussions!

Determined to thwart him, she steamrollered on in a relentlessly light and frivolous vein until she saw his eyes begin to glaze over and his jaw stiffen against a yawn. Only when she was certain that she had successfully bored him to distraction did she lapse into silence. She turned back to the window to hide a small smile of satisfaction as he quickly opened his laptop on his knee and buried his nose safely in his own business again.

She took a crumpled flight magazine out of the seat pocket in front of her and pretended to read, but as the plane angled out across the South China Sea she found herself seduced by the hypnotic flash and leap of the sun, dancing dimples of silver brilliance across the restless blue mantle. An occasional small fishing vessel and, as they neared Tioman, a sprinkling of raw, windswept rocks and tiny green-tipped islands jutting out of the sea provided the only visual interruptions.

The plane banked for its approach and Rosalind caught her first glimpse of their destination. The narrow tongue of land widened as the plane continued to turn, revealing the full vista—low, rock-strewn cliffs rising to steep, jungle-clad slopes which marched upwards and onwards into the hazy, mountainous interior.

She pressed her nose against the window so that she could watch as the tumbled boulders and stony cliffs gave way to long, wide streaks of smooth, pale sand. The exotic greenery grew thickly to the very edge of the beaches, and was broken only here and there by clearings for human habitation.

They descended further, flying across a bay where a long white jetty jutted out across the water. In the space of a few minutes the sea had changed dramatically, from a solid, opaque blue of fathomless depths to an exquisite, translucent cobalt as it skimmed over the sandy shallows to melt with scarcely a ripple onto the silky beaches.

Exactly like the brochures! Rosalind thought with a rush of pleasure, sending out a mental apology to her mother for doubting that her enthusiasm would bear comparison with reality.

The airport, when it hove into view, was tiny—a couple of alarmingly short concrete runways nestling at the base of the forested hills. A quicksilver thrill of exhilaration threaded through her veins. She couldn't help a quick glance over at Luke James to check how he was coping with the idea of landing in a patch of cleared jungle the size of a postage stamp.

He wasn't. Instead, he was watching her, his back turned to the solid wall of greenery now whipping past the window. She was surprised by his cool composure until she realised that his fixed fascination was more likely to be a state of controlled panic. By focusing his concentration on Rosalind he was blocking out his awareness of what was happening outside the plane.

Her own eyes were vividly bright, betraying the love of excitement that was intrinsic to her impulsive nature.

By the time they had bumped down onto the uneven runway and shuddered to a smooth halt beside the small, open-sided wooden building which served as a terminal Rosalind's earlier annoyance with Luke was forgotten in her eagerness to explore her new environment.

'It wasn't so bad after all, was it?' She grinned at him as they carried their bags the few metres from the shady terminal to the narrow, dusty road just outside the chain-link gates. 'I thought that landing was going to be a hair-raising roller-coaster ride, but it was actually quite smooth and easy.'

'Yes, I could see you were disappointed,' murmured Luke acidly as he set his suitcase down under the shade of a leafy palm and watched most of their fellow passengers board a small blue and white resort bus parked outside the wire gates.

'Well, maybe a little bit,' she confessed, looking around for their own transport. 'I happen to love roller coasters.'

'That figures.'

A typical accountant's reply, thought Rosalind in amusement. Everything reduced to numbers. He'd probably never even been on one himself. Roller coasters definitely came under the heading of entertainment!

She strolled over to where a snazzy-looking red motor scooter was leaning against one of the fence posts and ran her fingers wistfully over the white seat. 'You don't suppose...?'

'No, I do not!' He gave her hopeful suggestion short shrift.

'Pity,' she said, imagining how good the breeze would feel as they zipped along in the open. The air around them was very sultry and still, and she could feel the sweat beginning to trickle down her spine. She fanned herself with her hat. She couldn't wait to get into her bikini and fall into that azure sea.

They didn't have long to wait. Just as the resort bus pulled away a large green and silver open-topped Jeep with a palm-tree logo embossed on the door tooled up in a cloud of dust and a slim young Malaysian man dressed in cool whites vaulted out with profuse apologies for his lateness. He had had to stop to assist a tourist who had had an accident with his bicycle.

'I am Razak,' he said, his dark, almond-shaped eyes widening at the sight of Rosalind's hair glowing like molten lava in the full glare of the sun. 'From the Tioman Palms...and you are Mr and Mrs...?' He paused to look at the clipboard he had tucked under his arm.

'He's definitely a Mr but I'm still a Miss,' Rosalind laughed. 'We're not married.' The idea was deliciously absurd.

'Oh!' Razak's curious gaze darted from Rosalind's irrepressible grin to Luke's smooth, unrevealing visage. He looked down at his list and frowned. 'But—'

'We merely travelled on the same flight.' Luke cut him off abruptly. 'We aren't together. We're total strangers to each other.'

His attempt to distance himself from her provoked Rosalind into pure mischief.

'Yes, Luke and I have never seen each other before in our lives,' she purred, with an innocent flutter of her lashes that was more telling than any number of torrid looks.

A faint flush rose on Luke's neck as Razak regarded him with a brief flare of masculine envy before hurriedly consulting his list and ticking off their names.

'If you'd like to get into the Jeep, I'll just go and find the other two people I have come to meet,' he said as he loaded their bags and directed them to the open back seat. 'Please enjoy the ride. There is very beautiful scenery all the way to the hotel...'

Everything was beautiful, thought Rosalind an hour later as she stepped out onto her bedroom balcony and inhaled a heady brew of tropical scents. The hotel accommodation consisted of a sprawling arrangement of wooden chalets, each containing two-storeyed suites. The rooms themselves cleverly combined stark simplicity with exquisite luxury, so that the guests could pretend that they were roughing it without suffering any of the attendant inconveniences.

By leaning further over the sturdy balcony rail Rosalind could see past the thicket of towering coconut palms and weeping casuarina trees to the broad white smile of the beach with its scattering of wooden sun-loungers and huge, thatched umbrellas.

She turned her head at the sound of a slight scrape, and sighed as she saw a man leaning over the rail of the next-door balcony, which was screened from hers by a wooden lattice panel thickly covered with a glossy dark green creeper.

Instead of some exciting, sexy, fun-loving foreign millionaire, her neighbour was an accountant with an overdeveloped intellect and an underdeveloped social life.

Luke James had a lot to answer for!

CHAPTER FOUR

His luck certainly wasn't improving, thought Rosalind in exasperation as she watched the slinkily clad woman sidle away from the man at the bar with an insincere smile pinned to her glossy lips.

She just couldn't take it any more. She picked up her tall glass and sauntered over to plonk herself down on the next bar stool.

'You really have to do something about that technique of yours,' she announced.

Luke James stiffened, almost spilling his drink as he turned towards her, his dark eyes flicking over her shimmering green tube-top and flimsy wraparound skirt before darting past her to the crowded table of laid-back revellers which she had just abandoned.

The fiery sunset had provided a magnificent backdrop for diners at the hotel's open-air terrace restaurant but the thick, velvety darkness had long since fallen and most people had drifted away to the disco or to watch the nightly 'entertainment extravaganza' provided by staff and local cultural groups. Others, pursuing quieter interests, were strolling the moonlit beach, or entertaining privately in their chalets.

'I beg your pardon?'

Rosalind plucked a cherry from the bristling array of fruit decorating her Mai Tai, tossing it into her mouth and enjoying the lush burst of alcoholic flavour on her tongue as she studied his wary expression with faint amusement. She couldn't blame him for being suspicious; after all, she had been rather obviously ignoring him ever since they'd arrived.

But she had magnanimously decided to stop trying to avoid him. In a resort as small and exclusive as the Palms it was virtually impossible anyway. Instead of fading obligingly into the background in the past couple of days, eclipsed by the far more colourful company at the hotel, Luke James had managed to snag at her attention constantly. He was almost always alone, undoubtedly hampered by the shyness which those who didn't know him might easily interpret as off-putting aloofness.

Rosalind felt sorry for him, aware of his frequent, surreptitious glances in her direction. While she had been merrily acquiring new friends and acquaintances with her usual speed he had remained uncomfortably out of place amidst the relaxed holidaymakers. At least tonight he had left his laptop in his room—this afternoon he had been using it under one of the umbrellas down on the beach, a solitary figure absorbed in his own little world, seemingly oblivious to the fun going on around him. The man obviously needed taking in hand!

'Your technique for picking up women,' she explained, licking her cherry-slick fingers. 'Although I must admit you seem to have the picking-up part down pat. It's what happens afterwards that seems to be your problem.'

'Afterwards?' His winged eyebrows whipped into a steeply defensive slant.

Rosalind's eyes creased with amusement as she realised that he had placed a sexual connotation on her innocent words.

'After you've delivered your opening lines,' she said demurely. 'You're supposed to follow them up with some witty banter that fans the sparks of attraction into a mutual conflagration. You're acting more like a wet blanket than a bellows. What made her suddenly change her mind?'

'Who?'

'*Her.*' She jerked her head in the direction of the woman who had now zeroed in on another solitary male at the other end of the open-air bar. 'The hot-looking lady who was chatting you up just now.'

'She wasn't chatting me up,' he denied irritably. 'We were merely having a polite conversation.'

Wow! Talk about being uptight! Rosalind rolled her eyes at his obtuseness. '*She* bought *you* a *drink*, for goodness' sake; how much more of an invitation do you need?' She tilted her bright head towards him, lowering her voice confidingly so that he had, perforce, to lean towards her. 'She was coming on to you, Luke—I recognised the body language even if you didn't. She was zinging you with those coy up-and-under looks, snuggling up to your side, making sure you got an eyeful of that impressive cleavage…and there you were, as stiff as a post—'

'I *beg* your pardon?'

Rosalind collapsed into giggles at his outraged growl.

'I meant your *facial* expression,' she told him when she'd finally managed to stuff the laughter back down her throat. 'The way you were holding yourself.' She went off into another spate of giggles, almost falling off the stool, as she realised she had uttered another unintentional *double entendre*.

He looked as though he would like to throttle her, had he possessed the courage. 'Really?' he muttered sceptically through clenched white teeth.

'Yes, really. I…er…kept my body-language observations strictly above the waist,' she said, straight-faced, and then she couldn't resist teasing him by looking down at his shoes and stroking her gaze slowly up the long masculine legs, encased in pale cotton trousers, which were wrapped around his bar stool.

All his casual clothing had an expensive kind of crumpled elegance that suited his lanky frame. He looked a far cry from the dithering nerd-in-a-suit she had met at the airport, but that was still the image of him that she carried foremost in her mind. However, she had noticed on the

beach that his modest swimming boxers exposed some surprisingly well-defined leg muscles and her breath caught in
her throat as her eyes reached his splayed thighs and the
taut fabric across his hips revealed another unexpectedly
well-defined aspect of his masculinity.

Her eyes skipped a survey of his short-sleeved white shirt
and shot to his face, which, she discovered with a jolt,
looked as heated as she felt. His slight flush gave her back
the confidence to laugh huskily, as if she hadn't almost
been hoist by her own petard.

'So...one minute you and she are having a nice, polite
conversation and the next she's backing off as if you have
the plague,' she said, propping her elbow on the bar and
picking out more fruit from her glass. 'You were the one
doing most of the talking. What on earth did you *say* to
her?'

His eyes narrowed as he watched her devour a slice of
pineapple with voluptuous pleasure. 'If you must know, I
was merely telling her about one of my more intricate
cases.'

The pineapple nearly flew out of her appalled mouth.
'Accountancy?' she squeaked. 'You have a beautiful
woman flirting madly with you and you talk *books and
ledgers*?'

'It was a very interesting case,' he said mildly.

'Maybe to another accountant! She wasn't, was she...an
accountant, I mean?'

'She said she was an exotic dancer.'

There was a small, incredulous silence. 'Safe to assume
she isn't one of life's intellectual giants, then,' Rosalind
said drily. An exotic dancer on the make and Luke had
managed to let her slip through his fingers. If he had *tried*
he couldn't have done a better job of lousing up! 'For goodness' sake, couldn't you find something more exciting to
talk about...like the weather?'

'But she asked me about my work,' he protested.

'Yes, but she didn't really want to know all the gruesome details,' Rosalind told him. 'It was just an opening gambit, like asking what star sign you are or whether you have a light for her cigarette…'

'I don't believe in astrology and smoking damages your health.'

Rosalind kept a firm grip on her sense of humour. This was going to prove more of a challenge than she had thought. 'Do you have to take everything so *literally*? Boy, do you ever need help! Luckily I'm on hand to give you a few lessons.'

'Lessons?' His hair was ruffled by the warm off-shore breeze, a few glossy strands stirring and lifting to fall forward in twin curves on either side of the central widow's peak. He looked endearingly untidy for a few seconds before an absent hand slicked his hair back into its former neatness. Rosalind resisted the urge to reach up and restore the tousled look, which softened the sweeping angles of his narrow face and made him look more relaxed and casual…even rather sexy in a rumpled kind of way!

'In the fine art of flirtation. And don't say you don't need any because tonight was a rerun of what happened to you last night at the poolside buffet and today on the beach: initial feminine advance followed by hasty retreat. So far you seem to have a perfect strike-out rate where women are concerned.'

'I didn't realise anyone was keeping score,' he said tightly.

'Just call it a neighbourly interest.' She grinned, draining the rest of her drink. 'Don't take it too personally. People-watching is one of the accepted pleasures of being on holiday. The trick is not to let the watching take the place of healthy interaction—'

'Of which *you've* been having plenty, without apparent discrimination against age *or* sex!' he shot back. His mouth immediately compressed, as if he was angry at himself for the acid outburst. Following his brooding gaze to the un-inhibited group of men and women with whom she had enjoyed her dinner, Rosalind guessed that his words had been prompted by a combination of wounded male pride and envy of her easy popularity. She forgave him instantly and defused the comment by dropping into character.

'Mmm, being irresistibly likeable is *such* a trial,' she drawled in an impeccable aristocratic whine. 'One is constantly in demand, but one must do one's duty, mustn't one, dear chap? *Noblesse oblige* and all that...'

Anyone else would have gratefully picked up the cue to gloss over a *faux pas*, but Luke's smile was a perfunctory twitch. 'I'm sorry if I offended you. I didn't mean to imply that I thought you were promiscuous.'

Didn't you? popped into Rosalind's head as she met his unblinking gaze and wondered at the challenging gleam in the obsidian depths. But then she noticed his hands swivelling his drink round and around on its paper coaster, and the tension inherent in the gesture reassured her that the defiant glimmer in his eye was merely a reflection of one of the flaming torches which provided the hotel's beach frontage with its romantic ambience.

She sighed and shook her head. 'You take life too seriously, Luke—no wonder you're having trouble handling a simple holiday flirtation! Unless... You *are* interested in women, aren't you?'

Now he did blink, shattering the illusion of steely-eyed concentration. His olive skin darkened a tinge. 'Of course I am!'

'These days it pays to check.' She grinned, patting his bare forearm. She was surprised to feel the same electric hum that she had felt when she'd touched him on the plane. Last time she'd put it down to engine vibration; this time it must be the delayed punch of the Mai Tais she had been drinking.

'So, Luke,' she said, removing her hand and flexing her tingling fingers, 'do you want my help or not?'

His look, under the reckless brows, was unreadable. 'And if I said "not"?'

She tilted her chin and stared down her pert nose at him. 'Then naturally I'd steer clear of you for the rest of my stay. After all, I wouldn't want to interfere with your enjoyment of the wonderful, fun-filled, friend-crammed holiday you appear to be having.'

She wasn't surprised to see a brief flare of alarm in his eyes. 'Er...exactly what would this "help" of yours entail?' he enquired cautiously.

'You mean what would you be letting yourself in for?' The temptation to be outrageous was too much. She batted her eyelashes at him and said throatily, 'Why don't you buy me a drink, big boy, and find out?'

'Big boy?' He was startled into a dark chuckle. It was smooth yet rasping, a very masculine sound of appreciation that was all the more appealing for its undertone of reluctance.

At last she was getting somewhere! 'Too blatant?' she asked impishly.

'Erina was much more subtle,' he admitted, hiding the curve of his mouth against his glass. Rosalind watched the transparent liquid break against his lips and thought that if he was running true to form he was probably drinking mineral water.

'Oh, right! Miss Exotic Dancer was subtlety personified...in a dress that was cut to her navel!' she said sarcastically. 'What did *she* call you?'

'Darling.'

Rosalind snorted, conveniently forgetting how often the word was abused by her profession. 'How hackneyed. She obviously has no imagination. No wonder you gave her the brush-off.'

'It was vice versa, remember?'

'Only because you didn't give her a chance to glimpse the debonair man of the world beneath the accountant,' she said, already busily working out scenarios in her head.

He looked down into his glass, obviously struggling with some strong emotion. Gratitude, probably, thought Rosalind. 'It's very kind of you to take pity on me, but I don't like to encroach too much on your own holiday…'

'Oh, it won't take me more than a few days to whip you into shape,' said Rosalind confidently, wishing he would be less self-effacing.

'It sounds painful.'

'Stop being so negative. It'll be fun! You get a chance to explore your hidden potential and I get to play *Pygmalion*.'

'As long as you don't start giving me elocution lessons,' he said, so drily that for once she missed the joke.

'Oh, no, your speaking voice is one of your strong points…smooth and mellow, with just a hint of gravel in the undertone. And you have a sexy little hitch to some of your words. No, we definitely want to keep the voice.'

One eyebrow rose in an ironic slant, independent of the other. 'Thank you.'

Rosalind was impressed afresh by the whimsical charm of those wayward brows. 'Stick with me, kid, and this time next week women like Erina will be *begging* you to debit their balance sheets!' She gave him a lascivious wink and was amused to see him flush as he uttered another abrupt, almost unwilling laugh. It gave her a surge of odd, almost possessive satisfaction to watch his tightly compressed personality visibly unfold, although he obviously had a long way to go yet!

'I'm scarcely a kid,' he said stiltedly.

'Why, how old are you?'

'Twenty-eight.'

'Wow! *That* old, huh?' Dancing green eyes mocked his claim to maturity. 'How old do you think *I* am?'

His eyes flicked over her with unflattering speed. 'Thirty-five?'

'Ouch!' She laughed. With her supple, energetic body and elfin features she knew very well that she looked younger than her years. She licked her finger to place an imaginary stroke beside him in the air. 'Score one to me, Grandpa. I'm twenty-seven.'

'So I should be the one calling *you* kid,' he shot back with commendable speed.

'I may be younger in years but I suspect I'm decades older in worldly experience.' She chuckled, slyly swiping his glass in lieu of the Mai Tai he had failed to replenish. He made a half-hearted attempt at retrieval which she avoided by leaning back, giggling when the tube-top stretched alarmingly low over the smooth swell of her breasts, threatening to let them pop free. He froze and she directed a teasing look at him over the brim of the stolen glass before throwing back her head and dispatching the contents in a single swallow.

Mineral water it was not!

Rosalind choked on the ball of fire that exploded when the thick, oily fluid came in violent contact with the back of her throat, and grabbed gratefully at the cocktail napkin that appeared under her streaming eyes.

'My God, what in the hell was that?' she spluttered when she had recovered sufficiently to discover she still had a voice, albeit one that was cracked and croaky.

'Russian vodka, straight.'

Rosalind shuddered. 'You drink it raw? What are you, some kind of masochist?'

'It's an acquired taste, I agree.'

'Acquired taste! It's amazing you have any tastebuds left after drinking that stuff. It's like liquid fire. And it has a kick like a kangaroo!'

'I have a high tolerance for alcohol...something to do with my biochemistry, I believe.'

Trust Luke to have a boringly logical explanation for his dangerous taste in drinks. 'Lost opportunity there, Luke,' she chided wheezingly. 'You should have hinted at a shadowed past…that you *may* have acquired your liking for Russian vodka in Moscow, but the circumstances are not something you're at liberty to discuss.'

'You mean I should lie?'

'I said *may*, didn't I? It's not lying, exactly. It's weaving a romantic tale around the truth to make it a bit more interesting.' She sniffed. It was a mistake. The potent fumes lingering in her throat expanded into her nasal passages and made her eyes water furiously again. She abandoned the ridiculous argument over semantics and mopped at the brimming tears before remembering that she had applied a bold amount of mascara to her dark-brown-dyed eyelashes to make them look thicker and longer. 'Oh, no!' She raised her face to his. 'Has my mascara run?'

'Yes.' There was a trace of malice in his inspection. 'You look like a racoon.' She scowled at him and he tagged on hurriedly, 'A very pretty racoon, of course.'

She was torn between laughter and offended dignity. 'Oh, nice save, Mr Suave. Very debonair!' She slid off her stool. 'Since I haven't got my instant-repair kit with me I'd better take a face-saving stroll back to the chalet.'

Luke rose, sliding a discreet tip across the polished wood of the bar. 'I'll come with you. After all, it was my vodka that did the damage…and I wouldn't like anyone to take a swipe at you in the dark, mistaking you for a pretty, noxious pest.'

Rosalind groaned. 'You pick up the art of stinging banter awfully fast for a beginner. I hope I'm not unleashing a monster on the unsuspecting women of the world!'

'Perish the thought, Dr Frankenstein,' he murmured in her ear as they turned onto the crushed-shell pathway that branched off under the palms towards their small grouping of chalets.

When they reached her chalet she lingered on the door-step, relaxed in the certainty that her escort wasn't suddenly going to turn into an over-amorous octopus. If there was any pouncing to be done she suspected she was the one who would have to do it!

Smiling at the thought, she ordered him to call for her the next morning, so they could plan out their day over breakfast at the elegant little coffee-bar on the balcony of the hotel's marine sports pavilion.

'But—'

'But what?' she said impatiently as she opened the door. 'You don't eat breakfast?' She turned to look at him, standing at the bottom of the wooden steps. 'Or did Erina make you a more attractive offer? Were you planning on having breakfast in bed, maybe?'

She couldn't see, because his face was shadowed by the night, but she would have bet that he was blushing as he growled, 'Of course not. I just wondered why it had to be so early, that's all.'

'You'll see.' She grinned and turned to trundle upstairs to the bedroom, uttering a shriek of horrified mirth as she saw her black-ringed eyes in the bathroom mirror. Rosalind Racoon indeed! Ah, well, tomorrow she would get her revenge...

She scrubbed her face till it was pink and shiny and fell into bed, drifting off to sleep to the hushed sounds of the sea and the tropical night breeze whispering in the palms outside her window.

CHAPTER FIVE

ROSALIND woke to a furious thunderstorm.

No, not thunder. It was definitely a man-made racket, she decided as she opened her eyes to a room awash with light. Someone was hammering at the front door of the chalet.

Rosalind sat bolt upright and immediately fell back on the pillows, groaning, but it was too late—her stomach had already been set in unsteady motion. Waves of nausea washed over her and she closed her eyes, swallowing frantically, trying to think calming thoughts, but it was difficult to concentrate with the thumping going on downstairs, the sound vibrating through the wooden walls of the chalet. She held off for a few more miserable seconds but then had to make a heart-pounding dive for the bathroom.

She only just made it. She slumped to her knees by the toilet bowl, retching violently, feeling the sweat break out all over her tortured body. Even when she could bring up no more she still retched. She flushed the toilet and moaned as the churning of the water triggered a fresh bout. Death seemed a very attractive alternative.

The thumping had stopped and suddenly she became aware of a questioning voice echoing inside the chalet.

'Uh…Rosalind? I'm here! Are you ready to go?'

Luke! She lurched to her feet. She could hear the footfalls crossing the polished wood floor below. His next call was stronger as it came floating up the narrow stairway.

'Rosalind? Are you still up there?'

In a panic, Rosalind realised that if he came up the stairs he would find her in the nude. She preferred to sleep without the rumble of the air-conditioner and it was too hot to wear anything in bed but the flimsy sheets. She tried to call out but her voice emerged from her burning, bile-coated throat as a dry croak. She grabbed the green hotel robe hanging on a brass hook on the wall and wrapped it around her, her fingers fumbling with the tie as she staggered towards the door.

'Rosalind? I can hear you moving around; I know you're awake. Please, won't you answer me?'

'Yes, yes, I'm here.' She hurried down to meet him, moving as fast as she dared, a supportive hand sliding along the wall to give her stomach the illusion of stability. As she had feared, he had already started up the stairs and they met on the small landing.

Luke looked insufferably fit and healthy in white trousers and a rather vivid island-print shirt, the jewel-bright colours stamped on a red background—a garment which at any other time she would have coveted. As it was, its vibrancy made her stomach wince and she quickly shifted her gaze. His damp hair was neatly combed back, his recently shaven jaw was smooth and glossy and the crisp, clean tang of a citrus-based cologne preceded him.

In contrast Rosalind felt grubby and smelly and desperate for a shower, and when Luke froze in his tracks she knew that she looked exactly the way she felt. She glared at him, wishing she had long, abundant curls to hide behind, rather than the perky, short, nakedly revealing cut that she ordinarily loved.

'I'm sorry; I overslept,' she rasped sullenly. 'Did you have to pound at my door like that? I thought it was an earthquake.'

His speculative dark eyes roamed from her bare toes curling against the cool floor to the sleep-crease marring one creamy cheek. 'You told me to be here at this time. I thought you meant that you'd be ready and waiting.' He looked at his watch—a menacing lump of black plastic studded with buttons. Why was it that the people who needed them least always boasted the most macho time-pieces? thought Rosalind sourly.

'So? Sue me,' she grunted.

'Are you always this grouchy in the morning?' For some reason the notion seemed to give him pleasure.

'No. I'm usually much worse,' she snapped.

He nodded, as if he could quite believe it. 'You left your door unlocked? Don't you think that's a bit unwise for a woman alone?'

'I do now,' she said, unable to think of anything wittier.

He looked at her as she leaned limply against the painted wall, and moved tentatively closer. 'Are you sure you're all right? Your face doesn't look so good.'

No wonder—her stomach was still trying to push itself up into her throat! 'Gee, Luke, you really know how to turn a girl's head.'

'No, I meant you don't look well,' he said. 'Have you changed your mind about an early breakfast? Last night you said something about bacon and eggs and waffles dripping with syrup—'

'*Oh, God!*'

Rosalind clapped her hand to her mouth and whirled about. She raced back up the stairs, almost killing herself as she tripped over the trailing belt of the huge, one-size-fits-all robe. This time she only made it as far as the hand-basin, hanging onto it for grim life as she was shaken by another bout of violent nausea.

Lost in her misery, she was barely aware of the long arm swooping around her until it contracted to a tight band just beneath her breasts, gently supporting her bent-over body while her trembling legs were braced from behind by the warm cup of masculine hips and thighs. After she had finished her ignominious performance Luke forced her to sip a glass of water so that she could rinse the vile taste from her mouth.

Rosalind, a notoriously bad patient at the best of times, was purely ungrateful.

'Go away,' she groaned thickly as she tried to wrestle herself free of his tender mercies. Either she was as weak as a baby or Luke was a great deal stronger than he looked. 'Why can't you leave me alone? I don't want you here. I don't—mmph, mmph…' Her fretful wail was smothered in the folds of a deliciously cool flannel as it was firmly stroked over her sweaty face and then her hands.

'I can do that myself.' She glared at him from under damply spiked lashes and ruffled brows dyed the same colour.

'Too late; it's done. Come on. Back to bed.'

He was very good at giving orders all of a sudden, she thought grumpily, but still felt too fragile to make an issue of it. She meekly lay down on the tumbled bed and closed her eyes. She felt the mattress alongside her hip depress with Luke's weight as he sat down on the edge of the bed.

'I think I'll ring down to Reception for the hotel doctor. If you have food poisoning it could be serious—'

'Don't bother; I know what it is and it's *not* food poisoning,' she roused herself to protest.

'Oh. I see.' Luke's slow enunciation dripped with distaste. 'Perhaps a hair of the dog would help, then?'

Rosalind's eyelids cranked open to check the disapproving slant of the demon eyebrows. 'It's not a hangover, either,' she retorted. 'I wasn't drunk last night. You should know; *you* walked me home…'

'You could have gone out again after I left. Or hit the room-service bar.'

Maybe someone he knew was an alcoholic. It was the only reason Rosalind could think of for his unflattering suspicions. 'Well, I didn't. I went straight to bed.'

'Then why are you ill?'

'I just got up too suddenly, that's all,' she muttered petulantly. He would probably laugh if she told him. Hell, *she* would laugh if this was happening to someone else. But right now she didn't feel in the mood to provide anyone with amusement.

He frowned, propping one hand beside her head and leaning forward for a closer inspection of her unhealthy pallor. His hair fell over his forehead and this time he didn't bother to brush it back. His mouth was a thin, stern line, his face losing its puckish illusion of youthfulness as his expression became absorbed...intent.

Rosalind's skin prickled with self-awareness under the rough towelling. She was suddenly conscious that she was lying there, to all intents and purposes helpless, nude beneath her robe, while Luke bent over her, fully dressed. There was something uncomfortably erotic about the situation—a purely atavistic feminine response to the threat of male dominance.

Not that Luke was any worry to her in that direction, she told herself hurriedly, but she wondered at her own waywardness. Ever since her disaster with Justin she had preferred to be the controlling partner in her relationships with men. Even in her secret fantasies she had never felt excited by the idea of being sexually dominated, of being held captive by passion and aroused against her will by a skilful seducer...she was immune to the appeal of dashing sheikhs and silken bindings. So why such thoughts should sneak into her mind now, when she was feeling so thoroughly ghastly and totally unattractive, was difficult to comprehend.

She wondered exactly what was going through Luke's mind. Nothing as wildly inappropriate as what was going through her own, she decided as she watched the shift of his expression. What ever made her think that he was young for his age? Right now he looked every one of his twenty-eight years—and more...disconcertingly mature and sombre in his seriousness.

His eyes had that glaze of absent-minded, see-nothing

vagueness which Rosalind was coming to realise indicated a see-all state of mind. He was focusing on the big picture rather than on the one immediately in front of him, his brain adding up all the possibilities and cross-referencing them with what information he already had.

'Do you mean it's some form of motion sickness?' he asked puzzled. 'But how can that be…? You weren't sick on the flight.'

'Oh, for goodness sake! Not *motion—morning*,' she stressed weakly, realising that he wasn't going to give up until he had a satisfactory answer. 'Look, just pass me over one of those crackers just there on the bedside table and then toddle downstairs and make me a cup of tea…weak, with just a little milk and not too hot—'

'Morning? What do you—? *Morning sickness!*' He jack-knifed upright again, setting up an unpleasant vibration in the mattress. 'My God, do you mean—you're *pregnant*?'

'For God's sake, stop rocking the boat and pass me the damned cracker!' moaned Rosalind, wishing she were well enough to enjoy his shocked reaction.

'Pregnant!' he repeated, doing as he was bid, his face almost as pale as hers under the natural tan as he stood uncertainly next to the bed. 'Who's the father?' he asked abruptly.

'Jordan…my brother-in-law,' said Rosalind, munching experimentally.

'*What*?' If she had thought he looked devilish before, now he was Satan, King of Hell, come to fry her for every sin she had ever dreamed of committing. 'You've been having an affair with your own sister's *husband*?' he thundered accusingly, smoke practically pouring from his pinched nostrils.

'No, of course not!' she cried, stuffing the rest of the cracker in her mouth with kill-or-cure haste. Jordan would hit the roof if *that* rumour ever got around! 'Jordan's the father, but of *Olivia's*—my sister's—baby!'

His eyes went darkly opaque. 'My God,' he breathed. 'Are you acting as a surrogate mother—is that it? Are you carrying their child implanted in your womb because your sister can't carry a full-term pregnancy?'

His leap of imagination took her breath away. She was glad that she was already lying down. It wasn't often these days that she was taken so spectacularly off guard. She felt a deep, dangerous stirring of dark emotions which she ruthlessly repressed.

'*No*! Honestly, Luke, I don't know where you get such wild ideas from; you're as bad as the tabloids—' She bit her lip, hoping he hadn't noticed the slip. The cracker miraculously seemed to have settled down in comfortable residence and she pushed herself cautiously up against the pillows and took pity on his confusion.

'I'm not carrying *anyone's* child, OK? I'm not pregnant at all; I just have the symptoms.' She thumped the mattress with a frustrated fist and threatened fiercely, 'Oh, I'm going to *kill* her for doing this to me when I get back home!'

Sharp alarm briefly pierced the bewildered dark eyes. 'Kill who?' he said sharply.

'Olivia, my sister, that's who!' She braced herself for the usual scepticism as she attempted to explain as succinctly as possible, '*Olivia's* the one who's pregnant, not me. We're twins, you see, and we've always shared a really close mental and physical connection. When we were children, whenever Olivia got ill I did too…or I showed all the symptoms but not the illness…and vice versa. Fortunately it's faded quite a bit as we've grown older and become more separate in our lives. Sometimes it's just the echo of sympathetic feeling, a not-quite-rightness, but sometimes it's a real, rip-roaring snorter!'

'Like now.'

Strangers rarely took her affinity with her twin seriously and Rosalind's mouth formed a pink O at his apparently easy acceptance of the bizarre truth. But then, she reasoned, it was no more bizarre than *his* guess.

'Like now,' she conceded ruefully. She sat up further, and brightened as she realised the nausea had passed. She felt perfectly normal again. She grinned her relief. 'But, hey, it's just a temporary condition and it's not usually this drastic—at least not for me. Jordan told me it's far worse for poor Olivia, who throws up on and off for *hours* every single morning—and she hates being ill and helpless even more than I do!'

Thirty minutes later, at the balcony restaurant, Luke was watching in appalled fascination as she poured more syrup onto the plate of waffles next to her decimated serving of bacon, eggs, grilled tomato and hash browns.

'I don't know how you can do that,' he murmured, shuddering as she took a dreamy bite of the sticky-sweet concoction. 'Anyone else would have settled for dry toast.'

'I have a naturally high tolerance for food,' she grinned, paraphrasing his words from last night as she cast a disparaging look at his orange juice and the plain wholemeal toast that had followed his bowl of cereal and fruit. 'I think it's something to do with my body chemistry. And don't forget that Olivia's hormones are busily informing me that I'm now eating for two!'

'You'll have to make sure you start getting a bit of exercise today. You don't burn up many calories sunbathing.'

'Exactly my plan.' Rosalind's smug grin made him eye her warily. He was beginning to know the look that bespoke mischief. 'When we've finished eating we'll go downstairs and book our jet-skis. I hope we're still early enough to get a couple for this morning.'

He put down his orange juice. *'Jet-skis!'*

'They rent them out by the half-hour but I say we get them for a full hour. Surely you didn't think that we were just going to sit around and flirt with each other all day, did you, Luke?' she said sweetly, enjoying his startled consternation. 'That wouldn't burn up very many calories either. Flirting isn't a passive art, you know; it's as much physical as verbal. Being able to flirt on the wing, so to speak, increases your chances of success... Besides, if you do interesting things you set up opportunities to meet a more interesting type of woman. I take it you haven't ridden a jet-ski before.'

'No, nor ever wanted to,' he said, glancing down at the short jetty and pontoons which marked off the area of the beach which had been set aside for the safe use of power boats and jet-skis. 'Can't we do something less...noisy?'

'No, we can't.' She ruthlessly brushed aside his objection. 'I thought you said you didn't want to encroach on my holiday? Well, if we do things my way we'll both get what we want—I'll have some fun and you'll provide yourself with a stimulating new experience to talk about.

'Trust me—once you get the hang of it you'll love it,' she predicted, polishing off another waffle. Her green eyes shimmered with innocence as she leaned over the table to add in a low purr that made a flush streak across his cheekbones, 'Just think of the pleasure of having all that throbbing power between your legs. Who knows? It might prompt you to discover a totally new aspect of your personality!'

But it was Rosalind who was first to make that discovery a short time later as she prowled restlessly around Luke's chalet while she waited for him to change into his swimsuit and collect his beach gear. They were only going to have a short wait for their jet-skis and she didn't want to waste a minute of their allocated time. Since she was wearing a matching bikini under her sunflower-printed cotton Lycra swing-dress she had only needed to slip next door and fetch her beach bag, give her teeth a quick clean and slap on some sunscreen. Typically, Luke was obviously being more meticulous...or merely reinforcing his mistrust of her interpretation of fun.

Impatient with the wait and incurably nosy, Rosalind couldn't resist poking around his tidily arranged possessions to see what they revealed about his personality…other than the fact that he was a relentless neatnik. She was investigating his reading matter, noting the depressing lack of holiday trash amongst the pile on the small teak table, when she came across the torn-out pages of a magazine. It was the article about her that she had read on the flight from New Zealand, the story that rehashed the worst excesses of her 'wild child' exploits, carefully undated so that an uninformed reader might assume they had occurred weeks rather than years ago.

Luke must have torn it out of his copy of the magazine on the plane. Her heart began to thump as she realised the implications.

Rosalind was still staring at the crumpled pages when Luke came down the stairs, dressed as he had been before, except for the dark shadow of his swim-shorts showing under the white trousers and the sunglasses hanging out of his shirt pocket.

He halted abruptly when he saw what she had in her hand, his mouth closing over what he had been going to say, and Rosalind was stung by a sense of betrayal.

'You knew!' she attacked him, snapping her fist closed and balling up the offending paper with vicious, jerky movements of her fingers. 'Damn it—you read this and you knew who I was even before I sat down beside you on that first flight, didn't you? *Didn't you?*'

He shrugged, his eyes faintly hooded under the etched brows, his narrow face revealing nothing of what was going through his mind. And she had thought that he was so wonderfully transparent…had convinced herself that his air of bumbling helplessness was cute as well as harmless!

'Well, answer me, damn it!' she hissed at him, goaded by his silence, golden sunflowers flaring out around her slender hips as she stormed closer to impale him with the emerald fury of her eyes. God forbid that he should turn out to be a journalist after all.

'Why didn't you say you'd recognised me?' she demanded, spoiling for a reply that would allow her temper full rein.

But instead of looking guilty Luke casually bent over and picked up a white panama hat from a rattan chair, holding it loosely alongside his thigh as he answered. 'Because I received the very strong impression that you were travelling incognito, wanting to avoid drawing any attention to yourself or your identity,' he said, with the calmness of sincerity. 'Was I so wrong?'

'Well, no,' she admitted, unwilling to let go of her anger, or face the underlying emotion which had prompted her to lash out. 'But you still could have given me *some* indication—'

'How—without intruding on the privacy which was obviously so vital that you went to the trouble of disguising yourself?' he asked, with devastating logic.

She brooded on that one. He had managed to turn the tables very neatly, but that didn't mean that he was exonerated.

'What about later, when I told you I was an actress and you said you didn't go to the theatre? You could have mentioned the article; you didn't have to *still* pretend you didn't know anything about me,' she insisted sharply, the strong sense of pique she had felt at the time still mockingly clear in her memory.

'Ah…well, perhaps I couldn't help teasing you a little bit there—'

'Hah!'

He ignored the accusing sound. 'But by then it would have been awkward to admit otherwise without causing embarrassment,' he continued evenly. 'I thought it more diplomatic to behave as if we were strangers, which to all intents and purposes we still are…'

Rosalind's chin went up in a familiar gesture of dramatic defiance. '*I* wouldn't have been embarrassed!' she declared, her eyes blazing with the refusal to apologise for the way that she had lived. She had made mistakes, but she had paid the price for them too, and in one case would go *on* paying, for the rest of her life...

'Maybe not, but *I* would.' He made a self-deprecating gesture with his hands. 'I thought you might think I had done it with malice aforethought—pretending not to recognise you in order to scrape an acquaintance, so that I could boost my ego by boasting about our conversation later...selling my story, that kind of thing. I know there are some people like that...'

He looked down at the hat in his hand, sliding the brim between his fingers with his other hand. 'And I didn't think that particular story was something you would want to discuss, particularly with a stranger. Unless you brought up the subject yourself, I didn't see a way to mention it...'

'Hmm.' Rosalind summoned up her worst-case scenario to attack his aura of guilty innocence. 'So you're not in some kind of security intelligence service?'

His head jerked up. 'No!'

'Or a detective?'

He shook his head, the movement blurring the expression in the dark eyes.

'A reporter?'

'God forbid!' he blurted out.

He was either being honest or he was a spectacularly good liar. Rosalind only had her instincts to go on.

'Hmm.' She tapped her foot, reluctant to let him entirely off the hook as she tried to think whether there were any other unwelcome possibilities she hadn't covered.

'You needn't worry about your privacy being compromised,' he said, as if reading her scurrying thoughts. 'Accountants are, by the very nature of their work, trustworthy and discreet. We're often privy to extremely sensitive, pri-

vate information about people's lives and we'd soon find
ourselves out of work if we boasted about our inside knowledge. Not that I'm one for boasting anyway…'

Rosalind immediately felt like a paranoid witch. Of
course he wasn't, and that was part of the reason why he
couldn't hold a woman's interest beyond the first ten
minutes!

'There's nothing very private about *my* life at the moment!' She threw the ball of magazine pages at his chest,
amazed at the speed of his reflexes when his hand snapped
out and caught it before it hit him. 'I hope you don't believe
everything you read in that kind of publication!'

'I prefer to form my own opinions.'

'So? Aren't you even going to ask me how much of that
trash is true?' she taunted. 'Don't you want to know all the
gory little details that the story left out?'

'Only if you want to tell me,' he said, with just the right
touch of open-minded disinterest.

She wondered whether he expected his diffidence to result in a burst of confidence. She tossed her head. 'I don't!'

He passed the test with flying colours.

'In that case shall we go and try out those damned noise-
making machines you booked?' he said, settling his hat on
his head and indicating the door.

'Why on earth did you tear out the damned article anyway?' she brooded moments later as they skirted a fallen
coconut on the path.

'Impulse…I suppose as a kind of souvenir of our meeting.'

'You don't ask for much class in your souvenirs, do
you?'

'You mean like toothpicks and coffee-sachets have
class?' he shot back smoothly, making her laugh.

They cut down to the beach and strolled along the satiny
sand towards the jetty, skirting the early sunbathers and the
odd child with a bucket and spade. Families with teenagers

rather than young children or babies seemed to be predominant at the Palms, for which Rosalind was quietly thankful.

After they had picked up a couple of towels from the hotel's beach kiosk Rosalind veered towards the water's edge, hopping along as she removed her canvas slip-ons so that she could swish through the gently lapping waves. Without a word Luke took possession of her drawstring bag, paralleling her on the firm sand just above the waterline, keeping his beach sandals meticulously dry. The tide was fully in, the water so clear that Rosalind could see the rocks and pieces of dead coral dotting the sandy seabed as it sloped gently away from the wide beach.

The sun was already hot, beating down on her wide-brimmed straw sunhat, making her glad of its shade mantling her shoulders, which were left bare by her halter-necked dress and bikini. There was a slight breeze—just enough to stir the palm leaves fringing the beach and gently billow out the sail of a windsurfer sketching a lazy progress across the glittering plane of the water. They would do that next, Rosalind decided, admiring the skill of the briefly clad male as he deftly changed the direction of his board.

A sea-bird wheeled overhead and further out towards the line of yachts moored across the bay a pair of snorkels broke the surface. It was a picture-perfect moment and Rosalind took a deep breath, happy to be alive.

She placed a hand on the top of her hat and gave a small skip, enjoying the feel of the silky water creaming around her ankles and the spray of lukewarm droplets smattering up over her thighs and the flirty hem of her mini-dress. She was aware of Luke's easy, loose-limbed stride matching her brief burst of speed and glanced over to catch his eyes on her shaded face.

The white hat suited his olive complexion, she mused, and, tilted as it was on a slight angle, managed to give his face a rakish look that most women would find intriguing.

In fact, each time she saw him Rosalind was obliged to reassess her opinion of his potential.

'No more ill effects from this morning?' he said quickly, as if to forestall any comment on his watchfulness.

But Rosalind was used to being stared at and she merely shook her head with a rueful grin. 'Not me. Poor Olivia is probably still hung over a bowl, though. Even anti-nausea medication doesn't work; at least, not in the recommended doses. If Jordan could buy her way out of morning sickness I think he'd be prepared to spend the entire Pendragon family fortune!'

He removed his aviator sunglasses from his pocket and slipped them on, hiding his eyes. 'I hope not, since my livelihood depends on it.'

Rosalind was deceived by the casualness of his revelation. 'What do you mean?'

'I happen to work for his cousin, William.'

Rosalind nearly fell on her face in the water in mid-skip. 'You work for *Will*—?' she screeched inelegantly. Rosalind had dated Jordan's cousin a couple of times but purely on a friendly welcome-to-the-family basis, for he was a businessman to his fingertips, far too conservative for her taste, and she had been too *outré* for his.

Luke's stride didn't falter. 'For the Pendragon Corporation, yes.'

Rosalind was blown away by the coincidence. She splashed out of the water to trot after him on sandy feet. 'Where?'

'In Wellington.'

She shrugged off a frisson of unpleasant memory at the mention of the city. 'I didn't mean geographically. I meant—doing what?'

'I coordinate the preparation of various company accounts for taxation purposes.'

Taxes. She might have known!

'I can't get over what an incredible coincidence this is—

my sister is married to your boss's cousin!' she said as she waved to the young Malaysian up at the marine centre from whom she had hired the jet-skis and followed his pointing finger to the gleaming red and white machines being held in knee-deep water by another employee. 'Why, that makes us practically *family*!' She laughed, halting beneath a tall coconut palm that slanted out over the beach.

Luke spread out his towel in the shade of the fronds, carefully placing her bag on top of it. 'I wouldn't go quite that far.'

'Well, kissing cousins at the very least.' She gave him a sultry smile of sly mischief and tossed her hat down beside her bag. She tugged up the hem of her stretchy cotton Lycra dress and whipped it over her head. 'You should have mentioned the connection sooner, then I wouldn't have been so suspicious of you,' she said, amused by his half-step backwards at her sudden strip.

For a moment it seemed as if he wouldn't answer. In the black lenses of his sunglasses she could see twin images of herself reflected—slim, laughing figures in yellow floral bikinis that covered only the bare essentials.

Luke found his voice. 'I thought it might sound encroaching,' he murmured.

She planted one hand on the delicate arch of her hip and shook an exasperated finger at him. 'Luke James, you are the *least* encroaching man I have ever met! Stop worrying about what people might think and start taking a few chances. Now, get your gear off and let me show you how to give a woman a good time!'

He flushed, his jaw clenching, but he did what he was bid. His naked torso had perfect triangular proportions— strongly defined shoulders and compact, hairless chest tapering to a washboard abdomen and narrow waist. His hips and legs were as whipcord-lean as the rest of him.

She whistled at him to show that she was impressed, then chuckled as she led him down to the water, wading in to say to the man holding the jet-skis, 'We just want one for the first ten minutes or so.' She jerked her thumb over her shoulder. 'Luke's never ridden one before, so I'll take him out on the back of mine so he can see how it's done.'

'O.K. Did you read the rules at the centre?'

Rosalind nodded and he quickly reiterated the main ones and gave her a brief tour of the controls as she pulled herself up to straddle the red padded seat.

Luke hung back when Rosalind indicated for him to mount up behind her.

'Come on; time is money, as you accountants would say. This is a two-seater, see?' she said, scooting forward to show him there was ample room.

He still hesitated. 'If you drive as recklessly as you seem to do everything else I hope the hotel has adequate insurance.'

Her green eyes flared at the insult but she held onto her temper, telling herself he was merely being his usual cautious self. 'I promise you won't get hurt...the worst that can happen is that we'll both get wet. And this guy will come out in his Zodiac if the engine conks out.'

Her condescending tone and the glance of amused tolerance she exchanged with the hotel employee was impetus enough. With a grim smile Luke swung up into the seat.

'You can hang onto the handholds at the side or me— whichever feels more secure,' Rosalind yelled as she turned the key in the ignition and the engine roared to life. The front of the craft lifted as she gunned the throttle and they leapt forward to crest the swell of the incoming waves.

She could hear Luke's faint groans as they plunged from wave to wave; then they were out in the calm of deeper waters and after a few fancy turns and sharp, sweeping swathes she felt his hands snap around her waist. She laughed. She had known he wouldn't be able to keep his distance for long. For one thing hunching down to the handholds was uncomfortable for any length of time if you were above average height.

'If that's your idea of fun, I think I can do without it,' he said acidly when Rosalind finally sped back in and throttled down beside the other jet-ski.

'It's always uncomfortable riding pillion because you know you don't have any control over what's happening. Once you have the handlebars to grip onto you'll find it's quite a different feeling.' She grinned as he dropped into the waist-deep water. 'Did you see how I worked the throttle, or do you want it explained again?'

He placed a hand on the seat of the other jet-ski and vaulted onto it in a single, fluid movement. 'It seems to be not much different from riding a motorcycle.'

'You've ridden a motorcycle?' Rosalind blinked tangled wet lashes at a brief, shocking image of that lean, hard body encased in sexy black leathers insolently unzipped from throat to groin.

He seemed unreasonably irritated by her surprise. 'I owned one as a teenager,' he flung at her. 'A Harley, as a matter of fact. You don't have to be born to be wild like you to enjoy the occasional walk on the wild side, Roz!'

And with that he took off in a shower of spray, handling the powerful machine with only a slight clumsiness which vanished as soon as he hit the first wave, rising to his feet to absorb the impact of landing and leaning straight into a superbly flashy turn. Rosalind's gaping mouth closed as her ready sense of humour rescued her from the uncomfortable physical awareness of a few moments ago and she roared after him with a rebel yell of delight. Talk about being a fast learner! At this rate she was going to have trouble keeping pace with her protegé!

CHAPTER SIX

LUKE provided her with delightful sport for the next hour as they raced back and forth across the bay, circling the buoys and pontoons, taking it in turns to ride each other's wake and duelling with other jet-skis who dared challenge for supremacy of the waves.

It was the first time Rosalind had seen him completely uninhibited and she was startled by the streak of fierce competitiveness he revealed in their games. He liked to win, and when he did made no bones about enjoying his victory, punching a fist to the sky, his triumphant laugh ringing out over the water. She couldn't quite believe that it was the same man who would hardly say boo to a goose on dry land!

Even more surprisingly, Rosalind was the one to flag first. When their time was finally up she was glad to hand over her jet-ski to someone else and stagger up the beach, cheerfully admitting as she flopped down on her towel that her arms and legs felt like jelly from the constant strain of controlling all that horsepower.

'Not to mention another part of my anatomy that's taken a pounding,' she groaned as she wriggled on her back to make a nice contoured hollow in the sand for the tender region and propped her hat against the top of her head so that it shaded her face. 'I must have lost more condition than I thought on that wretched island!'

Luke, who seemed if anything to be *more* energised by the experience, shook his towel before settling down beside her, leaning back on braced arms, his knees drawn up in front of him, flicking his wet hair back with a sharp toss of his head.

'Are you talking about the film you've just finished?' His curiosity was no longer constrained by having to pretend ignorance of her background.

Rosalind pulled a wry face. 'You mean which almost finished *me*.'

She embarked on her humorously harrowing tale of woman-eating sharks, broken bones and mosquitoes the size of vampire bats. 'It was the sheer *incompetency* of the whole thing that I found so infuriating,' she finished, with an angry twist to her mobile mouth. 'I wouldn't have minded the deprivations so much if it had been a cracking script, but by the time the director had done a million rewrites the characters were practically incomprehensible. As a break into films it was *not* a good career move...'

'I thought you preferred the stage anyway,' he said, confirming that he had read the small print of the article, not just the trashy bits. 'What made you want to do *this* film?'

She sighed. He had an instinct for innocently framing awkward questions.

'Impulse. I was looking to expand my horizons. The original script was actually quite good...and the director begged me to!' She opened her eyes and found him regarding her thoughtfully. She moved her expressive hands restlessly. 'Trina was a friend of mine. Hell, I didn't know that since we left drama school she'd only done commercials and music videos!'

'You didn't think to check out her credentials before you committed yourself?' It was the accountant not the jet-ski speed pirate talking, and his incredulous tone put her on the defensive.

'I told you, she was an old friend. I liked her. It was a loyalty thing.'

'Misplaced loyalty as it turned out.'

Rosalind bristled at the hint of contempt. 'Yes, well, that's the whole point of loyalty, isn't it—sticking with people through the bad as well as the good? Trina did her best; her ambition simply overreached her abilities. At least she was willing to take the risk and try, and I respect her for *that*.'

His raised eyebrow was a taunt in itself and she thought that if he had been a calculating man she would have suspected him of playing the devil's advocate purely to provoke her impulsive retort. 'Maybe it was the element of risk that attracted you to the project in the first place.'

'Maybe it was,' she prevaricated. 'But at least I came out of it with a minimum wage. The investors must have taken a bath!'

As she'd suspected, the financial red herring was too tempting for him to resist, and they discussed the intricacies of film financing before Rosalind managed gradually to edge the conversation around to a subject of potentially greater interest—Luke's Harley-Davidson-owning days. However, they turned out to be disappointingly tame…a case of riding the motorcycle back and forth to university and to his part-time job. He had never even belonged to a motorcycle club, let alone a gang. As far as he was concerned, his grunt-machine had been merely a convenient and economical form of transport, with the added advantage of being a classic which would appreciate in value and therefore could be viewed in the light of an investment.

'A conformist without a cause!' Rosalind murmured, wistfully relinquishing the illicit vision of a leather-clad Luke lounging astride a sexy hunk of chrome and black, a cigarette and a sneer dangling from his lips.

She delved to find a replacement image but it was tough going trying to get Luke to open up about himself. On general subjects he was capable of being provoked into something bordering on eloquence but when it came to the personal stuff he retreated into his awkward shell.

She did manage to patch together the picture of an orphaned only child who became an adopted only child, then a conscientious student who had set himself a series of goals towards which he had worked with relentless dedication. Not for him the usual wild student frivolities. He had lived at home and, while his adoptive parents had been comfortably well off and prepared to pay generously for his education, they'd believed strongly in the work ethic, so that Luke had had to work at a variety of jobs while he was studying, to help ease the burden of his keep. Rosalind lazily admitted that since she was old enough to do walk-ons she had only ever worked in the theatre.

'And loved every minute of it,' she sighed. 'Up until now, anyway.'

She bit her lip as the self-pitying words slipped out, and Luke rolled onto his side, propping his temple on a loose fist. 'What's so different now?'

Rosalind looked straight up at the cloudless sky. Her mouth went dry at the thought of saying it…as dry as it had felt the last few times she'd been on stage, in those awful moments when her mind had gone totally blank, so that she hadn't even been able to remember what play she was in, let alone what her next lines were. All she had been conscious of was those eyes trained on her from the darkened auditorium—the eyes of friends, fans, strangers—and one stranger in particular who might be out there, watching, waiting for a word or gesture or a look which his psychosis could interpret as an invitation to fulfil his frightening fantasies…

'Oh, just a slight crisis of confidence. I'll get over it,' she forced herself to say lightly, with more optimism than she felt.

'Did you say confidence or conscience?'

She turned her head sharply. In spite of the increasing heat he hadn't replaced his hat or sunglasses, but the palm fronds stirring overhead dappled his sun-burnished face with fluttering shadows that made his expression difficult to read.

'*Confidence,*' she articulated, deciding to give him the

benefit of the doubt. Perhaps he still had water in his ears. 'I was talking about my *stage* confidence. When you're out there in front of an audience you have to be able to sub-merge yourself in the role. Once you start letting other things intrude you're in trouble. And worrying about whether you're going to have a panic attack in the middle of a performance can become a self-fulfilling prophecy—'

She broke off. She hadn't meant to reveal so much. She hadn't even spoken of her career concerns to her twin. She was tough, determined, a seasoned professional. She had expected to bounce back from adversity with her customary swift resilience. But what if she didn't?

She rolled over onto her stomach, burying her face in her folded arms to conceal the fleeting self-doubt which might be evident on her expressive features. She forced herself back into the role of carefree companion, her voice muffled as she said lightly, 'Speaking of confidence, you seemed to have plenty out there on the water. Now you've got to build on that image.

'The time-honoured ploy of the beach flirt is offering to rub sunscreen onto a woman's back. It gives you the chance to sound sexy *and* caring, and if she accepts then you can practically guarantee she's interested. But don't make the mistake of groping. The first time should be sensuous yet brisk. Your aim is to show her you're a man she can trust...'

There was a silence, several heartbeats long.

'Are you asking me to apply your sunscreen for you?' he said, in a distinctly edgy tone.

Rosalind grinned into her towel, her spirits revived. 'Well, I'm sure you need the practice and I'm prepared to sacrifice myself for the greater good of womankind,' she mocked. 'I'll even give you a critique when you're done! For a start you could show some enthusiasm. Try and sound eager to get your hands on my body...'

'Does your throat count?' he delighted her by muttering.

She turned her head to the side and, sure enough, found his eyes on the tender sweep of her neck, exposed in all its delicate vulnerability by her pixie haircut. 'Why, Luke, do you harbour erotic fantasies about being a vampire?'

His colour had darkened, although it could have been the heat of the sun on his bare head that was making him look flushed. 'I was thinking of strangling rather than biting!' he growled, reluctantly picking up the tube of sunscreen that was poking out of the top of her beach bag.

'Pity. Vampires are much sexier than common-or-garden stranglers!'

His subsequent wordless application of the sunscreen was far more brisk than sensuous but Rosalind didn't take him to task because she discovered the sensation of those firm hands massaging across her sun-warmed skin too disturbing for comfort. This time there was nothing to blame for the faint buzz that vibrated through her nerve-ends but her own bio-electrical system. Wherever Luke touched her it was as if a static discharge occurred—one that seemed to grow rather than to fade with continued contact. Rosalind was literally live to his touch!

Her amusement was mixed with chagrin at the unexpected physical attraction, especially as Luke gave no sign of being similarly affected. He was supposed to be an entertaining holiday distraction, not an added complication to her life. Still, as long as she kept that firmly in the forefront of her mind there could be no danger of her behaving like a real-life Pygmalion and falling in love with her own creation. She had made a promise to Luke, and she couldn't let him down. She would shake him up and turn him loose and in the meantime rely on her strong self-discipline to control any inconvenient pangs of lust!

So from then on Rosalind threw herself wholeheartedly into the task of making Luke seem irresistible to members of the opposite sex while quietly maintaining a discreet physical distance herself. She deliberately gave him no rest, filling every moment with activities which she hoped would so focus his concentration that he would forget the awkward self-consciousness that seemed to afflict him around other people.

Following their jet-skiing success, Rosalind took him snorkelling later the same afternoon and was relieved to find that he was as sleek as a seal in the water, though he regrettably seemed more interested in the teeming marine life on the reef than in the occasional eligible human female who drifted in his direction. They joined a dozen or so others in one of Tioman's distinctive, long wooden bumboats which plied for hire around the coast, to travel to a tiny, rocky off-shore island a scant few minutes from the hotel jetty.

Rosalind marvelled at the vivid fans of waving coral, and the iridescent colours of some of the fish that darted in and out of the rocks. There were gliding mantas and creeping crustaceans, flowing sea anemones and rocking sea urchins with jewel-like blue spots glowing between their long spines.

As they floated face down in the shallows around the island Rosalind was tempted by the idea of booking a scuba-dive and exploring the deeper riches of the sea, until Luke drew closer to her side and motioned towards the seabed, pointing out a young shark sleeking between the rocks. She decided then that perhaps she wasn't ready yet for another close encounter with any denizens of the deep!

The next day they took a three-hour guided walk through the forested valleys to the village of Juara, on the other side of the island. It was hot and still in the depths of the interior, the trunks of massive trees bearing such evocative names as sandalwood and camphor soaring skywards from the forest floor, their distant green canopy almost obscured by the lacy foliage of the palms and shrubs of the undergrowth through which they walked, and Rosalind was grateful to their guide for his frequent pauses on the banks of cool, boulder-strewn streams.

The steamy heat seemed to have little effect on Luke, who chafed at Rosalind's tendency to fall back amongst the stragglers and linger over every new orchid spike, every small lizard or exotic butterfly she spied.

In the afternoon they caught a bumboat back around the south coast, stopping off at Mukut village, from which they trekked up to the famous waterfall. Luke had never seen *South Pacific* and had been slightly contemptuous of the reason for Rosalind's eager pilgrimage, but he couldn't deny that the scenery itself was spectacular and Rosalind had her revenge for his sarcastic remarks about cultural imperialism in general and the silliness of musicals in particular by singing him every song from the show that she could remember, much to the amusement of others they passed on the walk.

Washing men out of her hair seemed particularly appealing, and she sang that one several times with special emphasis on their way back down to the boat, accompanying it with jaunty dance steps that criss-crossed in front of Luke's stride until he was goaded into begging her to stop.

Luke got his own back the next day, however, when Rosalind offered to teach him to windsurf. When he appeared ready to protest she overrode him with her usual bossy enthusiasm, stressing that everyone was clumsy at first but it was just a matter of persistence. She very kindly didn't say that she expected him to be a more clumsy beginner than most, but the message was subtly delivered by her condescending grin. And so it proved.

She made Luke walk parallel to her on the sand while she sailed the board along to the secluded end of the long beach to show him how it was done. The breeze was gentle but steady and the sea glass-like in its smoothness, so the conditions were as perfect as they could be for a beginner.

Given Luke's seal-like grace in the water, Rosalind was confident that once he got over his nervous fear of making a fool of himself he would soon pick up the basics, but to her frustration he proved so fumblingly inept that it took her ages merely to get him standing upright on the board. In the process she became his waterlogged sea anchor, her arms and hands aching from holding the board steady while he tried to find his elusive sense of balance.

When, finally, after more than an hour of careful coaching, he progressed to actually pulling the sail upright, he would invariably lose his stability before the wind had time to fill it and topple off again, usually in her direction, smacking down in a tangle of splayed limbs, sending yet another shock blast of salt water shooting up into her eyes, nose and mouth.

She couldn't lose her temper because each time it happened Luke was so very apologetic, so desperate to master the simple skill, so insistent that if she would just bear with him he would eventually succeed. She didn't have the heart to tell him that he might as well give it up as a lost cause, not after she had stressed the importance of persistence.

Even worse, his body seemed to be constantly bumping and rubbing up against hers as they struggled with the board and the wet sail. She had to help boost him up onto the deck and guide his legs into position and reach around him to show him the handholds. Every time she moved, his cool flesh somehow got in her way. Her hands slipped and slid against his smooth, wet skin, sometimes skidding off into dangerous territory, and the water proved a wonderful conductor for the zinging electrical awareness that intensified each time their bodies made contact.

Oh, for the temperate waters of New Zealand where most windsurfers wore demure wetsuits! Rosalind inwardly wailed as Luke took another tumble, one slick thigh fleetingly thrust between hers, its slight roughness rasping the highly sensitive skin and catching on the silky fabric of her bikini, giving it an intimate little nudge that, for Rosalind, was the last straw.

She faked, very professionally, standing on something sharp and painful. Just painful enough to necessitate her limping ashore to check the wound, not painful enough to require his assistance.

'It's not as if there's any blood. I'll be fine…you carry on with what you're doing,' she said, hastily wading beyond his long reach. 'Maybe you just need a bit of time fooling about on your own to get the hang of it, anyway…'

She limped up the beach to their towels in a masterful piece of underplaying, conscious of Luke's eyes boring into her back. She sat down and made a show of inspecting the sole of her foot before giving him a reassuring wave and relaxing back on her elbows with a grateful sigh. She watched him broodingly. This was ridiculous. Why was she running away? He was a perfectly nice man. Why on earth *shouldn't* she conduct this phony flirtation for real?

Her eyes drifted closed as she contemplated the idea. Although Luke might be inexperienced with women he was intellectually mature, a full-grown, well-educated adult holding down a highly responsible job. It wouldn't be as if she were seducing an innocent boy for her own amusement. And there would be no question of exploring the attraction if it didn't prove to be mutual…

She must have dozed off because when next she opened her eyes Luke was nowhere in sight. She sat up in alarm, her anxious gaze sweeping the bay, visions of finding him floating face down in the water dancing in her head. And it would be all her fault for pushing him beyond his physical capabilities!

Her jaw dropped when she finally spotted the distinctive green sail emblazoned with the hotel's palm logo breezing out towards the open sea. As she watched, Luke shifted his weight, swinging the sail around and moving back towards the shore, tacking to take best advantage of the light off-shore wind.

Hmm!

By the time he beached the board and strolled up the sand her suspicions were simmering.

'That was a pretty good run for an absolute beginner.'

He picked up his towel and mopped down his body with distracting thoroughness. 'Actually you were right—it was a lot easier without you there pointing out every mistake and making me nervous.' His face disappeared into the towel as he rubbed his hair.

'Oh, really?' she drawled, relaxing back on her elbows, dipping her head so that the straw brim of her hat concealed her study of the way the concave plane of his stomach flexed with his movements.

'Yes, once you figure out how to stay upright the rest just seems to fall into place!'

Her suspicions were unappeased by his muffled words. 'Luke James, is that the first time you've been windsurfing?'

His face emerged from the folds of the towel. 'Surely you should have asked me that question before we started? How's the foot?'

'Fine,' she said absently, trying to figure out whether his answer constituted a confession of exaggerated ineptitude.

'Is it? May I see?'

Before she realised what he was doing he had dropped to his knees in front of her feet, his buttocks resting on his heels, his fingers gripping her ankle.

'No!'

She tried to jerk away but his fingers tightened around the bone as he lifted her foot for inspection.

'Don't worry, I won't hurt you,' he murmured, brushing the grains of sand gently off her sole with the thumb of his free hand.

'I told you, it was nothing,' she said breathlessly as he

frowned, bending closer to the site, his damp hair fanning forward around the widow's peak, his thumb moving in another probing caress. His nail scraped lightly across her skin and her toes curled involuntarily towards the ball of her foot, a husky sound of protest issuing from her throat. He paused, his lids flicking up in instant enquiry.

'I'm ticklish.' Unbelievably she could feel her face pinken at the husky lie. She, the mistress of the mask, whose whole professional training had been aimed at the weaving of believable lies. She *never* blushed...except when it was written in the stage directions!

'I'll be careful.' His lids sank down again and Rosalind braced herself to have her silly deception exposed. 'I don't see— Ah, wait a moment, what's this...?' His short thumb-nail dug into the soft, resilient pad of flesh. 'It looks like...it could be a shell splinter, or some sort of spine...'

'Could it?' Rosalind hadn't really looked closely at her foot, knowing there was nothing there to see. 'Uh...it's not hurting now—'

'Did you feel a stinging or burning sensation when it happened?'

'Neither,' she said truthfully. But she could certainly feel something now! She wished he would stop rubbing his thumb back and forth like that; it was sending tingles of sensation shooting up the insides of her calves and thighs.

A heat that had nothing to do with the sun pooled in her stomach. Her fingers dug into the sand at her sides and her free leg shifted restlessly, drawing up slightly to hide the vulnerable triangle at the apex of her thighs. She could feel her nipples begin to firm and knew they would soon be evident through the thin, shiny fabric of her hot-pink bikini.

'Whatever it is I don't think we should leave it in there, do you?' he said gravely. 'In this climate infections can set in very quickly if you ignore a wound...'

'Unfortunately I don't happen to have a needle on me,' joked Rosalind weakly, patting her bare sides. She regretted

her mistake immediately as his eyes accepted the licence
to rove. A quick glance down confirmed that he couldn't
fail to notice the explicit outline of her breasts, the smooth
swells, gathered and lifted by the halter-neck of her bikini,
projecting the stiff little crowns forward into stark promi-
nence. And she couldn't even blame it on the chill of the
water!

His gaze took on a familiar blank, unfocused intensity
as it rose to her face, his fingers tightening on her ankle as
she instinctively tried again to twist it free.

'We'll just have to improvise, then…' he murmured.
And, still holding her gaze, he bent his head, shifting his
grip to cup her heel, tilting her foot delicately aslant with
his other hand as he placed it against his open mouth.
Rosalind gasped as she felt his teeth sink deep into the
tender pad of her sole and a hot, wet suction begin a rhyth-
mic tugging at her flesh.

'Luke!' Her exclamation of shocked protest was undermined by the insidious weakness that flooded through her
body. Her elbows collapsed and her shoulderblades hit the
sand, her hat rolling off her bright head, leaving her dazzled
by the sun. The second protest was even feebler than the
first. 'Luke…'

He sucked more strongly, his teeth grating against her
skin, creating tiny needles of pain that were instantly
soothed by the moist movements of his mouth. And she
lay there and submitted, watching him watching her over
the top of her toes. His gaze was intense with a dark concentration. She had never thought of her feet as erogenous
zones before, but the delicious sensation of bone-melting
pleasure she was experiencing made her re-evaluate her
thinking. No wonder people developed foot fetishes!

Suddenly she felt his tongue join the suckling, swirling
and rasping against her wet skin. One of his hands slid
lightly down the top of her foot and around behind her
ankle, to drift up the back of her supple calf, his spreading

fingers offering caressing support to the tautly extended muscle. The long, slow French kissing continued until Rosalind squirmed, a brief groan escaping her lips.

He lifted his mouth fractionally. 'Am I hurting you? Do you want me to stop?' His lips brushed against her sole as they formed the gruff words and she gave another little shivery moan. He was kneeling like a supplicant yet his eyes seemed to smoulder with the triumphant recognition of his own power. He knew *exactly* what he was doing to her...

Alarm bells started to ring in her distracted senses. The audacity of his action had been so out of character that it had caught her completely off guard, but she mustn't allow him to think that he could control and manipulate her through her passions.

'You're not hurting me...but I still think you'd better stop,' she asserted regretfully.

He lowered her foot onto his knee, holding her heel against the sun-warmed hardness of bone and muscle.

'I think whatever it was has come out anyway,' he said. His tongue appeared between his lips and he dabbed at it and then inspected his fingertip. 'Ah, yes, I'm sure it did...'

Rosalind suddenly remembered that her injury had supposedly been imaginary. 'Can I see?' She propped herself up on her hands but even as she spoke he was casually flicking whatever was on his fingertip into the breeze.

'Sorry, but it was hardly worth looking at. Such a tiny thing to cause you so much discomfort,' he said, so blandly that Rosalind's suspicions were reawakened.

But no, that was silly! Luke would never have summoned the nerve to make such an outrageously seductive move on purpose.

Would he?

'What made you want to try to get it out like that anyway?' she asked, thinking that tax avoidance was actually a fairly devious field requiring a certain amount of risk-taking by its practitioners. And Luke was a self-declared specialist.

'I saw it once…in a Bond movie,' he admitted.

Rosalind recalled the scene…and the way the woman's gratitude had been expressed afterwards, in typical Bond-girl fashion. She delivered him a tart warning. 'You should know that things you see done in the movies don't always work out the same in real life!'

'No, only sometimes,' he agreed meekly, his gaze briefly brushing her treacherously firm breasts. Rosalind shifted her foot hastily back onto the sand and as she did so the slight bristliness of his leg struck a familiar chord.

Her green eyes narrowed, squinting for a better look as she blurted out, 'For goodness' sake, Luke, do you *shave* your *legs*?'

'As a matter of fact, I do,' he said coolly, moving around beside her. 'I cycle, and shaving your legs makes treating the scrapes much less painful if you fall on the tarmac, not to mention reducing drag and chafing of the Lycra kit…'

'Oh.' Rosalind had discovered something else equally intriguing. 'You shave your chest too, don't you?'

She couldn't resist reaching over and touching it. His skin was like hot satin, slipping against her fingers, smooth but with a faint catch in a broad area from collar-to-breast-bone. She guessed that in his natural state he would be quite furry.

His voice also had a slight, uneven catch. 'We wear Lycra body-shirts as well.'

Rosalind drew back, her fingers drifting absently to her parted lips, and the clean, salty tang of him suddenly filled her nostrils, creating an unexpected hunger. Her tongue crept out to touch her fingertips and now the taste of him was inside her too, lush and tempting…

Through a veil of lashes she watched Luke's eyes glaze at her action and then sink down her half-reclining body, drifting into intimate territory before faltering and returning to find the flaw in the otherwise pearly perfection of her skin.

His lips parted, his brows darting upwards in a slight frown. He bent over to trace the faint silvery line low down on her abdomen with his finger.

'What's this? Appendix?'

It was like being delicately brushed with a live wire. Rosalind's skin quivered and she could feel the downy-fine hair on her belly spring erect. His finger jerked away, only to return almost immediately to explore the tiny ridge. He was getting bolder by the minute.

'No!'

She had thought she had herself under control but suddenly she was fighting a fierce, almost overwhelming urge to plunge her fingers into the fine, silky hair that had slid across his temples, twine them amongst the sun-warmed strands and force his mouth slowly, slowly down to her body…to feel him move his open lips against that small, inoffensive, earth-shattering scar. And then, and then…

She put a flat hand just below his shoulder, hesitating when she felt his heart pumping as violently as hers, then she pushed him away—a hard shove that sent him sprawling on the sand.

He blinked up at her. 'What's the matter?'

'Nothing. I just think it's time we made a move!' she said, leaping up, her jerky movements revealing her inner agitation.

'I'm sorry; I didn't mean to dredge up bad memories for you,' he said, rolling lithely to his feet beside her, brushing the sand off his side.

'You didn't. It's just an operation scar—from years ago…when I was living in London.'

She could probably tell him the exact day if she wanted to dwell on it. But she had long ago decided that she wouldn't because that would mean dwelling on Justin—wonderful, laughing, handsome Justin—the first and last great love of her life, the shining knight of her dreams who had turned out to be utterly without honour or conscience.

Rosalind—young, passionately in love and blinded by her own romantic idealism—had been a willing victim of his forceful charm. Because her trust had been as absolute as her love she had ignored the most elementary precautions with the man she had expected to marry, only to find out that he had been unfaithful with a string of one-night stands.

She had been lucky. She could have faced a death sentence for her naïvety. As it was, the consequences of her liaison with Justin had sent her recklessly off the rails for a while, but she had quickly realised the self-destructive futility of her actions. Yes, something precious had been taken away from her, but she had since found other things, other blessings to put in its place...

'Were you involved in an accident?'

'No. Pelvic inflammatory disease.'

Her bluntness didn't embarrass him into silence. He frowned. 'It must have been serious for them to operate.'

'It was. And no, before you ask, I didn't get it by being promiscuous,' she bit out. Many people associated PID with sexual profligacy, but until Justin had charmed his way into her heart Rosalind had been remarkably chaste. Ironically her innocence had probably been her downfall. If she *had* been more sexually experienced she might have been less submissive to Justin's seductive wiles.

'What made it so serious?'

'There were complications...'

'What kind of complications?'

She looked at him incredulously. He seemed utterly in earnest. For a shy man he was showing a hell of a nerve! She began to laugh. 'Do you just want the highlights or should I get my doctor to send you a complete gynaecological history?'

He flushed, reverting to type, and she was reassured sufficiently to tease, 'Don't worry Luke, the only thing you've risked with me so far is foot-and-mouth disease.'

His flush deepened and she took advantage of his confusion to tell him that, since he had suddenly turned out to be such a hotshot windsurfer, *he* could sail the board back, while she strolled leisurely back to the hotel for some much needed R and R.

The School for Flirts was out for the day!

CHAPTER SEVEN

FROM her vantage point beside a pillar in the glass wall Rosalind watched the man in shorts and singlet sweating on one of the ferocious torture machines inside the air-conditioned hotel gym.

'Crazy guy, huh?'

She jumped as someone came up beside her—a bouncy young Australian woman who had been taking an early-morning dip in the pool when Rosalind had passed it on her way to the reception desk to pick up some more of her money from her safety-deposit box.

'He looks in pain,' said Rosalind, wincing as Luke moved over to a free-weight bench-press and began another set of punishing exercises.

'Nah, I don't think those guys know what pain is—push a button and they just keep going and going. Most of them look as if you could knock them over with a feather…but their strength is in their incredible stamina—'

'What guys?' interrupted Rosalind, bewildered.

'Triathletes.'

'Did *he* tell you he was a triathlete?' she asked, hiding her amusement. If Luke had been practising some creative self-aggrandisement she didn't want to ruin it for him by blowing his cover.

'No, but I was in Hawaii last year when my father was doing PR work for one of the sponsors of the Ironman… I remember him—' she jerked her bleached-blonde head towards the gym '—because he was staying at the same hotel, scarfing up mountains of pasta and cake at the carbo-loading the day before the race. I actually saw him finish, too, quite well up in the field…'

113

Her words took a few moments to sink in properly. 'Luke was in the *Ironman*?' Rosalind repeated feebly.

Her Luke? The man she had privately voted the most likely to have sand kicked in his face…taking part in the most gruelling athletic event in the world?

Rosalind stormed through the glass doors into the gym and marched across to loom over Luke's supine figure on the padded bench-press.

'So this is why we have to have a late breakfast—so you can hang out with the rest of the jocks!' she flung at him accusingly, ignoring the fact that except for Luke the gym was deserted.

His hands almost slipped on the bar he was holding at the full extension of his arms. 'Roz! What are you doing here?' He lowered the weights on straining arms until the bar rested across his chest, his expression glazing protectively as he took in her glittering fury. 'Uh, you know the only reason I suggested breakfasting a bit later was to give you time to get over your nausea—'

'Oh, really?' She produced an exquisite sneer, unappeased. 'Not because you wanted to sneak out and pump some *iron* on the sly?'

His hair had flopped sweatily over his eyebrows and Rosalind was infuriated by a strong urge to comb it back. Even lying there clutching a set of massive weights, he still managed to project an air of defencelessness. 'Well, no, I—'

'Not because you're feeling deprived of your daily dose of self-flagellation?' she said, reminding herself that he was a hardened athlete. Physically, he was about as defenceless as a tank!

'Huh?'

'You know…those things you mild-mannered tax accountants do for a bit of relaxation…swimming, cycling, running? Hawaii Ironman?' she crunched out. 'Am I ringing any bells here yet, Mr Aw-gee-shucks-I'm-so-helpless James?'

Luke's chest contracted under his sweat-soaked singlet, his arms cording as he lifted the weight back onto the rack above him with only a faint grunt of effort. He sat up and swung his legs off the bench, using the small towel around his neck to blot his damp face and throat. 'That was your opinion. I never claimed to be helpless.'

Rosalind slapped her hands onto the hips of her ribbed cotton shorts. 'Oh, right,' she agreed with acid disbelief. 'And I suppose you'd never windsurfed before yesterday either!'

He had the grace to look guilty. 'Only once or twice, although I did quite a bit of board-surfing when I was young. We lived near a beach and I was a member of the local surf club. That's where I first got interested in triathlons…'

An ex-surfie! Rosalind ground her teeth, thinking of all the time she had spent trying to get him to balance upright on the board.

'I suppose in triathletes' parlance ''once or twice'' means you did a return crossing of the Pacific!' she said, sarcasm dripping from every word as her suspicions were confirmed. 'So you *were* deliberately having me on yesterday.'

'Well, maybe just a little,' he admitted, carrying out a few discreet warm-down stretches against the bench as she stood glowering at him, her lemon-yellow shorts and vest-top shimmering with her heaving outrage. When Rosalind's temper was sparking she didn't hold anything back.

'Fair's fair, Rosalind—you've been having plenty of fun at *my* expense ever since we met,' he pointed out. 'And you never *asked* me if I played any sport. I told you I had a full life but all you seemed interested in was my lack of cultural and social pursuits.'

She hated it when he used logic to make her feel in the wrong. 'Triathletes don't *play* at what they do,' she countered. 'I've read all about it. It's not a sport, it's an obsession.'

'Not for me. I just do it as a hobby—for fun.'

'Fun?' She stared at him, her anger eclipsed by her horror. If his idea of fun was to try to push himself beyond the limits of human endurance then he was even more socially deprived than she had thought! Maybe this new perspective of him wasn't so different from the old one. How typical of Luke to choose a solo sport. The tightness inside her loosened further as she contemplated all the solitary hours he must spend in training. No wonder he didn't have time for any other activities.

'You needn't look as though I've admitted to some gross depravity.' His eyebrows quirked in amusement. 'You ought to try it some time, Roz—the running part, I mean. There's no drug that can match the natural high it gives you.'

She smothered an unwilling grin. 'Since I don't do drugs I wouldn't know,' she said, exploding another colourful media myth. 'As a matter of fact I have my own version of a natural high...I get it from performing in front of a live audience.'

'You must be suffering a few withdrawal symptoms by now, then,' he said, with more accuracy than he could know. He glanced down at the trendy white designer sports shoes she was wearing. 'Look, since you've cut short my programme, why don't you come on a little run with me now, along the track at the back of the beach?'

'Ha! What do I look like—a masochist? You'd run me into the ground!'

'I'll go at your pace,' he offered. 'Come on; if your connection with your twin is putting your body under stress you could probably do with a little extra conditioning.'

She snapped at the challenge. 'I'm in perfect shape for my lifestyle, thank you very much!'

It was meant as a haughty rejection, so how was it that

half an hour later she was bending over against the drunken U-shape of a wind-distorted palm tree at the side of the trail, desperately trying to suck another breath into her shattered lungs?

'Do you think you're going to be sick?' The fact that Luke's words were crisp and even, without the slightest hint of a puff, added insult to injury as far as Rosalind was concerned.

'This isn't morning sickness, it's exhaustion!' came tearing out of her throat between whistling breaths. 'I *told* you you'd run me into the ground.'

'But I was pacing myself to your stride—'

'Yes, well...I was showing off, wasn't I?' she wheezed, giving up on her dignity.

'Can't you catch your breath? Here, try this way.' Luke stood behind her and looped his arms under hers, lifting them straight up over her head so that she was forced into an upright, shoulders-back stance. 'Now try slow and deep rather than fast and shallow.'

Immediately the tightness in her chest eased and she found that her breathing slowed enough for her to joke, 'I guess that's me off the team, huh?'

'I should have realised you were pushing it, but you acted OK with the pace right up until you stopped.' His voice was rough with self-accusation.

'You've only now figured out what a great actress I am?' She tipped her bright head back against his shoulder, feeling the smooth power of his raised bicep brush her cheek. She could feel the heat and dampness of his chest through her thin top. His heart, she was chagrined to register, was barely skipping a beat, while hers was still going crazy.

'Do you ever switch off or are you always on, always acting a part for the person you're with?'

She stiffened at the unexpected thrust and tried to pull her arms down. '*You* can talk.'

His breath was hot on her nape as he steadied her in

position. 'Not yet; just wait until your heartbeat slows a little more. Trust me—you'll feel better in a minute.'

She realised that his fingers around her wrists could feel her pounding pulse. Trapped by her fresh awareness of his superior strength and fitness, she resorted to striking back with words.

'*Trust* you? Why should I trust someone who pretends to be something he's not…who can't even be open with me about something as innocent as what he does in his spare time?'

His fingers tightened briefly. 'I'm Luke James. I've never pretended to be anyone else. Unlike *you*—'

'I had good reasons.'

'Escaping publicity? Oh, come on; publicity is something you've always thrived on.' He suddenly let her wrists go, his loosely encircling hands sliding the length of her arms as she lowered them to her sides and felt her fingers tingle with the returning blood.

He gripped her shoulders and spun her around to face him. She was shocked by his darkly intense expression and the rigid tension that gripped his entire body. She realised that she had finally goaded him into real anger. There was no gentle diffidence in him now, no shy uncertainty. The adrenalin which had been pumping into his system during the run was still saturating his blood.

'No, there's much more to it than avoiding a few newspaper reporters, isn't there, Rosalind?' he said harshly. 'I'm an intelligent man. Do you think I haven't realised why you practically dragooned me into letting you take over my holiday? It isn't solely for my benefit, is it? All I am to you is a distraction to keep your mind off whatever it is you're running away from…'

'That's not true—'

'Isn't it? *Isn't it?*'

'No!' Her gaze faltered, even though she realised at that

moment that it was indeed the literal truth. That *wasn't* all he was to her, not by a long chalk...

She stepped back, and found her buttocks coming hard up against the dipping curve of the misshapen palm that she had grabbed to catch her breath. She clutched at it again as Luke simultaneously mirrored her movement, leaning forward to brace his hands on either side of her hips, trapping her even more effectively than he had a few moments before, this time in a position in which he could read every nuance of her expression.

'Your personality shines with such incandescent brightness that most people are too dazzled to see the shadows,' he said quietly. 'What are they, Roz? What is it that makes you run?'

'Apart from you, you mean?' She couldn't look away from the hypnotic black gaze. She had an odd sensation of falling and the even odder one of knowing that she could rely on Luke to catch her, that he would be a steady, rock-solid support. Perhaps he did have the right to some answers, she thought, and by giving them to him perhaps she might find out something she needed to know.

So she told him about the bombardment of letters and gifts she had been receiving from an unknown fan, about her efforts to ignore the growing sense of menace in his attentions. This time she made no attempt to make her experience sound amusing and, lured on by Luke's silence she found herself impulsively exposing the heart of her anxiety—the stage fright that had caused her to question the core of her belief in herself.

'All my life all I've ever wanted to be is an actress,' she said starkly. 'It's what I've worked for. It's what I *am*.'

'You mean it's the only thing in your life that you take seriously.' Luke broke his silence with a sudden, shrewd insight into the essence of her bright, bubbly, fun-loving character. He felt a savage rush of pure adrenalin as he fitted a major piece into the elusive puzzle that was Roz

Marlow. No wonder she had so few inhibitions about enjoying the pleasures of life—because she knew how truly inessential such things were to her happiness. The social butterfly flitted compulsively not because she was unable to care deeply enough about anyone or anything to commit but because she was already committed elsewhere.

'If I can't perform, if I'm not Rosalind Marlow the actress, who am I? My parents offered me this holiday as a kind of escape, but I suppose the one thing that I'm never going to escape is myself...'

'And you have absolutely no idea who this Peter is...?'

She almost—*almost*—said a name.

The relief would have been enormous.

But she couldn't permit herself the luxury. If Rosalind mentioned Peter Noble by name, Luke would want to know why she hadn't reported him to the police. He would want to know who he was and how Rosalind had found out about him.

How could she tell him that Peter was Peggy Staines's illegitimate son, given up for adoption after a secret teenage pregnancy? Peggy had been adamant that no one else was to know. She had never even told her husband about the bitter mistake that haunted her past and she had been appalled when her adult son had somehow traced her and confronted her one day when she was out shopping.

For weeks she had been torn between curiosity about the baby she had been forced to give up all those years ago and fear of the moody adult that he had become. She'd been especially afraid that Peter's persistent attempts to make her accept him in her life would result in the old shame becoming public and thus jeopardise her marriage and her husband's all-important career. To add to her guilt, she had found out that Peter had not been happy with his adoptive family, which had broken up and dispersed when he was a teenager.

In an attempt to placate both Peter and her conscience,

Peggy had agreed to visit him at his flat, but the more she'd seen of him, the more disturbed she had become by his erratic behaviour. She'd discovered that he had been an outpatient at a psychiatric clinic and her fears about his mental stability had seemed to be confirmed after she'd seen his bizarrely decorated flat and realised the extent to which his fan-worship of his favourite actress had taken over his life.

Peter had no job and was on limited medical benefit, yet in his closet he'd had a complete wardrobe of expensive new clothes in Rosalind's size, still with their sales tags attached, and a range of her favourite make-up and toiletries lined up beside his razor in the bathroom. A home-made pin-up calendar of Rosalind had been marked with a detailed log of her activities, and when Peggy had found copies of his letters to Rosalind she had panicked at the thought of what would happen if Peter got into trouble and was exposed to the public spotlight.

Rosalind's knowledge from here on was very sketchy, because by the time she had met Peggy in that infamous hotel room the distraught woman had worked herself into such a state that she had only had time to sob out the bare bones of her story before she had succumbed to the pain of her heart attack, gasping incoherently about something that Peter had done that had made all her soul-searching and suffering pointless...

Rosalind, who had just got out of the shower and had still been in her damp robe when her visitor had arrived at her hotel room fully two hours early for their meeting, hadn't been quite quick enough when Peggy had suddenly crumpled to the floor. In spite of the choking pain, she had struggled vainly to communicate, only subsiding when a frightened Rosalind had firmly promised that she wouldn't do or say anything to anyone about Peter until she had Peggy's permission.

Now she was trapped by the integrity that the Press

claimed she didn't possess. It was ironic that in order to produce proof of her honour she would have to violate it.

'I know that it's someone who's much more disturbed than I wanted to believe,' she sighed, hoping that Luke hadn't read the long pause as significant.

'Then why haven't you *done* something about it?' he demanded, his impatience reeking of disapproval.

'I guess I felt—feel—sort of sorry for the guy,' she admitted, the mingled scents of cologne and male sweat rising between their bodies making her aware of how close they were standing. With Luke leaning in on her, his arms splayed around her sides, anyone coming up the trail behind them would think that they were embracing...

'*Sorry* for him?' Luke's exasperation with her tolerance was almost identical to Jordan's and expressed equally forcefully. 'He doesn't need your sympathy, Roz; what he *needs* is to be stopped before he can harm you or himself.'

Rosalind shivered in the steamy morning heat. 'I know.' She pulled a face. 'Jordan suggested I acquire a bodyguard for the duration.'

He frowned. 'Which you refused, of course.'

He was much better at predicting her behaviour than she was at guessing his reactions. She gave a defensive shrug.

'I already have too many people following me everywhere. If a crazed fan did try an abduction the reporters would descend like a cloud of locusts. They'd soon scare him off!'

'And ruin the chance to spin out a good story? More likely they'd stand back and take pictures,' he said grimly. 'You're lucky you've got the Staines affair hanging over your head, or you wouldn't even have the minimal protection of press surveillance.'

Her eyes flashed at the unexpected callousness of the remark. 'There's nothing lucky about it! Mrs Staines is still seriously ill in hospital, you know.'

'*Mrs Staines?*' he repeated, his eyebrows flicking derisively upwards. 'Isn't that a rather formal way to refer to someone you've been having secret assignations with— surely you're on first-name terms with each other?'

The sting in his tone hit her on the raw. 'It was only *one* assignation, damn it!' she blurted out. 'It was the first time we'd ever met!'

His seething impatience seemed to still, his voice easing to a toneless neutrality. 'That must have made it all the more traumatic for you when she collapsed like that.'

Rosalind lowered her head, biting her bottom lip as she replayed her own actions in her mind. 'I suppose I can't help feeling as if it was my fault, even though the whole thing was her idea...' She was so intent on the disturbing memory that she didn't notice Luke stiffen slightly. 'I've never seen anyone have a heart attack before. There was so little I could do. It was *dreadful*. I hated being so help-less...'

'I know the feeling.'

His quiet anger jolted Rosalind out of her self-absorption. 'Do you?' She lifted her face to his and saw a bleakness in his brooding countenance that pierced her to the heart. Without thinking she reached up and laid a comforting hand against his rigid cheek. He froze, and his eyes searched hers, then dropped to her pink mouth, which was slightly swollen from her thoughtful nibbling, and she was suddenly breathless all over again, taking shallow sips of air that gave her no respite from the tightness in her chest.

'Luke...?'

'What?' His voice was thick, his cheek heavy in her hand as he leaned his head into her touch, rubbing at her like a giant cat being petted, the corner of his mouth brushing the sensitive mound at the base of her thumb as he spoke.

'I think...'

'What?' He turned his head completely, his mouth open-ing against the centre of her palm, his eyes flaring darkly at the taste of her, the cold bleakness in their depths disappearing, leaving a smouldering awareness in its wake. He moved abruptly closer, bringing his hips firmly against hers, pushing her backwards against the trunk of the palm, his arms closing in until they brushed her sides.

'What do you think, Rosalind…?'

His hoarse, muffled whisper made her head spin. Whatever it was no longer seemed important. The important thing was that Luke's breath was moist and hot in her cupped hand and his bent knee was softly insinuating itself between hers, pressing forward and then retreating until, unable to bear the sensual torment any more, she widened her stance, eagerly inviting the added intimacy. He came the rest of the way in a rush, roughly pushing into the space she had created for him and drawing his other leg sharply against her flank, compressing her thigh between warm pillars of taut muscle.

For some perverse reason she kept her hand over his mouth while the centres of their bodies kissed, shifted and kissed again, her other hand applying pressure to his chest, preventing his torso from crushing against her breasts. She was excited by the stormy look in Luke's eyes as he submitted reluctantly to the delicate restraint. She was playing power games with him and they both knew it. They knew that he was stronger and fitter and could easily overcome her token resistance if he chose. But he didn't choose, because he was too much of a gentleman, and maybe because he was a little in awe of her feminine power, thought Rosalind exultantly.

That didn't mean, however, that he didn't possess other means of persuasion. Denied the luxury of taste, he resorted to his other most potent sense to appease their mutual craving for contact, holding her gaze as he rocked against her, grinding her soft buttocks into the rough palm-trunk, his muscles quivering with strain. He was wild for more, and so was Rosalind, but she wanted to tease, to withhold the pleasure that she knew was awaiting them for another few, dizzyingly delicious moments.

He made a deep, smothered sound in his chest and she felt his stiffened tongue dart into a crease between her clamped fingers—a blunt, wet probe that she resisted, even as it made her go weak at the knees. His eyes were sullen, raging with a strange mixture of anger and desire, and hints of a sultry male challenge that thrilled her to her toes. This was Luke the athlete, superbly self-disciplined and intensely focused on his own state of physical readiness. Her mouth went dry, a swimmy heat hazing everything but the man sharply centred in her vision.

Rosalind licked her lips, unconsciously tempting him with what she had denied him. His tongue thrust again at her fingers and she felt his thighs simultaneously tense around her trapped leg, squeezing and releasing in a graphic rhythm that made her arch her hips in the instinctive feminine response.

His control slipped a notch and his hands released their white-knuckled grip on the tree-trunk beside her hips and contracted around her waist, his fingers sizzling on her skin where her vest-top had ridden up from the waistband of her shorts. He angled his body, bending Rosalind further back over the curving beam of the palm, until the tendons in her neck ached with the effort of keeping him in sight and every cell and nerve-end between her knees and her waist was imprinted with the indelible evidence of his masculinity.

'All right!' she gasped, whipping her hand from his mouth.

'All right what?' he growled savagely.

She slid her arms around his taut neck, her fingers linking tightly across his strong nape, supporting herself while at the same time attempting to pull him down. 'All right, you can kiss me,' she ordered flatly, and was shocked to find him suddenly resisting. 'What's the matter?' she husked, rotating the bony jut of her hip against the hard resilience between his spread thighs. 'Changed your mind?'

'Lost it, more like,' was the ragged answer, half under his breath. His head dipped closer at her urging. 'Why am I letting you do this to me?'

Her eyes glowed with cat-like satisfaction at his whisper of helpless fascination. He was admitting that he was hers, to do with as she pleased...

'Don't tell me I have to teach you how to kiss as well as how to flirt?' she murmured invitingly.

He was breathing harshly, his black eyes riveted on her pouting mouth as he struggled with his self-control. 'What's to teach? A kiss is just a kiss...'

She laughed—a sound of pure feminine provocation. 'Oh, Luke, do you have a *lot* to learn...'

Her condescending mockery was smothered by his urgent mouth. It was hot and hard and surprisingly tart. His lips slanted across hers, his tongue smoothing inside the velvety interior of her mouth, sucking at the sweetness he found there.

Rosalind's eyes fluttered shut, unable to cope with the sensual overload. She was in a dark world of heat and tumultuous sensation which intensified when she felt his hands drifting up and down her satiny sides under the thin vest-top, his thumbs shaping the tender outer swell of her breasts exposed by her skimpy bra.

His teeth grazed her lips, his hardness lodged tightly in the hollow of her groin, and his fingertips slid under her lacy straps on their next casual journey, curling around the narrow ribbons and peeling the stretchy fabric down, leaving her breasts peaking against the soft abrasion of her top.

Rosalind's hands slid up into his hair, gripping him hard and deepening the kiss as she waited in exquisite agony for the explorative touch to steal back up to the flesh he had daringly exposed, but his hands stayed inexplicably at her waist, fingers kneading the soft indentation with an almost

painful thoroughness. She twisted restlessly. She couldn't
bear him to turn tentative and shy on her, not *now*... She
clutched at his wrists, dragging his hands up under her top
and moulding them around her naked breasts.

Fireworks went off in her head. A convulsion of inde-
scribable pleasure rolled over her, enveloping every milli-
metre of her skin from the top of her tingling scalp to the
tips of her reflexively curled-up toes. The heated darkness
came rushing up at her like a physical force, sweeping away
any semblance of thought or will, sucking her into a black
hole of pure, concentrated sensation. Time warped and
stretched, turning fluid and meaningless. The universe
shrank at an accelerating rate until it was composed of
nothing but a warm body and a violently beating heart...
one man at the centre of eternity.

It was Luke who broke the blindingly erotic spell, Luke
who dragged his mouth away from hers, his hands still
moving compulsively on her breasts, violent tremors shaking his body as he fought the gravitational pull of their
mutual desire.

'God, what am I doing?' he muttered harshly, dragging
his hands from her bare flesh but unable to prevent his
fingers trailing a final, reluctant farewell across her
stiffened nipples as he did so, his eyes burning at the sight
of her instinctive little shudder of response.

Rosalind stared up at him in dazed confusion until the
tortured self-contempt in his expression brought reality
crashing back down on her. She too was trembling, only
the palm tree behind her hips preventing her from sinking
bonelessly to her knees in front of the man who had kid-
napped her senses and held them so ravishingly to ransom.

She hadn't wanted to be rescued, she realised helplessly.
She hadn't cared what they were doing, or where, or why.
One minute she had been a playful temptress confident of
her control, the next she had been a maelstrom of chaotic

emotions, utterly at the mercy of her feelings for this one man. Luke James.

His thin mouth twisted at her wide-eyed stare, mistaking it for challenge. 'Well, teacher, I guess you made your point,' he said, stepping back.

'Did I?' It was Rosalind who had learned a lesson, and she was still grappling with the terrifying implications.

'I'm sorry if I hurt you.'

'What?' She had pulled her bra back over her breasts and now her hands flattened defensively over their aching tenderness, protecting her lingering arousal from his mockery.

To her shock he touched her throbbing mouth with his thumb, his face grave. 'I didn't realise I was being so rough...you have a little cut...'

'It doesn't hurt,' she said hastily, turning aside, so that his touch slid to the outer point of her jaw, a brief streak of fire across her soft cheek.

He straightened, putting his hands behind his back, and Rosalind didn't doubt that his fists were clenched as he said tightly, 'I suppose I should thank all your previous lovers for providing my teacher with her expertise.'

Previous lovers? That implied that she had a current one. A jealous lover who had the right to delve into all the secrets of her soul, who would seduce her from her emotional independence with the promise of something infinitely more rewarding, something she yearned for beyond the expression of words. Panic rose in Rosalind's throat and she resorted to her protective cloak of flippancy.

'Oh, not *all* of them,' she drawled. 'Out of the legion of men I've had in my bed there were one or two who were totally uninspiring.'

'Has there really been a legion?' he asked, his eyes narrowing at the defiant glitter in hers.

'At least!'

'Do you know how much a legion is, according to the dictionary definition?'

She shrugged airily. 'A lot.'

'Three to six thousand.'

Rosalind's jaw dropped and so did Luke's eyelids.

'That's an awful lot of lovers for any one woman,' he said smoothly.

'Well, maybe that's a little on the high side,' she said weakly.

'Only a little?' His eyebrow etched the daring question. It wasn't often that he had Rosalind so thoroughly off balance and he intended to press his advantage.

'Shall we just say I'm considerably less experienced than most people seem to think?' she said, wryly conceding him his victory.

He showed an unfortunate tendency to rub it in. 'How much less?'

'I don't think that's any of your business, do you?' she retorted, ruffled by his persistence. She wondered what Luke would say if she told him that the reason why she was such an expert in light-hearted flirtation was that she had been celibate for years. Turning aside propositions without wounding egos or losing valued friendships took a practised sleight of tongue.

'After what nearly happened just now I think it is,' he said with a quiet, unnerving certainty that prompted an instant, knee-jerk objection.

'Nothing *happened*—'

'I said *nearly*,' he corrected her, his eyes dropping to where her nipples still thrust against her thin top. 'But I don't happen to think that what we did was ''nothing''. It certainly felt like something to me. I'm afraid I don't have your sophistication—I don't quite know how to handle this...attraction between us...I don't know what to do.'

For a shattering moment she took him literally. 'You don't mean that you've never—? That you're a...a...?' She stepped away from the mind-blowing thought and trod on a cylindrical piece of coral on the uneven track. Her ankle twisted as her foot skated away, sending her down on one knee amongst the crushed shells.

'Steady!' He picked her up and set her on her slender legs again, bending to brush at the shell-dust that mingled with the blood that seeped from the minor scrape. 'You don't have to propose to get me into your bed,' he said, straight-faced. 'I didn't mean I was *that* innocent. Is your ankle all right?'

'It's fine,' she said dismissively, ignoring the slight stinging of her grazed flesh as she watched him straighten and reveal his lightly flushed face. 'Then what *did* you mean? How many lovers have there been in *your* murky past?'

He hesitated before answering briefly. 'One.'

Rosalind felt instantly light-headed. 'One what? One important one? One legion?'

He didn't smile. 'One lover. My wife.'

'You're *married*?' she whispered, her honey-coloured complexion paling, making her incredulous green eyes look enormous. She was profoundly shocked, even more so than when she had gone to a party she had thought she would have to miss and surprised Justin in the act of infidelity with one of his nameless pick-ups. At least with Justin she had been prepared by her growing suspicions. And somehow Luke seemed to be the type to wear a wedding ring…strait-laced, strictly honourable…

'I was. She died.'

Rosalind was appalled by her sense of relief and rushed to atone for her inappropriate emotions. 'I'm sorry.'

'It was a long time ago.' He put a hand under her elbow, turning her in the direction of the hotel. 'Come on, we'll walk the rest of the way back. I've got some antibiotic cream I can use to clean up that cut.'

'If it was a long time ago you must have married very young…' Curiosity crawled through Rosalind's veins as she limped gracefully along beside him. What had his wife been like? she wondered.

Was she pretty? she asked him silently. Did she make you laugh? Did she make you happy? If she was alive would you still love her?

'I was nineteen and Christie was eighteen.'

She turned that over in her mind. He would still have been at university. Hadn't he said he had lived with his parents?

'Did you *have* to get married?'

As soon as the question left her lips Rosalind's curiosity faltered. What if Christie had had a baby? Children? Luke could be a father, for all she knew. A family man. Someone who loved children and believed that procreation was the essential purpose of marriage.

'Quite the reverse,' he said firmly. 'Christie and I were sweethearts all through our teens but she came from a very religious family, even stricter than mine. There was no question of sex before marriage.'

'Oh.'

He intercepted her sideways glance and judged it correctly. 'And yes, that *is* one of the reasons we got married so young,' he admitted drily. 'We were both mature for our age and very sure of our feelings, and our parents realised that we were having more and more difficulty in refraining from the full expression of our love. They were happy to approve a marriage that would avert a sin.'

The chalets were in sight and Rosalind shortened her steps to a dawdle, forcing Luke to do the same as she tried to keep him talking. 'So how long were you married?'

'A year.' The casualness with which he spoke belied the horror of what he was saying as he added matter-of-factly, 'Although we only spent five days actually living together as husband and wife. Christie was critically injured in a car accident on the way back from our honeymoon. A man had a heart attack at the wheel and slammed into us from a side-road. Christie never regained consciousness.'

Rosalind felt some vital yet nameless defence crumble inside her, his words issuing from a well of loneliness that echoed in the empty chambers of her heart. 'Oh, Luke, no…'

They had reached his door, but he made no attempt to use the fact as an excuse to bring the conversation to a polite conclusion. He used his key and ushered Rosalind inside, then continued in that mildly detached voice, as if the tragic story related to an acquaintance rather than himself.

'What we had was so brief, yet so special… Christie and I always seemed to be utterly attuned to each other—heart, mind and soul. I knew I wouldn't find that kind of perfection with anyone else, so I never bothered to try. I just wasn't interested in platonic female companionship or empty physical release. Neither seemed to matter. If I ever looked at another woman in lust it was only because she reminded me in some way of Christie—'

'And me? Do *I* remind you of Christie?' she interrupted as he sat her down on the bamboo couch and handed her a tissue from the hotel-branded box on the coffee-table. How could she be expected to worry about something as mundane as a minor scrape on her knee when he was performing open-heart surgery?

Her mouth went dry as she waited for him to tell her that, yes, Christie had been a slim, green-eyed redhead.

'There's no resemblance whatsoever.'

But as she started to breathe again his brutal scalpel of truth continued to flash. 'Yet I find myself wanting to have sex with you. I can't seem to stop myself thinking about it. Whenever I look at you, I imagine you—' He clenched his teeth and his hands at his sides, forcing the difficult words out. 'I think of how it would be with you…I think of doing things with you that I—' A light sheen of sweat that had nothing to do with their run had broken out on his upper lip. 'And at night I have dreams—'

He broke off, but he didn't need to go on. Rosalind's hand trembled as she dabbed the tissue ineffectually against her knee, trying to look her most blasé when inside she was turning cartwheels like a giddy teenager. She had had a few fairly intense dreams herself...

'I see.'

He swept the hair impatiently off his forehead. 'I wish *I* did.' He looked angry, bewildered by his inability to explain his own behaviour, aggressive in his vulnerability.

Rosalind's defences dropped even further.

'Maybe it's *because* I'm so very different,' she offered gently. 'Maybe you've allowed yourself to feel desire for me because you know I'm not a threat to your memories of Christie.'

'But you are. I told you, Christie is the only woman I've ever made love to—'

'But it would be only sex with me, wouldn't it?' She proudly pointed out what he himself had made very clear. 'You can't *make love* with someone you don't love.'

'"Only sex",' he mimicked roughly. 'Is that all it is to you, Roz—"only" another incidental encounter with a person you fleetingly fancy?'

'As a matter of fact, no,' she said steadily, noting his careful use of language. 'I won't deny I did go through a brief period in my life when I wasn't very discriminating about *men*—' she hoped he noticed the special stress '—but I'd just been terribly hurt by someone whom I believed was the love of my life, and in typically flamboyant style I decided to show everyone how much I didn't care. I didn't want to be pitied. I thought that if I acted like Justin had it would somehow make *me* feel better. It didn't, so I stopped. I may flirt, but I don't sleep around.'

Her tilted chin and the thread of steely pride in her voice

told him that he could take or leave it—she wasn't going to beg for his respect.

'I'll get that ointment for your knee,' he said quietly, and went up the stairs to his bathroom without further comment.

Rosalind brushed at the stupid blurring in her eyes and got up, thinking that a little flexing would stop her caked knee from hardening over and making it more difficult to treat. She walked over to the small dining table where Luke's computer lay open, plugged into the electrical outlet in the wall, a screen-saver busily at work. Maybe Luke had left it on because he was expecting a fax or some electronic mail, she thought.

The computer looked highly sophisticated, but appeared to have no mouse or trackball. Rosalind leaned over and ran her finger over the flat pad where she had expected the trackball to be. The screen-saver suddenly dissolved and she realised that the pad was a miniature touch-sensitive screen. She dragged her finger across it again and sure enough the little cursor arrow moved in a parallel course. She tapped and a file opened full-screen.

Guiltily, because she hadn't realised that the cursor was hovering over any particular icon, she dragged the arrow up to the 'close' box, and was about to tap when a name leapt out at her from the mass of single-spaced text.

Her own name...things that she had said...things that she had done.

Luke, it seemed, had been making detailed notes of their association from the day they had first met.

CHAPTER EIGHT

'SPECTACULAR, isn't it?'

Rosalind didn't turn as the shadowy figure materialised on the ground beside her. Deep in the inky shadows of the casuarina tree, in her midnight-blue dress, she had thought she was invisible, but Luke evidently had eyes like a cat.

She kept her gaze fixed on the dark horizon. On Tioman the night was star-studded and clear but far out across the sea a distant electrical storm played out its fury. Sheet lightning flickered incessantly, brilliant flashes of varying intensity illuminating the rim of the world, throwing the billowing clouds high above the horizon into pulsating relief. There was no thunder, only the hushed breath of the sea to accompany the theatrical light-show, the violence of nature seeming all the more impressive for its silence.

When she didn't respond to his opening question she heard Luke shift on the soft carpet of dried casuarina needles scattered across the sandy soil.

'Where did you rush off to this morning? I looked for you. I thought we had plans...'

Rosalind could almost smell the ozone in the air, but it wasn't from the distant lightning. She felt electricity crackling through her veins, but, unlike the storm, her rage couldn't remain silent for long.

'I went on a parasailing trip. With the hunk from the pool bar,' she added with savage bite, not taking her eyes off nature's fireworks display.

There was a heartbeat's silence, then he said softly, and without a trace of jealousy, 'Trying to show me how much you don't care, in your typically flamboyant fashion, Roz?'

'Don't flatter yourself! It had nothing to do with you,'

she lied desperately, appalled at how easily he'd turned her own words against her.

'Then why won't you talk to me?'

'Why? So you can make some more *notes*?' she spat, her skin crawling at the memory of scrolling through the screens of information about herself—her habits and likes and dislikes, what she'd worn and what she'd said—the conversations with Luke reported almost verbatim.

Until she'd seen it coldly written down she hadn't realised how much she'd unwittingly revealed during their harmless 'flirtation', not only about herself but about her family and friends, a number of whom were famous in their own right. She had *trusted* Luke at a time when her life was ripe with paranoia and this was how he'd repaid her!

Damn it, he was as bad as Justin…worse, because she knew now that what she had felt for Justin had been a romantic yearning that had ignored reality. She had been in love with the idea of being in love, with the notion of finding her perfect match, and Justin had seemed conveniently to fit the bill.

Luke was far from perfect and he had never tried to be her ideal. He was irritating and engaging, obstinate and agreeable, shy and bold, blunt and evasive…in short, a mass of contradictions that should have sent her screaming in the opposite direction. Instead she had been perversely fascinated, seduced by her growing appreciation of his complexity of character, his breadth of mind and the smouldering power of his subdued sexuality. Somewhere along the line, without even realising what was happening, Rosalind had started falling in love with him!

'Damn you, you've been *dissecting* me like some character in a *play*!' She blinked hard, grateful for the darkness and appalled at her pathetic desire to cry on the shoulder of the very man who had caused her pain.

His sharp counter-attack vanquished the momentary weakness. 'Oh, come on, Roz, you do exactly the same thing with everyone you meet. A gesture here, a character trait there…they're all grist to your actor's mill. As I *was going* to explain to you this morning, clarifying my thoughts about a person or a problem by writing them down is a habit of mine—my observations were purely for my own benefit. I have—*had*—no intention of showing my personal jottings to anyone else.'

His grim self-correction told her he now knew that she had not only wiped the file off his hard disk but had also stolen the back-up floppy which had been in the drive.

'For God's sake, Roz, surely you can't *still* think I'm an undercover journalist?'

She wished she did. At this point she would have been relieved to find out that he was simply an over-enthusiastic hack, because a far more disturbing alternative had arisen.

Luke's word-processing program had been personalized with his full name. When Rosalind had inadvertently opened her file the copyright box had appeared for several seconds, but only later in the day had the impact of it exploded on her consciousness like a bomb.

Luke Peter James.

One of his names was *Peter*.

It could be just a coincidence. It probably *was* just a coincidence, she had feverishly tried to convince herself.

He *couldn't* be Peter Noble. Peggy's son was unemployed and on benefit, and even if he had been tracking Rosalind's movements as precisely as Peggy had claimed he wouldn't have had access to the kind of information or money that would have enabled him to follow her to Tioman. Unless he included fraud amongst his obsessions…

But what if everything Peggy had told Rosalind about her son was wrong? After all, she only knew what Peter had chosen to tell her. Peggy had been far too afraid of stirring up the murky past to make any independent investigation into his background…she didn't even know if his story about his adoptive family was true. What if he had told Peggy a pack of lies? What if *Luke* was telling a pack of lies to Rosalind?

He himself had pointed out the dangers of making assumptions. Just because Rosalind had independent verification that he was a triathlete, that didn't mean that he couldn't also be a borderline psychotic. Maybe all that heartbreaking stuff about his wife dying was a scam to arouse her sympathy.

Of course, it was all absurdly unlikely, but the circumstantial evidence was very unnerving: Luke's name was also Peter, he was adopted and the same age that Peggy's son would be, he had torn out an article about Rosalind—perhaps to add to his extensive collection at home—and was keeping a detailed account of her every move.

If ridiculing the idea out of existence didn't work, she could just *ask* him—but if Luke *was* Peter Noble she might be safer pretending to be unaware. To acknowledge his obsession might be to validate it. Oh, *why* hadn't she spoken to the psychologist whom Jordan had urged her to consult about handling a personal confrontation with her psychotic fan? Because she had been too busy hoping it would never happen...

'Rosalind?' Luke persisted. Wasn't relentless persistence a sign of an obsessive mind? 'I said, you surely can't still believe I'm compiling a sleazy kiss-and-tell for some moronic magazine?'

At the reminder of the kisses they had shared an icy thrill of erotic fear coursed down her spine. Even now, wondering if Luke was her stalker, she felt the powerful tug of attraction, the insidious stirring of sexual curiosity.

Maybe *she* was the one who was deranged! Rosalind scrambled hastily to her feet, away from the temptation.

'There's nothing for you to tell anyway!' she said, hearing the amused contempt ring false in her own ears.

'Isn't there?' He rose more slowly, like a hunter wary of

frightening his skittish prey. He seemed larger in the darkness and Rosalind's heart began to beat up into her throat.

'We kissed a few times, had a few laughs together—it didn't mean anything to either of us!' She quietly put one sandalled foot behind the other and began to shift her weight backwards.

'Didn't it?'

He was circling around her, and she turned to keep him within her night-blurred sight. She could hear her pulse in her ears, could feel but not see his eyes boring into her, and experienced the tingling of her scalp that usually presaged a severe attack of stage fright. Oh, God, if he *was* Peter she mustn't let him paralyse her in real life as she had let him do to her on stage.

'No!'

'Then why are you spitting at me like a cornered vixen? Could it be that you feel threatened by how much you enjoyed those *few laughs*...?'

It was such an apt description of her feelings that she recoiled. 'Damn you!'

His voice oozed with heavy satisfaction as he continued to pad softly around her, increasing his speed so that her head began to whirl as she tried to keep up with him, the hem of her halter-necked slip-dress flaring around her knees. 'No, damn *you* Roz. *You* started this game; we're not going to stop now, just because you've discovered that you don't get to make all the rules.'

She lifted her hands in a fierce warding-off gesture, some words from Shakespeare sliding unbidden into her mind. 'He was furnished like a hunter/O, ominous! he comes to kill my heart.'

'What game?' she said desperately. 'I don't know what you're talking about—'

His soft laugh was grim with determination.

'I'm talking about this...'

His mouth was as warm and exciting as she remembered,

his body as hard, and once more her passionate nature was hostage to his fervent enthusiasm. She stopped struggling, her fear dissolving in the heat of a seductive yearning. What Luke lacked in finesse he certainly made up for in zeal. How could she be afraid of someone who made her feel so beautiful, so powerful, so desirable and, uniquely in her recent experience, so utterly *complete*?

Her trapped hands fluttered briefly against his lean flanks before her fingers curled into the rough linen weave of his softly gathered trousers, not tugging him closer, but not pushing him away either. Like her dress, Luke's shirt was made of silk, and the two whisper-thin surfaces were slippery against each other, generating a slick friction which, with every movement, every wild breath and ripple of muscle, made parts of Rosalind ache for a similar caress.

His mouth suddenly broke away and Luke leaned his forehead against hers, resting it there while his arms fell loosely to her hips, cradling them against his fierce arousal.

'You're right—however it started this isn't a game for us any more,' he panted raggedly. 'Let's stop teasing each other...to hell with all the rest. Come to bed with me, Roz...please... I won't hurt you, I'll protect you... Come back with me now and dazzle me with your splendour...'

The hunter was disarming himself before his captive prey.

'Come...dazzle me with your splendour...'

How could any woman resist such a poetic, impassioned plea?

Hours later Rosalind was still reliving the pleasure of that exquisite moment, and cursing the self-doubt which had smothered her impulse to accept his invitation. She had wanted to fling herself headlong into the reckless glory of loving Luke, but for the first time in her life her steadfast optimism had failed her. She had been afraid to trust her instincts, afraid that her judgement was warped by her feelings.

Rosalind Marlow, the wild child of tabloid journalism, afraid to take a risk. What a laugh!

Rosalind paced back and forth in her bedroom, her heart aching for the man she had deserted under the casuarina tree. Had he been hurt by the fierceness of her rejection? Maybe she had gone overboard in her attempt to sound as if she was still angry with him. Luke hadn't even tried to follow her...surely if he was obsessed with her he wouldn't have let her just walk away?

She stopped and pressed her ear against the wall. Still not a single sound or vibration from the next chalet. She rested her hot cheek against the cool paintwork and closed her eyes. Damn it, where *was* he? Why the hell wasn't he knocking at her door, pestering her to change her mind?

Because he wasn't Peter, that was why, her guilty conscience whispered. Luke was simply an honest man who had got out of his depth with a witchy woman who blew inexplicably hot and cold and acted mortally insulted when he paid her the supreme compliment of trying to understand her.

Where on earth could he have gone? To the bar, to drown his humiliation in vodka? Or...more likely from what she knew of Luke...had he gone for a long, solitary walk to brood over his sorrows?

Rosalind jerked upright. What if Luke fell victim to the dreaded ricochet effect? What if, in his wanderings, he encountered some shameless, man-eating hussy who offered him the opportunity to soothe his wounded male ego with some mindless sex? Her blood boiled with jealousy at the idea. She felt sick at the thought of him with any other woman.

Her green eyes narrowed grimly as she made up her mind. Luke had stopped short of making any emotional declarations but she sensed that he had strong feelings for her, otherwise he wouldn't be in such a turmoil.

This definitely wasn't just a physical attraction. If Rosalind loved him she couldn't keep running away from the responsibility, but nor could she blind herself to her suspicions, as she had done with Justin. The Justin she had thought she was in love with had been a flawless young god who had turned out to have feet of clay. Luke was a flesh-and-blood man who had attracted her *because* of his flaws, rather than in spite of them.

Still, this time she had much more to lose than her girlish dreams and Rosalind had to be certain with her heart *and* her head that she was doing the right thing for Luke as well as for herself. If she couldn't bring herself to take him on trust, well, she would have to take him without, and hope to make up for her lack of faith later…

First, and most important of all, she needed to reread what he had written about her—properly, from start to finish this time, instead of relying on the few jumbled extracts that had leapt at her from the screen that morning. She wanted to know just how much of his own feelings and motives he had recorded in his so-called 'diary'.

Grabbing the small computer disk from her bedside table, Rosalind went out onto the balcony and peered around the edge of the lattice screen at his darkened bedroom. She knew Luke would have locked the front door of his chalet when he'd gone out, but, as she had hoped, he had left his balcony sliding door slightly open.

For someone as nimble as Rosalind it was a matter of seconds to kick off her sandals and swing herself over the sturdy wooden rail. The computer disk between her teeth, she edged along the narrow wooden parapet until she was on the other side of the screen and clambered back over the rail.

The sliding door moved silently on its smooth track and Rosalind uttered a smothered giggle of nervous fright as the filmy white curtain suddenly billowed out of the widened gap to wrap itself around her. She fought her way free only to stub her toe on the raised track and stumble into the room with a whispered curse.

She would make a hopeless cat burglar, she thought, realising that she had dropped the precious disk and would have to waste time fumbling around on the floor in the darkness. She put out a hand and knocked it against the back of a cane chair. If only she could turn on a light...

The light clicked on beside the bed and she found herself staring at Luke, who was rumple-haired and crumple-eyed as he pushed himself upright, the sheet slithering down his bare chest to settle around his waist.

'Roz?'

'Luke!' she said faintly, shocked by the sight of him. He had been here all along! *Sleeping*, for God's sake, while she had been miserably pacing her chalet, agonising over his whereabouts! She put her hand up to her frantically beating heart, wondering how she was going to explain her presence in his bedroom.

It seemed that an explanation was not required. A beatific expression stole into his sleep-darkened eyes.

'Rosalind, you came!' He pushed back the bedclothes and rose to greet her, splendidly naked.

'I knew you would,' he said warmly, strolling towards her, his mouth curving in delighted welcome. 'I knew you'd change your mind and come to me...'

Not only naked, but also magnificently aroused and completely unselfconscious about it, thought Rosalind hazily as she watched his graceful stride eat up the distance between them. Poetry in motion...every muscle moving in well-oiled symmetry under his burnished skin, the smooth hairlessness of his chest, belly and legs accentuating the thick, dark brown cloud of curly hair at the juncture of his thighs.

With difficulty Rosalind tore her eyes away from the fluid ripple of his thighs and met his gaze, suddenly understanding the reason for his total lack of shyness.

He wasn't quite awake, she realised as he blinked lazily

at her, his naked arms sliding around her waist as he bent his head to seek a leisurely kiss. His eyes still had that distant, dream-dark look and his mouth was tenderly whimsical as it nuzzled her startled lips apart. His eyelids fluttered shut again. Aside from the rigid thrust of masculinity nudging against her thighs he was utterly relaxed, and his warm body seemed to envelop hers like a butter-soft glove, absorbing her into his languorous dream-world.

'Touch me,' he invited, his tongue slipping inside her mouth and rubbing sensuously against hers. 'Everywhere, all over; I need to feel you all over me...wanting me... loving me...'

His flat hand slid up and down her silk-covered back, massaging her against his chest, his other hand finding hers and drawing it down between their bodies, pushing her fingers into the soft nest of hair. He groaned, racked by shudders as he curled her pliant fingers firmly around him, shaping her to his need, arching his back as he thrust graphically into her soft grasp. 'Oh, God, yes...like that...you know I love it when you touch me like that...'

Rosalind went liquid with pleasure. Luke might have gone to bed wanting to hate her but he obviously hadn't succeeded. She must have disturbed him in the middle of an intensely erotic dream—a dream about *her*...

In Luke's subconscious they were already lovers and now, if she didn't stop him, he was going to turn that dream into reality.

But she didn't want to stop him. She had forgotten the computer disk lying half-hidden under the bed. She no longer cared why she had come, only that she was here and that Luke, in his half-waking state, was open to her in a way he had never been before, expressing his deepest, most intimate needs with a frankness that was usually censored by his extreme reserve.

He was strong in his desire, yet vulnerable in a way that moved her to the depths of her being. Tenderness mingled with passion and she felt a surge of the old recklessness. In his dream Luke spoke of loving, not sex. In his dream he needed her, trusted her, believed that she would never disappoint him...

Rosalind wanted to share his dream. For however brief a time she too wanted to be free of the shackles of doubt, free to need and to trust and believe that love could conquer all. Whatever unwelcome knowledge lurked ahead, at least she could make of this consummation an untainted memory to hold in her heart...

Her hand moved on him and he moaned excitingly into her mouth. She eased their bodies closer together, the slow rotation of her hips replacing her stroking fingers as she caressed her hand back up his chest and over the strong column of his throat, sliding her arms over his shoulders and going on tiptoe to deepen the long, voluptuous kiss.

Her passionate response snapped him to full awareness. His mouth stilled and his eyes flew open, his hands pausing in their restless exploration, one splayed between her shoulderblades, the other shaped to the base of her spine.

His mouth lifted far enough for him to murmur a surprised question that wasn't really a question. 'Roz...?'

'Who else?' She pulled his head back down and flicked her tongue along his parted lips, savouring his delicious surprise as he struggled to comprehend that the woman he held was not the armful of dreams he had confidently embraced.

His gush of breath was warm and spicy, filling her senses with delight. 'I— What...what are you doing here?'

'Making love to you,' she vowed, tilting her head back so that she could see his face. Dark colour ran up under his skin, and his eyes flamed with a scorching hunger as his lips moved soundlessly.

'No...' She pressed a thumb to the soft curve of his lower lip, stilling the formation of another question. 'It doesn't matter how, or why...'

Confusion swirled in the smouldering heat of his gaze. 'But—earlier—you said—'

'Do you want to talk, or make love?' She cut him off huskily, impatient for the violent pleasure she knew he would give her, not wanting her gloriously reckless mood dissipated by cautious reminders.

His teeth nipped at her thumb, his mouth closing over it to suckle it briefly before releasing the moistened tip. 'Can't we do both?'

She shook her head, her rich voice mellowing to a slow, sexy drawl. 'I don't feel civilised enough for conversation. I tend to go a little wild when you touch me and tonight I want to let go completely; I want to set the wildness free. I only hope that you don't find me too uninhibited for your tastes…'

A pulse jolted in his left temple. 'I don't know what my tastes are,' he reminded her roughly, his lower hand unconsciously dragging her hips possessively against him. 'I know so little about women and their physical needs that it's far more likely that *you'll* be the one who's disappointed by my inexperienced performance…'

She cupped her hands over his slightly roughened jaw and slid them down his throat, feeling the ripple of nervous tension as he swallowed.

'This isn't an audition, Luke,' she chided him softly. 'Believe me, you have all the right instincts and that's all that matters. All you have to do is enjoy yourself and the rest will happen naturally.' Her eyes were very green as she assured him gravely, 'And just for the record it's been a long time for me too. Years… I guess I was waiting for a very special man to make *me* feel special…and that man is you, Luke…'

She kissed him and for a moment he was passive, but only for a moment. Then the power of her words shuddered through him and he tipped her head back with the devouring force of his hunger. He held her suffocatingly tight, kissing her with a savage eagerness that shattered the last boundaries of his restraint. His hands relentlessly explored her slender back, massaging lower and lower until the floaty hem of her dress was hiked up the back of her thighs, then sliding underneath to cup her lace-covered bottom, lifting her higher into his groin.

He pulled back, frowning as he watched the silk of her bodice peel off his chest and settle back over her taut breasts.

'I'm naked,' he said thickly, as if he had only just realised the fact.

'I know.' Rosalind playfully ran her fingertips across his shoulders and chest, sweeping them down his sides to linger on the tapered leanness of his muscled flanks. 'I'm glad you don't wear pyjamas. You're very beautiful in the nude; just looking at you excites me...'

His flush deepened and his nostrils flared. 'I usually wear boxers in bed,' he said vaguely, 'but tonight I couldn't—I didn't want anything next to my skin...'

The smile she gave him was sultry and knowing. She dropped her gaze to the point where their hips were sealed together, the erotic pressure preserving his modesty.

'Except me?'

'Except you,' he admitted heatedly, his expression becoming dark and devilish as he watched her smile curve with a hint of complacency, the feminine version of a flung-down gauntlet.

The male in him bristled at her confidence even as he exulted in a fierce sense of victory. The element of danger only added spice to the situation. Edgy, emotional, elegantly sensuous Roz Marlow had finally succeeded in luring herself into his net. Just when he had almost conceded defeat she turned around and did something like this. She was a riddle, wrapped inside a mystery.

But not for much longer. A night of unbridled passion might be all she thought she was offering, but he intended to take more…much more. He would unwrap her secrets just as surely as he intended to unwrap that dainty, delectable body.

His fingers moved provocatively, sliding down inside her fragile lace panties to smooth over the softly rounded cheeks of her bottom. Rosalind shivered and instinctively moved her hips into his touch, but instead of lingering to enjoy her acquiescence Luke continued to plunge his hands downwards, pushing her panties to her knees and then, with a sudden dip and a sideways twist, raking them roughly to her ankles.

He straightened, meeting her startled eyes with a look of blazing male triumph at his reckless daring. To her astonishment she felt herself blush and he gloated openly at the betraying crack in her façade of worldly sophistication. His hands settled firmly back on her waist, holding her steady as he ordered gruffly, 'Step out of them.'

Rosalind obeyed, her legs brushing against his, trembling slightly in response to his smouldering aura of suppressed sexual excitement. He liked giving her orders and her meek show of obedience was an incitement to his boldness.

'Are you wearing a bra?' he demanded in a low, smoky growl.

Rosalind nodded, even though they both knew an answer was unnecessary. He had traced the outline of it while he had been kissing her, his fingers meticulously investigating the seams and identifying the fastening between her shoulderblades. He had merely asked so as to tantalise her with the knowledge of what he was going to do next. He wanted her naked under the liquid silk dress, dressed yet undressed, vulnerable to his desire…

'It's strapless,' she told him unsteadily as his hand slipped through the wide armhole of her halter-necked dress to deal with the hooks. He took so long that she wanted to scream but the combination of taunting deliberation and fumbling difficulty was so much a part of the intensely erotic scenario that Rosalind forced herself to stand still until finally the flimsy undergarment gave way. He tugged and gravity obliged as her bra slithered out from under the loose A-line dress, landing with a hushed thud at her feet that seemed to quake through every nerve cell in her body.

Rosalind had never been so aware of her own sexuality as she was at that moment—never been more anxious for a man's approval.

Luke stared at the polished silk rippling over her skin like a midnight-blue waterfall, a provocative veil for the supple contours beneath. The thin sheen of the fabric was sculpted taut between her high breasts, her nipples jutting out as stiff peaks from which the graceful cut of the dress cascaded away to shimmer and swirl around her slender hips and honey-smooth legs. His chest rose and fell unevenly, his hands flexing violently at his sides, his manhood stirring and thickening against his flat belly. She had been mistaken in thinking that he had been fully aroused when he'd got out of bed, Rosalind realised with a flutter of apprehension.

She had the feeling that in his lovemaking, as in most other things, Luke was capable of a fierce concentration that brooked no distractions. She didn't think he would actually force her, but the familiar vague-eyed absorption with which he was studying her made her wonder if he might unintentionally hurt her in the throes of passion. Yet, oddly, her fear—of his size and the more nebulous threat of his identity—merely gave her own desire an added piquancy.

'Is this what happened in your dream?' she challenged, feeling a slow wave of heat wash through her body at the thought of being compelled to accommodate that potent hardness.

In answer he reached out and cupped her breasts through the silk, lifting the soft mounds and smoothing the fabric with his thumbs so that her distended nipples were outlined even more explicitly.

'This is much better than a dream,' he muttered as her breasts ripened and grew heavy in his cradling hands. He licked his lips and Rosalind unconsciously arched her back but he ignored the subtle invitation. His gaze lowered to her hem and his hands followed, gathering the flimsy fabric and slowly pushing it up her honey-coloured thighs until he exposed a tantalising glimpse of fiery red curls.

'Much better...' he whispered hoarsely, letting the dress fall again, veiling her femininity in a dark swirl of silk. His hands moved up over her belly, shaping the delicate imprint of her navel...up to her breasts again, and back down to toy with her hem...to slip his hand up underneath and delicately brush his fingertips over the unseen fleece...to reach around and massage the silk over the flare of her hips, tracing it into the sensitive crease between her quivering buttocks.

He was playing with her. This gorgeous, naked, *inexperienced* man was playing her like a master...drawing out the exquisite agony of desire until Rosalind thought she was going to explode with frustration at her passive role.

'Aren't you going to take it off?' she blurted out jerkily as he wound a swathe of silk around his fist, forming another shimmering perspective of her body. Luke's erotic absorption faltered and suddenly it occurred to her that perhaps he wasn't quite sure of his next move. 'Or would you like to watch me do it?' she said, reaching behind her neck and releasing the jewelled clasp that was the dress's only fastening.

'Yes, you do it,' he murmured thickly, his hard body glossy with a faint mist of perspiration as he watched her cross her arms and whisk the flared hemline up over her head.

She didn't get any further. Even before she had freed herself from the billowing silk Luke had swept Rosalind backwards onto the bed with a hoarse sound of inarticulate need. Blindfolded in midnight-blue, she found herself pulled beneath him, his mouth and hands eagerly roaming over her desperately squirming body.

He bit into her tender flesh, his groans and whispers of raw pleasure inflaming her smothered senses as he hungrily sought her swollen breasts and suckled fiercely on the engorged nipples while she struggled to free herself from the fabric surrounding her head and arms, succeeding only in entangling herself further. Her frantic writhing and gasps of helpless delight excited Luke to a frenzy and the full weight of his tightly compact body surged on top of her, his hands tugging at her thighs, prising them roughly apart, a groan tearing its way out of his chest as he settled himself heavily into the enticing wedge, his congested loins straining against her fiery heart, probing for its moist centre.

Rosalind finally managed to wrench the maddening dress over her head and toss it aside, but Luke was already rising above her on his arms, his chest rigid, his muscles bunching convulsively as he arched his back and threw his head back, blindly driving himself between her thighs with a guttural shout of gratification.

Rosalind echoed his cry, clutching his slippery, straining back as he sheathed himself to the hilt in her wet warmth. She barely had time to adjust to the agonising pleasure of being invaded and stretched to the brink of bursting before Luke was drawing back with a harsh moan and heaving convulsively forward again in a second, massively powerful thrust, his face contorting in a mask of pure ecstasy as he stiffened and then began to shudder in a violent spasm of completion that left him slumped heavily on top of her. She lay blinking over his lax shoulder at the panelled ceiling, stunned by the speed and intensity of his climax. She could feel him still pulsing hotly inside her tense body.

He shuddered again—a deep, sobbing breath. 'I'm sorry… Oh, God, Roz, I'm sorry…'

He withdrew before she could stop him and rolled onto his back, his chest heaving, his arm thrown across his eyes as he continued the choked litany of apologies. 'Couldn't help it…like some crass adolescent…'

'Luke… *Luke*!' She stroked his up-raised arm. 'It's all right—'

He jerked away from her touch. 'There's no need to pretend, damn it! I told you you might be disappointed.'

He sounded like a sulky boy. She wanted to peek under his arm but the grim line of his mouth warned her not to try. She raised herself on one elbow, her aching frustration turning to indulgent amusement mixed with heady anticipation. 'Are you kidding? For goodness' sake, Luke, I'm *flattered* that you exploded all over me like a firecracker.'

His chest stilled and the arm over his eyes tensed. 'A crazed sex maniac, more like.'

Her heart gave a little flip. 'I prefer to think of you more as a satyr…the combination of that Greek-god body and those eyebrows—well…you're bound to be governed by your earthy passions when you finally catch the nymph of your dreams!'

She could see the glitter of his eyes as his arm shifted slightly. She stretched her supple body and, when she was quite sure he was watching, casually turned her back and slid off the bed, bending to pick up her silk dress and slithering it over her head.

His arm whipped down as he pushed himself up against the disordered pillows. 'What are you doing? Are you leaving?'

She smiled at his mixture of outrage and anxiety as she strolled provocatively back to the bed and crawled onto it on her hands and knees. 'Certainly not. Now it's my turn.'

'Your turn?' he asked warily, watching her prowl across the rumpled sheets towards him.

'To explode all over *you*…' She daintily lifted a slender leg across his body and settled herself firmly astride his hips, modestly smoothing her silk dress down over his tight flanks, intrigued to note the visible ripple that undulated the length of his body. She squirmed herself slowly into a more comfortable position and lifted a haughty eyebrow at him as she felt the subtle male shift between her thighs.

A shadow of a smile quivered at the corner of his sexily narrow mouth. She wanted to kiss it but instead she leaned forward, folding her forearms provocatively across his collar-bone, making sure the unfastened neckline of her dress gaped to show him her softly swaying breasts, the erect tips almost touching his chest.

'The first time was for you…this is for me…' She looked at him through veiled lashes. 'Then it'll be your turn again,' she said, and laughed at the molten look he gave her. 'That's how it works, you see…it's called give and take…a very fertile ground for improvisation…'

His hunger congealed into shock. 'My God, I didn't even use a condom! Are you using anything?'

'No, but it's OK—'

He twisted his torso to fumble for the soft leather shaving case on the table beside the bed. 'No, it's *not* OK! I promised to protect you and I let us both down. It's *never* OK to leave these things to chance.'

He was so savagely upset by his lapse that it seemed natural to tell him, 'It is for me—*always*—that is, if it's pregnancy you're worried about,' she said quietly. 'My attack of pelvic disease left me permanently sterile. As for the other kind of protection…we both have that safety zone of celibacy, don't we…?'

'Oh, *Roz*…' He collapsed back on the pillows, his hands moving to cradle the classic oval of her face, his dark eyes filled with shocked regret. 'Oh, Roz…'

She shook her head, his unspoken sympathy sinking like music on her heart. 'I've got a big extended family, lots of money and an extremely challenging, fulfilling career. I can't expect to have all that and heaven too! Shakespeare had it right—''what's past help/Should be past grief''.' She nipped at his fingers and gave him her famous jaunty, gamine grin. 'And it does mean that I get to enjoy my sexy satyr in his raw, natural state.'

She wiggled her bottom and felt a fillip of joy when he instantly attuned himself to her mood and gave a mock growl, making wicked play with the eyebrows that so obviously enchanted her.

The second time they made love was far more shattering than the first. This time Luke kept careful pace with her, exercising a fierce self-control as she rode his iron-hard body to the pinnacle of bliss, withholding his own bucking release until he could use it to drive her over the edge into a wild, free-falling rapture of the senses.

He proved unquenchable in both curiosity and desire, his stamina equalled by his eager inventiveness, and by the time Rosalind fell asleep, curled against his gloriously sated body, she knew that she had found a precious gift.

When the telephone first rang she moaned, and tried to burrow deeper into warm, musky skin, but eventually the irritating intrusion into her cosy world became too much and she reached out to rake the receiver under the sheet, grunting sleepily into the mouthpiece.

'Luke? It's Jordan,' a terse, static-ridden voice rapped out. 'I just wanted to tell you that you don't have to keep an eye on Roz any more.'

A frown wrinkled her lightly tanned brow. 'Jordan? Jordan Pendragon—is that you?'

There was a small silence. 'Roz?'

'Jordan?' She was fully awake now, wriggling out from under Luke's heavy arm, meeting a gaze that sprang from sensuous approval to shrewd alertness as Luke registered the name on her lips. 'Jordan, what's going on?'

'You're five hours behind us...isn't this rather early for you to be answering Luke's phone?' he countered curiously.

'Maybe he's keeping a better eye on me than you thought,' she said bitingly. 'Would you mind answering my question?'

Thousands of kilometres away Jordan sighed. 'Now, Roz, you know how worried Olivia was about this letter business. All I did was ask a friend to discreetly watch over you—'

'A *friend*?' she repeated ominously, sharply slapping Luke's hand away as he tried to remove the telephone from her ear.

'Well, he and I knew each other quite well when I worked for the Corporation. He was the colleague I saw when you and I were at the airport. When I went over to say hello and found out that he was going to Tioman, well... I know what a straight-up guy he is—not street-smart but physically a tough cookie with a cautious brain that makes him cool-headed in a crisis—I'd trust his judgement of people any day of the week...so I told him about your stalking letters and how you refused to countenance protection and asked if he would mind keeping tabs on my favourite sister-in-law without making it too obvious what he was doing—'

'Well, he certainly stuck to orders on that one,' Rosalind grated, ignoring the blatant soft soap since she was Jordan's one and *only* sister-in-law. Her eyes were chips of emerald ice as they froze on the culprit's grim but unrepentant face. 'And now you've decided your *friend* isn't up to the job of minder after all?'

Tension crackled down the line. 'No, it's just not necessary any longer. I was going to ring you after I spoke to Luke.

'Roz, they've found your letter writer; they've found Peter...'

CHAPTER NINE

ROSALIND went clammy, an ugly premonition crawling across her skin.

'They?'

'The police. He's dead, Roz. He killed himself at his flat in Wellington a few weeks ago…but he was such an unsociable type that they only found the body yesterday. Peter Noble was his name. He took some sort of overdose on prescription medication, poor sod—they're not sure whether it was deliberate or not, because there wasn't any suicide note…'

Roz was vaguely aware of Jordan explaining the pitiful circumstances, and the fan paraphernalia, diaries and letters which led the police to approach the Marlows with their information.

Thank God they had nothing to connect Peter with Peggy through her, she thought, but she was sickened to realise that the police had dated his death at just days before that fateful meeting in the Wellington hotel. That might explain Peggy's mentally disorganised behaviour that day. Had she known Peter was dead—was that what she had been trying so hard to warn Rosalind through the pain of her heart attack?

Perhaps she had somehow got into Peter's flat and discovered his body, but had panicked at the prospect of reporting it, even anonymously. She might have been afraid to admit it to Rosalind, too—hence the elaborate, rambling lead-up. She would have been crazed with guilt and grief.

And ever since, all the time that Peggy had been lying unconscious in hospital, her son had been lying dead in his pathetic shrine to yet another woman from whom he had received nothing but rejection...

'Oh, God!' Rosalind curled over on herself on the bed, the morning sickness she'd thought she had beaten burning like acid in her throat.

'Rosalind, what is it? What's happened?'

Luke caught the telephone as it dropped from her suddenly nerveless grasp, his eyes on her white face as he lifted it, and after a short, staccato burst of speech conversed quietly with Jordan for several minutes. When he finally disconnected the call his face was as pale as Rosalind's.

'Roz—' He touched her bowed back tentatively, as if he expected her to lash out at him, but she was too caught up in the vivid horror she had created in her mind to resist as he put his arms around her and lifted her curled-up body gently into his lap, his hand cupping the back of her skull, his fingers ruffling her cropped locks as he held her against his naked chest.

'I was right to feel sorry for him, wasn't I?' she whispered, swamped by a fresh wave of guilt. 'But I don't feel sorry now; I just feel...*relieved*. Part of me is *glad* that he's dead, because that solves my petty little problem!' She hitched a half-sob into his strong shoulder, turning her face into the familiar musky scent of his skin. 'Oh, God, Luke, what if it *was* deliberate? What if he did it because of *me*...?'

'Shh, don't torture yourself about it,' Luke murmured, bending his head to brush his lips against her clammy forehead. 'You can't hold yourself responsible for the actions of a mentally disturbed stranger. Jordan said that he had a long history of psychiatric problems.'

'But if I'd looked on his letters as a cry for help—'

'Noble apparently had plenty of help over the years. He'd got very cunning at manipulating himself out of official programmes. You were *his* victim, Roz, not the other way around. He didn't even see you as a person. He didn't want you to know who he was because then he might have been forced to face the reality that he wasn't part of your life and never would be.

'He probably enjoyed the sense of power over you that his anonymity gave him and Jordan said that the police psychologist thought the things they found in his flat indicated a classic pattern of escalation. Sooner or later he would have felt the compulsion to act out his fantasies, and when he found that reality didn't match up he would have resorted to violence to punish whoever had disappointed his craving. If he hadn't been able to get access to you, he would probably have forced some other woman to act out your role…'

He dismissed each of Rosalind's hectic ifs and buts with the same calm logic and then, when her initial shock had passed and she broke into a storm of weeping, he held her, rocked her, softly kissing away her tears until the passiveness of grief became the militancy of passion and she made love to him with a wild fervour that blotted out the pain and reaffirmed in the most elemental way her fierce commitment to life, love and the pursuit of happiness. He was gentle, accepting her desperate desire for sensual oblivion, tempering her wildness with his ready responses, allowing her to use him to exorcise her demons.

Afterwards, as she lay tucked in the security of his arms, the perspiration cooling on her skin, she said croakily, the words raw in the swollen tissues of her throat, 'I should be furious with you.'

'Should you?'

He traced the shadows under her tear-puffed eyes with a light finger. The dawn had become day and the room was suffused with sunshine streaming in through the open curtains. They were lying face to face, their bodies still intertwined, and she could see every nuance of his expression. His deep satisfaction was underscored by a new aura of male confidence.

She sighed. 'I *would* be if I had any energy left!'

She felt as weak as a newborn kitten, aware of a pleasant all-over ache mingled with a bitter-sweet sense of melancholy.

'In that case I'd better do my best to maintain your current state of exhaustion,' Luke murmured, with the unique brand of playful gravity that had first confused her into thinking he had no sense of humour. Now her confusion deepened. She was grateful that her absurd suspicions about Luke being a crazed stalker had been squelched, but his feelings and motivations were even more of a mystery than ever.

When she failed to respond with her usual pertness to the subtle sexual banter Luke discarded his muted playfulness, a dark determination entering his gaze as he realised that Rosalind was trying to ease herself away from his disruptive proximity. His arm tightened around her waist, pinning her to the bed, her thigh still sandwiched between his.

'You can't blame Jordan for grabbing the chance to increase the odds on you being safe. Most people are rank opportunists when it comes to protecting their families. People compromise their own personal integrity—take chances—do things for the sake of people they love that under normal circumstances they would consider completely unacceptable.' His voice had hardened perceptibly, his eyes glittering with a restless fervency as he challenged, 'Haven't you ever done something you *knew* was wrong, for reasons that you believed were right?'

Rosalind thought of the time she had masqueraded as Olivia in order to qualify her twin for a portrait commission from the Pendragon Corporation. Olivia had been in a deep depression at the time and Rosalind hadn't even thought twice about perpetrating the fraud in order to promote her sister's stalled career. That Olivia had ended up with Jordan as well as the portrait commission had been sheer chance!

And now, too, there was Peggy Staines. She wasn't fam-

ily, but she had been in such desperate need that Rosalind
had found it impossible to callously turn her back.

'Well, yes—I have…but the ends don't always justify
the means,' she said, troubled by his intensity. 'Sometimes
the means are too painful, and who's really to judge
whether the ends are worthy of the hurt they cause?'

His mouth tightened. 'As far as that goes we all have to
make our own moral choices and decisions; ultimately—
right or wrong—we have to face the consequences of our
actions. All of us would like to believe that there is someone, somewhere, who would make the same sacrifices for
us. You're lucky; you obviously have plenty of people on
your side. When he asked me to help, Jordan was only
thinking of *you*—'

'Oh, I can understand *Jordan's* thinking,' said Rosalind,
her hair a brilliant splash against the white pillow as she
turned her head to confront him at eye-level. 'But what
about *you*? Why on earth should *you* want to get involved?
Especially after I'd given you the brush-off at the check-in
counter…'

'I was curious about you,' he admitted bluntly, dashing
her fond hopes. If he had told her he had fallen in love at
first sight—or even second—she might have been willing
to forgive him his secrets! 'I knew who you were so I
wasn't surprised that you wanted to avoid any curious
hangers-on, and when Jordan handed me a legitimate excuse to indulge my curiosity I couldn't resist. Although I
wasn't quite sure how to go about the introduction—'

'You could have tried the truth. You could have simply
said you were a friend of Jordan's and that he'd asked you
to look me up on the trip,' she pointed out sardonically. A
curiosity—was that all she'd been to him?

His eyes narrowed at the jab. 'Jordan said that if you
knew, or even suspected, that he'd asked me to keep you
out of trouble you'd lead me a hectic dance—deliberately

try to make it as difficult as possible for me to keep my promise.'

Keep her out of trouble?

Rosalind gritted her teeth at the condescending phrase, but since she would probably have reacted exactly as he'd described she could hardly argue.

She was suddenly diverted by his last words. 'You actually *promised* Jordan that you'd look after me?' Rosalind, of all people, was aware of the importance—and the cost—of keeping rash promises.

One eyebrow flared quizzically at her surprisingly subdued reaction. 'No, I don't make promises if there's a chance I won't be able to keep them.' Damn it, she had to respect him for *that*. 'I simply promised him that I'd do my best.'

Her eyes kindled at the irony. '*You'd* do your best? You didn't have to *do* anything. I practically presented myself to you on a plate!'

'Dropped into my hands like a ripe peach,' he agreed, for the sheer pleasure of annoying her. Rosalind angry was much less mindful of her tongue.

'And boy, did you take advantage of it!' she accused.

She struggled free of his arm and this time he let her go, watching as she sat up and hugged the sheet while she fished around in the bed for her dress. He finally found it for her—a sadly crumpled ball stuffed under the pillows.

'What are you so mad about, Roz?' he said as she snatched it away from him. He watched her silently debate whether to put it straight on, obviously remembering what had happened last time she had worn it without underwear. He sat up, leaning on one strong arm, and goaded, 'Are you afraid I only slept with you as a favour to your brother-in-law…to clip your flirty wings and keep you out of the beds of suspicious strangers?'

Rosalind pinkened with rage. She wasn't going to let him get away with that outrageous lie. 'The hell you did! Jordan's not a pimp and you know damned well I'm not a gullible tramp willing to sleep with any sleaze-bag who shows an interest! The only suspicious stranger around here has been you...and the only *favour* you were doing last night was for *yourself*!'

'And you, I hope,' he said, with an incendiary coolness that made her realise that he had been deliberately baiting her. 'So...I think we've established that you were curious about me too. The fact that it rapidly developed into something more complex was something neither of us could have foreseen. We both got more than we bargained for out of our curiosity, didn't we? I agree, I had a hidden agenda to mine, but *you* were the one making the decisions about where and how far the relationship was going to go—'

'Yes, but they weren't fully *informed* decisions!' she protested, clutching the balled-up dress to her chest to try to ease the tightness of her breathing. He didn't sound like a man gloating over his one-night stand with a minor celebrity. Men who were only after sex talked about complexity and relationships *before* they got the woman into bed, never afterwards...

His eyes narrowed on her white knuckles before moving back up to her defiant face. 'I hope you're not suggesting I seduced you against your will. If anyone was seduced it was definitely *me*. After all, *you* were the one who crept into *my* room last night—'

'Not because I wanted to seduce you,' she protested hotly.

'No?' He smirked sceptically.

'No! Because I wanted to check out your computer files again. Because I thought you might be Peter and I wanted to see if I could find any evidence to prove things either way!' she flung at him.

His smirk turned to shocked outrage. 'You *what*?'

'Well, what was I supposed to think?' she yelled defensively. 'I didn't know you were bosom buddies with my brother-in-law. I didn't know you were playing amateur bodyguard! I was just going to hack into your system to see if there was proof one way or the other—'

'You were going to *mess around* on my *hard disk?*' he howled. He seemed more affronted at the thought of his computer being tampered with than he was at the idea of being suspected as a psychotic stalker of women.

'I brought back the floppy I took,' she said, lifting her dainty chin aggressively. 'I was going to reread it, but I dropped it on the floor in the dark. And then you woke up and…and—'

'And you realised your suspicions were completely unfounded and utterly ridiculous!'

'Well…you took me by surprise and…uh…'

He read between the lines of her inarticulate stammer and swore with startling fluency.

'So you thought I might be dangerous, but you fluttered up to the flame anyway? Damn it, Roz, don't you have *any* sense of self-preservation?' Each sentence worked him into an even quieter fury. 'No wonder Jordan was worried! Do you realise what could have happened?'

'I thought it had,' she reminded him, with a trace of her old insouciance.

He stamped on it grimly. 'You know how strong I am. If I had been your stalker I could have hurt you, abused you in some perverted way to feed my sick obsession, *killed* you even,' he emphasised viciously. He took her by the arms, giving her an urgent little shake. 'You may act tough but sophistication is no protection against violence. You don't have the strength to fight a man who thinks he has nothing to lose—'

'P-Peter's dead, for goodness' sake!' she stuttered, her heart hammering at the fierceness of his reaction.

'You didn't know that last night! Just what the *hell* were you thinking, to take such a stupid risk?'

'I refuse to answer on the grounds it might incriminate me!'

His eyes sharpened. Too late Rosalind remembered the frighteningly perceptive observation amongst his diary of notes that she had a habit of resorting to flippancy whenever her emotions were in danger of being too deeply engaged. It was a self-protective mechanism that she had used a lot where Luke was concerned.

'Roz?'

His fingers sank deeper into the soft flesh of her upper arms and she dropped her dress, pushing against his chest to no avail. Unattended, the sheet across her breasts sagged, but Luke didn't take his eyes off her face as he pursued her with silken tenacity.

'Maybe you weren't thinking at all. Maybe you were operating on pure instinct. Your logic told you not to trust me until you'd checked me out, but you've never been guided by logic, have you? You invariably act from the heart. What was your heart saying to you last night, Rosalind?'

She shook her head slightly, her eyes flashing like rare jewels in the streaks of sunlight that lanced through the room. 'That I was crazy,' she said breathlessly.

'I know the feeling,' he murmured, vagueness suddenly blanking off his expression.

Was that a declaration? An admission? Why did she feel that she had disappointed him in some way? What did he expect from her?

'I keep discovering things about you that put a whole new spin on your character,' she blurted out in frustration. 'How can I trust the real you if I don't know who that is? What *other* secrets have you been keeping from me…?'

'Only one.' His eyes were hooded. 'But it's the most important one. Are you going to ask me to tell you what it is…?' His hands fell away, setting her free, as he lazed back down in the bed, tension evident in every muscle and sinew. Experiencing a strong premonition of danger, Rosalind drew the sheet back up over her breasts in an unconsciously symbolic gesture of concealment. 'You want us to be totally honest about ourselves?'

'Yes...of course I do,' she faltered.

Luke's lowered lashes flickered as he revealed the hook in his tantalising bait. 'Well, if you want to talk secrets, Rosalind, I'm quite willing...as long as it's mutual. Are you ready for that yet, do you think? Are you ready to bare the deepest, darkest, most important secrets of your soul on the strength of a one-night stand?'

Her whole being revolted at his brutal definition of their night together, even though she knew he had used it deliberately to provoke just such a reaction. 'That isn't how it was—'

'No.' He cut her off smoothly. 'I agree. So let's say we're lovers, then. And lovers are supposed to confide in each other, aren't they, Roz? To share their joys, their sorrows, their guilty secrets...'

Rosalind moistened her lips, knowing what was coming next, as he went on with insidious calm, 'So that must mean that you're going to tell me all about you and Peggy Staines and what led up to her having a heart attack in your room. Maybe you're going to tell me the rumours about blackmail were true...?'

Rosalind threw back her head proudly. 'I *wasn't* blackmailing her—'

'Then *she* was blackmailing *you*?'

'*No!*'

'Then what was all the money for?'

'It wasn't as much as the newspapers said—just a few hundred dollars—and it belonged to someone else. I was simply...minding it,' Rosalind said reluctantly. Peter Noble's last and most frighteningly direct gift had been a thick wad of banknotes stuffed in with his letter and she had intended to ask Peggy to return it. Peggy had had it in her hand when the pain had struck and in the ensuing panic the money had been scattered around the room.

'Was it some sort of drug deal gone wrong?'

She glared at him. 'No, of *course* not!'

'Then what?'

She remained silent, folding and refolding the top of the sheet across her chest. Even dead, Peter Noble had the power to create havoc in Peggy's life.

'Still want to keep your secrets, Roz?' Luke taunted softly as the silence stretched.

She swallowed the copper taste of fear. Why was he pressing her like this? Was it just a matter of principle, or did he have some deeper purpose? He must realise his flatly confrontational approach was bound to rankle. It was almost as if he *wanted* her to refuse...

'This one isn't mine to tell. My promises mean as much to me as yours do to you—'

He pounced. 'Who did you promise? Peggy Staines? Does that mean you know something that could be damaging to her or her husband?'

Rosalind looked away. Oh, he was sharp. So very, very sharp. If she wasn't careful, with a little more information he might piece the picture together. In a way she wished he *would* guess the truth and thus relieve her of the burdensome responsibility she had impulsively shouldered. His impartial, analytical brain might see an honourable resolution to her painful dilemma.

'I'm sorry...' Her expressive voice was redolent with weary regret. This was even harder than it had been denying her own family. The Marlow clan would always stand staunch for one of its members. Her family's love and private belief in her was strong enough to endure the slings and arrows of outrageous fortune. But the relationship between her and Luke was still very fragile and new and she might be damaging it beyond repair by demanding that he take her on faith. 'I can't tell you anything else.'

'Not ever?' he asked with equal quietness.

Her heart quivered with a faint pulse of excitement. 'Ever' was a world without end. His question implied a future that she feared to contemplate.

'Not *yet*,' she temporised.

'Soon?'

She looked back at him helplessly. 'I—no—maybe…I don't *know*!' She wrapped her arms about herself and shook her head. 'I just don't know! Can't we let it drop?'

'So you want us to go on as we are, then—no soul-searching confessions on either side…*yet*?' There was a tormented edge to his words, a duality that suggested that in spite of his attempts to persuade her otherwise he too welcomed the reprieve.

'Oh, you're very clever,' she said bitterly, recognising that he had brought her full circle, knowing no more about him than before, whereas he had managed to eke some valuable information out of her.

She flinched at his sudden movement, but he was only reaching for one of her fretting hands, lifting it unexpectedly to his lips.

'Clever enough to accept the wisdom of the Bible when it says that there is a season to everything,' he said, a strange serenity replacing the aggressive curiosity in his eyes as he kissed the underside of her encircled wrist and placed her hand against his warm chest, his rapid heartbeat providing a counterpoint to his slow words. '"A time to every purpose under heaven…a time to keep silence, and a time to speak…"'

'"A time to love, and a time to hate"?' she quoted shakily as he ran his hand caressingly up her arm and cupped her shoulder, gently tugging.

'Is that what you're afraid of, Roz? Do you think I might hate you when you finally unveil your secrets?' he whispered as he drew her inexorably down on top of his outstretched body.

A sudden smile chased the brooding shadows from her eyes and relaxed her supple body. Of course not. Why would he? 'No...' He might love her, though, if she gave him sufficient encouragement.

'Well, then...' Luke reached up to trace the outline of her soft lips. 'Maybe you're right...maybe this is our time for silence...our season for loving.' His fingers stroked up over her temple and threaded into the shimmering red halo of her hair. 'But that other time *will* come for us, Rosalind...' He lifted his head and exerted just enough pressure on the back of her delicate skull to breathe his vow against her lips. 'One day soon we'll have our reckoning...'

It was a promise Rosalind tried hard to forget over the next few days. After calling Jordan later that same evening to reaffirm the details of Peter Noble's death and check that Peggy Staines's condition remained unchanged, she determinedly dismissed the tangled past and uncertain future from her mind. She decided that for the remainder of her holiday she would live in the golden present, storing up emotional treasures, stringing memories like priceless pearls—pure, precious, unique in their joyous lustre.

The long, blazing Tioman days gave way to equally long, blazing nights with Luke. For all his inexperience, he was a wonderful lover, tender yet fierce, hungry for everything that she could offer and disconcertingly eager to experiment, delighting in his ability to sometimes fluster the unshockable Roz Marlow.

Instead of easing with familiarity, their passion strengthened and deepened, and as they lazed away the days Rosalind knew with utter certainty that her instincts hadn't betrayed her. Luke had melted into her heart until he was an indivisible part of it—part of her...

With Luke she could be gregarious and playful or silent and moody or broody and restless and he would simply be...Luke. He taught her to drink vodka without choking and she taught him to dance. He showed her how to tone her body with weights and she taught him how to abuse his with wickedly licentious desserts. He taught her astronomy while she quoted Shakespearian sonnets beneath the stars.

And they talked, not of important things but of the vital trivialities that bound people in intimacy—the foods they liked and music they preferred, the places they had been to and the books they had read as children. Emotions, like the immediate past and future, were a taboo subject, but Rosalind never doubted that, like her, Luke was discovering a part of himself that he hadn't hitherto realised existed.

Once they came upon some young island children playing on an isolated beach and, as Rosalind stood there wondering what Olivia's children would look like, she felt Luke's hand slip warmly into hers and squeeze. She hadn't been conscious of her melancholy expression and she banished it by flinging herself into the children's chasing game, making them giggle and Luke laugh at her mad antics.

She had thought she had finally come to terms with her sterility long ago, but now she knew what her doctor of the time had meant when he'd talked warningly about cycles of acceptance. Loving Luke had made her aware that, no matter how full and contented a life she created for herself, a secret sorrow would always lurk in some hidden corner of her heart. Any man who loved her enough to be faithful would forfeit his only chance of immortality. She could offer him everything…everything but a child born out of their love.

The days slipped past with ever greater speed but the end of Rosalind's holiday was still a small eternity away when the bubble of wonderful unreality abruptly burst.

Rosalind had breezed into Luke's chalet, laden with new clothes that she had picked out for him from the hideously expensive hotel boutique, to find him on the telephone. He had been going through some of his electronic mail when she had left, as he did most afternoons, and he was still seated in front of his laptop at the small dining table, his reading glasses dangling from his hand as he pinched the bridge of his nose between forefinger and thumb, uttering brief, monosyllabic replies to whoever was on the other end.

Rosalind put down her packages quietly and as Luke looked up sharply at the crackle of the carrier bags she was shocked by the greyness of his face. His hand clenched on the receiver and she hesitantly mimed herself going out again but he shook his head abruptly, his attention snapping back to the last few words of his call. After hanging up he sat for a moment, staring into nothingness, his cheeks hollowed with strain.

'Luke? What's happened? Is something wrong?'

He stood up jerkily, looking at her but not seeing her, tossing his glasses down on the table with unaccustomed contempt for the lenses. 'That was my father.'

'Oh,' she said, taken aback by his harshness. Had they had an argument? 'What did he want?'

She wondered whether the elder Mr James was anything like his adopted son. Had Luke still been young and impressionable enough to be moulded in his new father's image?

'Sit down.' She blinked at the order, a little trickle of coldness running down her spine. 'I've never told you much about my parents, have I?'

She shook her head as she perched uneasily on the edge of the couch, watching him prowl round the room tidying things that didn't need to be tidied. He hadn't told her anything but the bare fact of his adoption. Thinking it must be an ultra-sensitive subject, she had respected his silence.

'Actually, my adoptive father is related to me, but only by marriage. My mother was his stepsister.'

Rosalind opened her mouth to protest that he had told her he had been orphaned without a family but snapped it shut again as he continued flatly, 'My parents left a hell of a lot of debts when they died—my father had just mortgaged everything to go into business. His only legacy to me was his name; that was why I kept it when my aunt and uncle adopted me. They couldn't have any children themselves and I've always felt I disappointed them by not taking on their name, but I just couldn't bring myself to reject my last link with Mum and Dad.

'They certainly loved me as if I was their own and I never lacked security, financial or otherwise, and although they demanded strict standards of behaviour of me I knew it was no more than they expected of themselves. When I was at school they never missed a sports day or a play, and they always welcomed my friends. They bought me the best education money could buy and gave me all the support I ever needed in my studies…'

Rosalind sat there listening to him describe how wonderful his adoptive parents were and how much he owed them, gradually feeling colder and colder until her core was solid ice—numb and blessedly unfeeling. He still hadn't mentioned any names, but as he rambled jerkily on she knew…she *knew*…with a black fatalism that made her wonder if she'd *always* known…

'It's Peggy, isn't it?' she uttered through white lips, when she could stand the torture no longer. 'Donald and Peggy Staines are your uncle and aunt…'

He swung around, knocking one of her packages over, and out spilled a green silk shirt she had bought him because it was the colour of her eyes and she'd thought it would remind him of her when she wasn't around.

'She regained consciousness yesterday morning. Don didn't ring me until now because her condition hadn't stabilised, but now they've had time to make an assessment… The stroke has affected the movement down her left side and distorted her speech but she can make herself understood.'

Peggy was awake and starting to communicate! Rosalind could hardly take it in. She felt as if *she* was having a heart attack, the squeezing in her chest almost too much to bear. She looked up at the towering figure…at the adoptive half-brother of Peter Noble. Poor Peggy—she had had two sons and neither bore her name! She had been forced to give up her first-born child for adoption, who, it had turned out, was destined to be her *only* born, and then through a tragedy she had gained another son, whom she herself had adopted. Luke's love and respect for Peggy bordered on reverence. What would it do to him to learn that she had been too ashamed to appeal to him for help?

'It wasn't just an incredible coincidence that you were on that Tioman flight, was it?' she whispered. 'Somehow you found out and you *were* following me.'

'Don begged me to find out what kind of trouble Peggy was in. He wanted to know if he ought to resign before the scandal breaks. He's that kind of man—painfully honourable,' Luke said grimly. 'He couldn't remember anything of what you'd said at the hospital, only that you'd been vague and evasive, and you'd disappeared pretty sharply. He couldn't leave Peggy so I said I'd track you down and find out what he needed to know.

'Don's police connections were of the opinion that you were certainly hiding something, but they had nothing to work on and they suspected you would bolt at the first sign of pressure, so I put some feelers out at Pendragon before I flew up to Auckland and, thanks to my security rating, I found out about Jordan's extremely confidential travel booking…non-tax deductable.' The typically meticulous addition was made totally without humour. 'I knew the best chance I had to persuade you to help me was to be on that plane.'

Rosalind massaged her aching chest. 'But—I can't believe that Jordan—'

He cut her off with an impatient shrug. 'Our friendship

was largely confined to the Pendragon offices; he has no idea who my parents are. Seeing him at the airport—now that *was* pure coincidence. And a profound piece of luck for me. But unfortunately he couldn't tell me anything more than the police, so I knew then that if you weren't even talking to the people you trusted most you certainly weren't going to open up to me. Given what you were being accused of, I didn't think compassion would be one of your strong points. I was wrong about that, wasn't I?'

His sober question threw her off balance for a moment but she quickly regained it. 'Did you think you might have a better chance conning me into some pillow talk?' she flung at him bitterly.

His eyes narrowed. 'It occurred to me—especially considering your royal reputation for reckless behaviour.'

She went white, leaping to her feet, her hand itching to hit him. 'You *bastard*!'

He was equally pale. 'I told you how much Peggy and Don mean to me—'

'And that excuses what you did? I suppose you're going to say the ends justified the means!' she spat furiously. 'And how proud of you would your parents feel now, knowing that you prostituted yourself with a little slut for nothing?'

His complexion flooded with brilliant colour. 'I said it *occurred* to me, that's all,' he said roughly. 'Damn it, Roz, I'm trying to be as honest as I can with you, for *both* our sakes. I didn't know you back then. I do now…probably better than you would like me to. You know damned well I *made love* to you because it seemed the utterly natural thing to do. There was no ulterior motive, except maybe to build an intimate bond between us that was strong enough to survive whatever truths we had to tell each other.

'And it is, isn't it, Rosalind? Yes, we're angry with each other, and yes, you're feeling frustrated and hurt, and so am I, and yes, *yes*, I'm going to use every argument in the book to get you to tell me what I need to know, but whether you do or not *this is not over*…I won't *let* it be…'

Rosalind had had plenty of flamboyant rows in her time, but never one in which she had felt the pain of the attacker as acutely as her own defensive wounds. On the ferry to Singapore the next morning, clutching only her small overnight bag, she shakily congratulated herself for withstanding Luke's powerful assault on her conscience, on her seesawing emotions and…finally…on her body. They had made love all night long with a fierce, bruising urgency that should have left her feeling fragile and vulnerable but instead had left her charged with a furious energy. Luke seemed hell-bent on staking a claim to Rosalind's loyalty, both in bed and out. Well, first she would have to clear the decks of *prior* claims…

She had left him still sleeping and signed an early checkout, arranging for the rest of her luggage to be packed and sent on to her the next day, hoping that her scattered belongings would fool Luke long enough for her to make a clean getaway. Unfortunately, when she got to the tiny airport there wasn't a spare seat until an afternoon flight to Kuala Lumpur, so instead she headed for the wharf and gained a last-minute berth on the high-speed catamaran.

As the twin granite peaks of Tioman receded into the glassy South China Sea Rosalind refused to look back. No regrets, she told herself. She had made her decision; now she had to stick to it.

Don't look back, she told herself half a day later as she boarded a first-class flight from Singapore to Auckland via a couple of long, tiresome stop-overs which had not figured in Jordan's original flight plans. She sat bolt upright as they chased the daylight all the way down the Pacific rim, rehearsing scenarios over and over in her head until she thought she was prepared for every eventuality.

Nearly twenty-seven hours after she had blown a farewell kiss to the sleeping man on a tumbled bed in a faraway paradise she stumbled into the starkly modern clinical ward in the Wellington hospital where Peggy Staines was listed as not receiving visitors and immediately got into a full-blown argument with a tank commander in nurse's drag.

'It's all right, Sister, I know she looks dangerous, but she's with me.'

Rosalind gasped at the mirage hovering before her in a faintly rumpled suit, his hair flopping over his tanned forehead, his eyes almost as bloodshot as hers.

'How did you—?'

'Because I told you—I know you almost as well as you know yourself, Roz Marlow. This is exactly your extravagant style—the hotheaded decision, the dramatic exit, the flamboyant gesture of self-sacrifice! Did you think I didn't know the instant you left the bed? Did you think I didn't immediately pick up the phone and ask Reception to let me know if you checked out? Did you think I couldn't spin a good enough sob story to touch the heart of the woman on the flight-information desk at Singapore?

'You taught me well, Roz—you should have stuck with me then you wouldn't look such a total wreck,' he said cruelly, his eyes flicking over her jeans and travel-stained T-shirt topped with her denim jacket. 'I pleaded a family emergency and got priority-bumped all the way from Tioman. I understand you took the scenic route…'

Her blood sugar shot sky-high—quite a feat since she hadn't eaten for a day and a night. 'Why, you—!'

The sergeant major harrumphed. 'Don't disturb her for too long, Mr James. She needs her rest.'

'Uh, that's very kind of you…' Rosalind was mortified. How could the woman be so caring about someone who had been so insulting? She flashed her a brilliantly apologetic smile.

'She's talking about Peggy, Roz,' Luke reproved her as the nurse trod heavily away.

'Oh.' Her eyes darted to his. 'How is she?' He hadn't tried to stop her leaving Tioman or entering the hospital, yet he was here lying in wait for her. Was he now going to show her how futile any cunning attempt to see his aunt would be?

He took her elbow and turned her down the long corridor, shortening his stride to match her wobbly steps. 'Well enough to see you.'

She just stopped herself leaning on him. 'You *told* her I was coming?'

'She's in no condition to take any shocks. Don't worry,' he said wearily. 'I reassured her that although we know each other we haven't discussed anything that happened between you two. She seemed pathetically relieved.

'She told me that she was horribly embarrassed…that she's been a closet fan of yours for years and got carried away having recognised you having coffee at the hotel. She said she followed you up to your room and got you to ask her in by pretending to be a hospital employee, and that you kindly let her stay for a drink and a chat while you got ready for your appointment. She said she thought Don would be angry with her for behaving like a teenager and she's sorry that she put you in such an awkward position by making you promise not to tell anyone of her foolishness when she started having pains.

'I didn't mention the extent of the publicity but I did say the press interest had put quite a lot of pressure on your silence, and she said she had no idea that her silliness would get blown so out of proportion or she would never have asked such a thing of you…'

Rosalind's heart sank at the blow. Peggy was scarcely awake yet she was already frantically covering her tracks. She expected them to continue their charade for ever! The story actually sounded quite plausible but it was obvious from Luke's toneless delivery that he knew Rosalind too well to believe that so frivolous a reason was behind her unshakeable show of loyalty.

'That's what she's going to tell Don, anyway, and since they both hold that lying is a sin he'll believe it.' He wiped a hand across his face. 'Problem solved for everyone...as long as it's not going to blow up later in his face...'

Rosalind said nothing. What could she say? She couldn't guarantee that the truth wouldn't eventually leak out; she could only remove herself from the situation to ensure that it didn't come from her. Unless she could persuade Peggy to make a clean breast of it, so that they could *all* begin again with a clean slate...

'I hate it that she has to suffer like this,' he went on savagely. 'She's always seemed so strong...and to see her lying there so...so...'

His voice thickened to a halt as they stopped before a plain swing-door with a square panel of reinforced glass, and he placed his palm against it, blocking out her view of the bed within.

'Luke—' She was shocked to see the glitter of tears in his eyes, the way the skin was stretched taut across his cheekbones and jaw. God, he was hurting, and part of his pain was because of her. By coming here like this was she making things worse for Luke and his family just for the sake of her own selfish needs? 'Luke, I—'

'I know...I know...you want to go in alone,' he said, misunderstanding her inarticulate plea. He released her elbow reluctantly. 'For God's sake, Roz, whatever this is about, please try not to hurt her any more than she already has been. She's going to need every ounce of hope and courage to tackle her recovery.'

There was a hot stinging in her own eyes at the irony of his plea. He didn't know what he was asking. To have any sort of future with Luke she might *have* to force Peggy's hand. And if she did she might very well lose him anyway. 'Of course I won't!'

She turned to go in and felt him touch her shoulder.

'And Roz?'

'What?' She looked back, her chin brushing the back of his hand. Unable to resist, she tilted her head and rubbed her cheek yearningly against it, until he turned his hand over and ran his fingers down the line of her jaw to tap them on her chin.

'I love you,' he said huskily.

'What?' She was hallucinating from lack of sleep. Having a waking dream...

'Never mind. Later. Go on...' He flattened his hand between her shoulderblades and pushed, so that she stumbled forward, instinctively reaching out and bumping open the door. 'I'll be waiting for you...'

A long, slow, painfully intense half-hour later he was true to his word, getting up from a hard wooden chair in the small, sterile waiting room at the end of the hallway as she trudged across the wavering floor towards him.

'Well?'

She closed her dry, gritty eyes, unwilling to face the dream that had become a tangled nightmare of lies.

'I have to go.'

'Go? Go where?' His voice sounded as if it was coming from the end of a long tunnel.

'Home.'

'Home?'

'To Auckland...my apartment... I have an audition to study for...' Damn it, she was going to take that Shakespearian role! she thought, trying to summon her enthusiasm. Peter was gone...no more stalker to distract her stage persona, to paralyse her vocal cords with nameless fears. Her career had taken the place of children in her life; now she would stretch it over the gaping hole left by Luke. She would be the fiercest, most bloodthirstily ambitious, most utterly wretched Lady Macbeth in the history of the Scottish play!

There was a long silence and she opened her eyes, to be confronted with the intense black conflagration in his.

'What happened in there?'

She tried to smile, failed and settled for a shrug. 'Nothing. We talked. It's over—I don't have to feel any more horrible guilt or responsibility on Peggy's behalf…she said she'd been having chest twinges for some time but had put them down to indigestion. As for the rest…well…' She found a wall at her shoulder and leaned gratefully against it. Why did her legs seem not to work? 'It was just as she told you…'

Peggy's struggle with language had reminded her uneasily of those terrible minutes in the hotel room and Rosalind had been no more proof against the agitated pleading of her eyes and the working of her distorted face than she had been on the last occasion.

Peggy was deathly afraid of losing her family and, trapped by her disability, more vulnerable than ever to her deeply rooted feelings of shame. She *had* found Peter's body, after calling in at his flat on the way to the hotel, and, as Rosalind had surmised, had fled in shock and panic. But she was under the impression that she had managed to redeem her wickedness by blurting everything out in the confused moments before she'd finally lost consciousness.

Rosalind had tactfully glossed over the facts, hoping that the poor woman need never know of the true circumstances surrounding the discovery of her son's body. Her grief over his death was muted by a shamed sense of relief and, true to the spirit which had characterised her behaviour all along, Peggy was desperate to have the past swept safely back under the carpet where it belonged.

Rosalind hated it but she had been too exhausted to remember her rehearsed arguments, even if she could have brought herself to unleash them on the fragile bundle of humanity on the bed. She had the feeling that in years to come Peggy would continue to struggle with her conscience and ultimately pay the price of suppressing her unresolved grief.

'And where does that leave us?' Luke broke harshly into her anguished thoughts by placing a hand on the wall beside her head and dipping his face to force her to look at him.

'Us?' She was still an actress, wasn't she? Maybe that was *all* she would ever be as far as Luke was concerned…but at least she could be the *best*.

Rosalind summoned all her remaining courage and gave a tinkling laugh. 'Oh, Luke, don't be so *intense*. There is no *us*…that was just holiday fever…spiced up with intrigue and all our suspicions about each other. It's a shame that it had to end in the way it did, but maybe it was for the best, because we're back in the real world now and I really don't think we have much in common—'

She yelped as he shot out his other hand to slam it against the wall. 'Oh, no, you don't!' he hammered out. 'I didn't chase you halfway across the world to be fobbed off with your flighty-actress routine! I told you before you walked in there that I love you. That *meant* something to you—I could *see* it; stop trying to deny it, damn it— *I love you*!'

'Maybe you *think* you do,' she said desperately, aware of the sick woman hovering like a spectre between them.

Maybe in time, as she got stronger and better able to cope, Peggy would relent, but what if she didn't? Rosalind imagined loving Luke, sharing his life, coming into contact with Peggy and Don, always walking on a knife-edge, aware that one careless word might sow the seeds of destruction in his adoptive parents' marriage. She would stifle. In love, as in everything else, Rosalind was an all-or-nothing person. She would love freely and completely or not at all.

'But you're a realist, Luke; you know that isn't always

enough,' she continued. 'We…we want such different things from life—'

'Yes—I want you and you want me,' he said bluntly. 'Different, and yet the same. We complement each other, Rosalind, we know that we *fit* together…like the two halves of a whole.' His hands bunched into fists on the shiny white wall as he looked down into the carved stillness of her coldly classic features. 'If you want this to be our final reckoning, so be it. Look at me and tell me you feel nothing for me. Convince me. Look into my eyes, damn you, and tell me that you don't love me and never could.'

She lifted tragic green eyes, rage breaking through the marble-like stillness of her façade. 'I don't love you, Luke, and I never could,' she snarled, hating him for forcing her to be brutal.

He drew a breath, and his hands fell heavily to her shoulders. His eyebrows slanted and his mouth quirked.

'And people *pay* to see you do this?' He cocked his head. 'Oh, Roz, I hope nobody ever asks me for my opinion of you as an actress.'

His response was so unexpected that she began to slide down the wall. How could he not believe her? She thought she deserved an Academy award for her performance. 'I don't love you!' she repeated feverishly. 'I really don't!'

He caught her by the waist, preventing her from falling off the crazy tilt of the world. 'We've done things round the wrong way, haven't we, Roz…had the honeymoon before the wedding?'

She held her hands up in a warding-off gesture, only to have them captured and kissed. 'Luke, for God's sake, it wouldn't work—'

'Why not?'

A million reasons…most of them to do with other people, she thought.

'It just wouldn't. I have a career that takes me all over the place and I like to move around—have plenty of excitement going on in my life. You wouldn't like it…you're too conventional…you need to be settled…have a fixed home, family…children…' A light went on in her overloaded brain. 'You'd make a wonderful father; you should have a big, loving family of kids to make up for all you missed in being an only child. I can't even give you *one* child's love…'

She went on to tell him that he hadn't thought it through; she listed all the reasons why he would come to resent her childlessness and announced that she never intended to get married anyway because she didn't see the point if there were no children to protect.

'Fine. We'll just live together for the rest of our lives.'

'Luke!'

He cupped her face tenderly. 'Look, Rosalind, I know what you're doing and it's very kind of you, but you can't protect me from my own emotions. Let *me* bear the responsibility for a change. I *have* thought this through. For the last twenty-four hours I've thought of nothing else. I know damned well that you and my aunt are linked in some way that she doesn't want you to reveal, probably by something that happened in her past, something she's bitterly ashamed of—and, for someone of her generation and religious upbringing, it's probably to do with sex.

'Now, I know that you can't possibly be her daughter but maybe you're her connection to someone else— No!' He pinned her mouth shut with his thumb. 'Let me finish. I'm not going to ask you about it again—I won't *ever* ask you. I don't have to. It's between you and Peggy, not you and me.

'Can't you see that telling you I loved you before you walked into that room was an expression of faith? I will *never* lose faith in you, Roz. I *believe* in you. You're a passionate idealist, a true and honest friend, never venal or self-serving at the expense of others, and because I have that certainty in my heart I can accept everything else on trust…

'I love you for *all* your qualities…for your joy and your stubbornness, your fiery dramatics and your deep humanity—yes…even for your sterility.'

There were tears again in the dark eyes, tears and something else that vanquished her doubts and fatigue—a deep, passionately held commitment to what he was saying.

'The pain that you carry from your past is the part of the compassion you bring to the present. I'd love to heal that pain for you but I know I can't; I can only do as you do for those you love: be there when the hurt is too much to bear alone. There might not be children from our love but— oh, Roz, there'll still be love…so much *love*…'

He leaned his forehead against hers and whispered prayerfully, 'I need you to be there for me too, Roz. Through good and bad, in sickness and in health. That's what this is all about. Trust. If you love me, then *believe* in me. Keep your secrets, and believe that nothing will make me betray our love. Please…'

Rosalind's arms went around him, tight and hard. It had taken magnificent courage for him to say all that, to open himself up so completely before she had uttered a single word of love, and she could feel the shock of it shivering through his entire body.

Trust. Betrayal. Rosalind knew which of the two words she associated with Luke. He was intelligent, resourceful, sensitive and strong and deeply thoughtful…of course she trusted his judgement and the depth of his compassionate understanding. He would never betray those he loved, any more than Rosalind would. In that sense they were two of a kind. There would be difficulties ahead but Rosalind knew that there was no secret that she couldn't share with him, no problem or sorrow they couldn't discuss. For now, she was content to hug the revelation to herself, but she knew that one day soon she would talk to him about Peggy and Peter, and in doing so she would create not a gulf but another bridge of understanding…

'The most important scene in my life and it's being played out in an empty hospital waiting room,' she said in a choked voice. 'I somehow expected a revolving set and maybe a full orchestra and chorus. You're a cheap guy with a proposal, Luke James!'

His head lifted. 'Is that an "I believe"?' he asked rawly, a dark splendour dawning in his eyes at her flippant reply.

She began laughing through her tears. Her dear, darling, cautious Luke wanted the i's dotted and the t's crossed.

'Oh, yes, it's an *I believe*. I love you, Luke James. Now and for always, *I believe*…'

CAPTIVE HEART

CAROLINE ANDERSON

CHAPTER ONE

HE LOOKED like something out of an old B-movie.

Faded khaki shirt and shorts, feet propped up on the veranda, hat tipped over his face, chair tilted onto its back legs—and he was in the shade, which was another reason to dislike him on sight.

Gabby could feel the heat of the sun scorching down on her unprotected shoulders—the skin would probably be burned already. No doubt her nose was covered in a smattering of little freckles, with the rest of her programmed to follow in short order, but that was what you got for being a green-eyed redhead—sunburn and a lousy disposition!

She studied the man on the veranda again as she drew closer. As there was no one else around and no other dwellings in the vicinity, it must be him she was looking for, and he was every bit as clichéd close up as he'd been from a distance. She stifled a little laugh. She'd come all the way across the world and she'd stepped into the set of a Trevor Howard film, with the neighbourhood MO cast in the leading part!

He was quite well put together, however, despite the air of old-Colonial dissipation that hung over him. No doubt some Hollywood director would be thrilled to have him, she thought, examining him with clinical detachment. 'In fact, forget Trevor Howard,' she mumbled to herself, losing her clinical detachment, 'think Harrison Ford as Indiana Jones...'

His shirtsleeves were rolled up to expose deeply tanned and hair-strewn forearms, rippling with lean muscle, and long, rangy legs, strewn with more of the same gold-tinged wiry hair, stuck out of the bottoms of crumpled shorts. His feet were bare and bony, with strong high arches and little tufts of hair on the toes. They were at her eye level as she approached the steps to the veranda, and a little imp inside her wondered if they were ticklish.

She couldn't see his face because of the battered Panama hat tipped over his eyes, but his fingers were curled loosely around a long, tall glass of something that looked suspiciously like gin and tonic. The outside of the glass was beaded with tiny droplets of water, and in the unrelenting tropical heat it drew her eyes like a magnet. She swallowed drily and wondered if he'd mind if she pinched it.

Mind? Of course he wouldn't mind—he wouldn't know! He was fast asleep, a soft snore drifting out from under the hat at intervals—he looked so relaxed that Gabby had an insane urge to kick out the two legs of the chair on which he was balancing and knock him onto his indolent behind.

Only two things stopped her. One was her natural good manners. The other was the fact that he was a darned sight bigger than she was and would almost certainly get just a tad cross about it.

So she plopped down onto the edge of the wooden veranda, propped her back against the nearest post and cleared her throat.

Nothing. Not a flicker of reaction.

Damn. She was going to have to kick the legs—

'I'm asleep.'

She blinked at the deep growl that emerged from under the hat. She thought she saw the gleam of an eye, but she wasn't sure. He hadn't moved so much as a single well-honed muscle.

She swallowed. 'I know. I'm sorry. I hate to disturb you—'

'So why do it? I don't entertain bored tourists,' he drawled. 'It's not in my job description.'

'Well, excuse me,' she muttered under her breath. She stood up, banging the dust off her bottom and stomping down the steps, pausing on the rough track to turn and glare up at him. All she got for her pains was a view up the leg of his shorts which her grandmother wouldn't have approved of and which did nothing for her blood pressure.

'For the record,' she said tersely—petulantly? Probably. Oh, heck. She dragged her eyes away from his shorts. 'For the record,' she began again, 'I'm not a tourist, I'm Gabrielle Andrews—Jonathan's cousin. Penny sent me up here to tell you lunch will be ready—'

The chair legs crashed to the floor, making her jump, and he tipped back the hat with one finger and studied her out of startling blue eyes.

'In a minute,' she finished.

'Well, why didn't you say so?'

She scowled at him. 'I just did,' she said crossly.

His grin was lazy and did further damage to her blood pressure. So did his eyes, tracking equally lazily over her body and back to her face. That did it. She wondered if she looked as angry as she felt, standing there in the muddy road with her head tipped back at a crazy angle and her hair—the red hair that was a dead give-away for her temper—clinging to her forehead in sweaty tangles.

She brushed it impatiently back out of her eyes and glared at him. 'Well?'

'Well, what?'

'Are you coming?'

'To lunch?' He leant forward and propped his elbows on the railings, the cool, inviting glass dangling from those lean and very masculine fingers, and grinned that lazy grin again. 'Tell Penny I wouldn't miss it for the world. And by the way…'

'Yes?'

'You shouldn't stand about in that sun with your fair skin—you'll burn in seconds.'

Gabby had noticed. She stifled the little scream of frustration and smiled viciously at him. She thought she probably looked more closely related to a barracuda than to her mild-mannered cousin at the moment, but she was too hot and too cross to be nice—not to mention exhausted. 'Thank you. I had realised,' she retorted and, spinning on her heel, she walked back down the rough track to the bungalow where her cousin lived.

What a pain! Idle, indolent, laconic, self-serving pig! Doctor? 'Huh! Not in this lifetime,' Gabby muttered crossly.

Penny greeted her with a glass of something cold, tropical and absolutely delicious that improved her humour immediately. 'Mmm, yum,' she murmured, pressing it against her hot cheeks. She'd only been in the country since early that morning, and it would take her a while, she imagined, to get used to the heat. In the meantime, the icy glass felt wonderful—

'Did you find Jed all right?'

She stifled the urge to tell her cousin's wife what she thought of the cliché she'd found sprawled on the veranda. 'Yes—he said he'd come. I would have thought he'd be here now—he wasn't exactly busy.'

'I expect he'll be taking a *mandi*—a bath.'

Gabby blinked. 'In this heat? Surely he'd shower.'

Penny laughed. 'He hasn't got a shower—the bungalow's not that sophisticated, I'm afraid. He's using the *mandi* at the back of the bungalow—it's a bamboo enclosure with a big tank of water in it. You stand in it and bail water all over yourself out of the tank with a big scoop. Actually, it's wonderful.'

It sounded wonderful—more refreshing than the shower she'd taken just before she'd wandered up the road to call Jed for lunch, and which had already lost its impact in the tropical humidity.

Penny settled down beside her in the rattan lounger, took a long swallow of her drink and turned to face Gabby. 'So, how was the journey? You don't look too bad, considering how tired you must be. Are you sure you don't want to lie down?'

Gabby shook her head. 'I'm still too wound up. Perhaps later.' She thought of the flight from London to Kuala Lumpur, the two-hour stopover for fuelling, the short flight to Jakarta, and then stepping out onto the runway at the airport at two in the morning. It had been like walking into a sauna, and the five-hour wait with little Katie had been hot, smelly and at the wrong end of an exhausting journey.

They had had to transfer to the other airport for the local island service, and even in the middle of the night Jakarta had been seething. The airports had been crowded with travellers and they had spent the last couple of hours perched on their cases, dozing against each other.

That had been the easy bit. Their arrival shortly after dawn in the unbelievable crate in which they had made the last short leg of the journey had been nothing short of a miracle. Her heart had been in her mouth most of the way as she'd listened to the engine cough and splutter—

'So, how was the journey?' Penny asked again, breaking into her thoughts.

How was it? 'OK,' she replied, always the master of understatement. 'Although I would have had more faith in the last plane if I hadn't seen the pilot tinkering around under the engine cowling with a spanner just before we took off.'

Penny laughed. 'They're quite safe—well, mostly. Some of them are a bit rough, but it's not exactly a hot tourist route—well, not yet.'

Gabby looked around her. Below them, stretched out into the muddy estuary on stilts, was a bustling little wooden town, the shacks roofed with corrugated iron or palm leaves, the fishing boats tied up at the makeshift piers rocking gently in the swell.

A seedy hotel, a handful of shops, a bank and not much else comprised the westernised part of the town, legacy of the Dutch influence which had also been responsible for the few bungalows at the top of the hill, in one of which they were sitting. That was it, however. Behind them, just yards away, the jungle began and civilisation, such as it was, ended.

'Not exactly on the beaten track,' she agreed drily.

Penny laughed, and for a moment Gabby thought she sounded a little strained. 'Hence the resort. It's going to be very expensive and very exclusive, so we're told, and with minimal impact. That's why they want the hydro-electric power plant instead of generators—so they don't have the noise in the resort village.'

'Where will it be?'

Penny waved an arm at the little headland beyond the town. 'Over there, in the next bay. It's a fabulous spot, I can see the attraction for the tourists once it's done.'

'But not now,' Gabby said softly, instinctively reading Penny's unspoken words.

She shrugged. 'Perhaps not while it's quite so primitive. Jonathan loves it here, and the little ones are very happy. I just hope Katie settles down like the others have—I can't thank you enough for bringing her back to us.'

Gabby chuckled. 'She was no trouble at all—and, anyway, I got a free tropical holiday in the middle of winter out of it! What more could a girl want?'

'A swimming pool?'

'What, with a bar in the middle and some fancy waiter in a grass skirt, serving bizarre blue cocktails with parasols floating in them?' She shuddered theatrically, and Penny relaxed and smiled.

'Yes, they can be pretty tacky, some of those pools— and they aren't necessary really. The sea's wonderful if you don't mind the odd jellyfish. Still, sometimes I wonder if this doesn't go too far the other way. It will get busier, of course, once Jonathan's built the power station and we have real electricity—then the resort will get under way and prosperity will happen and, whatever they say, it'll get just like Bali in the end, which will be a shame in a way because it is beautiful like this, so unspoilt.'

'Will it be spoilt? I thought the developer wanted to keep it very low impact.'

She shrugged. 'He does. He's quite emphatic about that, but it might just open the floodgates for other firms to come in the slipstream, so to speak. He's supposed to have an arrangement with the government, but things change with time. Still, a little more civilisation wouldn't go amiss. It would be nice to be able to buy butter that wasn't rancid, for instance, but they haven't got a cold storage facility here yet, and they won't until they have a proper and reliable source of power.'

Gabby laughed. 'Something to look forward to.'

Penny shrugged. 'By the time they have I expect we will have moved on to another primitive site in Brazil or Africa.'

Was that a wistful longing Gabby could see in her eyes? 'Don't you ever wish Jonathan had a proper job— you know, nine to five, Monday to Friday, in Basingstoke or wherever?'

Penny smiled, and again for a second the strain showed. 'Of course, but he wouldn't be happy doing that so here we all are. If we didn't have Jed I'd probably refuse to live here, but having a doctor on the spot makes it much safer and there are wonderful hospitals in Jakarta and Singapore.'

Gabby thought of their 'doctor on the spot', and hoped no one was about to be ill. He looked much too laid-back to cope with anything faster than ingrowing toe-nails.

She remembered her last job, a three-month stint in A and E, and almost laughed aloud at the thought of Pulau Panjang's resident MO caught up the hurly-burly of real medicine. Still, what did she expect? No doctor worth his salt would give up a decent job to live out here quite literally at the edge of civilisation, if not somewhat beyond it—but, anyway, he was quite decorative in a rather rough-hewn sort of way so she could probably forgive him so long as she remained healthy!

The object of her musings ambled into view, dressed in equally faded but freshly pressed shorts and shirt, his dark blond hair still wet from his bath, and bounded up the veranda steps with a grin that, to Gabby's utter disgust, did stupid things to her insides.

He looked even more like Indiana Jones, and she regretted the weakness she had for the type. She thought of all the old-fashioned and appropriate words, like 'cad' and 'bounder' and 'rascal'—all oddly flattering. Damn.

He grinned at her, waggled his fingers and turned to their hostess.

'Hiya, Pen. How are you doing?' he said cheerfully

and, bending over, dropped a casual kiss on Penny's cheek.

She caught his hand and patted it. 'Hi, yourself. Can I get you a glass of juice?'

'I'll get it.' He wandered into the house and emerged a few moments later with a tall clinking glass and a jug. 'Top-up?' he asked the two women.

Gabby held her glass out and wondered if she hadn't judged him a little too harshly, but then he blew it all away by dropping into a chair, hooking his feet over the veranda and closing his eyes.

'Bliss,' he said with a muffled groan, and within seconds he was asleep. Gabby was astonished at the rudeness of the man. Didn't he have more respect for his hostess than to come for lunch and go to sleep?

'He's been up all night,' Penny said under her breath, as if reading Gabby's mind. 'Jon'll be here in a minute— I'll wake him up then.' She settled back in her chair, sipped her drink and levelled a searching look at Gabby. 'So, tell me about your job,' she demanded. 'Got anything lined up yet?'

Gabby shrugged. 'Not yet. I don't want to go back to London, and there's nothing in my line anywhere else at the moment.'

Well, there was, but she would have had to cancel her holiday to attend the interview and wouldn't have been able to escort little Katie home. After the bout of appendicitis which had struck Katie while they had been on leave Gabby's temporary lack of employment had seemed like a godsend. It had meant that Katie hadn't had to travel alone once she was fit—for which service, Gabby reminded herself, she had been well paid despite all her protests that it wasn't necessary.

And there was no way she would have passed up the opportunity to see this wonderful tropical island, a tiny jewel in the Indonesian archipelago. Called Pulau Panjang, or Long Island, in Bahasa, the universal language of Indonesia, it was easy to see why from a map— and indeed from the air. Several times longer than it was wide, her first view had been of a huge, vivid green crescent in the turquoise sea.

As the ancient little plane had circled overhead she had had the most spectacular view of the thick unbroken green of the jungle with its winding rivers, slicing through the hillside on their way down the mountain, the deserted sandy coves and the isolated little settlements scattered here and there.

It was like something out of *Robinson Crusoe*, she'd thought, only bigger, and then at one end, clustered round an estuary, she'd spotted a larger settlement with an airstrip no bigger than a pencil line.

Around the town there was a terraced area of *padi* fields where she was told the locals grew rice and soya beans in rotation, but apart from that there was little sign of cultivation on the island. Because of the shape it was also known as Pulau Pisang, or Banana Island. Apparently, so Penny told her, Indonesian places often had more than one name, which just added to the delightful confusion.

The airstrip lay to the south of the town, on a spit of land sticking out into the sea, and although it was a little bigger than it had appeared from the air it was still barely adequate. What would happen if the plane failed to stop didn't bear thinking about, but it was hardly a jet. The little twin-engined monstrosity would probably just bellyflop into the sea and be towed back to land by a group of cheerful Indonesian children, yelling, 'Hello, Mister!'

It was the sum total of their English, apart from 'Give me money, give me sweets', which was the tail end of the refrain she had heard ever since her arrival in Jakarta that morning. Katie had been wide-eyed. For Gabby, it summed up the influence of the west on the innocent children of the east, and she felt faintly ashamed.

This island, though, had been unlike that, the children simply friendly and curious and the adults likewise. They had been courteous, voluble and charming—which was more than could be said for the company doctor.

A soft snore rippled the air, and she glowered at him and willed him to wake up and not just lie there.

She got her way. As she watched, his fingers relaxed their grip on the almost full glass of juice and ice and it tipped up on his chest. He gave a startled yelp and sat up, blinking and swatting at his shirt, but the damage was done.

That'll teach you, Gabby thought, stifling a laugh, but she was the one who suffered in the end because he stripped off his shirt, mopped the hair-tangled expanse of his deep, muscular chest with the soggy bundle and dropped back into the chair with a sigh.

'I suppose you want another one,' Penny said with a grin.

He flashed her a smile full of wry self-disgust, and to her horror Gabby found herself warming towards the rogue.

'Shirt or drink?' he asked ruefully. 'It was my last clean shirt. Last night was a bit heavy on them.'

Penny stood up. 'I'll get you one of Jon's. Can't have you frightening the natives—or Gabby. Help yourself to the drink.'

She left them, and Gabby felt his eyes graze her skin, sending a shiver over it. 'I don't think I frighten you, do I, Gabrielle?' he murmured, his voice a little husky. 'Rather the opposite, I feel.'

She blushed and glared at him, and he chuckled, a

deep, warm sound that was nearly as attractive as the expanse of bronzed skin that filled Gabby's line of sight. She shifted slightly and turned her eyes to the little town below them, the houses clustered along the curve of the bay and stretching up towards the brilliant green of the terraced *padi* fields.

She hoped he would leave her in peace, but no chance. That deep, slightly husky voice teased at her senses again like a caress. 'Pretty, isn't it? Especially if you don't have to live here.'

She turned back to him and tried to avoid ogling his body. 'Don't you like it?'

He shrugged. 'It's where the work is. You do what you have to do.'

Like sleep on verandas. Gabby was less than sympathetic, and it probably showed, but she really didn't care. As far as she was concerned, what he seemed to be doing couldn't possibly be construed as work. She thought of the sick people of the world, and of him passing the prime of his life with his feet on the railing of some tropical veranda, and despaired of the waste of talent.

If he was, indeed, talented. Perhaps he'd been struck off?

'How long are you here for?' he asked after a pregnant pause that she refused to fill.

'Three weeks—and, don't worry, I won't expect you to entertain me.'

He said something under his breath—not an apology, she was sure. She turned and met his eyes, her own glittering with challenge, and that sapphire gaze locked with hers. The same sparkling blue as the tropical sea beneath them, they issued their own challenge.

'That's just as well,' he said mildly. 'I'm much too busy to play nursemaid to a tourist—even if she is related to the boss.'

'Busy?' Gabby couldn't keep the scepticism out of her voice, but he either chose to ignore it or it went over his head, which she doubted. Most likely he had a skin like a rhinoceros.

Penny re-emerged, clean shirt in hand, sparing them the necessity of any further conversation. He stood up and pulled it on, and Gabby noticed with interest that it was a little on the tight side, compared to his other one. Not surprising, really. He was somewhat larger than her cousin, better muscled—heavens, she must stop looking at his body!

She was just wondering how she was going to get through lunch, without disgracing herself by being rude or ogling him, when a Jeep appeared on the horizon, horn blaring, bearing down on them in a hurry.

With a muffled exclamation Jed was on his feet and running over the lawn to meet the Jeep before it came to a halt. Penny and Gabby followed a little more slowly, and arrived at the Jeep to see Jonathan in earnest conversation with Jed.

'Just serviced two days ago,' Jonathan was saying worriedly. 'I can't understand it.'

'Where are the men?'

'Up at the compound. I didn't think it was safe to move them without you. Derek's giving them first aid.'

'Right. I'll get some gear. What injuries are we talking about?'

He was getting into the Jeep, and Gabby put a hand on Jonathan's arm. 'Can I help?' she asked.

'I hardly think this is going to be a spectator sport,' Jed growled, but Jonathan ignored him.

'Thanks. Get a hat and put on something with sleeves—we'll pick you up shortly. Oh, and wear sensible shoes.'

She ran back to the bungalow with Penny, opened her

case and pulled out thin cotton trousers, a long-sleeved cotton shirt and trainers. She was back in the road in seconds, Penny following her to plonk a hat on her head, and as the Jeep came careering past she jumped in before the vehicle had even come to rest.

'Pity about lunch,' Jed said. 'You should have stayed and kept Penny company.'

Jonathan, she noticed, was missing. Ignoring Jed's barbed remark, she asked where her cousin had gone.

'Phoning for an air ambulance to take the men out—sounds like it might be necessary. God knows why you wanted to come—I expect it'll be somewhat gory. Just keep out of the way and don't faint on me, all right? I don't need any more casualties and if you're anything like your cousin you'll go green at the first drop of blood.'

'I think I can cope,' she told him drily. 'After three months in A and E as staff nurse, I'm sure one more accident won't turn my stomach.'

His head snapped round and he stared at her in amazement. 'You're a nurse? God, woman, why didn't you say so?'

'You didn't ask—and don't call me "woman".'

A brow climbed into his hairline, and those full, firm, well-shaped lips quirked at the corners. 'Yessir,' he said with a grin. 'Right, hang on tight, it gets a bit rough here.'

For the next twenty minutes she was heartily relieved that she didn't have a roof over her head because she would have smacked into it countless times. She was also glad that she hadn't had her lunch. 'A bit rough' turned out to be the understatement of the century.

'The road's the next thing on the list, once we've established where the plant's going to be,' he yelled over the scrabbling of the tyres and the grinding roar of the engine. 'Obviously we can't do anything in the way of construction with the road like this, but until the feasibility study's been completed there's no point.'

Gabby just hung on and wondered if anyone had done a feasibility study about staying in bouncing Jeeps at fifty miles an hour on jungle tracks.

And it really was jungle, she realised when the mud forced Jed to slow down enough for her to focus on her surroundings. All around them the trees soared skywards to the canopy, their trunks straight and tall and leafless, and at the edges of the road the undergrowth was rioting in the light and air let in by the narrow channel the road had cut through the canopy.

She didn't recognise a single plant—not that she was much of a botanist but, even so, she was surprised that things were so strange and different.

'What's happened to the men?' she asked belatedly.

'Nobody's quite sure. They were driving back from town this morning and crashed.'

She wasn't surprised. It didn't take a genius to work out that the road was dangerous. They passed the tangled remains of a Jeep in the undergrowth on a bend, and then suddenly she could see light and they were in a clearing. Wooden prefabricated huts clustered round a central square, and Jed slid to a halt outside a hut labelled somewhat grandly INFIRMARY just as the rapidly blackening sky opened.

Gabby gave a little shriek as the first fat, heavy drops hit her, and then Jed was jumping out of the Jeep and telling her to hurry. 'Bring the rest, could you?' he yelled, and then, grabbing bags and boxes of equipment, he ran up the steps and inside, leaving Gabby to follow. She straightened her hat, scooped up the last remaining supplies and went after him at a run.

It was like an oven inside, and the sound of rain on

the tin roof was deafening. She looked out of the window and saw it fall in a solid sheet, flattening the exposed plants at the edge of the clearing and turning the area to a sea of mud in seconds. She felt sweat break out on her skin and run in rivers down her spine, and she longed for a cool shower or the *mandi* Penny had spoken about. No time for that, though, there was work to be done.

The hut was dimly lit, with four beds arranged around the single room. Men lay on three of them with others clustered around, trying to help. Two seemed reasonably comfortable, if a little bloody. The third, the one Jed had gone straight to, looked awful. A young Indonesian, he was pale and sweating, his lips were blue, his eyes were rolling and he was obviously very seriously injured.

'Thank God you're here,' an Englishman yelled over the noise of the rain. Derek presumably, Gabby thought. About thirty years old, lean and bespectacled, he was covered in blood and dirt, and he looked harrassed and weary. 'Right out of my league,' he continued. 'I'll go and tell Ismail to bring boiled water. Anything else you need?'

Jed shook his head and bent over the man, examining him quickly. 'Chest,' he said economically, and proceeded to sound it, his face impassive. 'Tension pneumothorax—we'll have to put a drain in before we can move him. I've got some stuff in there somewhere that we can use.'

'I'll set up—you check the other two,' Gabby said quickly. 'Is there somewhere I can wash?'

He rattled off instructions in Bahasa, and one of the men left the room and reappeared moments later with a bowl, fresh water and a towel that looked reasonably clean. She used one end and left the other for Jed, and went back to prepare their patient.

She knew where he would want to enter the chest wall, and she swabbed and wiped it, washed it with iodine solution and left it to dry while she fished around in the bag he'd shown her. All she could find of any use was a urinary catheter, some tape, a couple of pairs of rubber gloves, a scalpel, a pair of scissors and some local anaesthetic and suturing equipment.

She drew up the lignocaine into one of the syringes, recapped the needle and turned to him. 'Ready when you are.'

He nodded, came over and checked the things she'd set out on a sterile paper towel and then injected the local into the area around the fourth rib space, before washing his hands. Gloved up, he swabbed the area again, sliced neatly with the scalpel and then inserted the point of the scissors, twisted and opened.

There was a hissing sigh of air out of the chest cavity, and behind them a dull thunk over the noise of the rain. 'Hello, one of the boys has bitten the dust,' Jed said softly. 'Can we find a bottle of water to put the end of the catheter in? Boiled water, tell them.'

'I can't,' she reminded him, handing over the catheter. 'I don't speak a word of Indonesian.'

There followed another stream of instructions, thrown over his shoulder as he deftly pushed the catheter in, taped it to the chest wall and stood up. 'Right, let's get this air out.' He pushed gently on the chest, listening to the sighing exhalation of air from the tube, and as he released the pressure he folded the end of the tube over to prevent air re-entering the chest cavity.

Immediately their patient started to look better. His colour improved, and he groaned and his eyes fluttered open. '*Obat*,' he whispered.

'What's that?'

'Medicine—he wants some painkiller, I expect.' She

drew up a shot of pethidine while he spoke quietly to the man in his own language, running his hands lightly over the bruised and battered limbs and gently palpating the abdomen.

'Seems to be fairly all right, apart from the chest and a broken arm. I'll just check the others again—give him the pethidine and watch him, would you?'

He turned to the man who'd fainted on the floor behind them and was now coming round, leaving her to her own devices. Gabby found herself lost without a language in which to communicate so she spoke in English, murmuring gentle reassurance. It seemed to work. The man relaxed his death grip on her hand, but when she soothed his head and touched his forehead his eyes widened.

'Careful—the head is sacred. You never touch it unless you've asked permission, and never with your left hand—it's an insult. Never take or give anything with your left hand, either. Always use the right.'

Jed's quiet advice made her aware of how little she knew. How could she really be of help amongst these people about whom she knew nothing? She could offend so easily without any idea of what she had said or done. Perhaps she should just go outside, sit down and wait for him before she did something truly awful—

He was beside her again. 'Don't get bent out of shape—it doesn't matter. I'll explain.' He broke into the native tongue again, and the man relaxed and almost smiled.

A few moments later Jed beckoned to her and they went out onto the veranda. The rain had stopped, and the air was cooler and fresher. It felt wonderful. She turned to Jed. 'Sorry about that—I didn't realise about the head. What did you say to him?'

His grin was wicked and did silly things to her insides. 'I told him you were a healer. Healers can do anything.'

She gave a hollow laugh. 'I wish. It would come in awfully handy sometimes.'

'Tell me about it,' he muttered. 'Right, we need to get these limbs splinted up for the journey down to the airstrip. Both these others have got fractures—one arm, one leg.'

They worked side by side without comment, strapping limbs to makeshift splints made of bits of wood wrapped in clean towels. They padded them and supported them as well as they could, but even so Gabby knew it was going to hurt, bouncing down that hillside to the town.

They laid two of them in the back of the Jeep, but the third, the man who had the chest drain, Jed propped up on the front seat between them so Gabby could keep an eye on him and the bottle of water as they travelled slowly and carefully down the hill.

It took nearly an hour, almost three times as long as it had taken to drive up, and when they arrived they could see the little plane just taxiing to the end of the runway. Jed drove along the edge of the strip to the plane, and then they loaded their patients, handed them over to the medical crew and sent them off to Jakarta for treatment.

As they watched the little plane climb into the sky and bank away towards Jakarta, Jed turned to her. 'Thank you for your help—it was invaluable,' he said quietly. 'Most things I can manage on my own, but there are times like this when a skilled assistant makes all the difference.'

She felt heat brush her already warm skin, and looked away, confused by the sudden rush of pleasure his words had given her. 'It was nothing—I only did what I'm trained to do,' she replied diffidently.

'Nevertheless, you did it well. Thanks.'

A silly grin crept onto her lips and she turned away, walking back to the Jeep so that he wouldn't see her response. Why would those few words of praise mean so much?

Because he was competent and skilled himself, of course. She'd seen that in the quick, precise movements of his hands, the assessing eyes, the searching fingers— he was a natural physician, and his praise did matter.

She grinned again, and swung up into the Jeep. 'Get a move on, I'm hungry,' she told him as he ambled up.

'Typical woman—always complaining.'

'Typical man—always providing something to complain about,' she returned.

It was almost four o'clock when they got back to Jonathan's and Penny's house, and as Gabby went to have a shower and change into clean clothes she heard Jonathan and Jed in conversation.

They were talking in low tones about the accident, too quietly for her to grasp more than the general drift, but one word jumped out of the urgent exchange.

Sabotage…

CHAPTER TWO

LUNCH turned into an early supper.

They sat on the veranda and ate their delayed meal of cold chicken in spicy sauce, rice and avocado salad and wonderfully exotic fruit. It was delicious, but Gabby couldn't concentrate on it. She was too tired to enjoy the food, and all she could think about was the three injured men who had been airlifted to hospital, and the possibility that their injuries had been caused deliberately.

It was the sole topic of conversation, in any case.

'It seems that the brakes failed,' Jonathan told them. 'The driver told Derek that they were working one minute, and the next there was nothing there at all. He was completely helpless. You know that stretch of road—all hills and bends. It's lethal enough with brakes. Without them it's suicide.'

Jed frowned. 'Has anybody checked out the vehicle?'

Jonathan shook his head. 'No, not yet. Derek's going to do it now.'

'But surely it could just have been a simple failure. Why would anybody want to tamper with the brakes?' Gabby asked, puzzled.

'To frighten us off?' Jonathan suggested.

'But why?'

'That's what we don't know,' he replied. 'It's the third or fourth incident in the past couple of weeks. The first was nothing much—a generator was smashed. It was irritating vandalism, we thought. Perhaps some of the boys from the town out looking for mischief. Then the

25

cookhouse was burned down. It could have been an accident—a spark lodged in the roof or something. Then one of the Indonesian engineers left suddenly without explanation. We still don't know why, but he seemed very frightened and it spooked the others.'

'And now this,' Gabby said thoughtfully.

'And Mohamed last night.'

They looked at Jed. 'Mo?' Jonathan said. 'I thought he slipped and fell?'

'But why? He won't talk about it. By the time he went out on the plane this morning he was still refusing to discuss it, and he seemed scared. I think he either saw or heard something, or someone pushed him. Whatever, I don't think he just fell down that cliff.'

Penny licked her lips nervously. 'But why? Why are they being targeted? Do they want us to use workmen and engineers from the island?'

'Or do they just want us to go away?' Jed said quietly.

'But why?' Penny asked again. 'What are we doing that's upsetting them?'

Jonathan shoved his hands through his hair and sighed. 'Lord knows, darling, but I don't think you need to worry. It seems to be restricted to the Indonesians at the moment—I think it must be some local thing. There's a lot of rivalry between the different areas, but I'm sure we're all quite safe.'

Gabby shot Jed a look and saw him shake his head slightly, as if in mute disagreement. Did he think they were in danger?

She didn't have a chance to find out because at that moment the children finished their nap and came and joined them, and the topic was dropped instantly. Later, though, a messenger came from the compound and Jonathan excused himself and left, his face troubled.

Jed went too, and Gabby, exhausted from her trip,

suddenly ran out of steam. 'Penny, I need to go to bed,' she told her hostess.

'Oh, heavens, how dreadful of me, you must be exhausted!' Penny exclaimed. 'Oh, Gabby, I'm so sorry. I'll take you up there now.'

'Up?' she asked, puzzled. There was no 'up' in the bungalow.

'To the guest house. I'm afraid you'll have to share it with Jed,' she said apologetically, 'but it's got two quite separate bedrooms and a large living area and veranda in between. I don't think you'll be too much on top of each other. It's just that both our bedrooms in this house are already overstretched, but it's a very nice bungalow—I'm sure you'll be quite comfortable.'

Share. With Jed.

Great.

She dredged up a smile, heaved her case off the veranda steps, swung her flight bag over her shoulder and followed Penny up the uneven road to the bungalow where she had found Jed that morning.

'Rom has made your bed up ready—if you want anything just ring and one of the servants will come and see to you. We all eat at our house—it's got the only decent kitchen. Make sure you put plenty of insect repellent on—and have you started a course of anti-malarials?'

Gabby nodded. 'Of course. So's Katie.'

'Oh, yes. Right. Well, here you are...'

She threw open the door of a plain but spotlessly clean room. The windows were open but had mesh screens over them, as did all the doors and windows, and there was a fan on the ceiling that creaked slowly into life when Penny pushed a switch.

The bed was made up with crisp white sheets, and dangling over it was a thick, net rope suspended from the ceiling.

'That's a mosquito net—you spread it out and tuck it into the edge of the mattress when you go to bed. It cuts the air circulation down a bit, but it's better than being eaten alive and, although the screens help, the odd bug gets in through the doors. When the power station's built we'll get air conditioning, of course, but the generator can't manage it.'

Gabby didn't care about air conditioning. She just wanted to get her head down and get some sleep. First, though, she was going to explore the *mandi*.

She opened her case, found a cool cotton nightshirt and some fresh underwear, grabbed the thick white towel off the end of the bed and padded out to look for the bathroom.

There was a loo and basin off a corridor at the back of the bungalow, but the *mandi* was located, as Penny had said, outside the back door. There was a wooden walkway and a bamboo structure like a little shed, and she opened the door and peered in.

A cold stone floor and a big tank of deliciously cool water convinced her she wanted to try it. She shed her clothes and looked about for somewhere to put them, but there didn't seem to be anywhere. 'Oh, well,' she shrugged, put them on the floor in the corner, piled the fresh ones on top and tipped a scoop of water over her head.

A little shriek escaped before she could control it, but she was expecting the next scoopful. It was cold against her hot skin, but wonderfully refreshing. There was a bar of soap that smelt like Jed, and she rubbed it over her body and wondered if he'd done the same.

What a curiously intoxicating thought, she thought, humming cheerfully. Strangely intimate.

She rinsed, grabbed the towel from over the door and

rubbed her hair, threw it back out of her eyes and then looked at her clothes.

Soaked. Not just damp, but sodden. She must have been flinging the water around with even more abandon than she'd realised!

Oh, well, there was no one about. She wound the towel around her body and tucked it in over her breasts like a sarong, scooped up her soggy clothes and went back inside.

It was getting dark rapidly now at the end of the day. The light was fading fast, night literally falling, plummeting her into a velvet blackness.

She paused for a moment, listening to the sounds of the night from the jungle behind her, and a shiver went down her spine.

Primeval forest, full of strange plants and even stranger creatures. She felt as if someone was watching her, and a shiver ran through her again. Clutching the towel tighter round her, she hurried inside.

The bungalow was gloomy without lights, the rooms almost completely dark now, so the sudden movement of a white-clad figure startled her. With a little scream she stepped back, thumped her heel against a low table and sat down on it with a bump.

'Feeling a little jumpy?' Jed said mildly.

She swore somewhat colourfully under her breath, and rubbed her heel. 'Where did you come from?' she snapped. 'I didn't hear you drive up.'

She could hear the laughter in his voice, though. 'I'm not surprised, with all the splashing and singing,' he teased. 'I gather you enjoyed it.'

She hoped it really was dark and that it wasn't just her eyes because she could feel the heat scorching her cheeks. Had she really been singing? Oh, Lord.

'It was wonderful, but my clothes got wet.'

'You're supposed to take them off—'

'On the floor,' she said drily.

'Before you go in.'

'Oh.' She had a sudden vision of Jed going to the *mandi* stark naked, and the colour in her cheeks grew yet brighter—just as he flicked the lights on.

'You've caught the sun,' he said softly, bending to brush her burning skin with his knuckles. The light touch against her cheeks sent a tiny shock wave through her, and she stood up, dodging past him, and went to her room.

'I'm going to bed,' she told him. 'I'll see you in the morning.'

'Running away?' he asked with gentle mockery.

She turned back to him, hanging onto her temper with difficulty. 'I'm tired. I've had an incredibly long and trying forty-eight hours, and I'm wiped. Anyway, I thought you didn't want to entertain me.'

'I don't,' he said bluntly. 'It appears, however, that I don't have a choice.' His face was stony and he was clearly unimpressed, but there was nothing she could do about it.

She tried again. 'Look, I don't like the idea of having to share your accommodation either, but we're just going to have to be civilised about it. I'm sure if we try hard we can manage to act like grown-ups,' she said sweetly, and, going into her room, she shut the door with a definite little click, looked for a bolt and was disappointed.

Well, she'd just have to rely on his good manners— if he had any. So far she hadn't seen much evidence of them, but she'd give him the benefit of the doubt for now. She was too tired to do anything else.

She dragged a comb through her hair, spread a dry towel over her pillow and lay down on the bed, arranging the mosquito net over herself as Penny had said.

It was the last conscious thing she did for eleven hours.

'Tea, mem.'

Gabby's eyes struggled open and she sat up, fighting the layers of mosquito net that were tangled round her.

'Come in,' she called, and the door swung open to admit a young Indonesian girl with a smiling face and a very welcome pot of tea on a tray.

'Where's Jed?' she asked, wondering if it was safe to use the *mandi*.

'*Jalan-jalan*,' the girl replied, and then with a little bob and a smile she was gone, leaving Gabby with her tea.

She wondered where Jalan Jalan was. The compound? The town? She looked at her watch, and discovered it was six o'clock. Plenty early enough not to worry, she thought, and sipped her tea with gratitude. It was flavoured with the powdered milk she was beginning to get used to, and which she dimly remembered from a short spell in Sarawak in her early childhood.

She looked out of the window and saw that it was light again. Wonderful. She felt better—positively energetic. She disentangled herself from the mosquito net, stripped and wrapped herself in a towel and went out to the *mandi* for another delicious slosh around.

This time she managed to get back to her room without being caught, and she dressed quickly and went down the road to Penny's and Jonathan's bungalow. There the same girl who had brought her tea informed her that *Tuan* had gone out and *Mem* and the children were still in bed.

'*Doktor* come back,' she was told and, looking over her shoulder, she saw Jed strolling up the road from the town, a string bag dangling from his fingers.

'Morning,' he called, and she went down off the veranda towards him.

'Morning. I gather you've been to Jalan Jalan—is that the town?'

He laughed, showing even white teeth that gleamed against his tan. '*Jalan-jalan* means to go for a walk but, you're right, I have been to town. I wandered down to the market in Telok Panjang for some fruit. Join me for breakfast?'

Join Jed? She was astonished at the invitation after last night's cool rebuttal, but she was starving and it sounded wonderful. 'Sure you've got enough?'

He grinned, showing those teeth again. 'If I ate all this lot I'd be really ill,' he said with a chuckle.

Gabby fell into step beside him, thinking that if she wasn't so busy being critical of him professionally she could probably enjoy the man's company—and why was she thinking that? He'd already made it clear how unwelcome her presence was, from the comment about entertaining tourists through to his lack of enthusiasm the night before over having her as a house guest.

She was probably the last person he'd seek out as a companion—and, anyway, she wouldn't want him to because she couldn't separate Jed the doctor from Jed the Hollywood cliché. She'd seen him at work the day before, after all, and knew he was capable of working efficiently and well—so why wasn't he?

Unless, of course, they were going to continue to have accidents like that one, in which case his expertise would be well and truly put to the test.

'Did you find out what happened about the brakes?' she asked as they climbed the veranda steps.

His face clouded. 'No. The Jeep was burned out.'

She frowned. 'No, it wasn't. We saw it.'

'They must have done it after we came down again

with the casualties. When Derek went to look at it, it was a heap of smouldering ash. They were lucky there wasn't a forest fire, but I suppose the rain would have made it safer by damping everything down.'

'Damping?' She laughed, thinking of the slashing torrents of water that had fallen. 'Does it always rain like that?' she asked, amazed yet again that the sky could hold such vast quantities of water.

Jed grinned. 'Every afternoon. That's the beauty of it—you can get about in the sun in the morning, even in the monsoon season. It just makes the mud a bit deeper and the roads even worse.'

That was hard to imagine. The thought of the track up to the compound getting any worse was mind-boggling. She just hoped she wouldn't have to travel it again if it did.

She followed him into the kitchen area at the back, and he washed the fruit, piled it into a bowl, picked up two plates and some knives and spoons and headed back to the veranda, leaving her to bring from the fridge the glasses of juice he had poured.

They settled themselves down on the veranda out of the direct heat of the sun, already scorching at only eight in the morning. The fruit looked wonderful, and Gabby realised she was ravenous. She had hardly eaten anything the day before, and it seemed for ever since she'd had a decent meal.

'What's this?' she asked, picking up a fuzzy little pinkish red fruit.

'Rambutan—it means hairy. Just peel it and eat it, but be careful. There's a stone inside.'

She pulled off the skin, bit into the translucent white flesh and sighed with delight. 'Oh, wow.'

He chuckled. 'Lovely, aren't they? I managed to get a couple of mangosteens, too,' he said, proffering a dark purple ball the size of a small orange. 'It's a bit early in the season for them, but one of the traders owed me a favour. Crush it in your hands to split the skin, then it's easy to peel.'

Gabby found herself wondering what sort of favour he'd been owed as she peeled one of the precious mangosteens, then promptly forgot to worry about it as she tried the fruit. Segmented like an orange and with firm white flesh like the rambutan, it, too, tasted wonderful. Silently thanking Jed's favour-owing friend at the market, she moved on to sample a wedge of mango, a slice of papaya and a pomelo, before admitting defeat.

'I'll be ill if I have too much before I'm used to it,' she said and, sipping her drink, she lay back in the chair and opened her mouth to quiz him about local customs.

She didn't get a chance, though, because he smacked down his glass and stood up with lazy grace.

'Right, I must get on. See you later—and don't forget to cover up if you go out, remember to take your anti-malarials and drown yourself in insect repellent—and don't go near the jungle. There are snakes.'

'Yes, Mum,' she replied, trying not to look at those well-made legs only inches away from her face.

'Just doing my job as camp MO,' he said mildly, then left her to it, bounding down the veranda steps and heading off towards a battered old Jeep. It started with a cough and a rattle, and set off up the road with a little spurt of dust. The clutch was obviously less than subtle—or else it was Jed's driving.

She leant back, closed her eyes and dozed for a while, then Penny came and found her. 'Hi. How are you feeling?'

'Tired—it hit me last night and my system's all confused. All I want to do is sleep!'

'So sleep. We aren't doing anything today—Jon wants

to sort out this business of the crash yesterday, put out a few feelers. I'm sorry you had to go and work when you're supposed to be on holiday. It was very kind of you.'

She dismissed the remark with a wave. 'It was nothing. I couldn't sit here and twiddle my thumbs and let people bleed to death, could I?'

Penny laughed. 'No, I suppose not. Why don't you come down and spend the day with me? I don't want to leave the children, and Katie's still catching up on her sleep. Perhaps later we can go and explore the town.'

They did, at four in the afternoon when the worst of the heat had worn off. They walked down because the Jeeps were now one short, and the children skipped and scuffed up stones and seemed full of energy.

Gabby was too hot to skip, but she felt a bubbling excitement just the same. The noises and smells and sights were all strange and yet familiar from her very early childhood, and they saw things she'd forgotten.

On one street corner a man was grating ice over a huge plane, then packing the chips into a ball and covering it in hideously pink raspberry juice. He put it inside a folded cone of newspaper, then prepared another with condensed milk, grated coconut and chopped banana over the top.

'Gross,' Penny said with a shudder, but to Gabby, who was steaming gently in the tropical heat, it looked unbelievably inviting.

'The ice isn't safe, I suppose,' she said wistfully.

'Absolutely not. The water's probably straight out of the river. Come on, I want to go to the draper's and get some white cotton. I've run out.'

They went into a tiny shop, run by a wizened little Chinese woman with quick fingers and more wrinkles than Gabby had ever seen, and then they came back along the main street.

Penny indicated a sort of café, with people eating at tables on the pavement. 'This is a *rumah makan*—literally a food house. It's our only restaurant, and the food's brilliant. Indonesian and Chinese, and the kitchen's so clean you can see your face in the counters, so we're told. It's the only place to eat so it's just as well! We'll take you one night. It's a real treat, and ridiculously cheap.'

As they walked on Gabby was sure she could hear the unmistakable roar of a football crowd. 'It's the satellite TV over the restaurant,' Penny explained. 'They rent out space to watch it—the Indonesians are all football-crazy, and they love the Australian and American soaps. After the restaurant it's the town's most popular venue!'

'Do they have *Children's BBC*?' Katie asked hopefully.

'Sorry, darling, no,' Penny told her oldest daughter. 'When we get electricity we can have a TV with a satellite dish, and you can watch cartoons—OK?'

'But we've got electricity,' Katie reasoned.

'But only a tiny generator and it's not big enough to run a television. Sorry, darling.'

But it didn't pacify her. Katie trailed up the hill behind them, scuffing her toes and looking mournful.

'Oh, dear. It's one of the adjustments she's going to have to make,' Penny said. 'There's so much that's different. Still, the others managed to get used to it quite quickly. I expect she will.'

They made their way slowly back to the bungalow and were greeted by Rom with a brimming jug of freshly made lemonade for the children and steaming tea for the adults.

Gabby eyed the lemonade longingly but, as Penny assured her she would, she found the tea actually very refreshing.

Not so refreshing that she didn't very soon excuse herself and go back to bed until supper, and then escape again to return to her bed as early as she could decently do so.

It was worth it, though. She emerged the following morning after her *mandi* and early morning tea feeling refreshed and ready to start enjoying her holiday at last.

Jed was stretched out on the veranda, sipping fruit juice, with a little heap of papaya skins beside him on the table. She greeted him cheerfully, and he turned his head and looked up at her, without moving.

'Morning,' he said, and his voice sounded husky and interesting.

All that gin, Gabby thought. It probably wrecks the throat. She didn't dare look into those astonishingly blue eyes.

She helped herself to some fruit and sat down, nibbling as she looked out over the bay. It looked sparkling clear and inviting, and she longed to be out on it.

'We're going out in the launch today, I think,' he told her, as if he'd read her mind. 'There's nothing more we can do about the Jeep, and Derek's making some discreet enquiries about the other incidents. Until we find out what's wrong Jon thinks we should just carry on and not pay too much attention to it.'

'Do you agree?' she asked him, sensing that he was reluctant to criticise her cousin in front of her.

'I think he might be underestimating the situation,' he said carefully. 'I don't know what's wrong, but something's making them jumpy and someone's going to get badly hurt before long if this goes on.'

She remembered something her cousin had said the

night before last. 'Do you think it's just the Indonesians being targeted?' she asked.

There was a second's pause and then he shook his head. 'No. Anybody could have been driving that Jeep. Derek's wife could have been in the cookhouse—she's living up there with the others. She's an engineer too, and part of the team. They got married two months ago.'

'A female engineer? Doesn't that cause problems?'

He raised an eyebrow. 'Sexist?' he said softly.

She blushed. 'Not at all. I just thought, with all those men in the primitive conditions up there—well, bathrooms and that sort of thing—it's a bit difficult, I should think.'

'It's better now they've tied the knot. Indonesians can be a bit funny about women on their own. Married women, on the other hand, are quite safe. That was why I was a bit wary about you sharing the bungalow with me—I didn't want your reputation to suffer so that you lost respect.'

'My reputation matters to you?' she asked, feeling guilty for judging him so harshly last night but not at all convinced that he was genuinely concerned for her virtue and it wasn't just an excuse to get out of entertaining her.

'Well, perhaps not directly,' he said with a lazy grin. 'It might enhance mine, of course, which could be good news, but Jon's reputation could be affected and he needs to remain in a strong position to lead the team.' He stretched out his legs and propped them up on the veranda rail right in front of her eyes.

'As for the safety thing, I think we should all be vigilant. Jon's checking over the launch now, and making sure it hasn't been tampered with. The last thing we want is for it to break down and leave us adrift in the sea in the middle of the day in this heat.'

He eyed her bare arms critically. 'You'll need to cover up and smother yourself in sunblock,' he warned. 'And don't forget to take your anti-malarials.'

'Yes, Mummy,' she teased. 'Am I going to get this lecture every morning?'

He gave a wry grin. 'You can't be too careful. What pills are you taking?'

'Mefloquine—now you're going to tell me that's wrong.'

He laughed. 'I'm not—it's fine. It's the recommended drug. Just watch out for side-effects, but even they're better than dying of falciparum malaria.'

'What do you take?' she asked, somehow knowing it would be different.

He grinned. 'I'm trying a combination of other remedies.'

'What—marinading yourself in sweat and gin?' she said before she could stop herself.

To her relief he gave a short bark of laughter. 'Don't forget the tonic. The quinine in tonic was an early attempt to kill the malaria parasite spread by the *Anopheles* mosquito—you do know it's the female of the species that causes all the problems, typically?'

'Sexist?' she said softly, returning his little barb, and he grinned.

'Only mildly, and it is true. The female is the carrier of the parasite. Quinine was first used as an anti-malarial by the Indonesian folk doctors or *dukun*. Unfortunately this means it's been around for ages and so there's a lot of immunity to it now.'

'Hence the introduction of mefloquine.'

'Exactly. Chloroquine combined with proguanil, or alternatively doxycycline, causes fewer problems than mefloquine, but since none of them are especially desirable long term I'm trying to find out if anything else works any better—'

'Hence the gin and tonic.'

'Amongst other things.' He grinned. 'Hey, a man has to have some recreational activities, and what else do you see around here? Anyway, it's a good idea to take in plenty of fluids to replace the huge amount lost in sweat, and the juniper oil in gin acts as a natural insect repellent. Of course, rubbing yourself with a solution of tobacco juice is also effective—'

She wrinkled her nose. 'Nice,' she said with a grin. 'I could go off the tropics.'

He laughed again. 'There are hazards. The best thing to do is stay in the shade, cover up, use insect repellent and stay inside a screened area at dusk and during the night to avoid being bitten. The fluids are the easy bit. Want another drink?'

He was on his feet, heading for the kitchen, when Penny hailed them from down the road. 'We're off soon—are you ready?'

'Be with you in two shakes,' he called back. He looked at Gabby's arms and frowned. 'Cover up—have you got any long-sleeved shirts?'

'Only one clean one, and it's tight fitting and quite thick—and black.'

He rolled his eyes. 'Borrow one of my shirts. You can roll the sleeves up and tie the bottom, but it'll give you more protection. The sun shining off the sea will burn you in no time flat—and don't forget to put sunscreen on under your eyebrows and chin. Everybody gets sun-burned there because they forget about reflections up from the water.'

'Mothering me again?' she said drily, heading for the kitchen with their plates.

He followed her. 'Just a little friendly medical advice.

I don't want to end up having to nurse you through malaria or heatstroke—and don't forget the hat.'

She rolled her eyes and he threw up his hands in mock surrender and backed out of the kitchen. 'OK, just don't say you weren't warned.'

She did cover up—in one of his shirts, freshly laundered and pressed to perfection, tied at the waist over loose cotton trousers and cotton tennis shoes.

'All right?' she asked, appearing outside her bedroom as he emerged from his.

He scanned her quickly, then those gloriously blue eyes locked with hers. 'Fine,' he said, and she wondered if it was her imagination or if he had sounded a bit curt.

He crammed the Panama hat down over his eyes so she couldn't really see them any more, and looked down at the bag in her hand. 'Got your swimming togs?'

'Of course—they're on, and I have spares. Now you're going to tell me I have to swim in a wetsuit because of jellyfish, and I'm probably going to hit you.'

'Oh, I love a bit of violence in a woman,' he teased, and pushed her gently out of the door. 'Come on, they'll be waiting.'

She was glad he couldn't see her face because the touch of his hand against her back had brought soft colour flooding to it. She had to fight the urge to lean back against him—and as much to escape from herself as from him—she hurried down the hill to where the others were now waiting.

'Where are we going?' she asked Penny as they drove down the road to the town. They were all squeezed into the Jeep, the children chattering excitedly beside them.

'A little island called Pulau Tengkorak—Monkey-Skull Island—so called because of the shape. It's fabulous—unpopulated except for a few monkeys and lizards, and of course the jellyfish, but they're mostly further out. Just keep your eyes open.'

She did, looking over the side of the launch into the sparkling clear water as they sliced through it on their way out to the island. She could see jellyfish, and flying fish jumping just yards from the launch, and she thought of the freezing fog and grey drizzle of England in November and forgave Indonesia its malaria mosquitoes. 'I can hardly wait to get in the water,' she told Penny. 'It looks so inviting.'

Penny nodded. 'It is. Warm and refreshing and wonderful, and of course there's plenty of shade from the palm trees. There are coconuts on the island—if any have fallen we can eat them with our lunch. The fresh ones are delicious, nothing like the dried-up remains that get into English supermarkets.' She pointed ahead of them. 'There it is.'

Gabby saw a little green dot growing on the horizon, and then within minutes they were there, pulling up near the beach and anchoring the launch to a buoy that floated in the surf.

'We have to wade the last few yards,' Penny told her. 'Keep your shoes on—in fact, keep them on the whole time, even for swimming. You never know what you might tread on.'

She climbed over the side into the knee-deep water, and found herself in Jed's warm and firm grip. 'OK?' he asked gruffly, before releasing her, and she could hardly function enough to nod in reply.

What was it about the man that every time he touched her she turned into an inferno? She shook her head slightly, scooped Katie up into her arms and carried her up the gently shelving slope to the shore. 'OK?' she asked her little travelling companion.

Katie nodded and grinned, quite happy to be carried

to the beach by the woman who had become her friend
over the past few weeks. 'Yes, thanks,' she grinned. 'Are
you going to swim with me?'

'I expect so. Shall we ask Mummy where we should
put all our things?'

'They're up there,' she said, nodding up the beach to
the edge of the treeline.

They walked up the sandy slope to the others, and
Gabby wondered if she'd get away with spending all day
with the children so she didn't have to spend any of it
with Jed because she honestly thought she'd make a fool
of herself if left to her own devices.

She wasn't to be that lucky. He appeared at her elbow
with a bottle of factor 25 sunscreen, and ordered her to
undress to her swimsuit.

'Even if you put your clothes back on it's a good
idea,' he told her, and then stood waiting until she'd
stripped off his shirt and her trousers and was standing
in just a skimpy costume. Had she known he was going
to do this she'd have worn the more modest one, but it
was too late now. He turned her round, spread a dollop
of cream over her neck and shoulders and smoothed it
down her arms and back, then turned her round again,
did her face and throat and down her chest until she
pushed his hands away.

'I can manage now,' she told him firmly, and finished
off the low neckline herself. Not for all the tea in China
was he getting his fingertips down the neck of her costume!

He handed her the bottle. 'Return the favour?' he
asked, and, as if it hadn't been bad enough to have him
touching her, she now had to run her hands over acres
of bronzed Hollywood potential. 'I'll do your back,' she
muttered, and went round behind him.

She was a little on the rough side in self-defence, but

it was either that or linger longingly on the supple, satiny skin that her fingers itched to explore. She finished off with a last defiant swipe, squirted enough into her hand to do her legs and handed the bottle back to him.

'Thanks,' he said, and she could have sworn his voice was a little gruff.

Him too, eh? That could make life interesting. Too interesting. She wasn't into holiday romances, and she had no doubts about Jed. He was a love 'em and leave 'em man if ever she'd met one, and there was no way he was loving and leaving *her*.

She slapped on the last of the sun cream, helped Penny spread some on the children and then went to explore the sea.

She was just about to dive into the gently rippling surf when a hand clamped on her shoulder, making her jump. 'Mind—there's a jellyfish beside you.'

She looked down to where Jed pointed, and saw a soft, pale parachute, undulating gently in the water. Almost invisible, it was beautiful to watch.

'Are they dangerous?' she asked, fascinated by the slow movement.

'Not those. They sting a bit—and they sting where they're washed up on the beach, too, so be careful where you walk. You should also keep an eye out for rocks under the sand and avoid them. This beach is fine, but others have stonefish and sea urchins, and they're deadly, quite literally. Remember to keep your shoes on and your eyes open.'

He drew her to the side. 'Here, I've checked this bit. Just wallow. It's wonderful.'

She sank down under the water, revelling in its gentle caress, and sighed with delight. 'Oh, it's glorious.'

'Glad you came?' he asked softly.

'Oh, yes.'

'Despite the malaria and the flukes and the leeches and the hepatitis and the rabies and the filariasis and—'

'Yes!' she said with a laugh. 'Even so! Are you trying to put me off?'

He grinned, his head floating above the water just inches from hers. 'Would I?'

'Probably,' she said drily.

'Oh, I don't know. I'm beginning to think having you over here for a holiday may not be all bad after all. If all else fails, you can always help me with the sick list.'

'What sick list?' she scoffed. 'You don't have a sick list. You ship them all off to Jakarta!'

He grinned. 'Rumbled. Ah, well. You can help me with my malaria research—'

She chucked a handful of water in his face and swam away from him, laughing. She thought she'd got away with it until she felt long, strong fingers close around her ankle and jerk her backwards. She shot through the water and cannoned into him, and the sudden contrast of coarse hair against her back and legs did nothing for her composure.

He stood up, drawing her to her feet, and turned her into his arms. 'Forfeit,' he said softly, and then before she could move his lips were on hers and her mouth was opening to him. Heat flooded her, and with a little moan she leant into him and felt the solid pressure of his response.

That nearly finished her. With a little cry she pushed him away, and turned and swam back to the others, wondering if they'd seen and if so what they'd make of it.

They were all engrossed in a game of water polo, and she went and joined in. Jed, she noticed out of the corner of her eye, went up the beach to their bags, took out a towel and lay down in the shade with his hat over his eyes.

Good. She didn't need any more challenges to her nervous system like that one. She was beginning to think that in terms of mortal danger malaria was the least of her worries!

CHAPTER THREE

THEY stayed all day on the tiny island, playing in the water until it was too hot, then lurking in the shade at the fringe of the palm trees and eating the picnic that Rom had prepared for them.

There were little sticks of spicy chicken satay with a tasty peanut sauce, cold roasted chicken legs, avocados and, of course, lots of fresh fruit and plenty to drink. Jed wandered off and came back with a couple of fresh, young coconuts, and with a vicious-looking knife called a *parang* he laid about the green husks, poked out the three eyes in the top of each nut and poured the sweet, translucent coconut milk into a jug.

Then he hacked the coconuts into chunks and handed them out, and they used their teeth to scrape off the tender white flesh from the hard shell. Gabby couldn't believe the flavour.

'Good?' Penny asked with a smile.

'Amazing—it's nothing like the ones you can buy in supermarkets in England!'

'Told you. You'll be spoilt now—you'll have to keep coming back.'

Gabby stretched out on her towel and sighed. 'It could certainly be addictive,' she agreed. 'Just think, back home it's cold and rainy—foul!' She wriggled a little on the towel, rearranging the soft sand under her back to conform better to her contours, and shut her eyes.

The conversation droned quietly around her, and she lay completely relaxed and tried to follow the words, but it was too much like hard work. Perhaps she'd just lie there…

The next thing she knew was a tickling sensation around her ribs. Her eyes flew open and she lifted her head to find Jed, sitting next to her dribbling fine sand over her midriff. There were little piles of it all over her costume, tiny slithering pyramids that ran together when she moved.

His smile had a slightly alarming quality, rather like the smile of a tiger. There was no sign of the others, she noted with a little shiver of panic as she looked around.

'They've gone for a wander round the island,' he told her, as if he'd read her mind, and made another pyramid on her stomach. 'I volunteered to babysit.' His teasing grin did silly things to her, and her memory would keep re-running the kiss, which did her no good at all.

'Why do I need to be sat on?' she asked a little breathlessly, watching the sand. 'I'm hardly going to get into mischief.'

'Snakes,' he said calmly. 'They come down out of the jungle and curl up on you when you're sleeping—I had to guard you.'

She gave him a sceptical look. 'You, guard me?' She snorted softly. 'You're joking, of course.'

He grinned that devastating grin of his. 'Of course—there aren't any snakes that dangerous on the island, but it was worth a try just to get you looking adoringly at me as your saviour.'

'I didn't,' she said dampeningly.

The grin widened. 'No—great shame. Still, I'll keep trying. Want a drink?'

She sat up, spilling sand all over her legs. 'Yes, please. What is there?'

'Beer, lemonade, coconut milk, fruit juice.'

She opted for lemonade as the safest choice. She'd

had a great deal of fruit already, and until her system adjusted she didn't want to push her luck.

It was freshly made, cold and sharp and gorgeous. He was pretty gorgeous, too, she had to admit. He was wearing his shirt open over his swimming trunks, and the little glimpses she had of his chest were almost more enticing than the lemonade.

'Fancy a stroll?' he suggested, and she dragged her mind back under control.

'Around the island? Is it far?'

He didn't answer because Jon came running back just at that moment, carrying little Tom who was screaming and thrashing in his arms.

'Uh-oh. Looks like he's been stung by something,' Jed said, getting to his feet. 'Problems?' he called, sprinting towards them.

'Jellyfish—he stood right in the middle of one on the beach. I told him not to, but he didn't realise it would squelch over the top of his shoes.'

They came back to Gabby, Jed examining Tom's foot as they hurried over the sand. 'Any idea what sort?' Jed asked, rummaging in a bag.

'Not really—big pink job.'

He nodded and, taking off the shoe, held Tom's foot firmly in a bowl and sloshed something dark brown over it.

'What's that?' Gabby asked, peering over his shoulder and sniffing.

'Vinegar—it's the cheapest and most effective remedy. That and meat tenderiser paste—don't ask me why, I haven't got a clue, but it really takes the sting out. It's brilliant for Portuguese man-of-war stings, too.'

'Whatever happened to good old-fashioned antihistamine cream?' Gabby said wryly.

'It's a bit low-key for some of these things. I do use

conventional antihistamines and adrenaline in case of emergency and anaphylactic shock, and I always carry it with me wherever I go just to be on the safe side, but for this sort of thing cooking ingredients seem to have it licked. Right, Tom, my old son, how does that feel now?'

'Better,' the boy said with a sorrowful sniff. 'It hurt vewwy badly.'

Jed ruffled the boy's hair and stood up. 'Where are the girls?' he asked, searching the beach.

'Probably looking for us. I didn't have time to let them know what was happening, I just picked him up and ran. I don't suppose you'd like to go and find them? They were just near that rocky outcrop when we saw them last.'

Jed screwed the lid on the vinegar and turned to Gabby. 'Fancy that stroll now?' he asked.

Alone? With him?

'I dare you,' he said softly, so softly that Jon and Tom didn't hear over the little boy's sniffling.

Their eyes locked. 'Really daring,' she murmured somewhat scathingly, and pretended that her heart wasn't thumping at the thought of being alone with him. Nevertheless, she got to her feet, brushed the sand off her legs and put her shoes back on.

Murphy's law being what it was, she lost her balance and swayed against him, and felt the hard thrust of his thigh against her hip. By the time she'd straightened up she'd coloured beautifully and, being the gentleman he was, he grinned knowingly at her and made the situation worse.

She stepped well away from him, looked back over her shoulder and tipped her chin up a touch. 'Well? Are you coming?'

He bent over Tom. 'All right now, little man?'

Tom nodded, and Jed straightened, picking up a bottle of the lemonade and dangling it from his fingers. 'Let's go, then.'

She put his shirt on again to protect herself from the sun, then fell into step, although not quite beside him. She maintained a careful distance between them, but if she thought she'd got away with it, without him noticing, she was wrong.

'I don't bite,' he said mildly, strolling some ten feet away from her. 'You'll be walking in the water to get away from me soon, and you shouldn't be in the sun anyway. Come back here in the shade and stop behaving like a Victorian virgin. I promise you, I'm quite harmless.'

She snorted. Jed, harmless? And she was a monkey's uncle!

He did behave, though, after she came back in the shade, and then she had to deal with an emotion that felt suspiciously like disappointment.

It didn't last long. Gabby was too busy enjoying the strange vegetation and the sparkling clear blue sea and the cloudless sky—except that it wasn't cloudless. Rainclouds were building fast over Pulau Panjang and heading towards them, and she got the distinct feeling it was about to rain very, very heavily—

'We're going to get caught in that,' Jed said as she thought it, and, taking her hand, he led her at a run along the beach to the place Jon had mentioned where the rocks stuck out into the sea. There was a big outcrop with an overhang, and clustered underneath it they saw Penny and the girls.

'Hi,' she called. 'Have you seen Jon and Tom?'

'Back at base camp—Tom's trodden in a jellyfish,' Jed told her. 'It didn't seem too bad—I've dealt with it.

They sent us to tell you where they are and make sure you were all right.'

'We're fine. We've been puddling about in rock pools, haven't we, girls?'

The girls nodded excitedly and began to tell them about all the funny things they'd seen.

'You didn't put your hands or feet into the water, did you?' Jed warned.

Penny shook her head. 'No. We know about nasties that live in rock pools. Anyway, we looked up and saw the sky, and came in here to shelter from the rain when it comes.'

'Which is now,' Jed said with a laugh, and pulled Gabby down and under the shelter of the rock just as the rain swept up the beach from the sea and flung itself against the little island. Once again she was amazed at the torrential streams that fell, blocking out their view of the sea and turning the beach to a river.

They played games and told stories to keep the children's minds off the storm, but it was short-lived. It stopped after about half an hour, and they crawled out from under their rocky umbrella into glorious sunshine.

'Look, a rainbow!' Daisy said excitedly, and pointed at the horizon.

'Oh, Mummy, wow!' Katie breathed.

Gabby could have echoed her. There was a perfect arch spanning the sky, the colours more radiant and glorious than she had ever seen. She stared at it, spellbound, for endless seconds, before sighing and turning to Penny. 'Why is it that the colours here are brighter and more— more *coloured* than they are at home?'

Penny laughed. 'I suppose they are—I don't know why. It must be something to do with the light.'

'Perhaps you're just more relaxed?' Jed suggested.

Relaxed? With him two feet away?

'I think it must be something to do with the angle of the sun,' Gabby said, ignoring his suggestion.

'Possibly. Come on, girls, let's go back to Daddy and let Jed and Gabby get on with their walk,' Penny said to the children, and herded them gently back in the direction of the boat, ignoring Katie's protests.

Jed turned to Gabby. 'Want to carry on round? It'll take about half an hour.'

'What about Tom's foot?'

Jed shrugged. 'It was a simple sting. He'll be fine. Anyway, I want to talk to you. I've got a proposition to put to you.'

Gabby's eyes widened and she backed up slightly, making his lips quirk.

'Don't jump to conclusions,' he teased. 'Come on, let's walk and talk.'

They walked, but for a long time they didn't talk—or at least not about what Jed wanted to discuss. Gabby was so busy being fascinated that she wasn't really paying attention, and he didn't seem to be in a tearing hurry to broach whatever subject he had in mind.

Perhaps, she thought with mild curiosity, he was biding his time—or perhaps it had just been an excuse to get her alone on the other side of the island, away from the others.

And do what? she scoffed at herself. Seduce her?

She was being ridiculous. Whatever else he was, he was easygoing and good-natured. If seduction was in his mind and she said no, he'd accept it, she was sure. She was less sure that she'd say no, and that worried her just a touch. Maybe he knew that, too? Even more worrying!

She managed to convince herself that he didn't want to talk to her at all but just wanted to get her alone, and so she continued to plague him with questions about the trees and undergrowth and the composition of the sand, which was smooth and tracked with rivulets after the downpour—anything rather than silence.

Not that there was much of that, either. Lizards scuttled about, birds flashed overhead and she saw and heard monkeys screeching in the trees and swinging from branch to branch with casual ease. Every now and then one would stop for a moment and watch them with bright, intelligent eyes.

'I wonder what they think of us?' she murmured, returning the level stare of a young male.

'Not a lot, if they've got any sense. We either ruin their habitat or eat them, depending on how civilised our culture is. Either way, I don't suppose they're exactly grateful.'

Gabby laughed softly. 'If you put it like that, I suppose you're probably right. I wonder if they can philosophise?'

He rolled his eyes and carried on walking, and she fell into step beside him again and wondered when he was going to make his move.

She didn't have to wait long. Apparently the time was right because he turned to her and tipped his head towards the trunk of a fallen tree. 'Come and sit down,' he suggested, and made himself comfortable on the trunk. He uncapped the bottle of lemonade and handed it to her.

Warily, she sat a discreet distance away from him and took a swig, then handed it back and waited.

He drank deeply, recapped the bottle and put it down. 'Do you like it out here?' he asked after a second or two.

'On this island?' she asked, surprised. This was not what she'd expected.

'Pulau Panjang.'

She shrugged. 'It's only been three days. I suppose

it's all right. The scenery's gorgeous, the town's colourful and noisy and smelly, and the people seem friendly enough if you discount the trouble up at the power station compound—why?'

He shrugged and grinned at her. 'I was just wondering. I heard you talking to Penny about not having a job so there's no need for you to rush back, I imagine, unless there's some significant other you haven't told me about?'

'No significant other.' Or insignificant, come to that, she thought with an internal sigh. Nobody that cared or mattered at all, depressing though it was. 'Why?'

He shrugged again. 'I could do with a research assistant,' he told her with a lazy smile.

'Research assistant?' she exclaimed, staring at him in amazement. 'What on earth for?'

'My anti-malarial research project, of course,' he said as if it was obvious. He was totally deadpan, and she thought again what a loss he was to the film industry—or poker.

Research project indeed, she thought, and laughed. 'You must be joking! You seriously imagine you can persuade me to stay out here and join you on that veranda, sousing myself in gin and tonic and watching the world go by while I wait to get malaria? Get real, Jed! Life's too short to spend playing Hollywood bit-parts to the natives.'

'There is rather more to it than that,' he said mildly, but she didn't let him finish because the light had dawned and she suddenly realised exactly what he was suggesting. Yes, his aim had been seduction, only not now but later, longer term and pre-arranged. Rather more to it, indeed! She hung onto her temper with difficulty.

'No, thank you,' she said firmly.

'Sure I can't persuade you? The terms and conditions are very flexible,' he said with a grin.

'I'll bet.' She gave a huffy sigh. 'Look, Jed, I'm not in the market for an affair. I want a real job, thank you, not some thinly disguised excuse to get me into bed. Find a nice little native girl to cuddle up to if you're lonely at night, but leave me out of it. I'm sorry, I'm not buying. You don't interest me.'

He stared at her in stunned amazement. 'My God, you're arrogant,' he murmured.

She exploded. 'Me, arrogant? Just where the hell do you get off calling *me* arrogant? You have the infernal nerve to suggest setting up some cosy little love nest in the name of your bogus research—research, for heaven's sake! What research? You're such a fraud, Jed Daniels— and, for the record, you leave me cold.'

She stalked off but he followed her, grasped her arm and turned her back, pulling her hard up against his chest.

'Liar,' he said softly. His eyes glittered dangerously, and she wondered what she'd done, angering him when they were so far from the others. After all, what did she really know of him?

'I am not,' she protested, pushing feebly against his rock-hard chest. It didn't budge an inch. 'Idle lounge-lizards are not at all my type,' she added, just to ram the point home.

'Is that why you kissed me back this morning?' he murmured just inches from her mouth.

'I didn't,' she protested, but he cut off her argument by the simple expedient of sealing his lips over hers and stifling the words. His mouth was firm and yet soft, and after a few moments it softened further, coaxing, sipping and teasing, and she felt her resistance ebbing away.

She was powerless to resist the probe of his tongue,

and her mouth opened to him, giving him what he so gently demanded. She felt the silken stroke of his tongue over hers, hot and salty with a faint trace of lemon from the drink they'd shared, and then her body exploded into molten heat and she sagged against him with a little cry.

He might have been a gentleman, but he wasn't a saint. He took only what she offered, and when his large, hot palm closed over her breast she gasped and leant on him even harder. His other hand cupped her bottom and lifted her hard against him, and the tattered remains of her mind seemed to flutter to the sand at their feet.

'Yes,' he sighed against her throat as she trailed her tongue over his jaw. Her fingertips threaded through the hair on his chest, seeking the hot, damp skin beneath. Everything was hot, she thought vaguely. Hot and humid and torrid and a little like a dream, not quite connected to reality. What on earth was she doing?

His fingers were kneading her breast and her head felt too heavy. It fell back, and she felt the heat of his mouth on the vulnerable slope of her throat. There was a gentle suck, and a nip, then the soothing sweep of his tongue over the tender skin.

It nearly drove her wild. She felt herself clawing at his clothes, pushing the open shirt off his shoulders, whimpering slightly as the fabric resisted, and then suddenly he was releasing her and stepping back.

She nearly fell at his feet.

'Now tell me you're not interested,' he said dangerously softly, and, turning on his heel, he walked ahead, leaving her standing there rooted to the spot.

'Damn you, Jed,' she muttered under her breath. 'Damn you to hell and back—*I am not interested*!' she yelled after him.

She trudged after him through the soft, thick sand that sucked at her feet and made her calves ache. She didn't dare take her eyes off the ground she was walking on unless she trod on a snake or lizard. Beside her the monkeys screeched and ripped through the trees with ridiculous ease, and she wished she could do that. At least she wouldn't have to walk through the sand!

It probably only took about ten minutes to get back to the others, but it seemed more like hours. She was hot, she was tired and she was ready to kill. She was also embarrassed at herself.

Penny shot her a searching look but she avoided the other woman's eyes and wouldn't be drawn. 'How's Tom's foot?' she asked, exhibiting a professional interest.

'Oh, Jed's dealt with it—it's fine. It's so reassuring having him around.'

She heard a soft snort from the man in question, but she didn't look at him either. They were packing up to go home, and she helped with the loading of the bags onto the boat and the ferrying of the children.

Once on the launch she found herself a nice secluded spot in front of the wheelhouse, well away from Jed and Penny and the children, and sat under her hat, enjoying the cool breeze as they chugged across the stretch of water to Telok Panjang.

The water was magical. As they were approaching the town the sun was low in the sky, and the phosphorescence in the water was wonderful. She imagined at night it would be stunning, the sparkling green trails left by the flying fish and the wake of the boat quite spectacular.

It would be wonderfully romantic to share it with a lover, she thought in a moment of weakness, and then remembered Jed and his proposition. Maybe she ought to stop being such a prude and take him up on it?

Although she was by no means the Victorian virgin he'd accused her of being, she was very far from liberal in her morals. Perhaps it was time to make a change, she thought, and then remembered that she'd rather burned her boats in that department.

And they had to go back to the bungalow and live together for the next three weeks! She groaned inwardly, wondering how she could have put him down without being quite so forceful so that they were both left with a shred of dignity instead of the awkward and uneasy silence that had existed between them ever since their 'talk'.

Penny came and sat beside her and smiled a little warily. 'OK?' she asked.

'Fine. It's beautiful up here, I'm enjoying the view.'

'Good. Um—look, Gabby, is everything all right with you and Jed?'

She stared at the island, feigning interest. 'Of course. Why wouldn't it be?'

'I just wondered,' the other woman said softly. 'Only Jed seems a bit crusty and irritable, which isn't like him at all. He's normally so easygoing. I just wondered if anything happened on your walk—but it's none of my business. Ignore me.'

'Good heavens,' Gabby said with a false little laugh. 'Whatever could have happened on our walk? Penny, relax, everything's fine.'

And the moon was made of cheese.

Oh, hell.

As they drew near the jetty they could see a cluster of people, waving and shouting, and Jed came round beside the wheelhouse and held his hand above his eyes, peering at the crowd. His mouth was tight, and Gabby looked away. Was he still mad with her? Or was he worried?

She looked at the jetty and saw people were gesticulating at them to hurry.

'Something's wrong,' Jed murmured, squinting at the crowd. 'What the hell's happened now?'

Penny came up beside her and joined the inspection. 'Oh, no. Whatever can it be?'

They scrambled to their feet and headed back to the well of the boat, ready to disembark as soon as possible, and as they drew up alongside the jetty she saw Rom, the pretty young Indonesian servant who worked for Jon and Penny, weeping and calling out to Penny.

There was also a crowd of men in uniforms, and as they tied up and climbed out of the boat, one of the men with more gold braid than the others stepped forward, his eyes flicking from Jed to Jon.

'Tuan Andrews?'

'That's me,' Jonathan said. 'What's the matter?'

The man looked unhappy. 'We have a situation,' he said in stilted English. 'Some of your engineers—they seem to have been captured by men from the hill tribe.'

Gabby felt the blood drain from her face.

'Captured?' Jon said in a shocked voice. 'Who?'

'Tuan and Ibu Beckers, Ismail Barrung, Jumani Tandak and Luther Tarupadang.'

'Derek and Sue,' Penny said with a wail. 'But Sue's pregnant!'

'Sorry, mem,' the chief of police said to her. 'It's a bad business. Very bad.'

'Mummy, what's happened?' Katie was asking. 'What's wrong?'

'Nothing, darling,' she assured her, and gathered the children close. 'Nothing at all.'

But her eyes were wide with fear, and Gabby knew this was what she'd been dreading for two days. It was no longer just the Indonesians. They could no longer pretend.

All of them were in danger.

CHAPTER FOUR

'I WANT you to leave the island.'

Jonathan's voice was rough with worry, but Penny was implacable.

'I'm not leaving you,' she said firmly. 'I think we should all go. It clearly isn't safe—'

'I can't leave,' Jonathan said just as firmly. 'I have to stay here and get to the bottom of this. The engineers' lives could depend on it.'

'Your life could depend on you getting away,' Penny replied, and they could tell the strain was getting to her by the shake in her voice. Jed shook his head and looked across at Gabby, sitting with him on the veranda just outside the bedroom where Jon and Penny were having their argument.

'Do you think we should all leave?' Gabby asked softly.

Jed shrugged. 'Who knows? Until the chief of police comes and we find out more about what happened, I don't think we can tell, but I have to say I'm not concerned about the children. Indonesians dote on children, they wouldn't hurt them. Children are sacred, whatever their parents may have done.'

'You seem very sure.'

His smile flashed white in the darkness. 'I am sure. They're quite safe. Jonathan is probably most at risk of the five of them.'

'What about you?'

'Me?' He sounded surprised. 'I'm not at risk—I'm just the doctor, I'm not really anything to do with the project.' He tipped back his chair, propped his feet on the rail and stared out over the dark sea. A boat carved a gleaming, greenish wake in the phosphorescence, and here and there lights twinkled.

Behind them she could hear Penny weeping quietly, and her cousin's gentle reassurance.

Gabby's mind stayed locked on their problem. 'Will the developer come out to see what's going on?' she asked.

'Bill Freeman?' Jed shrugged again. 'Maybe. He's been quite involved up to now. It depends what the problem is, but I don't think Jon's told him about the sabotage attempts yet.'

The lights of a vehicle appeared on the track up from the town, and the battered old police car spluttered to a halt near the veranda.

Jed unfolded himself from his chair and ambled down the steps to greet the police chief, while Gabby went in to tell Jonathan of his arrival.

'Stay with Penny, she's upset,' her cousin pleaded, and so she went in to the other woman and comforted her. Outside on the veranda they could hear the murmured conversation of the three men, and then the sound of a vehicle clattering to life signalled the end of the police visit.

Jonathan came in again and sat heavily on the end of the bed. 'No news. They still don't know why it's happened, but they're sending an officer up to the next village to find out what he can. They expect him back by tomorrow night, and in the meantime they've left an armed guard to protect us, just as a precaution.'

Penny's eyes widened. 'Armed?' she whispered.

'Just to be on the safe side—he's not convinced it's necessary. I had to talk him into leaving the man at all.'

Gabby eyed her cousin thoughtfully. He was lying,

she could tell. Was the situation worse than they'd been told at first?

'Excuse me, I think I'll go back to the bungalow now,' she said to them, and slipped out. Jed was on the veranda, as she'd expected, and she beckoned him.

He stood and followed her up the track. Out of the corner of her eye she could see the guard, lolling against a tree, and she could smell the sweet, heavy scent of the clove tobacco he was smoking. He didn't look much of a deterrent to determined and desperate men, Gabby thought with a little shiver of nerves.

'What did he say?' she asked once they were out of earshot.

'They came at two in the afternoon when the men were resting. They always lie down for a while after lunch and start work again after the rain when it's a bit cooler. They came while they were asleep, and took them.'

'How?' Gabby asked. 'Surely the road doesn't go very far.'

'They were on foot, so had the alarm been raised quickly it might have been possible to catch up with them, but by the time the cook-boy got back from town at five they were long gone and the trail had been destroyed by the rain.'

'So how do they know when they were taken?'

'A note from Derek, apparently dictated by the captors and translated by one of the engineers.' He stopped, obviously reluctant to say any more, but Gabby pressed him.

'What did it say apart from that?'

Jed sighed quietly. 'Just a threat to kill them if the project proceeds.'

'Oh, my God.'

'Quite. These boys aren't messing around, they mean business.'

He looked at his watch. 'Fancy dinner?'

'But Rom isn't up to cooking—wasn't her husband one of the engineers who was captured? I thought Penny had given her the night off so she could go home to her family?'

'I meant in town, at the *rumah makan*.'

She stared at him in amazement. 'They could be killed and you want to go out for dinner?' she exclaimed, her voice rising. 'Anyway, I thought you didn't entertain tourists.'

He gave her a level look. 'I don't, but I still have to eat. Anyway, before you get carried away about why I want your company, I want to go down to town and sound out a few people I know, but I don't want to leave you here on your own and I think Jon and Penny could do with a little privacy right now.'

'I'd be all right on my own—'

'No, and, anyway, you have to eat as well. We'll go to the *rumah makan* and have a meal, and then wander through the town as if I'm giving you a guided tour. We'll be quite safe, but I can casually make a few enquiries while we're down there.'

'More people who owe you favours?' she asked with a thread of sarcasm. The last thing she felt like doing was going out for a meal to celebrate. 'What did you do, save their children's lives?'

'Actually, yes.'

Colour scorched her cheeks and she was suddenly ashamed of her suspicious mind. 'Sorry. That was un-called-for. Yes, of course I'll come.'

They set off in the Jeep, after telling the others where they were going, and Gabby discovered to her surprise that she was actually starving. While they were waiting for the food to be put in front of them they sat at a table on the street outside amongst the other customers and the smoking mosquito coils, and while her stomach grumbled quietly to itself Gabby marvelled at the way Jed networked the locals.

'Nobody wants to talk,' he confided under his breath at one point. 'They all know more than they're saying, but they're keeping out of it.'

The food arrived then, great heaps of *nasi goreng* or fried rice, with *satay* and dried salt fish and curry and sweet and sour chicken and innumerable other side dishes, all spicy and tasty and quite delicious.

'Save some room,' Jed warned as she piled in, eating—as he did—with her fingers, balling the rice into neat pellets with her right hand and popping them into her mouth. It was, in fact, an easy way to eat once she'd mastered the art of making the grains of rice stick together, but again there was the question of the right and left hand—the right for eating and greeting, the left for toilet purposes.

So much to remember, she thought as she ate yet another strip of the salty dried fish.

'Why do I need to save room?' she mumbled around the tasty fragments.

'Because we're going visiting, and the Indonesians are such hospitable people they just have to feed visitors.'

Gabby groaned, thinking of the vast amount she'd just put away. 'You might have warned me sooner!'

'You'll cope.' He caught the waiter's eye, haggled for a moment over the bill and then paid up once honour was satisfied on both sides. They took the Jeep and drove down to the harbour, then parked it and wandered along the seafront.

The town was slightly L-shaped, wrapped around the mouth of the river on one side. On the other side was a small *kampung*, or village, a much poorer community altogether. It was to there they were headed, she discovered.

Jed hailed a water-taxi, a rickety little boat with a hissing kerosene lantern, hanging from a bamboo pole, and an outboard that had seen better days. It spluttered to life once they were seated, and the boat chugged across the estuary to the little settlement on the other side. Jed asked the boatman to wait, and then handed Gabby ashore and ushered her along the jetty, a makeshift raft linked to the wooden walkways that stretched out over the water like fingers.

Between them were simple houses, lit with the yellow glow of kerosene, all family life taking place behind the open doorways. 'They don't go much on privacy, do they?' Gabby murmured.

'Only for certain things. Men and women never touch each other in public except in a very asexual way, and they never hold hands or kiss like we do in the west, but they have much more contact between people of the same sex. Indonesians are great touchers and huggers.'

He turned left and right and left, and then finally stopped outside a sorry little shack with a thin, tired-looking woman sitting on the step nursing a baby.

Jed crouched down and greeted her, and she scrambled to her feet and ran inside, calling to the others and beckoning the visitors in.

'Take off your shoes—and don't touch the children's heads,' Jed muttered, and then they were inside the little room and being greeted by all the family.

There was the now familiar smell of mosquito coils smouldering quietly near the doorway to deter the worst of the villains, and also the sweet, cloying scent of the clove cigarettes that were so popular. Drinks were brought out—the incredibly strong and sickly sweet coffee she'd learnt to avoid—and tiny cakes, nuts and other delicacies were spread out in front of them on the floor. Although she couldn't understand a word, the women kept giving her sidelong glances and giggling behind their hands.

'Do they think we're an item?' she asked Jed in a lull, and he laughed.

'Probably. You might be kind and play along with it—I've been religiously celibate and they think there's something wrong with me.'

She chuckled. Jed, celibate? Surely there was no need. The young women were looking at him as if they could eat him, and at least two of them were nursing babies!

Finally, after all the social niceties had been satisfied and Gabby had eaten more sickly little cakes than she thought she could keep down, Jed and Jamal, the head of the house, seemed to turn their talk to other things. They went into a huddle in the corner, and Gabby suddenly found herself the centre of attention.

The young women touched her clothes and smiled shyly, and one fingered her hair, marvelling at the colour and texture, so unlike their own. A baby crept onto her lap and tugged at a curl, and she laughed and hugged it, just stopping herself from kissing its head.

It used her as a climbing frame, pulling itself up and bouncing on her lap just like her nieces and nephews did, and she held onto the chubby little brown arms and let it bounce, laughing when it sat down with a plonk.

She looked up then to find the other children clustered round her, all reaching out to touch her hair. They didn't seem to have the same inhibitions as the adults about touching heads, and as she had none at all she sat there and let them maul her gently.

A hand on her shoulder made her turn her head, and

she looked round to find Jed standing behind her, an enigmatic look on his face.

'Time to go?' she asked wistfully.

'If you can tear yourself away.'

She stood up, and one of the young women went out the back and returned with a length of batik cloth, beautifully dyed in the most wonderful jewel colours, and pressed it into Gabby's hands.

She turned to Jed. 'It's lovely—why's she showing it to me? Did she make it?'

'It's a gift,' Jed told her. 'A sarong.'

'A gift? Oh, but I couldn't possibly accept!' she protested, stunned by the girl's generosity.

'You have to. They'd be desperately insulted if you refused it.'

'Really? Could I offer to pay for it?'

He shook his head. 'Absolutely not. Just take it, Gabby.'

She turned back to the girl, unbearably touched, and hugged her. 'Thank you,' she said simply, blinking away the tears that filled her eyes, and all the women hugged her and patted her and sent her on her way with a warm glow she hadn't felt in years.

She clutched the cloth against her chest all the way home, amazed that she should have been made such a gift.

She stroked the fabric, and found it was fine and soft and felt quite wonderful against her skin. 'Why did they give it to me?' she asked Jed as they climbed the road out of the town.

'The man with the pneumothorax is her intended— you helped to save his life. They've heard you're a healer, and your unusual colouring backs that up.' He shrugged and grinned. 'Seems like they just wanted to say thank you.'

'I wonder where they got the idea from that I'm a healer?' she murmured drily, still stroking the cloth.

He laughed and pulled the Jeep to a halt outside her cousin's bungalow. Lights were burning brightly in the sitting room, spilling out across the veranda. 'They're still up—let's go and tell them what we've found out,' Jed suggested.

The security guard was asleep under a tree and jumped as they approached. Jed spoke to him in rapid Indonesian and he struggled to his feet and straightened his uniform, grinning sheepishly.

'Useless,' Jed growled. 'They just aren't taking this seriously, but they'd better.'

Gabby shot him a keen look in the dim light from the windows. 'Why? You still haven't told me what you found out. Why do we need to take this so seriously?'

'Because they mean business. Come on.'

He pushed open the screen door and went in, to find Jonathan and Penny sitting together on the sofa. Penny had been crying, and Jon looked distracted and tired. They both jumped up as Jed and Gabby went in.

'You're back—thank God,' Penny said, looking relieved. 'I was worried about you.'

'There's no need,' Jed assured her. He folded himself into a chair, crossed one leg over the other and sighed, dropping his head back against the cushions.

'Well? Did you find anything out?' Jon asked urgently, clearly irritated by his casual attitude and impatient to hear the news.

'Oh, yes. Jamal wouldn't tell me why they want us to stop, but these hill people apparently are quite fierce and have powerful magic.'

'Magic? I thought this lot were Christians?' Jon said, looking confused.

'They are—after a fashion. Indonesian beliefs are all

a little tangled. Anyway, everyone's a little afraid of this lot, although they very rarely venture down to the town. They're hunter-gatherers in the main, rather like the Dyaks, and their religion is largely animist with the odd fragment of Christianity.'

'Are the two compatible?'

Jed laughed softly. 'In Indonesia almost all religions are compatible, and if they aren't they alter them until they fit. Whatever, these people could be dangerous, and they mean to stop us building the dam. What we don't know is why, but you can bet your life it's tied up in *adat*.'

'*Adat*?' Gabby repeated. 'What's that?'

'Custom, tradition, social order and behaviour patterns, ways that things are done or not done. There's a tremendous amount of ceremonial attached to all their religious practices, whatever the religion. What we need to do is find out whose toes we're treading on and why, and then we might stand a chance of negotiating a settlement.'

'Did Jamal think—? Are they—? Oh, Lord, Jed, they will be all right, won't they? I can't bear to think of Sue pregnant and going through all this.'

'I'm more worried about Derek and his diabetes. If he didn't take insulin with him he could be in trouble already,' Jed told them.

'Bill phoned—he's arriving tomorrow afternoon. He's bringing his plane so you can overfly the site and get a closer look, see if that sheds any light.'

'We might also see if we can spot any woodsmoke or signs of habitation further up—give us an idea of where to start looking.' Jed jackknifed out of the chair and looked at Gabby. 'Time for bed, I think. Tomorrow could be a very long day.'

She nodded and stood up, following him out past the dozing security guard.

'That man's a waste of space,' Jed muttered as they went into the bungalow. 'I think it might be a good idea to sleep together tonight.'

Gabby shot him a look. 'Excuse me?'

'Relax, I have no designs on your virtue. Actually, I think it's probably me taking the risk, but I'll tough it out if you promise to be gentle with me.'

She had to laugh. It was that or scream. 'Do as you wish. I shall be in my room, in my bed, alone. Where you choose to sleep is up to you.'

She went into her room, undressed and wrapped herself in a towel and went out to the *mandi*. When she came back it was to find Jed sprawled on another bed apparently dragged in from his room, wearing nothing but a sarong fastened round his waist.

She raised an eyebrow witheringly—she hoped. It didn't wither him. He smirked, vaulted off the bed and snagged his towel on the way out of the door. 'Yell if you need me,' he said with a grin.

'In your dreams,' she muttered under her breath, and he laughed and shut the door. She pulled on her night-shirt, slid under the covers and arranged her mosquito net over her mattress, then lay down to wait. Five minutes later he was back, his body beaded with moisture from the *mandi*, the sarong clinging to his damp body and leaving little to the imagination.

She dragged her eyes away and hauled in a breath, and turned firmly on her side away from him. 'I think you're being ridiculous. We've got a security guard—'

'Who's asleep again. I just checked. He's about as much use as a eunuch in a brothel.'

'That's disgusting.'

'Oh, Gabby, give over. We need some rest. Your virtue's safe. Just go to sleep.'

She couldn't, though, not for ages. She lay and listened to every creak, every scream and wail from the jungle just yards away, and then there were the soft snores that drifted out from under Jed's makeshift mosquito net.

Dawn seemed to take ages to break, and when it did she fell into a deep and dreamless sleep. Jed woke her at nine with a cup of tea and the news that he and Jon were going up to the compound to look around, and he was then going back to town to continue his sleuthing.

'More people who owe you favours?' she asked without any real rancour, and he grinned.

'Comes in handy at times. I'll see you later.'

The day dragged without him around. She spent most of it with Penny, trying to amuse the children and distract them and Penny from their worries. Despite her protests of the previous day, Penny was packing to leave the island, taking just a few things and going to Jakarta with the children for a while until things settled down. She persuaded Gabby to pack and come with her and, as she could see little point in staying without Penny, she agreed.

They were to leave late next morning on the little local plane. Jon was relieved that they had both seen sense, and Jed, too, nodded his agreement when he came back at ten that night. They talked with Bill, the developer, for some time, and then Jed rose to his feet and stretched.

'Bedtime,' he said to the assembled company. 'Tomorrow could be quite eventful.'

Gabby was happy to agree. The sleepless night before had taken its toll, and she slept like a log, comforted this time by Jed's presence.

He'd said nothing about what he'd discovered the previous day, but he'd had a thoughtful look on his face, and she wasn't surprised when she woke at dawn and found he was gone. She slid her feet over the edge of the bed, ducked under the mosquito net and padded softly out into the sitting-room area in the centre of the bungalow. She could hear him moving around in his bedroom, and she looked through the open door to see him packing medicines into a flight bag.

'What are you doing?' she asked.

His head whipped round and he searched her eyes, as if he wasn't sure how much to tell her.

Eventually he spoke, measuring every word. 'Derek needs insulin. The others need anti-malarials, probably antibiotics and anti-inflammatories, and there could be all sorts of other emergencies—dysentery, fungal infections, burns and wounds that won't heal—the jungle's a nasty place.'

'And how do you intend to get this little Red Cross parcel to them?' Gabby asked, plopping down on the edge of a chest and waiting.

He hesitated again, and she felt a sinking feeling inside. 'You're going to try and go to them, aren't you?' she said, following her unerring nurse's instinct.

'There's a scout gone up there—he may be able to get a message to them.'

'And pigs fly. You're going to walk up there, aren't you, if you can get an idea of where it is?'

He sighed and sat back on his heels. 'Yes. I think I stand a better chance of negotiating than your cousin or Bill and, anyway, I'm a bachelor. It's reasonable I should be the one to go.'

'And how will you know the way?'

He shifted, and she fixed him with a steely glare. 'How, Jed?'

'Jamal knows a man from there—he's an outcast, but he knows the way. He'll be able to show me how to get there. We'll set off later this morning.'

'So why didn't you tell Jon last night?'

He laughed softly. 'Because he would have had a fit, and so would Penny. I went up with Bill yesterday to fly over the site and see what we could see but, as I suspected, it was nothing. Before they get up I want to go and look at the site from the ground—the compound, the area where they've been drilling and blasting for the feasibility study—all of it. See if I can work out what the problem is.'

'Can I come?'

He quirked a brow. 'Can't keep away from me?'

She blushed. 'Not at all. I just thought two pairs of eyes might be better than one, and our plane doesn't go for ages.'

'Do you know what to look for?'

'Do you?'

He shrugged in submission and grinned. 'No, not really. It might just be a holy place—there might be nothing *to* see. I just want to look, that's all—and, yes, you can come if you're ready now.'

She glanced down at her nightshirt. 'Give me ten seconds.'

She was back in about ninety, just as he put the last of his pills and potions into the flight bag and zipped it up. 'I'll take this with me—there are one or two things up at the compound I need to pick up as well.'

The Jeep, bursting into life, woke the security guard with a start, and he grinned and waved and rubbed his eyes.

'What a waste of a good skin,' Jed muttered, and gunned the engine.

Gabby said nothing. She was too busy hanging on like

grim death because Jed clearly didn't intend to waste any time on this trip. They hurtled up to the compound, disturbing another security guard who slept peacefully in the shade of a veranda, and then, after collecting a few more drugs and supplies from the infirmary and making a cursory check around the immediate area, they set off again for the proposed site of the power station.

It wasn't far, a third of a mile at the most, but the road was every bit as bad as the other one, and as they grew nearer so it became worse, more winding and twisting as they negotiated rocky outcrops and the huge trunks of fallen trees.

Finally Jed pulled the Jeep up in a little clearing and turned off the ignition. The silence was deafening. Gradually, sounds began to return—birds screeching, monkeys whooping and yelling, the chirring of the cicadas, and underlying it all the dull roar of water. The sounds all seemed distant, though, as if there was an uneasy silence over the area.

'Come on,' he said briskly, and slid out from behind the wheel. She followed him, almost running to keep up with his long stride, and then finally they emerged on the edge of a rocky cliff.

Below them, falling almost vertically for fifty feet or more, the river crashed downwards towards Telok Panjang and the sea, a foaming torrent of water that threw up a veil of mist. Gabby could quite see how harnessing its power would provide electricity for the town and the new resort.

'The plan is to divert some of the water over here, and build a turbine house to take the generators,' Jed yelled over the roar of the waterfall. 'That will mean damming it and putting weirs in the side of the lake— it might be that there's something here that's sacred. Let's take a look.'

They retreated from the edge of the cliff, to Gabby's relief, and studied the area Jed indicated. A little lake lay sparkling in the sunlight, a natural weir-pool and the perfect pick-up point for the water they would need to power the turbines.

It was beautiful, peaceful and cool and restful, and there didn't seem to be anything—any artefacts or man-made structures—that could be shrines or tombs or any such thing that might be of significance. The only strange thing was the wonderful peace she felt steal over her as she stood there in the dim light of the jungle.

Gabby tipped her head and looked up through the soaring trunks of the jungle giants that fringed the edges of the lake. They were amazing, great gnarled trees with massive boles and leaves so far removed from the roots she wondered how they could possibly pump the water such a long way.

Some of them had a strange chequered effect on the bark—an almost square pattern of astonishing symmetry that clothed the lower part of the trunks.

She nudged Jed. 'Look at those trees—the bark's really weird.'

He looked, and his eyes narrowed for a second. 'My God—I think that might be the answer.'

'What might?'

He looked at her, his eyes strangely bright in the artificial twilight. 'Grave trees,' he said.

'What?'

'They have them in Tanatoraja, in Sulawesi. They're animists, too, and it's possible the two tribes could be related. One might be an offshoot of the other. Whatever. They believe that if infants die without touching the earth their souls go directly to heaven, and so for the first few months of their lives they're carried everywhere and never put down. If a baby dies they cut a hole in the bark of a grave tree, chisel out a cavity and put the baby's body inside, then replace the bark and put a little door over the hole. That way the baby never has to touch the ground.'

Gabby swallowed. 'So those trees contain dead babies?'

He peered closely at them. 'Could be.'

She laid a hand over her chest, conscious of a great feeling of sadness. A cold chill ran over her. 'Oh, Jed. No wonder they want to protect them.'

'They're right in the line of the turbine house and the weirs. They'd have to be felled without a doubt if the plant was to be sited here.'

'But it can't!' Gabby protested. 'They can't be allowed to cut them down!'

'They could be hundreds of years old. Those marks aren't new by any stretch of the imagination, Gabby. It might be a red herring.'

She knew it wasn't, though, just as she knew that the strange feeling of peace came from the souls of those children.

Tears welled in her eyes. 'Jed, they can't cut them down, no matter how old they are. They must be left in peace.'

He turned to her, saw her tears and cupped her face gently in his big hands, smoothing the tears away with his thumbs. 'I think I'll let you negotiate with Bill. He's a sucker for pretty women.'

She smacked his hands away and turned, wrapping her arms around her chest. 'I mean it. They can't be allowed to desecrate this area, Jed. Can't you feel it?'

His hands closed over her shoulders. 'Oh, yes, I can feel it. I agree with you. I'm just wondering how Bill will feel about all the money he's spent on this project so far, and how much it would cost to relocate it.'

'Tough,' Gabby said uncompromisingly.

Jed squeezed her shoulders and she heard a soft laugh. 'I think we'll definitely let you tell him.'

Her shoulders drooped, and he eased her back against his chest and rubbed the tense muscles of her neck with his thumbs. 'We'll talk to him. With the lives of the others on line I'm sure he'll see reason—if we're right and that is the problem.'

She looked up at the trees again, and sighed. 'Why didn't anybody notice before?'

'Because nobody was looking. The area's uninhabited now—Jamal told me the hill tribe moved north years ago when the Dutch arrived. What seemed like a natural clearing where we parked the Jeep is probably the site of the old village. This graveyard is all of a hundred years old, if not more.'

'That doesn't stop it being sacred.'

'No, but nevertheless I don't suppose anyone was looking for grave trees when they did the feasibility studies. Like I said, they're exclusively Torajan, or I thought they were. Obviously these people have never been studied.'

'Perhaps because of their powerful magic?'

'Maybe.'

'Or perhaps just because they're very fierce.'

His hands fell to his sides. 'Perhaps. Come on, let's get back and tell Jon.'

They turned, and then stopped dead. Five men stood around the Jeep, naked except for bark loincloths and tattoos. Their skins were smeared with what looked like ash, and they held long things in their hands, not spears but something else. Blowpipes?

'Hell,' Jed said quietly.

'I'll go for that,' Gabby mumbled from beside him.

One of the men stepped forwards. '*Docktor*?'

Jed nodded and pointed to his chest. '*Docktor*,' he repeated.

The man jabbed his blowpipe upriver, at a barely discernible path in the jungle. '*Jalan-jalan*,' he growled.

'I don't think he's negotiating,' Gabby said softly.

'No. I'll take the medicine and go with them, you get in the Jeep and go like hell for the town. Tell them what we've found out, and start the negotiations rolling. OK? And get them to follow us.'

She nodded, and he winked. 'Attagirl.'

He stepped forward, picked up the bag from the Jeep and turned to the waiting men. As he moved, Gabby got into the Jeep and reached for the ignition, but there was a yell and one of them pulled her out. There was an urgent exchange, and she felt the press of cold steel at her back.

'I think they want me to come too,' she said as steadily as she could manage. Her heart was pounding, her mouth was dry and she thought her legs were about to give way, but she was damned if any of them would know that.

She lifted her chin a notch and noted the approval in Jed's eyes. A lot of good that would do her.

'No problem. I'll try and talk to them.'

He spoke in Bahasa, then in the native dialect of Pulau Panjang, but he was met with a blank wall of silence. Incomprehension, or just a stubborn refusal to listen?

The ringleader jabbed his blowpipe at Gabby. '*Jalan-jalan*,' he repeated, sounding angry now, and the man holding her thrust her forward so that she staggered against Jed.

They were looking at the flight bag, and Jed unzipped it. '*Obat*,' he told them. Medicine. They nodded, and they turned towards the jungle. Three of them went first, melting into the jungle along an almost invisible path. Jed turned to her. 'Stay close,' he ordered.

The others fell in behind, and within seconds the undergrowth closed in behind them and the last trace of civilisation vanished...

CHAPTER FIVE

IT TOOK Gabby about two seconds to work out that if they went any further into the jungle she wouldn't be able to find her way back to the Jeep.

It took about another two seconds to tell herself it was a crazy idea, but so what? So she was crazy. So they had blowpipes. One quick poison dart was probably preferable to walking all day in the jungle in nothing but a pair of thin trousers, trainers and a long-sleeved shirt.

She was too hot, and she'd already discovered that the trousers gave little protection against the whipping stems of some of the more vicious jungle plants she'd already encountered—and they'd hardly started their journey, she was sure of that! And, anyway, she might be the last chance the hostages had. She had to get back to Jon and explain about the grave trees and do something positive before the situation escalated out of control.

She scuffed her shoe heel down, loosened it, then casually walked out of it and stopped dead. As she bent over to refasten it Jed and three of their captors had moved ahead, and there were only the two men following her.

They looked reasonably harmless, she thought, if one ignored the blowpipes and nose-bones. She smiled and made a great production of putting her shoe on again, then, as the others disappeared from view ahead of them, she turned and threw herself against one, catching him by surprise and knocking him over. Using her old netball skills, she ducked past the other and ran back down the path towards the Jeep.

At least, she'd meant to, but in her haste the jungle blurred into a mat of foliage and the path vanished. She pushed the stems aside, hurling herself forwards against the vegetation to cleave a path through it, and ran straight into a mass of thorny stems.

The vicious spikes ripped her clothes and skin, and with a scream of frustration and pain she fought to free herself.

Hands stopped her, trapping her arms and pulling her backwards out of the savage clutches of the monster plant and back against a hard, muscled chest. The arms were like steel bands, and once she was free of the plant they half dragged, half carried her back towards the others.

'Let me go!' she protested, but the arms didn't move and she was propelled relentlessly back through the undergrowth, kicking and screaming.

Not that it did any good. Her captor's arms simply tightened and, apart from a grunt of pain when her heel connected with his shin, she slowed him down so little she might as well have been a gnat.

She could hear yelling in the distance, and as they neared the rest of the group she was released and thrust forward so that she fell at the feet of the ringleader.

'That was a bit bloody stupid,' Jed said angrily, and, ignoring the men, he pulled her roughly to her feet, hauled her up against him and hit her hard across the face.

She screamed, blood trickling down her lip, and raised her fists to pound on his chest. He caught them with one large hand, trapped them and then glared at her—but not angrily. 'Don't say a word,' he growled. 'Just play along. You're my wife, you do as I tell you, I'm responsible for you. It's the only way you'll be safe.'

'The Indonesian didn't hit me,' she grated back at him.

'No, he's just ready to rape you, and if you get away from the others again he probably will. He's looking at you as if he'd like to eat you. Now cast your eyes down, look ashamed and I'll try and explain that you're a difficult wife but I'm taming you gradually.'

He pulled her round to his side none too gently, looked at the boss-man and gave a man-to-man shrug, then he grasped a vine and indicated to one of the men that he would like it chopped. With a quick twisting motion he wound it around her right wrist and shackled her to his left.

'What the hell are you doing?' she muttered furiously.

'Ensuring your safety and proving that you're my chattel. Now shut up!' He held up their wrists, rolled his eyes expressively and winked.

To her relief and fury, they laughed and the party set off again. There was no further chance of escape, of course, but it seemed there was none anyway so she probably hadn't lost anything except her dignity and several inches of skin.

Bitter disappointment settled like a lead weight in her chest, and gradually as the sweat trickled down her body into the cuts and scratches the pain became almost unbearable. Her mouth hurt where he'd hit her, the vine was chafing on her wrist and she was sick of trailing just behind Jed with one arm outstretched to accommodate her shackle. It wasn't necessary anyway, she thought crossly, but at least, being so close behind him, his big body took most of the sting from the undergrowth.

Then she stumbled over a root and fell, only Jed's arm tied to hers preventing her from falling right down.

A little sob broke from her lips, and he turned and helped her up again, then tipped her chin and winked at her.

'Keep going,' he murmured comfortingly. 'You're doing well.'

'Liar,' she grumbled.

'I'm sorry about your face. I had to make it look real.'

'That real?' she said bitterly.

His thumb brushed the bruise on her swollen lip. 'I'll make it up to you. Just hang on in there, it can't last for ever—the island's not that big.'

But it was, of course. She'd seen it from the air, and she knew just how big it was. Anyway, distances couldn't be measured in normal ways because progress was so slow.

She tried a smile, and he dropped a hard, quick kiss on her lips and turned away again. As he did she caught the eyes of the man who'd chased her, and realised with a chill that Jed had been right. His eyes were glittering with a strange fever, and she just knew that given the slightest chance he'd try and get her alone.

Which was a problem because just then she wanted to be alone, just for a moment or two. She tugged at Jed.

'I need the loo,' she hissed.

'Fine. Can you hang on? They have to stop soon.'

'I hope you're right.'

They trudged on, however. The heat was relentless, steamy and intolerable. Her mouth was dry, and she thought she'd have given her eye teeth for a long glass of ice-cold beer.

She began to fantasise about it, to such an extent that when their captors called a halt she didn't even notice and cannoned into Jed's hot, sweaty back.

It was probably no hotter and sweatier than her front

so she leant against it, exhausted, and waited for some instructions.

As she listened she heard the sound of rushing water, and realised they were still near the river. The cold, wet, clean, thirst-quenching river—

'I think he's saying we can drink and bathe, and I think they've got some food,' Jed said softly over his shoulder.

She straightened and looked around, and found they were in a little clearing beside the river. The air was cooler, and the water looked wonderful. Just then the men disappeared one at a time and came back, adjusting their loincloths.

'Jed, I need to go!' she muttered. 'Take this thing off—'

'No. We'll go together.'

Jed waved his arms about in some ghastly sign language, and the ringleader nodded. Unfortunately he also accompanied them out of the clearing, standing over them with his arms folded.

'Jed, I can't—'

'I think you're going to have to. I'll stand between you and him.'

'What makes you think you're any better than he is? Jed, I want a private pee! Is that so much to ask?'

He grinned. 'If it's any consolation so do I, and I'm not going to get one. I'll turn round and face him, and you can turn your back to me—'

'Can't you just untie me?' she pleaded for the nth time, but he was emphatic about it.

She was too hot and tired to flounce so she turned round and then discovered the impossibility of undoing her clothes with her left hand and squatting down over prickly undergrowth full of unmentionable creepy-crawlies—

With a yelp she catapulted to her feet, forgetting the shackle and almost dragging Jed over on top of her.

'What the hell?' He turned towards her to steady her, and then looked down. 'You've forgotten something.'

She yanked up her knickers and trousers and to her embarrassment had to enlist Jed's help in refastening them.

'Want to tell me what that was all about?' he asked calmly when she was reassembled.

'I felt something tickling me,' she muttered, furiously embarrassed.

'Is that all?' he asked with a chuckle. 'I thought at the very least you'd been bitten on the bottom by a cobra.'

Her eyes widened. 'A what?'

'Forget it. I needed cheering up.'

'At my expense?'

There was a wicked twinkle in his eye and if she hadn't been so damn tired she would have hit him. As it was she leant her head on his chest for a second, then straightened again, tilted her chin and nodded.

'Any chance of a wash?' she said wistfully.

Again Jed went through the pantomime, and they were led through the trees to the river. It tumbled over rocks, looking clear and cool and absolutely the best thing in the world to Gabby, and she almost fell into it in her haste.

'Steady,' Jed murmured, and then he was beside her on the rocks, sloshing water over his head and face with one hand while the other went up and down to hers, shackled to her arm.

One particular scratch was stinging furiously, and she turned back her cuff to look at it.

'When did you do that?'

'When I tried to play the hero,' she said drily. 'There was a great spiky vine thing—'

'Rattan. It's wicked. Let me look.'

He rolled up her sleeves, tutting and mumbling, and washed all the scratches thoroughly—too thoroughly in some cases. Then he rolled up her trouser legs and did the same thing with those, and by the time he'd finished and smeared antiseptic over them from his box of tricks the hill men were looking bored and irritated.

They were each handed a little bunch of bright yellow fig-shaped fruits, and then nudged on the way.

'Can't we sit and rest?' Gabby pleaded, but apparently they couldn't.

She fell in behind Jed, examining the fruits with suspicion. 'What do you suppose they are?'

'Figs. They'll probably give you the runs, but they taste good.'

The runs? While she was shackled to him and in front of an audience? Not in this lifetime!

She lobbed them into the forest and trudged on, ignoring the rumbling of her stomach. She'd rather starve than go through that.

Four hours later she was regretting her impulse. They'd had another quick pitstop, but there was nothing else to eat and she thought if she didn't wrap herself around something substantial soon she was going to fade right away.

Melt, in fact. She remembered the old saying, 'Ladies glow, men perspire, pigs sweat.' Clearly she was a pig.

A tired pig. She put one foot in front of the other without any real awareness of where she was going, except that she was following Jed. She couldn't see for the sweat and dirt that was running down her face, although that was probably marginally preferable to the rain that had fallen. The air was still soaked, a fine misting drizzle falling from the canopy, and every third or fourth step some kind-hearted leaf generously poured a couple of pints of water down the back of her neck as she went underneath, but at least the unrelenting downpour had stopped.

The path was slippery now, and there was something on her wrist which she had an idea was a leech.

'They're medicinal,' she told herself, and ignored it. Some while later it had dropped off, and there was a little red spot where it had been, with a thin trail of blood leaking from it.

'I'm going to bleed to death and Jed won't know until he looks round and finds my corpse, dangling behind his wrist,' she mumbled.

He stopped dead and she crashed into his back. 'What?'

'Nothing. I'm bleeding to death.'

He turned abruptly. 'What? Where?'

She showed him her wrist, and he gave a huff of laughter that sounded suspiciously relieved and ruffled her hair. 'Chin up. You're doing fine. Look, we must be nearly at the village, the path's much clearer now.'

She looked and, lo and behold, she could actually see where they were heading for the first time since they'd set off on their tortuous journey.

Not that she'd been exactly looking hard.

'Yippee,' she said expressionlessly, and he gave her a quick hug and turned back, setting off again. Their captors, who had stood patiently waiting during this exchange, picked up the pace and within minutes they were surrounded by a group of chattering children, darting back and forth and giggling.

'This must be it,' Jed murmured, and moments later they were in a clearing in the forest. A few large huts clustered around the fringes under the shade of the canopy, simple huts roofed with leaves of some sort, capable of sleeping several families.

The families themselves were standing round, studying them, their bodies all smeared with ash like their captors', and then into the throng came a white woman Gabby had never met.

'Jed—oh, thank God!' she wept, and threw herself at him.

He hugged her, a little awkwardly because of the shackle that still tied him to Gabby, and then eased her away. 'How are you, Sue?'

'Sick as a pig but that's just because of the baby. Derek's awful—I don't suppose by a miracle you've got any insulin?'

He nodded, and Sue's eyes closed with relief. 'Thank God—he's almost in a coma, Jed. Come on...'

She started to drag him forward, and together they were herded into one of the huts. They had to climb a ladder to reach the entrance. Once inside it was gloomy and Gabby had to blink and screw up her eyes to see.

What she saw did nothing for her. Derek was pale and sweating, his eyes sunken in his grey and slightly stubbled face, and his breath was an instant give-away.

'Pear drops—his blood sugar must be sky high,' Gabby mumbled, and Jed nodded. Kneeling down beside the sick man, Jed untied the vine from his wrist to free Gabby, told her to stay close and quickly examined him.

'Has he been vomiting?'

'Yes.'

'Drowsy?'

'Yes—and slurred speech. He sounds drunk—well, he did. He hasn't spoken for an hour or so, but I don't think he's in a coma. I can rouse him still, just about,' Sue told them.

Jed passed Gabby the bag of goodies and asked her

to pull up a very high dose of insulin, about twice or three times the normal amount. This was to deal with the high level of blood sugar that was causing Derek's symptoms and would push him before long, if Gabby wasn't mistaken, into a coma.

She'd seen diabetic comas, both hypo- and hyperglycaemic, and knew exactly what to do. It was a good job she did because she was definitely on autopilot.

She drew up the insulin and looked at what Jed was doing. Her eyes widened when she saw the dark green-blue of the testing stick on which he had put a drop of Derek's blood.

'That's dark.'

'Almost black. It's well off the scale, which goes up to 44. Normal should be about 8. That's what I'm aiming for in the next twenty-four hours. Got that insulin ready?'

She handed him the syringe and watched as he injected it. 'There—he should be feeling better in an hour or so, and within twenty-four hours he should be fine.'

He looked up. 'What about the rest of you?'

The three Indonesian engineers were sitting around on the other side of Derek, watching Jed anxiously. At his question one proffered a foot with a nasty cut on the ankle, but that was the only problem. Jed cleaned it and squirted it with antibiotic spray, gave him an injection of antibiotics and dished out anti-malarials to everyone. Then finally, when everyone had been seen to, he turned to Sue.

'We need to wash and have some food—how strictly are you guarded?'

She gave a hollow laugh. 'Guarded? Where would we go?' She scrambled to her feet. 'Come with me, I'll show you where you can wash—have you got any clean clothes?'

He shook his head. 'No. Nothing except the drugs, by a miracle. I was just getting them ready in case I got a chance to get them up to you somehow, and we'd just collected the last few things from the compound. They took us from the power-station site—and I've got something to tell you about that, as well, after we've washed. I don't suppose you could rustle up some food?'

'Sure. It might be a little strange but none of us have been sick yet. They seem to be taking good care of us. They've almost been hospitable, crazy though it seems. I don't think they want to harm us.'

'No. I don't think they do—I think that's why they came for me. They must have been waiting at the compound and followed us on foot.'

'They knew Derek was sick right from the start. He grabbed what insulin he could, but of course there wasn't enough up at the compound and it ran out yesterday morning. They seemed to understand he was ill, and we saw the men who brought you leaving the village by the path we'd come on. They might have had time to get down there before dark.'

Jed nodded. 'Makes sense. Without us they would have made better time, and downhill as well would have been easier.'

Gabby wasn't sure about that. She almost fell down the ladder she was so tired, but the sight of a clear pool in the rocks at the foot of a long sloping waterfall was enough to wake her up. 'Let me in,' she mumbled, and, pulling off her shoes, she walked straight into the water without stopping.

It was freezing on her hot skin, but the pain of her scratches and bites faded instantly and she lay back in the water with a sigh of relief and shut her eyes.

'Wow,' Jed murmured from beside her, and disappeared under the water for endless seconds. He came up just when she was starting to panic, shooting up through the surface and shaking his head like a dog, sending water droplets flying.

Then he grinned, and he looked as fresh as a daisy.

She wanted to kill him.

She also wanted another bathroom stop, but she thought she might wait and ask Sue about that. She sluiced her hair again, squeezed the water out of it and then wondered what to do about her dripping clothes.

'Take them off and wring them out, then put them back on. They'll soon dry and they'll keep you cool.'

She gave him a sideways glance and saw he was following his own advice, standing on the rocks at the edge of the pool in a pair of skimpy briefs, looking more delicious than he had any right to look after the day they'd just gone through.

She pulled herself out of the water, peeled off the sodden clothes and squeezed them out and then, after her skin had stopped streaming, she went to put them on again.

'Hang on.'

Jed's hands touched her gently, turning her this way and that in the soft green light, and he shook his head. 'You're a mess—why didn't you say how bad the scratches were?'

She shrugged, standing there in her soggy undies, all but naked. 'What would you have done—admitted me to hospital? It wouldn't have made any difference.'

He looked at her and through her bleary haze she thought she saw respect in his eyes. 'Come on,' he said gently, and helped her into her clothes. He had scratches and bites too, she noticed as she returned the favour. He hadn't said anything either. She promised herself she'd put some cream on them once they were back at the hut.

Sue was waiting for them. She showed them what

passed for a bathroom, then on their return greeted them with some food—vegetables baked in leaves, boiled rice and some sauce, which Gabby avoided because it smelt so strongly of chilli she thought it would finish her off.

The meal was strange but palatable, and as they ate it darkness fell. The temperature fell with it, dropping sharply up here in the hills as it didn't nearer the coast. She remembered climbing Ben Nevis once and being astonished at the temperature difference. Somehow in the tropics she just hadn't expected it.

Someone lit a candle, a makeshift affair that smelt vile but probably kept the mosquitoes out. By its meagre light Jed told the others about the grave trees they had found. The Indonesians particularly were very excited at this.

'I think it must be the reason they want us to stop,' Luther said. 'They have been chanting and the priest has been wearing ceremonial robes and dancing and they sacrificed a pig today. I think they are using their strongest magic.'

'All we need to do is tell the others,' Sue said. 'Got any bright ideas?'

Jed grinned and, like a conjurer pulling a rabbit out of a hat, he produced a thing like a mobile phone from the bottom of the flight bag.

'The Magellan GCS! Jed, you're wonderful!' Sue cried.

'What?' Gabby asked, confused. 'Surely a mobile phone won't work.'

'No, it won't—but this will. It's a global communications system, and I can send an e-mail to anywhere in the world, telling them where we are and what's going on. All I have to do is remember the e-mail number—and that's the problem. I can't. The only one I can remember is my own, and I don't know if anyone will check my e-mail at work, or how often. My secretary might, but perhaps not for a day or two. Still, it's the best chance we've got.'

He keyed in a few brief words about the grave trees, their reunion with the other hostages and their state of health, and sent the message winging on its way, before shutting the machine down. 'I must keep the batteries going as long as possible—we have no idea how long we'll be here,' he told them all. 'If I remember a more relevant number I'll try sending our whereabouts to that.'

'Our whereabouts?' Gabby said with a laugh. 'A jungle hut in the middle of God knows where? How precise.'

'It is. It's a satellite GPS—a global positioning system. It tells them where we are to within fifteen metres.'

Gabby's jaw dropped. 'It's that precise, and you've just done it? Just like that?'

He nodded.

'So they might come and rescue us?'

He looked thoughtful.

'Well? Will they?' she pressed.

'Yes—when the message is picked up. And that's the problem. I don't know when the message will be picked up, or even if it will. I'm sorry.'

'Doesn't it have a memory for addresses?' Sue asked.

'Yes—but I haven't got round to programming them in yet. I've only had it a few days.'

Sue's face fell. 'It isn't Derek's?'

Jed shook his head, and she dropped her face into her hands for a moment. When she straightened she looked calm but tired. 'I suppose we'll just have to wait, then,' she said pragmatically. 'It can't take for ever. How much insulin did you bring?'

'Enough for two weeks.'

Sue perked up immediately. 'Well, it won't be that long, will it?' she said more brightly, and then turned to Derek. 'How are you?' she asked him.

'Horrible—I need Jed.'

'Jed's here—he's brought his Magellan. We're going to be all right, Derek. They'll find us soon. It's OK, love, we're going to be all right.'

Gabby, hearing the optimism in the other woman's voice, felt a cold shiver of fear run over her. Perhaps it was her still-damp clothes, or perhaps the fact that two weeks wasn't really all that long in the great scheme of things. If the e-mail didn't get picked up—

'OK?'

Jed's voice was soft and right beside her, and she looked up at him and tried to smile.

'I'll be better once I've got some cream on these scratches and I can go to sleep,' she told him.

'Easily done. I gather we're all sleeping here together in this hut. The men are together in one part, then Sue and Derek, and we get the last bit. We'll stick to the myth that we're married—you'll be safer that way.'

'Definitely,' Sue assured them. 'They might not want to do us any harm, but there are plenty of healthy young men here who would be fascinated to sleep with a white woman. I think telling them you're married is an excellent idea.'

Gabby yawned and Jed unfolded himself and stood up, then pulled her to her feet. 'We'll go and settle down now. See you in the morning. Call me if you're worried about Derek—I've given him another shot of insulin and his blood sugar level's falling steadily. I think he'll be all right soon.'

They padded along the little corridor to the room at the end, a small area screened off by a beaten bark curtain over the doorway, and in the middle of the floor was a heap of bedding—rush mats, sarongs and a couple of woven rugs.

They sorted out the beds and Gabby took off her outer clothes, pulled on the sarong she'd been left and fastened it. Then Jed, as much by touch as by sight, spread cream over her lacerated arms and legs, and around her wrist where the vine had cut in during the day.

'You're a mess,' he said huskily, and she remembered the sun cream. It seemed weeks ago—months. In fact, it had been only forty-eight hours earlier. She was exhausted, she had aches where she hadn't known she had muscles, and yet at his touch her body seemed to find another life.

She felt the pain ebbing, the aches soothing, and a mellow warmth seeped through her. She lay bonelessly, letting him move her arms and legs around, rolling onto her front when he prodded her, and all she could think about was the feel of his hand on her skin.

All too soon he stopped, and she rolled over and looked up at him in the darkness. A candle was burning in the little passage outside, and in its dim light she could make out his shadowed features. She reached up a hand and cupped his cheek.

'Thanks,' she murmured languorously.

He capped the tube and turned away. 'You're welcome.'

'How about you?'

He made a choked sound and looked back at her over his shoulder. 'How about me?'

'Want me to do your scratches?'

He looked at her for endless moments, before turning away. 'I'll do them. You rest.'

She lay and watched him, then took the tube and did his shoulders and back, anyway, where the occasional particularly determined vine had coiled round him. His skin was hot, like damp silk, and she had to struggle to resist the urge to lay her lips against it—

'That'll do,' he muttered, and his voice sounded slightly strangled.

She lay back and watched as he got ready for bed, then lay down beside her. The noises of the jungle seemed incredibly loud and close, and they could hear the shufflings and soft snores of the others on the other side of the wall.

He turned his head towards her. 'You did well today, Gabby,' he said quietly. 'Well done.'

'What about you? You must have been exhausted when we arrived, but you dealt with Derek straight away.'

He laughed softly. 'I didn't think Derek had time to wait while we freshened up—and, anyway, you helped.'

'Only a bit. I don't think I could have walked any further, though,' she told him.

'No, nor me. Good job we didn't have to.' His hand reached out and squeezed her shoulder. ''Night,' he said softly.

'Goodnight.' She turned on her side to face him, but she didn't sleep. Tired as she was, too much had happened for her to relax. She lay for ages, then she thought she heard him sigh.

'Jed?' she whispered.

'Mmm?'

'I can't sleep.'

'I can't sleep either,' he murmured. 'Too much to think about.'

The candle had gone out, and in the darkness the noises all seemed louder. Knowing the others were close by was strangely comforting, but she still felt very alone. She wriggled a little closer to Jed. It was chilly now,

and she wished she'd got something a little thicker than
the mat and a sarong and little woven rug to cover her.

'Penny will be worried sick,' she said.

'If she knows. She might have thought you'd changed
your mind, and gone without you. Jon and Bill will be
worrying, though, and I expect the chief of police will
put another dozy security guard on the case, for all the
good it'll do.'

Gabby thought back to their capture and the appear-
ance of the men in the clearing by the Jeep. 'I wonder
how they knew who you were and where to find you?'

'They have their contacts, I expect—Jamal's exile
friend for one. Anyway, it's a good job they did. Without
medical help for Derek, he would have been dead in
twenty-four hours. I expect they realised how sick he
was and couldn't afford to risk him dying. Anyway, as
Sue said, they don't seem to mean us any harm.'

Gabby gave a hollow laugh. 'I wish I had your confidence. My legs and arms certainly feel harmed, and my
feet are killing me.'

He laughed gently at her, then reached out a hand.
'Are you warm enough?'

'Not really.'

'Nor am I. Come over here and warm up.'

She hesitated for a nanosecond—certainly not long
enough for decency—and then shuffled across the mats
to his side. He pulled her light covering across them
both, tucked her bottom into his lap and draped an arm
round her waist. 'Better?' he murmured.

'Mmm.' She snuggled closer, comforted by the solid
warmth of his body at her back, and fell instantly asleep.

CHAPTER SIX

GABBY woke to find her head cradled on Jed's shoulder, her hair spread across his chest and cramp in her foot.

'Ow,' she moaned, and he pitched her off him and sat bolt upright.

'Wha—?'

She flapped a hand at him to shush him. 'Nothing exciting,' she whispered. 'I've got cramp.' She folded over and grabbed the offending foot, and Jed took it from her and stretched the toes up towards her knee, straightening her leg and pulling the muscles tight in her arch. Then he dug his thumb into the offending muscle and she wailed softly.

Pig that he was, he laughed at her, a kindly laugh but a laugh for all that. She decided he needed punishing so she put her foot in the middle of his chest and pushed.

Unfortunately he still had hold of her foot so he didn't fall. Instead a dangerous glint appeared in his eyes and he dodged her foot and sprawled across her, pinning her to the floor, his stubbled face hovering just inches from hers.

'Want to play games, do you?' he asked softly, and there was a curious rasp to his voice that did crazy things to her nerves.

She couldn't move, couldn't speak, couldn't do anything. She was trapped, pinned down as much by the look in his eyes as by his arms. Against her leg she felt his body stir, coming to life in response to her closeness, and with a tiny moan she closed her eyes and accepted his kiss. His beard scraped her face softly, sensitising her skin further, making her forget common sense.

Her sarong had ridden up around her hips and he shifted, one hard-muscled thigh nudging between her legs and settling against the ache that was growing with every touch of his lips on hers. She was conscious of the coarse, wiry hair against the tender skin of her thighs, the contrast of his hard, masculine frame aligned with her softer, more yielding body.

He shifted so he could gain access to her breasts, tugging the sarong down and closing one large, hard hand over her softness. She had never felt so much a woman, or been touched by so much a man. She arched against him, against that thigh that chafed with such devastating accuracy against her, and as she did so the cramp that had woken her returned with interest.

She wrenched her mouth from his with a yelp and reached for her foot, and he rolled away and took it from her, stretching and kneading it again in a strained silence broken only by their ragged breathing.

Finally, when the knot had dissolved and her foot was relaxed again, he set it down with great care and looked at her.

His eyes were smouldering, and she was suddenly aware of the sarong rucked up around her waist, the top unfastened to expose the soft swell of her breasts...

She covered herself hastily and sat up, pushing the hair out of her eyes, and saw him withdraw into himself.

'Saved by the bell, eh?' he murmured softly.

He stood up and turned away from her, but not before she'd seen that he was still aroused. His briefs hid nothing, and the ache returned, slamming into her so hard that she had to bite back the moan that rose in her throat.

He pulled on his clothes, slid his feet into his shoes

and went out, leaving her sitting there in the midst of their bedding, frustration her only companion.

She could hear the others moving about, and next door through the thin bamboo wall she could hear Jed murmuring to Derek and Sue.

Had they heard everything? Oh, Lord. She buried her face in her hands and sighed. Why had she tried to push him over? When would she learn not to bait the tiger?

She scrambled to her feet, pulled on her clothes and dragged her fingers through her hair. Then, on the principle of getting unpleasant things over and out of the way, she went along the hut to the end where Sue and Derek were sitting, staring out of the doorway.

'How's the patient?' she asked brightly, avoiding Jed's eyes.

'Which one?' Sue said weakly. 'Derek's better but any second now I'm going to throw up.'

'No, you're not,' Jed said reassuringly. 'Come on, have some fruit. That'll stay down.'

Gabby saw they had fruit and cold rice and bamboo tubes filled with coconut milk set out on the floor in front of them. As they settled down to eat, Sue eyed the food with horror and then covered her mouth.

She leapt to her feet and ran, threw herself down the ladder and fell to her knees in the dirt, retching helplessly.

'Ginger,' Jed said, standing with Gabby in the doorway of the hut and regarding the poor woman dispassionately, a banana skin dangling from his fingers.

'Ginger?' Gabby repeated.

'Mmm. Good anti-emetic. It's used a lot now for travel sickness. I wonder if we can get any—would you like to ask the women? They might know.'

She stared at his retreating back. Ask the women. Just like that. No language barrier, of course!

She went down the ladder to Sue, put a comforting arm round her shoulders and helped her back to her bed, then went out into the village again. A pregnant woman was sitting with her back propped against the stilts of her house, pounding something in a coconut shell.

She was beautiful, her black hair long and lustrous, her flawless skin a deep golden brown. She was wearing only a loosely woven skirt, slung around her hips under the prominent swelling of her baby, and Gabby approached her with a cautious smile.

The woman put down her makeshift pestle and mortar and smiled back at Gabby, then pointed to the place where Sue had been sick and said something unintelligible.

Gabby made a cradle with her arms to show it was pregnancy sickness, wondering as she did so if these very healthy-looking people actually had such a thing.

Evidently they did. The woman smiled and nodded, then beckoned to Gabby and led her into the hut. She gestured to her to wait in the first room, went off and came back a few minutes later with a gnarled piece of root.

She indicated that Sue should chew it, and handed it to Gabby. She remembered to take it with her right hand, thanked her with a bow and smile and went back to Jed. 'A pregnant woman gave me this when I explained the problem. Do you suppose it's ginger? It looks a bit like it.'

He frowned at it, turned it this way and that and tried to break it, but it was too tough and fibrous. One of the Indonesian engineers pulled out a penknife and Jed cut into the root and sniffed, then chewed the little piece he'd removed.

'Hmm. It tastes a little different, but it's very similar.

It might be a wild form. Did she understand? I mean, it's not an abortifacient, I hope?'

Gabby shook her head. 'No, I'm sure it's not. Hang on.'

She took the root back and returned to the woman, who was pounding again. She held it out and pointed back to the hut, then pointed to her stomach and mimed retching. The woman nodded happily. Then Gabby pointed to her stomach, cradled her arms again and made a flushing away gesture with her hands to indicate losing the baby. The woman shook her head vigorously and started to talk nineteen to the dozen, miming chewing and pointing to her own distended abdomen.

Gabby nodded, sure she was now understood, and went back to the others. 'She got very agitated when I mimed losing the baby, and indicated that she'd taken it. I'm sure it's just to stop the sickness.'

'I think we could risk it, then,' Jed said slowly, and Sue waved a hand at him.

'In which case, for God's sake let's do it. I can't cope with this,' Sue muttered, and Jed cut her off a small piece and handed it to her.

After a few minutes she sighed with relief and lay down again. 'Thank God,' she said fervently.

'Better?' Jed asked.

'Much.'

'So much for drug trials,' Gabby said with a laugh. 'I'll go and thank our friend.'

The woman had finished her pounding and was sitting with a wicked-looking *parang* and chopping up strange oval fruit of some kind, prickly and olive-green. She beckoned to Gabby and patted the ground beside her.

It was cool and shady, the house behind casting a shadow just wide enough to sit in. Gabby smiled and sat down cross-legged next to her new friend and inspected the food she was preparing.

The green things looked like aubergines inside, and Gabby thought they might be jackfruit. Whatever they were, they were all cut up and put in a huge iron pot. The woman moved on to slice some lengths of what looked like young bamboo, and then some other things, the identity of which Gabby couldn't even begin to guess at. She imagined it was all edible, provided too many of those bright little chillies didn't end up in the dish!

Garlic she recognised, going into the pot with the other ingredients, and then the pot was set on some hot embers and given a stir, and the paste that had been pounded earlier was scraped into the pot. Water from a jug was poured over the top, and Gabby reckoned she'd seen her first native Indonesian vegetable stew created.

The girl then sat back on her heels, grinned at Gabby and said, '*Makan*.'

At last! An Indonesian word she had heard before! She smiled and nodded, then pointed to herself. 'Gabby,' she said. Jed was wandering across the open area and she beckoned him over. 'Jed,' she said, pointing to him, then to herself, 'Gabby.'

The girl smiled and pointed to herself. 'Gabby,' she repeated.

Gabby shook her head. 'No.' She pointed to her breasts, then to the girl's, and said, 'Woman.' Then she pointed to Jed in the region of his shorts, and said, 'Man.'

The girl giggled deliciously and covered her face with her hands. Then Gabby did the Gabby and Jed routine again, and the penny dropped.

She pointed to Gabby and repeated her name, then to Jed and repeated his, then to herself. 'Hari,' she said.

Gabby felt a grin almost split her face. 'Hari,' she

repeated, pointing at the girl, and laughed with delight. Such a simple accomplishment, to learn someone's name, but what an achievement.

She almost forgot that the girl's tribe was responsible for her capture. She pointed to the bubbling cook-pot, repeated, '*Makan*,' and turned to Jed. 'I'm learning,' she said with a grin.

His smile was indulgent. He took her arm and drew her gently to her feet, then bowed at Hari and led Gabby away from the village to the bathing pool.

'Do I smell or something?' she asked with a grin, still ridiculously pleased with herself.

He returned her grin. 'No worse than me. I wanted to talk to you out of range of the others.' He stripped off to his briefs, slid into the chilly water and beckoned to her. 'Come on, then.'

She did, only because the water looked so inviting and not because he said so. She pulled off her shoes, shirt and trousers and went into the water in her underwear. To hell with modesty—she was steaming.

'What did you want to talk to me about?' she said, once she'd got her breath back from the shock of the water.

'I want to get Derek stable, then I think we need to get him out of here. I have no idea when my e-mail will get picked up or even if it will. I'm relying on my secretary to use her initiative. She usually does, but I don't want to take her for granted. I've been sending her research results by e-mail so she may be on the lookout, but I have a horrible sinking feeling she has a week's holiday some time now.'

Gabby rolled her eyes. 'Great. Isn't there anyone else?'

He gave a shrug. 'Not offhand. I don't suppose you know anyone's e-mail number?'

'By heart?' She shook her head. 'No. I've tried, but I can't think of anyone. I'm not really a computery sort of person.'

He tutted at her and she poked her tongue out at him and lay back in the water. 'Just imagine, these people live here without any of these so-called necessities, eking out their simple existence by gathering food from the forest—'

'Nature's bountiful harvest?' Jed said with a little snort. 'They're riddled with parasites, plagued by malaria and filariasis, dysentery and malnutrition. They have no health service, no surgery, no antenatal care, dentists don't exist—'

'But if they don't eat refined sugars they probably don't need dentists,' Gabby reasoned. 'And, anyway, it's probably better than dying of stress-related illnesses like we do in the West. I'm sure they have all sorts of herbal remedies that are very effective—probably some of them even more effective than the ones we've come to rely on. You can bet your life no Indonesian village in the mountains is plagued by the MRSA bug!'

He laughed. 'You're just an optimist. You wait till you get sick and see what you want, western medicine or Indonesian *jamu*.'

She sobered, thinking of Derek for whom the Indonesians would have no treatment. 'How's Derek's blood sugar?' she asked.

'Coming down. It's still a little high, but I want to get the last bit down gradually. He's all right now, just a little queasy, but that's natural. I've given him some of Hari's ginger, too. It seemed to help a little.' He climbed out of the pool and sat on the rocks by the side, dripping all over the stone and giving Gabby altogether too much to look at.

'I want to have a meeting with the priest,' he was

saying. 'He seems to be the doctor as well, and I might be able to impress on him the need to have us released. I also want to tell them about the grave trees and ask if they're the reason, but without language it's a little tricky. I don't suppose you can draw?'

'Me?' She shrugged. 'A little—but do we have any paper?'

'Derek brought some, and a pen. We could try drawing the lake and the trees, and see if we get a reaction—'

Something flew low over his head and he ducked, flinging his arms up instinctively and losing his balance so he fell back into the water. When he came up Gabby was laughing. 'Well, that certainly got a reaction,' she choked.

He was at her side in two lazy strokes, and pushed her under the water. She came up spluttering and fighting, her fists connecting with his chest and her legs tangling with his, so that she could feel—

'Oh,' she said softly, her eyes widening with surprise.

He stared into her eyes for an age, then his head lowered and his mouth brushed hers. 'Gabby, I want you,' he said softly, 'but it isn't going to happen. There's too much else going on—we need to keep our heads clear.'

She pushed away from him, treading water while their eyes locked, and then with a sigh she turned and swam to the edge and climbed out. 'Fine,' she said in a choked voice. 'Just stop getting me alone and winding me up and it'll be easy.'

She pulled on her clothes and left him there in the water, cooling off. Do him good. Who did he think he was talking to? So he wanted her, did he?

And she wanted him. She bit back a little moan of frustration and stomped back towards the clearing. She saw a shadow above her, and ducked from another of the swooping whatevers, glanced over her shoulder and then suppressed a shriek.

A bat nearly two feet across?

She headed back to the hut almost at a run, and went up the ladder and into the relative sanctuary of the dimly lit interior like a rat out of a trap.

'Hi, folks!' she said brightly, and plopped down on a heap of folded bedding near Derek. He was lounging against a post, looking better than he had at breakfast and infinitely more human than he had the night before, and she considered again the miracle of modern medicine while her heart settled down again.

'How are you feeling?' she asked him, sure of what the answer would be.

He smiled wanly. 'Almost back to normal, thanks to you two. I'm sorry you got dragged into this mess.'

Gabby grinned. 'Actually, daft though it might seem, I'm almost enjoying myself. It's an opportunity to see an untouched culture and get to know a genuinely friendly people—'

'Very friendly,' Jed said drily, entering the hut behind her. 'So friendly they insist on you coming to stay with them.'

She swivelled round and fixed him with a look. 'We want to desecrate the graves of their children,' she said very slowly and clearly. 'I think they have a right to be a little bit antsy about it!'

'There are ways of communicating—'

'By e-mail?' she said sweetly. 'Anyway, talking of communication, I thought you were going to have a chat to the doctor-priest fellow.'

'I am. I want you to come too. Let's scrounge up some paper and go to it.'

She got reluctantly to her feet and did as he suggested, then they went out and stood at the bottom of the ladder and looked around. 'OK, so which one is he?' Gabby asked.

Jed shrugged. 'Let's ask your friend, Hari.'

She was busy parcelling up little pieces of some indeterminate meat in leaves and burying them in the ashes around the pot as they approached her. She sat back on her heels and gave them her lovely smile.

'Gabby,' she said.

Gabby smiled. 'Hello, Hari.' She squatted down beside the woman and waved a questioning hand at the village. 'Doctor?' she said hopefully.

Hari looked puzzled so Jed crouched down too and pointed at himself. 'Jed, doctor,' he told her. '*Obat—jamu—dukun.*'

'*Dukun!*' Hari exclaimed, and broke into a torrent of her unintelligible native tongue.

'What's a *dukun*?' Gabby asked Jed.

'An Indonesian folk-doctor—like a sort of witch-doctor with an amazing battery of natural remedies. Some of them are quacks, but some are fantastic. Your friend seems to be getting very excited so we might be in luck.'

'Hari, is there a *dukun*?' Gabby asked, pointing round the village.

She scrambled to her feet, wiped her hands on her skirt and led them over to a hut. Gesturing to them to wait, she approached a gnarled old man sitting in the shade under the ladder, fanning himself with a huge leaf.

She spoke to him rapidly, waving at Gabby and Jed, and then the old man stood up and drew himself to his full height.

He reached almost to Gabby's chin, and he was dressed like all the other men in a hammered bark loin-cloth and tattoos. He had a gleaming white bone through his nose and ash over his dark, withered skin, and he looked ancient. His eyes, however, were like polished conkers, bright and lively and incongruous in so lined and venerable a face.

He looked only at Jed, giving Gabby a cursory once-over and dismissing her. Taking Jed's arm, he led him under the hut into the shade and they sat down cross-legged. Gabby, standing in the full sun, began to wonder about the natural order of things that dictated that women toiled in the sun while men sat in the shade, smoked their evil clove cigarettes and drank out of tubes of bamboo.

Perhaps there were things about this wonderful and untouched culture that weren't quite perfect!

Jed caught her eye and winked, and she smiled sweetly and stood there until he beckoned her.

'Draw the lake and the trees for him. I've tried and I can't do it well enough. I don't think they're exposed enough to 2-D images to understand.'

She tried not to smile at his efforts. Art was obviously not his forte, but one couldn't be good at everything and he was a hell of a kisser...

She dragged her mind back to the subject at hand and thought for a moment, then tried to recreate the scene from memory. As she drew the trees and put the squares on the trunks the old man seemed to become very agitated, and when she drew a baby and pointed from the baby to the tree he nodded vigorously.

Then she drew the trees cut down and lying on their sides and a building in their place, and he got very angry and started to mutter and chant.

Gabby touched his arm gently, took the page and screwed it up then put it into Hari's fire. When she returned he was looking puzzled. She drew the scene again, extended the river and drew the power station at a different site. She didn't know where she'd drawn it, and just hoped it wasn't on the site of some other burial ground or sacred spot.

Obviously it wasn't. He stared at the paper for a long while, turned it this way and that and then took the paper, folded it and tucked it into his loincloth. He turned away, and Hari touched them on the arm and beckoned them away, indicating that their audience was over.

'I suppose that means he's going to think about it,' Jed said drily as they walked back to their hut.

'He'll probably do what an Anglican priest would do and pray over it, only I expect he'll sacrifice something and wait for the gods to tell him the way forward. Not so very different.'

'At least he seemed to understand the drawing.'

'By a miracle. I thought he was going to have us killed when I cut the trees down and put the power station there.'

Jed laughed softly. 'You and me both. That might have been a little rash.'

'It told us what we needed to know, though. It *is* the trees that are the problem. I should add an addendum to your e-mail.'

'For all the good it'll do us.' He sighed and sat down in the shade near the hut. 'I wonder what's for lunch? It seems a long time since we had that fruit for breakfast.'

'I wonder what the meat was in those parcels?' she said speculatively.

'Don't ask,' Jed advised sagely. 'Probably bat or monkey.'

She shuddered. 'Just as long as it isn't snake or frogs, I don't care.'

He laughed. 'I remember listening to a radio programme about some scientists who were taken hostage on Irian Jaya. They said that rat was tough, pig was fatty but the frogs were delicious.'

Gabby gave him a sceptical look, firmly unconvinced. 'How many of them died?' she asked drily.

'None from food poisoning. I think if the natives eat it we can assume it's safe for us to, but we need to boil water for teeth and drinking unless we stick to coconut milk and *tuak*. Rather nice stuff, that. The *dukun* gave me some.'

'I saw you drinking away with him,' she sniped, remembering being left out in the sun. 'Was it nice and cool?'

'What's the matter—didn't you like standing in the background, being servile?'

She threw a bit of twig at him and laughed. 'Tell me about this *tuak*. What is it?'

'Palm wine. They tap the sap from a palm tree and pour it into lengths of bamboo and seal it for a day or so. It ferments naturally and gives a lovely warm glow.' He grinned. 'A sort of naturally occurring gin and tonic without the quinine.'

'No doubt you'll have to research it heavily,' she said innocently.

'Oh, of course. Perhaps you can persuade your friend, Hari, to show you how to make it for me as befits your station. After all, you are supposed to be my wife.'

She snorted. 'Don't hold your breath. My acting skills aren't that brilliant.' She doodled in the sand. 'So, anyway, now they know we know about the trees, do you think they'll let us go?'

He shrugged. 'Depends on what the gods tell our friend, I guess. Maybe, maybe not. We'll have to play it by ear. I wouldn't hold your breath, though, we could still be here for weeks. What we need, of course,' he continued after a pause, 'is an interpreter—some way of communicating with them. We could also do with having a chance to talk to Bill about the possibility of re-siting the power station.'

'I wouldn't have thought he could refuse—not with seven lives at stake,' Gabby pointed out, but Jed shrugged again.

'The Indonesian government gave him consent and passed all the plans. He's got permission for his holiday resort because he was going to provide free electricity to Telok Panjang. At the moment it struggles on kerosene and the odd generator, and the government obviously thought it were getting a good deal. They may decide to throw their weight behind Bill and send troops in to deal with this little insurrection.'

'And we'll all get caught in the crossfire. Great.' Gabby stood up. 'I want to go for a walk around the village.'

'To see if you can find a way out?' Jed said wryly.

'Oh, yeah. Absolutely.'

He stood up and brushed the dirt off his trousers. 'I'll come. Your friend still seems to be watching you so I'd be careful about being alone anywhere too isolated.'

They wandered down to the mountain pool where they had swum that morning and turned left, following the river downhill for a while. There was a path which was quite well used, and it crossed others, a veritable network of tracks and trails that criss-crossed the area around the village.

They wove through them, keeping an ear out all the time for the sounds of children playing and making sure they didn't go too far.

Not that it would have mattered. They were followed at a discreet distance by a gang of little children, tittering and squeaking like a litter of baby mice. They pretended to ignore them, and looked around at the forest.

One tree caught Gabby's attention because of its strange structure. It had a network of stems stretching up in a circle around a hollow core, as if the tree had grown up like a fungus from a ring of roots, and the children were playing hide and seek inside it.

'It's a strangler fig,' Jed told her. 'They germinate halfway up one of the forest trees, send down aerial roots to the soil and then continue to grow upwards. Eventually they link up with each other in a band and strangle the host tree, which dies and rots down to provide nourishment for the growing fig trees. It's probably several trees, not just one. Look, there are figs on it.'

There were, but she shunned them, mindful of the effect they might have. They continued on their way, circling the village until they were almost back, then suddenly the children vanished and an eerie silence descended.

A chill ran over Gabby, and she moved instinctively closer to Jed. 'Everything's gone quiet,' she whispered. 'Even the monkeys are quiet.'

He pointed ahead of them at a tree, and there in the trunk she saw a number of neat, square patches on the bark. Most had started to heal but there was one, though, that was unhealed, indicating a grave tree in current use and, judging by the look of it, used very recently.

She closed her eyes and a tear slipped out. 'Oh, Jed,' she said and, turning, she buried her head in his chest and sobbed.

'Hey, softy, it's a fact of life,' he told her gently.

'I know,' she mumbled, wiping her eyes on his soggy shirtfront. 'I'm just being silly. It's because they're babies, and there seem to be so many little holes for so few people. They must lose their babies all the time.'

'Perhaps that's why the children that are still alive are

strong and healthy—perhaps nature sorts them out early
so that only the really tough ones make it.'

She sniffed and straightened up. 'Don't be logical,'
she told him, and with a last lingering look at the quiet
glade with its sad little secrets she turned away and carried on with her walk.

Jed fell into step beside her. 'If you get so emotional
and weepy about a few babies you've never met, how
on earth do you cope with losing a child you've nursed?'

She gave a humourless grunt of laughter. 'Badly,' she
told him with characteristic honesty. 'Usually I fall apart
afterwards, but I have been known to cry at the time
more often than I care to remember.'

'How did I know that?' he murmured and, slinging
his arm around her shoulders, he gave her a quick
squeeze. 'Come on, my stomach tells me it must be
lunchtime. Let's go and find out what that meat was that
Hari was putting in the fire.'

'If it's fruit bat I'm not eating it,' she warned, and he
laughed.

'You could get awfully thin in the next few days.'

'So be it,' she said firmly. 'But I'm not eating bats
for anybody!'

They walked back into the clearing arm in arm and
laughing, to find two men on their knees in the middle
of the open ground. A cluster of what looked like village
elders stood around them with spears pointing menacingly at them, and at their head was the *dukun* in full
ceremonial dress, chanting tunelessly.

'Damn,' Jed said softly.

'What?'

'It's Jamal and his friend Johannis, the man who's an
outcast from this village.'

'Isn't that good?'

Jed looked from the group to her and back to the

group. 'I somehow don't think so,' he said softly. 'I think, if they aren't about to kill them, we've just got ourselves two more fellow-hostages.'

And with that he strode into the middle of the group of men, stood in front of the *dukun* and began, so Gabby imagined, to intercede.

CHAPTER SEVEN

'HE's off his trolley,' Sue said quietly, appearing at Gabby's elbow. 'Come into the hut out of the way—it could get nasty.'

Gabby needed no second bidding. She'd always thought Jed was a bit of an Indiana Jones, but surely he didn't have to take it quite so seriously? She followed Sue up the ladder and sat, watching anxiously from just inside the doorway through a crack in the bark-covered wall.

Jamal and his friend stayed where they were, but she noticed that Jed was speaking to the other man, who was in turn speaking to the *dukun* and relaying messages back.

The conversation was inaudible, but after a moment the *dukun* waved away the men with their spears and told Jamal and Johannis to get up. They were then led to a hut and thrown in, and a guard was posted outside the door.

Then the *dukun* waved his spear at Hari, who was standing on the fringe, and went back to his shady spot under his hut. The elders with their spears stood, looking disgruntled, for a moment, then turned away and shuffled back to their business, and Jed was left standing there in the middle alone.

After a second they saw him shrug and make his way towards them. Hari was serving food to the *dukun*, and nobody seemed to make any attempt to stop Jed. Within seconds he was up the ladder and they all pounced on him.

'Well?' Sue said impatiently. 'Are there others behind them? Are we going to be rescued?'

Jed sighed and shook his head. 'No. The elders were going to kill them, but I managed to persuade the *dukun* to spare them so we can use them as interpreters to negotiate between us and the tribe and the Indonesian government and Bill. I said it would be a terrible tragedy if they were unable to communicate their concerns and the trees were destroyed, without proper respect being shown for the burial site.'

'Crafty thing,' Derek said with a chuckle. 'I thought you'd had your chips, Jed. I thought for sure you were going to bite the dust back there.'

Jed gave a quirky little grin. '*You* thought that? How do you think *I* felt!'

Hari appeared in the doorway with a huge wooden platter laden with food, and passed it in to them. She gave Gabby a shy smile, bobbed her head at Jed as if he were some kind of spirit and backed away again.

'Great,' he said, reaching for one of the charred little leaf parcels they had seen being put on the fire. 'Let's see if it's rat or bat.'

Sue groaned, turned away and reached for another little piece of the ginger root. 'Jed, you are foul,' she muttered and, turning her back on them all, she chewed her way back to equilibrium.

If Gabby had thought the arrival of Jamal and Johannis signalled a change in their circumstances she was wrong. The days seemed to drag by with more of the same nothingness, and after a week everyone was getting crabby and difficult.

Every night Jed checked the Magellan instrument to see if he'd had a reply and every night he sighed, switched it off and put it away as their hopes crumbled in the dust.

He tried to talk the *dukun* into letting Jamal go back to Telok Panjang but he wouldn't hear of it, presumably because it would give away their whereabouts. The men were guarded night and day, although Jed seemed to be allowed to go and talk to them, and he discovered that everyone was convinced they had all been murdered.

Penny had been sent back to Jakarta as planned, he told them all, and Jon, a government official and Bill Freeman, the developer, were in endless meetings. At least they had been. By now they might have decided to track the tribe down but, since Johannis was the only man to know the way, it seemed unlikely they would be discovered.

Gabby found the waiting very difficult, and passed the time as well as possible by making friends. She spent time with Hari, getting to know her in a strangely silent way, and by observing her carefully through the days she realised Hari was very tired and uncomfortable, although she never complained.

She spoke to Jed about it one night, carefully separated by a foot of floor and maintaining a strict rule of no physical contact through the night. It was less frustrating that way, they'd discovered, and by an unspoken agreement had settled into the companionable but slightly distant routine.

Tonight, though, she didn't want to be distant. She rolled on her side to face him, pillowing her head on her arm, and tapped his shoulder to get his attention.

'Mmm?' he murmured drowsily.

'It's about Hari,' she said softly. 'She's huge and she doesn't seem to be showing any signs of going into labour, but she's very uncomfortable. Today she was really bad.'

His eyes flickered open in the half-dark. 'Yes, I'd noticed. I wonder if she's got a breech? It might not be triggering her uterus to contract if so, or just feebly.'

'So what will happen?'

'Nothing until it's too late, then weak contractions that get nowhere. She might have an antepartum haemorrhage and die, or the baby might turn and everything will be all right, or she might go into very strong labour and rupture her uterus and die that way. Or she might just work like stink and get away with it if there are enough people to help her who know what they're doing.'

'Like us?' Gabby suggested.

'Forget it,' he told her. 'Even if we could get near her, what could we do?'

Gabby rolled onto her front and propped herself up on her elbows, her head close to his so they could hear each other without disturbing the others. 'We have to do something, Jed. We can't just ignore her, can we? Surely we can do something?'

He snorted. 'How? We haven't got access to any diagnostic tools, we can't scan her or X-ray her or even examine her. I don't suppose for a moment I'd be allowed to perform an internal on a young pregnant woman, do you? Think about it. I bet the only birth attendants will be the older women—and the *dukun* if things get really bad. No way will they let me in there.'

'How about me?' she suggested.

'More likely, but still not very probable. It depends how desperate they get. Of course Jamal thinks you're a healer so that could work in our favour. I'll talk to him in the morning.'

He didn't get a chance, though, because they were woken later that night by a woman's screams.

Gabby leapt up instantly. 'Hari,' she said with conviction. 'Jed, I want to go to her.'

'Try getting dressed first, then,' he suggested, stopping her in her tracks.

Bemused, she turned back and pulled on her clothes in place of the sarong, freezing as the air was ripped again by another cry. A shiver ran down her spine. 'Jed, please come too. If they let me in I can perhaps talk to you through the wall, but something's dreadfully wrong. Women don't scream like that normally.'

'God, I haven't done obstetrics since I was twenty-seven—I doubt if I can remember what's what,' he muttered.

'Let's just hope you're better with obstetrics than you are with e-mail numbers, then, or I might be better off without you.'

'Ha-ha,' he growled, dragging on his trousers and following her out of the hut.

The action was all taking place in and around Hari's hut, they discovered. Her husband, a strong and healthy-looking young man, was sitting at the fire with another man, whom they recognised as the chief, smoking clove cigarettes and talking in muttered undertones.

'You know Hari is the chief's daughter, do you?' Jed murmured as they approached.

'Yes, I'd gathered. That must be why he's here. I wonder where the *dukun* is.'

'Inside, I expect, chanting and giving her ghastly potions. I should think he's given her something to speed up the contractions, hence the screams.'

'Don't,' Gabby said with a shudder. 'How am I going to get inside?'

'Just go in. You're a woman. If you're humble enough they might let you help. I'll see if I can talk them into letting Johannis out to interpret.'

She climbed the ladder and slipped into the hut unnoticed, and found everyone clustered round Hari who was lying on the floor, writhing. Everyone in the room was a woman, with the exception of the *dukun*, who was squatting beside her chanting as Jed had predicted.

He looked up at her and stopped, then pointed at the door and said something that was obviously telling her to leave. She shook her head and knelt down on the other side of Hari, facing him, and pointed to herself. 'Gabby, *dukun*,' she said, hoping he would believe her and enlist her aid, or at least allow her to help.

Would he feel threatened, as if his magic was no good?

He sat back on his heels, folded his arms and stared at her defiantly—challengingly. Gabby swallowed and bent over Hari, stroking her hair back from her face and murmuring soothingly to her.

A woman pressed a damp cloth into her hand and she used that, wiping away the beads of sweat on Hari's clammy skin. 'Hari? Hari, it's Gabby,' she told her, and the girl's eyes flickered open.

They were glazed with pain and fear, and she clutched Gabby's hand and began to weep silently. Gabby used the other hand and laid it on the hugely distended abdomen, palpating it thoughtfully. It was years since she'd done much obstetrics, but she knew that what she was feeling now wasn't run of the mill.

For a start, she realised with a shock as she palpated the edges of the woman's abdomen, Hari was having twins, and—if she wasn't very much mistaken—it was a double transverse lie, one baby in the lap of the other, both crosswise.

'Gabby?'

She lifted her head at Jed's voice. 'She's having

twins—a double transverse presentation. Jed, she doesn't stand a chance without a section.'

He swore, softly but succinctly, and called to her to come out. 'Johannis is here, he can interpret. We've been talking to the husband. Apparently she's been in labour for a day off and on, without complaining, but she's starting to have much stronger contractions.'

'I can tell,' she called, her hand still resting where it was. There was suddenly a tremendous tension under her palm, and Hari cried out and rolled up into a ball, tensing all her muscles.

Gabby stroked her back soothingly, talking reassuringly to her, and when the contraction was over she slipped out of the hut and went to see Jed. 'Her contractions are horrendously strong, and she's never going to make any progress. Jed, she's going to die unless we can operate.'

Jed stabbed his hands through his hair and looked up at the sky for inspiration. 'I can't, Gabby. There's no anaesthetic, no light, no after-care—she'd die anyway, and if we've interfered we'll probably die too.'

'So you're just going to leave her to it?' she said furiously. 'Jed, you can't. We can do it—surely you've got some painkillers in that box of tricks.'

He snorted. 'Nothing that strong. I've got a couple of phials of pethidine, that's all, and no antibiotics strong enough to dare risk it, not in these unsterile conditions.'

She twisted her hands together worriedly. 'There must be something we can do.'

'Only if the *dukun* has a narcotic available in his arsenal of natural remedies, and he might well have—and if he's prepared to help us, which he might not be.'

'Ask—get Johannis to tell the chief his daughter's going to die unless we help her. Get him to tell the man that we're healers too. Get him to order the *dukun* to help.'

'Just like that?' He shook his head in despair and turned to Johannis, and explained the situation to him through Jamal.

'Wah,' the man said, rolling his eyes in fear and starting to babble.

'I think what he means is he can't tell the chief that because he'll cut his head off,' Jed translated.

'I'll cut his head off—Johannis, please, tell the chief his daughter's dying,' she pleaded.

Just then another scream cut through the night, and the chief looked anxiously at the hut. Gabby, not one to hang about in the face of such an emergency, pushed Johannis over to the fireside. 'Tell him,' she snarled.

So the poor man, shaking and trembling, translated their message. The chief's eyes widened in fear, then glazed and filled and he started to sob. The husband fell on him and they wept together.

'Oh, this is hopeless,' Gabby said impatiently, and pulled the two men apart. 'Jed, *dukun*,' she told them firmly. 'Hari…' She pulled her finger over her throat. 'Jed help.'

They looked at her as if she were mad. 'Johannis,' she wailed, and he spoke again. She turned to Jed. 'Make sure he tells them about the operation.'

There was a muttered exchange between Jed, Jamal and Johannis, and then their intrepid translator tried again. This time the chief got to his feet and went to the door of the hut and called out.

The *dukun* appeared in the doorway and they had a brief, fierce exchange. Jed got Johannis to translate, and then relayed it to Gabby.

'The *dukun* doesn't want to help us. He's now admitted he can't do anything and, yes, she will die.'

At this the chief produced a knife and threatened the man.

'Things are hotting up—he might be on our side,' Jed muttered to Gabby, rubbing thoughtfully at the beard on his chin. He turned to Johannis and said something which the man then translated, and the *dukun* nodded, his face surly.

'I don't think he wants to help, but on the other hand I think he's quite happy being alive. The chief's just told him that if Hari dies he dies too.'

'So I guess the same will apply to us.'

Jed grinned at her. 'I love a challenge. We need to scrub, kiddo. I think we're about to do surgery al fresco style, and the anaesthetist has got a serious case of the sulks.'

Adrenaline, Gabby thought some half an hour later, was a wonderful thing. Talk about sharpening up your wits!

Hari had been washed and sedated with the *dukun*'s herbal remedy, and was now sleeping peacefully in her hut. The women had been herded out, only the woman's mother, the *dukun*, Jed and Gabby remaining, with Johannis outside the door to translate if necessary.

They had scrubbed as well as they could and sprayed their hands with antibiotic spray, and Jed used more of it to sterilise the incision site. 'I'll do a longitudinal section because I don't want to cut the babies, and this light's awful. Anyway, it's quicker and she's less likely to have problems later with another delivery.'

He picked up the knife he'd been given by their reluctant assistant and which he'd sterilised as well as possible by boiling it in water for ten minutes. 'Let's hope this sedation works,' he said to Gabby, and without further ado he ran the knife down the skin.

A thin beading of blood appeared along the line, and

Hari moaned and moved a little. Her mother soothed her with trembling hands, tears streaming silently down her wrinkled face, and Jed stroked again and again until he was through the muscle layer and the uterus was revealed.

'It's very thinned at the base—I think it would have ruptured within another hour or so. I wish I could do an ultrasound scan to find out where the placentas are,' he muttered. 'Let's just pray I don't hit one of them.'

He stroked the knife over the uterus, pierced it and then, by sliding his fingers under the knife the wrong way up, he opened the uterus far enough to reveal the babies.

'So far so good. Right, let's see what we've got here.'

'Wah!' the mother keened softly as Jed reached in and lifted the first tiny infant out. It squalled healthily, and he grinned and handed it to Gabby. She laid it on Hari's chest and waited for the second child. It wasn't long coming, and also squalled vigorously.

Jed turned to Johannis and asked something, which was relayed to the astonished *dukun*. He reached in his bag of potions and produced a root, which he slivered with a knife and handed to Hari's mother with an instruction.

She placed it under Hari's tongue, and a few minutes later the uterus contracted steadily and the placentas came naturally away.

'Well, I never. Oxytocin, as I live and breathe.'

Jed smiled grimly. 'So far so good. Right, let's separate these babies from their placentas, take them out and get her closed up before too many moths fall inside.'

He closed quickly, more quickly than Gabby had ever seen it done and probably nearly as neatly, using the antibiotic spray liberally as he went along. Then he cleaned up his hands, washed the site down and sprayed it again, before covering it with a non-adherent sterile dressing.

Then he sat back on his heels and looked at Gabby.

'Well? What have we got?'

'Two boys, both well and fit and hungry. I don't suppose he's got a natural antidote to that sedative so she can feed them?'

Jed laughed. 'I think we'd better let her sleep it off,' he said. 'The longer she's out of it the better. I'm sure another woman can be persuaded into service as a wet nurse.'

He spoke to Johannis, then turned to the *dukun* and held out his hand with a grin.

After a few seconds' hesitation he took it and smiled, and said something to Johannis who translated.

Jed relayed it back to Gabby. 'He says together we have powerful magic,' he said with a grin. 'I reckon we were just damned lucky.'

'So far,' Gabby agreed, looking at the sleeping woman who had been all but unaware of the procedure. 'Never mind the magic—thank goodness he had a powerful enough painkiller. Let's just pray she doesn't get an infection.'

'I'm sure our friend here has something as impressive in the way of a natural antibiotic. I'd make up a garlic paste dressing and lay it on if all else failed, but he's probably got a whole battery of goodies up his sleeve.'

He stood up, moved to Hari's head and squatted down by her mother, who was cradling the babies in her arms. They were both squalling furiously, and were quite obviously well and healthy. They were very certainly alive, at least.

Jed smiled at the woman who smiled back tearfully and hugged the babies even tighter, then she struggled to her feet and went over to the doorway, holding the babies up. There was a cheer from outside and she turned back to the *dukun*, obviously thanking him for his part.

He bowed graciously, then began chanting over Hari and the babies, sprinkling them with something from his bag. 'Doubtless thanking some powerful god for the safe deliverance not only of the babies and their mother but also himself,' Jed murmured to Gabby.

She laughed softly. 'And us. I think I might join in.'

Jed hugged her, dropping a quick kiss in her hair, and together they left the hut to the greetings of the women who were still waiting for a proper look at the babies.

They were led to the fire by the happy, laughing throng and asked to sit with the chief and Hari's husband, and they were brought strong, sickly coffee and even sicklier cakes made of palm syrup in order to celebrate.

The *dukun* came out about half an hour later, smiling and bearing the babies in his arms, and they were handed to the women, who immediately took charge.

'They'll be fed and washed and looked after now,' Jed said confidently. 'The Indonesians are wonderful with children. If parents die the children are always instantly absorbed into another part of the family, and they often seem almost to share their children. I'm quite sure those babies will be fine now.'

'And Hari?'

Jed turned and spoke to Johannis who was squatting on the fringe of the group, waiting to be asked to translate again, and after a brief discussion with the *dukun* he relayed that Hari was fine and sleeping peacefully.

'Should I stay with her?' Gabby asked.

'Perhaps we all should. I don't think he would, but the *dukun* has the power, I'm quite sure, to kill her and have the blame fixed on us. I think this guy is OK, but a lot of these healers are quacks and totally unscrupulous, and they'd stop at nothing to protect their own reputations.'

'Even murder?' Gabby murmured.

'Possibly. I think, just to be on the safe side, he should have an audience at all times and, anyway, I'd rather be near Hari just until she comes round.'

In the end they stayed up by the fire until the sky began to lighten, popping in and out of the hut every few minutes to see the sleeping woman and her relieved mother. Both were fine, and after a while Hari stirred and moaned a little. The *dukun* gave her a potion which quietened her, without sedating her, and Gabby and Jed were both happy with her condition as far as they could tell.

The babies, too, were cuddled and admired once they had been fed, and they were passed around the group at the fireside with pride.

Gabby held one and Jed the other, and Gabby felt a huge lump in her throat.

'I'm so glad they didn't end up in a tree,' she said and, without thinking, she held the baby tight against her and closed her eyes.

When she opened them and looked up at Jed, his eyes seemed very bright in the firelight. He took the baby from her and passed it on, then took Gabby by the hand and led her back to their hut.

'I think she'll be all right now,' he told her and, leading her along to their bedroom, he turned her into his arms and held her tight. 'Thank you for making me do that,' he mumbled into her hair. 'I really didn't want to but, you're right, she would have died. I just thought we were bound to kill her.'

'And we didn't. I just couldn't bear to see her die, she's such a lovely person.'

'So are you,' he murmured, and his lips closed over hers. Her tiredness was forgotten, the drama of the night behind her, and only she and Jed existed.

They lay down without a sound on the scattered bedding, and Jed undressed her with trembling fingers. Everywhere he touched her skin it turned to fire, and by the time she was naked she was shaking all over.

Her fingers didn't work, and he dragged his shirt over his head, ripped off his trousers and briefs and settled beside her with a tiny sigh.

'I love you, Gabrielle Andrews,' he murmured. 'You're my little angel, do you know that? I've wanted to hold you like this for so long…'

His mouth found hers, teasing and tormenting until she thought she'd go crazy for him. His hands moved over her, cupping and cradling and stroking, making her weak with longing. She searched his body, her own hands restlessly fluttering over his back, over the skin that was like hot, damp silk in the tropic dawn. So hot, lit with the fire that was consuming them both. Amazing that he could feel so hot—

He shifted slightly and her hand found its way around and down, cupping the heavy fullness of his masculinity, dragging a groan from deep inside him.

His own hand responded, stroking the damp nest of curls that hid such a wild need she thought she'd die of it.

'Jed, please,' she whispered, and then he shifted across her and buried himself deep inside her.

She couldn't hold back the cry, couldn't help the little sob of relief at being part of him at last. He dropped his head against her shoulder with a shudder, and was still for an endless moment.

Then he lifted his head and met her eyes in the pale

light of dawn. 'Oh, Gabby,' he breathed raggedly. 'It feels so right—it's like coming home.'

Tears filled her eyes and she blinked them away, anxious to see his face—to remember every moment of this precious union. 'Jed, I love you,' she whispered.

'Oh, angel, I love you, too, so very much.'

His lips touched her face like the wing of a bird, soft, open-mouthed kisses that left a trail of fire over her eyes, her nose, her jaw, and finally her lips.

Their mouths went wild then, hungry and demanding, clinging fiercely and searching as their bodies rose to meet each other and the relentless passion broke in a devastating climax that left them both weak and shaken.

Jed collapsed against her, his breath scorching against her neck.

'God, my head aches,' he murmured a few moments later, and then his body slumped bonelessly onto hers.

'Jed—Jed, get off, I can't breathe,' she whispered.

There was silence, broken only by the harsh rasp of his breathing, and it dawned on Gabby that something was horribly wrong…

CHAPTER EIGHT

'JED?'

He was heavy on her, so heavy she could hardly roll him off. She pushed him, hissed at him, shook him, all to no avail. He seemed oblivious to her, and now that the wild heat of passion had cooled in her Gabby could feel that the heat coming off him in waves was far from normal.

In fact, it was worryingly abnormal, coupled with his lack of reaction and the headache he'd spoken of. Now he seemed to be unconscious, his body shaking violently.

She gave a mighty heave and rolled his shuddering body off her, then knelt beside him. 'Jed? Talk to me, damn it!'

He mumbled something unintelligible and curled into a ball, hugging his arms around himself as if he was cold, and Gabby covered him with one of the loosely woven rugs, pulled on her clothes and went out to see the others. There was a deep chill of fear settling round her heart, and she needed Jed's advice.

Unfortunately he wasn't in a position to give it to her.

She found the others grouped round in the living area by the door, eating their breakfast. Conversation stopped dead as she walked in, and she realised that in the flimsy hut their love-making had probably been quite clearly audible.

Tough. She had other things to worry about.

'Have any of you ever seen cerebral malaria?' she asked them.

'I have,' Ismail said.

'I don't suppose you'd recognise it?'

'Jed?' Sue asked her, the curiosity on her face replaced by concern.

'I think so. He complained of a headache, and he's burning up and shivering and I can't seem to get through to him. He might just be very tired, but I don't think so.'

Sue was on her feet in an instant, following Gabby back to their bedroom, with Ismail behind her and the others trailing at a distance.

Jed was pale and sweaty, his sunken eyes shadowed in his bearded face. 'He looks awful,' Sue said bluntly, and knelt down beside him. 'Jed? Come on, wake up!'

He mumbled something and stirred, but his eyes didn't open and he didn't really respond.

'He's out of it—how long has he been like this?'

Gabby shrugged. How long was it? 'Twenty minutes? Half an hour? Not that long.'

'Looks bad, mem,' Ismail said, squatting down beside him and touching his hot skin with a tentative hand. 'My cousin died—'

'Thank you, Ismail, we can manage now,' Sue said quickly, but Gabby felt a chill run right through her.

'You don't suppose it could just be flu, do you?' she asked, knowing as she did so that she was clutching at straws.

'No. I think it's almost certainly malaria. There's a leaflet about treating all the different types in the medicines he brought with him, and I'm sure he would have brought the right things to treat it. We just have to get the drugs into him.'

And that, Gabby knew, would be almost impossible without his co-operation or an intravenous drip. She found the flight bag, dug about in it for the leaflet and then read it quickly.

'"Severe headache, fever, drowsiness, delirium or confusion may indicate impending cerebral malaria",' she read aloud. 'Blah blah—"chloroquine-resistant strains—quinine, pyrimethamine and a sulphonamide orally, or chloroquine dihydrochloride IV if unconscious".'

She looked up at Sue. 'I would say he's unconscious. I think I ought to try injecting him very slowly intravenously, just to get something into him, and then try orally as soon as he comes round a bit or we can get him to co-operate. Will you help me?'

'Of course. What do you want me to do?'

And that was the problem, of course. There was nothing she could do except provide moral support, and Gabby said so. 'Just stay with me. I'm so scared he'll die...'

She dropped her face into her hands and choked down a sob, then lifted her head, took a deep breath and dredged up a smile. She had to think—

'OK. The first hurdle is saline solution. There isn't any.'

'You'll have to use boiled water.'

Gabby rolled her eyes. 'I could be giving him God knows what. OK, I'll use boiled water. Could you organise some?'

While Sue went in search of boiled water in something reasonably sterile, Gabby read and reread the leaflet until she was sure she'd understood the treatment, then she looked through the medicines and found everything she needed.

'Thank God he brought it,' she muttered, and looked up just as Sue came back with not only a bowl of water but the *dukun* in tow.

She wasn't sure if she was relieved to see him or not, but he might have some magic cure up his sleeve that wouldn't hurt as adjuvant therapy, and just now Gabby would settle for all the help she could get!

He squatted down by Jed's head, laid a hand on his scorching forehead and then pulled up his eyelids. Jed moaned a little, and the old man shook his head slightly and turned to Gabby, pointing to his head and holding it as if in pain.

She nodded, and hugged her arms around herself to show he had been shivery, and then fanned her face to show he was hot.

The old man unfolded himself and disappeared, presumably to fetch something. Gabby watched him go, and turned back to Sue. 'Did you ask him to come?'

'No. He just followed me. I had to talk to Johannis to get him to explain what I wanted, and he must have got wind of it. I wonder what he's gone to get.'

'Hopefully Johannis, amongst other things, so we can have an intelligent conversation. Could you hold his arm for me?'

She pulled up some of the water in the syringe, prayed that it was all right and drew up the chloroquine. Then she tied Jed's belt around his arm to raise the vein, slid the needle in and checked she'd entered the vein, then released the belt. Then gradually, millilitre by millilitre, she squeezed the contents of the syringe into his arm.

She was about halfway through when the *dukun* came back, and he watched her impassively as she delivered the drug. When she had finished, withdrawn the needle and bent Jed's arm up over a pressure pad against the vein, he produced a small cup of liquid, lifted Jed's head and tipped it into his mouth.

He swallowed convulsively, the reflex triggered by the liquid in his throat, and Gabby was relieved to see he was not as deeply unconscious as she had feared. She thought it might be safer, that being the case, to give him medicines orally instead of intravenously in view of the absence of sterile saline solution as a carrier.

The *dukun* was now fishing about in his bag and pulling out a variety of things—brilliantly coloured feathers, a shrivelled frog, some claws off a nameless animal, a piece of fur—there seemed no end to the bizarre collection of items he came up with. He laid them in a ring around Jed's head and began to chant, and Gabby settled back to watch.

Clearly, this was the theatre of his work, the drink having been the real treatment. This spectacle was now for psychosomatic relief, the psychology of medicine that was so effective in witchcraft and African juju.

She knew it wouldn't hurt him, and there was nothing she could do. Who could tell—perhaps the ritual would invoke the help of some god she had never heard of? At this point, she wasn't prepared to turn away any aid at all—cerebral malaria could and did kill in six hours.

She closed her eyes and hugged her arms tight around her body. Please, no, don't let him die, she said silently. Don't take him away from me now when I've only just found him. Don't let me lose him like this.

There was a soft touch on her shoulder, like a butterfly, and she opened her eyes to find the *dukun* regarding her compassionately. He patted her hand and then, beckoning, he went out of the hut.

She followed him down the ladder and across to Hari's hut. Hari! Heavens, in the confusion she'd forgotten all about the young woman!

She was lying propped up on brightly coloured rugs, a baby in each arm, and she looked wide awake and well. When she saw Gabby she smiled broadly and beckoned her over. Gabby knelt down beside her and hugged her, then sat back and looked at the babies.

She wanted to say, 'How are you? The babies are beautiful, you're a lucky girl. I hope you aren't in too much pain.' But it was impossible. Perhaps her face said it for her. Whatever, she couldn't keep the smile off it.

She patted Hari's abdomen and raised her eyebrows in enquiry, and Hari pulled a little face. So she was in pain, but not so bad that she couldn't hold her babies and feed them, with help. Her mother was there, of course, beaming broadly and pressing Gabby's hand to her head in a gesture of gratitude.

Gabby checked the incision and found the dressing had been replaced by a poultice of leaves bruised in hot water, by the look of it, and the incision line under the leaves looked clean and healthy and without any sign of infection.

Yet. She hoped it would continue.

She smiled her satisfaction to Hari, who was obviously nearly as proud of her stitches as she was of her babies. They offered her coffee and more of the little palm cakes, and she was going to refuse before she saw the look in Hari's eyes. The new mother wanted company, and to show off her babies to her new friend who had helped to save their lives, and Gabby didn't have the heart to refuse.

So she sat and drank a quick cup of the thick coffee and ate two of the little cakes. Then, bowing to the *dukun* who was busy mixing something in the corner, she left them and went back to Jed.

'How is he?' she asked Sue anxiously. 'I had to go and see Hari and there didn't seem to be a polite way to get out of it.'

'He's the same. He doesn't seem any worse, anyway,

and he's a bit less fidgety. He's talking, though—something about angels?'

Gabby gave a shaky little laugh, wondering what on earth he'd said. 'Angels?'

His lids fluttered and he looked straight at her, his eyes sparkling a vivid blue. 'My favourite angel,' he slurred. 'The angel Gabrielle herself. I love you. C'm'ere, you sexy thing.'

They fluttered shut again, to Gabby's relief, and he went quiet.

Sue laughed. 'Oh, well, at least we know he's not dreaming about dying. He spooked me for a minute. Want any more help?'

Gabby looked around. The room was hot and stuffy, and she wondered if there was any way to ventilate it better.

'It's getting so hot,' she murmured to herself. 'I wonder if we can cool him down?'

'You might find it cooler under the hut in the shade—shall I get the men to carry him out for you? You probably ought to sponge him down too, he's still very hot.'

'I think so—yes, please, Sue, could you do that?'

She waited until Sue had left the room and then tugged Jed's briefs on more or less properly. He was heavy and uncooperative, though, and it wasn't easy. Sue came back with Ismail and Luther, and they took an end each and carried him, slung between them, out of the hut and down the ladder to the shady spot underneath.

Gabby carried the mats and rugs and made up a bed on the ground, and they laid him down in the cooler air and then sat beside her. Sue fetched cool water and a cloth, and Gabby sponged him down, keeping an eye on the time.

He would need oral therapy, if she could get it into

him, as soon as possible, but for now she wanted to keep sponging and see if she could lower his temperature. It seemed to be climbing even higher, and every now and then he had a rigor, a shuddering fit almost like a convulsion.

People came and went, sitting quietly with her for company and helping her with the endless little tasks. Hari's mother sat for a while, and her sister, and Sue was never far away.

Derek spent some time talking to Jamal about the situation back at base, but he was still quite weak and spent a lot of the day resting. Gabby, though, didn't rest. There wasn't time.

The *dukun* came and gave Jed more of the vile green decoction, and she managed to crush up the malaria pills and dissolve them in honey and coax him to swallow the mixture. That in itself took nearly an hour.

During the afternoon Sue came and sat down with her back against one of the posts and regarded Gabby thoughtfully. 'You look awful. Why don't you let me take over and go and have a sleep? You were up all night with Hari, and you'll have days of this ahead of you. You ought to pace yourself.'

It made sense, but she didn't dare leave him. She went down to the pool, though, and washed herself and her clothes by the simple expedient of walking into the water fully clothed. She washed out Jed's clothes as well, and then went back and changed into the sarong.

Her shoulders were bare, but in view of the near-nakedness of the other women she didn't think it would matter. She smothered herself in insect repellent, hung the clothes over a beam and went back out to Jed.

'Go and lie down for a while,' Sue ordered her.

'I can't. I won't sleep. I need to be with him.'

Sue sat back on her heels and regarded Gabby

thoughtfully. 'You love him very much, don't you?' she said shrewdly.

There was no point in lying. 'Yes,' she replied. 'I do. I can't let him die, I know that.'

She plucked at his skin. It was still plump and taut, but she needed to keep getting fluids into him if she could or he might become dehydrated. 'Help me give him a drink,' she said to Sue, and together they propped him up and dribbled cool boiled water into his mouth.

He swallowed barely any, most of it dribbling out of the corner of his mouth and running down his chest. Sometimes, though, he did swallow, and for those few times it was worth it.

She stayed with him all that day and all the following night, and as dawn broke on the second day the *dukun* came back and squatted down beside her in the hut. He said something she couldn't understand, and then some men came and lifted Jed up like a rag doll and carried him outside under the hut again.

She made as if to follow, but the old man pointed to her bed and ordered her to stay.

'But I need to look after him,' she argued.

However, he was having none of it. There was no need for language. He simply pointed to her, pointed to the bed and walked out, dropping the bark-cloth door curtain into place as he left. He might just as well have locked it, the meaning was so clear.

Exhausted, beyond thought, she lay down obediently and slept for two hours. Then she woke up in a panic and got up and went to Jed, to find a strange woman bathing him with cool water.

The woman smiled at her and patted the ground beside her, and she sat down and looked at him.

He was still alive, despite her desertion. Gabby's shoulders drooped with relief, and she opened the flight bag and took out the next dose of quinine, pyrimetha-mine and sulphonamide. She crushed the tablets into the honey and smeared the paste on his tongue, then stroked the underneath of his jaw to stimulate the swallowing reflex.

As she did so she noticed that his skin was beginning to show signs of dehydration, and he was still almost unconscious. She propped him up and gave him a drink, and was rewarded by him dribbling over her trousers.

'Really, Jed, I've just done the washing!' she grumbled, and to her surprise he turned towards her voice and mumbled something.

'Jed?'

'Head aches,' he said almost inaudibly. She bent and pressed her lips to his forehead, and he moaned softly and turned his face into the softness of her breasts.

'Gorgeous,' he mumbled. 'Sexy, sexy lady. I want to make love to you.'

She looked up to see Derek there, grinning, and went beetroot red.

'Don't be silly, you're sick,' she reminded him a little breathlessly.

'Not silly—love you. Marry me, angel.'

She smiled. 'Of course I will—just as soon as you're better. Now go to sleep.'

'Sick, Gabby,' he mumbled. 'Head hurts.'

'I know,' she murmured soothingly, and smoothed his hair back from his face, forgetting Derek. Jed was hot and she tried to move away a little but he hung on, and so she held him like that for ages while the tears ran down her face and dripped onto his hair. Eventually she felt the light touch of the *dunku* on her shoulder.

She lifted her head with a sigh, and he tutted at her and moved her out of the way. More of the vile green liquid was coaxed into Jed, and more incantations were said, and Gabby joined in with prayers of her own.

Then he gathered up his trappings and beckoned Gabby to follow him to his hut. There he gave her food and drink, and if there was anything in it she didn't care. She was sure now he was a good man, and any fears Jed might have had about him being a quack had been long dispelled. If he wanted to give her medicine for anything let him, she thought.

Anyway, she was starving.

She ate the rice and vegetables and some of the sauce, drank the coconut milk and stood up. 'I have to go back to Jed,' she told him, not expecting him to understand, but he nodded.

'Jed,' he said, and let her go.

He was hovering on the fringes constantly for the next few days, quietly coming and going, taking care of her and Jed and Hari, and she was immensely grateful for his loyal support.

Derek continued to recover and was much stronger, and the others seemed to be remaining well, to her relief. She had her hands more than full as it was.

Jed, meanwhile, continued to be oblivious of the rest of the world. He kept talking rubbish, some of it utter gibberish, some unfortunately quite easily understandable to the inevitable audience, keeping her company in the shade under the hut.

At one point he opened his eyes and looked at Gabby with a glazed expression. 'You are one hell of a sexy woman,' he told her gruffly. Derek and Luther, sitting nearby, laughed softly, and Gabby felt herself colouring.

'Jed, shut up, you don't know what you're talking about,' she told him.

'Yesido,' he slurred. 'Sexy legs, sexy eyes, sexy everything.'

'You sound drunk.'

'Because I fancy you? C'mere. I wanna hold you—'

'Jed,' she said warningly, and he giggled.

'Never learnt to take a compliment,' he told her, and lunged towards her.

She dodged out of the way and he collapsed on the mats and started to snore. She sighed and glared at him.

'I think I like you better unconscious,' she muttered at his comatose form. 'At least you're less embarrassing.'

He mumbled off and on for the next couple of days, coming and going like a tide as the drugs fought the parasite for supremacy. Then on the morning of the third day he opened his eyes and looked at her.

'I have got one hell of a headache,' he said gruffly. 'Have I been ill?'

To her humiliation she burst into tears, dropping her face into her hands and weeping silently with relief.

'Gabby?' he murmured. 'Gabby, what's the matter?'

She sniffed hard and pulled herself together with an effort. 'You've had malaria.'

'Again?' he said heavily. 'Damn. What sort?'

'Cerebral—falciparum malaria, we think.'

His eyes widened. 'Really? No wonder my head hurts.'

She nodded. 'I've been following the instructions and treating you, and the *dukun* has been giving you something green and gruesome and chanting over you—whatever, it seems to have worked...'

She swallowed the tears again and gave him a rather watery smile. 'It's nice to have you talking sense. You've been a bit—well, away with the fairies.'

He groaned and rolled his eyes. 'Sorry.' He moved his head and groaned again. 'Could I have a drink?' he asked.

'Sure.' She poured some cool, boiled water out of a big container into a coconut shell and held it to his lips, and he sipped it and lay back.

'Thanks,' he sighed, and then his eyes drifted shut and he slept again. He continued like that off and on for the rest of the day, and although there were no more episodes of delirium he was still a bit confused and obviously sick.

That night, though, for the first time he seemed to be sleeping normally and, when she checked it, his skin seemed to be a normal temperature.

Relieved that he seemed to have turned the corner, she relaxed and slept heavily for the first time in almost a week, and when she woke he was gone.

'Jed?' she called, scrambling out of bed and pulling on her clothes.

Sue stuck her head round the doorway. 'Derek's taken him down to the pool for a wash—he felt hot and sticky. He wants to know what drugs he's had so I told him he'd have to ask you. He seems fine.'

Gabby sighed with relief and sagged against the wall. 'I didn't know where he was. I thought he might have wandered in his sleep.'

Sue laughed. 'No, just gone to freshen up. I can hear them coming back now.'

Sue's head disappeared and Gabby gathered up the bedclothes and took them down under the hut in the shade. Jed was sitting against a post, looking exhausted after his exertions, but at least he looked a little fresher.

'Feel better?' she asked him, arranging the bedclothes.

'Much. Thanks—I think I'll have a rest. I feel so weak.'

'I'm not surprised, you've been at death's door,' Derek told him bluntly.

Jed rolled over onto his hands and knees and crawled

onto the bedding, then collapsed. 'Tell me about it,' he muttered.

The others left them so Gabby could settle him to sleep, but after a moment he opened his eyes again. 'I don't suppose there are any headache pills in that flight bag?' he asked her.

'Paracetamol,' she told him.

'I'll have two—and what treatment have you been giving me?'

She helped him take the pills, then sat down beside him with the drug chart she'd improvised on the back of the leaflet and told him what he'd had and when.

'How long have I been out of it?' he asked in puzzlement when she started to list the third day.

'Four days altogether,' she told him.

He looked thoughtful. 'Oh. Right. I can remember odd bits and pieces but I didn't realise it was that long.' He took her hand, but didn't meet her eyes. 'Look, Gabby, I don't know what I said and did—I gather some of it was pretty embarrassing. It's just the way I am with malaria. It makes me a bit unihibited—just ignore it, and if I offended you I'm sorry. I've been known to do all sorts of things in the past but it doesn't mean anything.'

She grinned. 'Forget it, Jed, you didn't do anything.'

'I didn't? Good. Only I wouldn't want to have embarrassed you.' He gave a wry laugh. 'I gather I asked you to marry me once—crazy. I hope you had the good sense to ignore it. It doesn't mean anything.'

Her heart jerked painfully. 'Yes, of course I did,' she said with a little laugh. Was it as hollow as it sounded to her?

He closed his eyes and sank back against the bedclothes. 'I don't suppose there's anything interesting to drink, is there?'

'Drink?' she said numbly. 'Yes, of course. I'll get you something.'

Just ignore it? she thought. It doesn't mean anything? Nothing? None of it? Not the love-making before, either?

Of course, she realised with a shock, he'd had malaria then. Probably Hari's operation was the last thing he'd done when in full control of his faculties. So when he'd told her he loved her was that just the malaria speaking?

Hot colour scorched her cheeks when she thought of the uninhibited way she'd responded. Well, if she was lucky he wouldn't remember any of it, and so she could pretend it hadn't happened and spare them both some embarrassment.

She got some fresh coconut milk in a cup and took it in to him, and he drank it eagerly—too eagerly.

'Steady, not too much at once,' she cautioned, taking it away, and he lay down again and gave her a wry grin.

'So, what's happened while I've been out of it?' he asked after a moment.

'Not much to anyone else. Hari's much better.'

'Hari?' He blinked. 'Did I dream it, or did we—? No, we couldn't have done.'

Do what? she wondered. Make love?

'Tell me we didn't do a Caesarean section by candlelight with only herbal anaesthesia.'

So he didn't remember—yet. 'We did. She's fine, incidentally, so are the babies.'

'Babies?' Jed repeated, half sitting up then falling back with a groan and clutching his head. 'Oh, God, I want to die.'

He rolled to his side and shut his eyes, and seemed to sleep for a while. She left him to sleep until it was time for his drugs again, then she washed his face and hands and changed the rug over him for a cooler, drier one.

'I gather you looked after me almost on your own.' he said quietly as she finished.

She avoided his eyes. 'Yes, most of the time. The *dukun* helped, and so did some of the women—they sponged you down and helped me give you drinks and medicines.'

'I don't remember it. I remember hearing people talking to me and making me drink something ghastly, but nothing else. I just know it seemed endless.' He looked up at her. 'You look bloody awful,' he told her bluntly. 'Have you had any sleep?'

Sexy legs, sexy eyes, sexy everything? Only in his delirium, evidently. 'A bit last night. You kept me rather busy before that,' she told him, perhaps rather sharply because he seemed to withdraw.

'I'm sorry. I'm very grateful. I would have died without your help.'

She choked back the sob of protest. 'You didn't, though. That's all that matters. Get some rest now.'

She scrambled to her feet and all but ran down to the pool, then, heedless of any eyes on her, she stripped and dived into the chilly water. Her heart was breaking. She couldn't pretend or hide it any longer, and the noise of the waterfall that filled the pool would at least muffle her grief.

He didn't remember.

She did, though. She thought of the tenderness of his hands, the light in his eyes, the care he had taken with her. She thought of him telling her it was like coming home, and a sob rose in her throat.

Meaningless, all of it. Just empty words.

'Marry me, angel.'

She cried for what seemed like ages, then the chill of

the water drove her out and she wiped the water off her arms and legs and dressed again. When she looked up the *dukun* was standing watching her with gentle, understanding eyes, and another sob tore its way out of her chest.

'I'm just so tired,' she said. She closed her eyes, and the next thing she felt was his arms around her, cradling her very gently as she wept. Then he wiped her eyes with his gnarled old thumbs, patted her shoulder and led her back to the village.

He sent her in to Hari, who took one look at her and made her lie down on a mat in the corner. She was asleep in seconds, and she must have slept for hours.

When she woke, it was to Sue shaking her shoulder and saying something excitedly.

She opened her eyes and struggled into a sitting position, fighting the pins and needles in her arm. 'What?' she mumbled. 'Is it Jed?'

'He's got an e-mail,' Sue told her. 'It's OK, Gabby—help's on its way. We're going to be rescued!'

CHAPTER NINE

GABBY went back to their hut and found everyone in a state of great excitement.

They were clustered round Jed in his bed under the hut, and he was grinning wearily. 'My secretary just got a rise,' he announced. 'Bless her heart, she checked the e-mail, contacted Bill Freeman's office and mobilised a search party, then replied to me, telling me what was happening.'

'What *is* happening?' Gabby asked, her feelings very mixed. She'd made friends in the village, despite the language barrier—Hari and the *dukun*, and some of the other women—and she had felt herself grow closer to Jed over the twelve days they had been there.

Now, it seemed, it was all going to come to an end—possibly in the next day or so—and she wasn't sure how she would go back to her ordinary life. She would miss them—especially Jed, and she was sure their relationship would be over. He'd as good as told her that.

Derek was explaining that a group including Jon and Bill were setting off from Telok Panjang and making their way on foot from the compound, following the river and using the Magellan GCS to communicate with base and with them.

'Unfortunately, I think our battery might be about to give up the ghost,' Derek said. 'Still, at least they know where we are and can make their way towards us.'

'I need to speak to Johannis,' Jed said from his pile of bedding. 'We need him primed to deal with their arrival, and he needs to be sure exactly what it is we're able to negotiate on.'

'I agree,' Derek put in. 'I'm sure the power station will have to go ahead. The only variable will be the positioning of it, and they need to understand that.'

'Don't get overtired,' Gabby warned them both. 'You've both been ill—you must be careful. You never know, you might have to walk out of here and just at the moment you, Jed, particularly, aren't in a fit state to do it.'

'I'm fine, don't fuss,' he told her, and turned back to Derek.

'OK,' she said under her breath. 'Suit yourself.'

She walked off, leaving the others to their endless confab. So he was quite happy to let her wait on him when it suited him, but as soon as it came to taking advice, oh, no, he was fine!

'Men!' she muttered. She walked out of the village along one of the paths, her feet instinctively leading her towards the grave trees. She needed the peace and tranquillity that she found there, the almost church-like atmosphere of hushed reverence.

She was still feeling bruised inside, angry with herself for thinking that all those tender words were real and not just the product of his illness. So she'd thought that the delirium had made him more honest and uninhibited? Apparently, it just made him lie and flatter—perhaps that was the man he really was after all, a womanising flirt with a laughing eye and a ready compliment.

Damn him.

She walked under the towering grave trees and turned her face up to them. They had a quiet dignity that she needed just now, and she sat down against the trunk of one and rested her head back against it.

They were about to be rescued, and she had no idea

how she was going to cope without him. Would she ever see him again? She doubted it somehow. All the camaraderie they'd built up in the week before his illness seemed to have gone out of the window, and he was almost like a stranger now.

She stared at the little squares on the trunk of the tree facing her, and wondered about the women who'd buried their babies in there. How had they coped?

How much less significant was her own sorrow.

The crackling of a twig startled her, and she saw the man who'd been so interested in her on the day of their capture standing a few feet away, his eyes fixed on her.

In his hand was a *parang*, a sharp jungle knife, hanging loosely by his side, and the light in his eyes was chilling. He must have been waiting all this time to get her alone.

She swallowed and tried to stare him out, but he didn't move, except to coil his fingers more tightly round the handle and slowly raise the knife above his head.

Fear clawed at her. He was going to throw the knife at her!

He said something, very softly, and held his other hand up as if telling her to sit still.

'You have to be joking,' she muttered, but then out of the corner of her eye she caught a movement, a slow, weaving movement, repetitive—

There was a *swoosh* beside her ear, and she screamed, darting away from the tree as something thrashed against her, and then the man caught her in his arms and stopped her headlong flight, turning her back to face the tree.

The blade of the *parang* was buried in the bark, blood staining it, and on the ground at the base of the trunk, still twitching, lay the body of a snake.

'Oh, Lord,' she whispered. Cold sweat broke out on

the palms of her hands, and she scrubbed them against her legs.

Her 'assailant' grinned, picked up the snake and slung it over his shoulder, then picked up the head off the ground and showed it to her, pulling out the flaps of skin on each side.

A cobra. Great. Marvellous.

She gave him a sickly smile. 'Thank you,' she said fervently, and he laughed cheerfully, obviously pleased that she was impressed.

He hooked the *parang* out of the trunk, wiped the blood off it on the undergrowth and turned away, beckoning her to follow him back to the village.

She needed no second bidding. She was right there with him, almost standing on his heels in her haste to get back to safety.

As she entered the clearing Jed looked up from talking to Johannis and his eyes narrowed. She smiled at the man who'd rescued her, and to her surprise he blushed beneath his dark skin and turned away with an embarrassed giggle.

He's just shy, she thought to herself, not shifty at all, and he's fascinated by me, poor deluded boy.

Suppressing a smile, she crossed over to Jed and he glowered at her.

'If you've quite finished consorting with the natives, we've got things to sort out,' he growled. 'I want to send a reply to this e-mail, and we'll need scouts unobtrusively circulating on the outskirts of the village to leave pointers, just in case they get lost. I want you and Sue to go to the washing pool, and take the track from there downstream towards the town. The rest of you take the other tracks—not all at once. Pace yourselves and take turns.

'Leave pointers if you can, footprints of your shoes in

the track—that sort of thing. Of course if it rains it'll mess things up, but they might come before then and if not we'll have to go out and do it again.'

He looked round at everyone. 'Any questions?'

Luther nodded. 'How long will it be before they come?'

'Any time in the next few hours or days, I would guess. That depends whether or not they can find the track, if they can follow it, how many of them there are and so forth. We'll just have to be patient.'

And that, of course, was the problem. Waiting was going to be hell on nerves already stretched taut. Leaving the others, Sue and Gabby set off for the pool and found children laughing and splashing in the water.

'I'll miss the little ones,' Sue told her. 'They're so sweet and friendly, and there's one in particular who keeps bringing me little stones and things as presents.'

Gabby laughed. 'My nephews and nieces do that on walks, and sometimes I can hardly get home for the weight in my pockets!' She lost her smile then, looking round at the women and children. 'I'll miss them, too, especially Hari. She's been really sweet to me, and her babies are so lovely. I hate leaving her before she's properly healed, just in case anything goes wrong, but I suppose we'll have to.'

'I think the *dukun* will look after her,' Sue said confidently. 'He's a wonderful man, they're very lucky to have him. I think Jed wants to get to know him and learn some of his secrets. I shouldn't be at all surprised if he doesn't come back, once we're all released, just to find out more.'

Gabby leant against a tree and toed the earth idly. 'What about you and Derek? Will you stay and finish off the power station if they can agree a new site?'

Sue shrugged. 'I don't know. I didn't intend to get

pregnant, but these things happen and neither of us are getting any younger. We're both thirty-four now so I suppose it's the right time for us. I don't want Derek out here on his own, but on the other hand I don't know how I'd feel about having a baby out here.'

'I wonder if Jon and Penny will stay?' Gabby mused.

'Who knows? If Penny's here it will be easier, of course, and more fun.' Sue shrugged away from her tree and headed off casually down the path. 'Come on, we've got to make tracks, so to speak.'

They were careful to leave pronounced tracks back towards the village, deliberately treading in muddy bits to leave lasting footprints, but, of course, there was no guarantee that they would survive the rain or even be noticed.

'Do try and keep Derek quiet,' Gabby advised as they returned to the village. 'I know he thinks he's better, but he really ought to be careful. He might be less stable now, and the insulin should have been refrigerated, of course, so it might not be as good as it ought to be.'

Sue sighed. 'I'll try, but he's every bit as stubborn as Jed in his way. I'll do my best, though. What are you going to do about Jed?'

Gabby gave a short laugh. 'I think I've been told my services are no longer required,' she said a little bitterly.

'Oh, dear. I wonder if that's Derek's doing? I think he told him this morning about what he'd been saying when he was delirious, and he was apparently very embarrassed and worried he'd humiliated you.'

Gabby laughed awkwardly. 'I think I'm made of sterner stuff than that.' Anyway, it wasn't humiliation that was her problem, it was losing him.

They rejoined the others, but Jed was deep in conversation with Derek, drawing plans and discussing alternative sites and so on, and so she went to see Hari.

She was up and about now, just doing a little bit here and there, but Gabby was very much afraid she'd do too much too soon and burst her stitches. She tried to explain that to Hari in mime, and ended up having to get Johannis, with Jed's help, so she could explain the importance of being careful for the first few weeks.

The wound was healing nicely, she saw when she examined Hari, and her uterus was going down well. The babies were positively blooming, and it seemed almost impossible that five days before they'd been on the point of death.

Gabby stayed with her for lunch, holding one of the babies while Hari ate, and after they'd finished their meal she went back to the others.

'How is she?' Jed asked without preamble.

'All right, I think. Healing well, babes both fine. You did a good job.'

Was it her imagination or did his skin colour? 'Just don't ask me to do anything like that again,' he said gruffly.

Raised voices behind them made him turn his head, then sigh. 'I think the tension's getting to everyone. Waiting now is going to be the hardest part.'

'Waiting is always the hardest part of anything. Waiting for you to come back to us was pretty hellish.'

He looked down at his hands, fiddling with a twig for a moment. 'Thanks for sticking by me,' he muttered. 'I'm sorry I said all those things.'

'Actually, some of them were quite complimentary,' she said with forced brightness.

He shot her a searching look. 'I doubt if any of them did you justice. I gather I was a bit crude at times.'

She blushed and trailed her fingers through the sand, sifting it. 'Look, just forget it, Jed, OK? I have.'

He looked as if he was about to say something else,

but then he shut his mouth and turned back to the twig,
tearing it into tiny little pieces. 'Luther's got a low-grade
fever and bloody diarrhoea. I think he's got dysentery.
Have we got anything to give him?'

'Nothing much. The rest has all been used up. I'll ask
the *dukun*.'

'He'll start charging,' Jed said with a smile, the first
one he'd given her all day, and she nearly cried.

'I'll bat my lashes.'

She went over to his hut and greeted him, and he put
down the stick he was whittling and unfolded his frail
form, following her back to the hut. She showed Luther
to him, and after laying his hands on him for a moment
he disappeared and came back with a few black seeds.

'Papaya seeds,' Luther said weakly. 'It's an old remedy. It works.'

'He's holding up two hands—is that ten a day? An
hour?'

'A day,' Luther said. 'You have to chew them.'

'We've got a couple of sachets of electrolyte solution,' Gabby told Jed. 'Shall I make one of them up for
him?'

'Yes—give him as much as he can cope with.
Hopefully we'll get out of here soon and he can have
proper medical attention.'

The papaya seeds seemed to help, and by the end of
the afternoon he was feeling a little better although he
still had a fever and diarrhoea. The *dukun* brought him
something else, a powder that made him sleep and that
she suspected might be related to opium. Whatever, he
wasn't going to be here long enough to get addicted and
sleep was the best thing for him.

It would have been the best thing for Jed, but he was
too busy planning to rest. He slept for an hour, but he
looked like death warmed up and wouldn't give in.

The rain had come after lunch, of course, drowning out conversation and washing away all their careful tracks, and because it was the start of the rainy season there was a spectacular thunderstorm so even if he'd wanted to sleep it would have been difficult.

Now it was evening, the sky darkening to a velvet blackness in minutes, and they gathered in their hut by the doorway and looked out at the village, settling down for the night.

'I thought we'd be gone,' Derek said, voicing everyone's thoughts and disappointments. 'I thought for sure they would have been here by now.'

'Maybe the rains have held them up,' Gabby suggested. 'Perhaps they've had landslides—some of the tracks round here are showing signs.'

'Maybe they've got lost.'

'With the technology they've got available to them? They could be put down anywhere on earth and know exactly where they were. They aren't lost,' Jed pointed out. 'I expect they've found the village and are waiting for the morning to make their move. I suggest we all get an early night so we're ready for whatever the morning brings.'

'And most particularly you,' Gabby told him firmly, and chivvied him off to bed.

It took some time to settle everyone down, but finally Gabby crawled into her bed next to Jed and lay there, listening to the jungle. After the threat with the snake earlier, it didn't seem quite the friendly place it had seemed before, and she found she was tense with the waiting and unable to sleep.

Jed, too, seemed to be wakeful. She turned her head and found him looking at her in the dim candle light. 'How's Luther?' he asked.

'Still suffering, although less so, and the powder

seemed to help. I'll have to get some more for him in the morning.'

'What about Derek?' he asked in a low undertone.

'I'm concerned about him. I think he's becoming a little hyperglycaemic. Perhaps the insulin's deteriorated with the heat.'

Jed nodded. 'That's what I was afraid of. Please, God, let them come tomorrow.'

She turned on her side, facing him. 'What do you think's holding them up?'

'Not knowing the route? There are lots of ravines and things—if you didn't know the way it could be quite tricky. It wasn't easy even on the right track.'

She chewed her lip for a second. 'What if they can't get to us? What if they never make it?'

'They'll make it,' he promised and, reaching out a hand, he cupped her cheek. His thumb idly stroked her temple, soothing her, and she felt silly tears well in her eyes. She closed them so he wouldn't see, but he must have sensed them because the next minute she was in his arms and he was cradling her against his chest.

'It's all right, Gabby,' he murmured. 'We'll be OK. You'll be out of here soon, you wait and see. It's nearly over, sweetheart.'

She slid an arm around him and moved closer, drawing comfort from his nearness. He was thinner, she realised with a shock. The malaria had drained his resources, and yet here he was, being strong for all of them when they should have been looking after him.

She felt him relax against her, and his breathing become more even. Then, when he was asleep, she let the silent tears slip down her cheeks and soak into his shirt. Was this the last time she'd ever hold him?

'If they don't come today I'm walking out of here.'

'Derek, don't be ridiculous,' Sue told him firmly.

'You'll do no such thing. Without any insulin you wouldn't get anywhere.'

'Well, I can't stay here without it, can I?' he snapped. 'I might as well take my chances in the jungle.'

'You're being absurd. Just rest and conserve your energy, and don't have too much sugary fruit.'

'I'll eat what I bloody well like—'

'Hey, hey, boys and girls, let's not fight. None of us wants to be here under these conditions, and it's almost over. Just bide your time.'

'I'm sure if we got Johannis and Jamal out of their hut we could make it back down—'

'Before they get us with their blowpipes? I don't think so,' Jed said drily. 'They might be friendly and pleasant at the moment because there's nothing at stake, but once they decide if they're going to go and negotiate this change of site we might find we're much more closely guarded. I think at the moment they're keeping us here to make Bill and the government sweat. It suits them to do so, and they know we won't do anything silly without Jamal or Johannis to guide us. That's why they're always so closely guarded.'

'They could have told us the way,' Derek argued. 'We haven't even asked them!'

'You can get lost in the middle of London with an A to Z!' Sue told him bluntly. 'What are they going to say—turn left at the big fern? Get real!'

'Well, we could try—'

'And die in the attempt. Thanks, but no thanks—'

'Hush! What's that?' Gabby said.

They all stopped talking then, cocking their heads and listening.

'Have I gone off my trolley or is that a helicopter?' Jed murmured quietly.

'My God!' Derek said. 'I'll stick my head out of the door and have a squint.'

He left the room, and they waited, listening, until it was obvious that, yes, it was a helicopter and, yes, it was coming in to land, or at least to hover just overhead.

They all ran to the door, to find Derek on the ground, waving frantically at a craft about fifty feet above the ground. The dust was swirling up around the huts, and the villagers were running, screaming, men, women and children scattering in all directions as a hatch opened and a ladder was thrown out.

Bill was the first to descend, followed by Jon, another man in shorts and T-shirt and a government official in a safari suit. As soon as the last one was off the ladder the helicopter lifted up and away, and as the dust settled so the villagers began to creep back out from their hiding places, spears and blowpipes at the ready.

Derek, Sue and the Indonesians ran towards them, but Jed hung back. 'Why couldn't they just walk in?' he muttered, and Gabby turned and looked at him.

'You look like death—you should be lying down.'

'And miss this? No way,' he replied, and then ruined it all by swaying against the ladder and nearly falling over.

'Stubborn fool,' she said firmly and, tucking herself into his armpit, she draped his arm over her shoulder, hung onto his wrist and almost carried him across the clearing to the others.

Then there was lots of hugging and backslapping before Jed called them all to order.

'I think, gentlemen, we should get down to business,' he said. 'Jamal and Johannis are here and ready to translate—I think it might be politically correct to introduce you to the key players. You do understand about the grave trees?'

'Oh, yes,' Bill assured him. 'We've examined the site and agree with you. We can't possibly build it there. We just have to negotiate an alternative.'

Gabby felt the tension drain out of her shoulders. She was sure it would now be all right.

With Gabby supporting him, Jed went over to the edge of the group of villagers, where the chief and the *dukun* were standing together in hastily donned ceremonial garb, and smiled and bowed at them.

'Jamal? Johannis?' Jed asked, and the chief waved at a man who brought the men to the edge of the circle.

'Jamal, ask Johannis to tell them these men have come to talk about the grave trees and to apologise for having threatened the sacred place.'

They waited while the translations were carried out, and then the chief and the *dukun* looked at Jon, Bill and the two other men and bowed their heads slightly.

'The chief says the trees must stay,' Jamal informed her.

'We understand that. There are other ways. Please will they talk about them?'

The message came back that, yes, they would talk.

Jed introduced the chief and the *dukun*, and Jon introduced himself, Bill and the other two, one of whom was from the government, the other from the International Red Cross. The men disappeared under the chief's hut, and Gabby, heart in mouth, followed them and sat down at a polite distance in case she was needed. The others joined her, straining their ears to listen to the conversation.

Coffee was served first, and once the ceremony had taken place the negotiating could begin. She saw the *dukun* produce her drawing, and the government inspector nodded and looked at Bill, who produced a sheaf of paper from his pocket.

The papers were handed backwards and forwards, considered and studied, thought about and argued over, and then once again the *dukun* took them and tucked them into his belt and turned away.

'OK, guys, I think your audience is over,' Jed told them softly. 'Come and see the others. The *dukun* will talk to the elders and consider it. It's all down to him now.'

Jon had brought insulin in case Derek had run out, and Jed tested him and found his blood sugar soaring again. Tutting, he gave him a double dose of the new, fresh insulin, and after an hour he began to feel better again.

Luther, though, was still causing concern and Gabby could tell Jed was worried. What they needed—what they all needed—was to get out of there and have a proper medical check-up. She met Jed's eyes and he winked reassuringly, as if to say, 'Don't worry, it's nearly over.'

Nothing in Indonesia moves fast. It took five hours for the elders to agree—five hours in which the tension rose to unbearable levels. They were closely guarded now, herded together into the hut with Jamal and Johannis, and by the time they were summoned tempers were well and truly frayed.

The key players disappeared again with Johannis and Jamal, and after another hour Jon came up the ladder, grinning.

'You're free to go. We're going to renegotiate the site—we're meeting the elders down there in a couple of days, and we're going to get you all airlifted out of here in the next couple of hours. Gabby, tell me, who's first?'

'Derek,' she said emphatically. 'He needs stabilising in hospital. Sue—she's pregnant and needs checking up.

Luther has dysentery, and Jed's been extremely ill with cerebral malaria and needs proper treatment. The rest of us are well.'

He nodded. 'I'll get those four sent out first, then, and next you and the others, and Bill and I can go last with the interpreter.'

He left the hut and went out to the others, and a very short time later they heard the whop-whop-whop of the returning helicopter.

It returned for Gabby after an hour, and she bid a tearful goodbye to Hari and the *dukun*. As they rose up in the air the village seemed to disappear, swallowed by the trees, vanishing like a myth.

'I'm sure it can't be anything serious.'

'You look awful—you're suffering from lassitude, nausea, tiredness, lack of appetite—you're coming in for a whole battery of tests, young lady, and that's all there is to it. You could have picked up anything.'

She looked at Jed, fit and well now, sitting on the edge of his desk in the tropical diseases hospital she gathered he worked in when he wasn't swanning about in the tropics, and sighed. 'All right, if you insist.'

'We'll keep you in overnight,' he told her, and her silly heart did a crazy leap. She'd see him! That was worth any amount of tests.

'What are you looking for?' she asked him.

'Anything unusual. My secretary will arrange your admission. I have to fly, I've got another clinic, but I'll see you later.'

He patted her shoulder on the way past, leaving her with a sense of emptiness when he had gone. Funny how it seemed so much colder without his presence.

'Miss Andrews?'

She stood up. 'Yes. I gather I have to come in.'

She'd met his secretary, the woman who had had the initiative to check his e-mails, and she now discovered she was extremely efficient. She flipped open a diary, ran her finger down the days and turned to her. 'Tuesday to Wednesday—all right?'

'That's tomorrow.'

'Yes. Is that too short notice? I think he wants to get the results quickly.'

She shook her head. 'That'll do. I've got my things with me, I was going to stay with a friend.'

'In which case, could you make it today? He thought you probably couldn't, but I think he'd prefer it if you were able to.'

'Fine. If I could just use the phone to ring my parents and my friend, I can stay now.'

'Good. Here, use Jed's phone. I'll come and get you in a minute—I'll just notify the ward.'

His office was functional but very pleasant. She wondered what kind of research assistant he was, and how he came to have his own secretary. Perhaps his research into malaria was a little more organised and well orchestrated than she'd realised…

The tests were apparently endless, involving copious blood-letting and samples from every conceivable part of her. They were sent off to labs, and her heart and brain waves were all charted and inspected and reported as normal.

On the Tuesday her parents arrived to visit her and wait with her for the results, and although some might not be available for a few more days they were going to take her home.

Jed didn't seem to be around much during all of this, to her disappointment. She'd missed him so badly in the past two weeks she couldn't imagine how she would get through the rest of her life, but she'd thought at least she'd see him while she was in the same hospital.

He'd popped in the evening before and told her that they'd agreed a new site for the power station and it was now going ahead with everyone's blessing. 'Johannis has apparently been forgiven for his indiscretion because of his part in the negotiations, and he's been allowed back into the tribe, so I'm going back there in a few days to try and find out what I can from the *dukun*. Anyway, someone has to take out Hari's stitches.'

'They will have dissolved by now.'

He grinned. 'Maybe. I ought to check, though.'

'You're a sucker for punishment,' she said with a smile. 'I knew you'd go back. Give Hari my love when you see her.'

'I will. You get some rest now, you're looking peaky.'

And he'd left her alone to consider the fact that he was leaving the country shortly for heaven knew how long. It was silly to feel so bereft. He'd never promised her anything, except, of course, in the throes of malaria, and she could hardly hold him to those extravagant words.

She'd slept fitfully in the strange bed, and now she was up and dressed, sitting on the edge of the bed talking to her parents about the tests and waiting. Would she see him today?

The Nigerian doctor who'd been dealing with her came in and smiled at her and her parents. 'Well, we've got all the results back that we need,' he told them cheerfully. 'There's nothing to worry about, you'll be pleased to know—'

The door opened and Jed came in, wearing a white coat and looking for the first time like a real doctor.

'Ah, Professor,' Dr Mgabe said.

Professor?

Jed? A professor?

'I was just telling your patient that we have all the results now and there's nothing wrong with her at all. In fact, she's a very fit and healthy woman. She is simply pregnant.'

'What?' Gabby took a deep, steadying breath and looked at Jed, hope flaring in her heart. 'What?' she said again.

'You're having a baby, my dear—nothing more complicated than that.'

Jed looked stunned. He stared at her as if he'd seen a ghost, and then with what looked like a huge effort he sucked in a breath and let it out again. 'Well—that's good, I suppose. Nothing nasty. Fine. Right. Well, ah— I suppose this is it. Um—take care. I'll send you a post-card.'

And he turned on his heel and walked out.

'Well, that's it, you can go home just as soon as you're ready,' Dr Mgabe told her with a smile, and he followed Jed out.

'Darling?' Mrs Andrews said softly.

Gabby stood up on wooden legs. 'We'd better go, then. Um—I've got a case—'

'I'll pack it,' her father said quietly. 'Meg, I think she needs a hug.'

'No!' She moved away, holding herself rigid with enormous effort. 'No. Don't touch me. I'm all right. Just get me out of here.'

They did. They put her in the car and drove her home to their farm in Gloucestershire, and her mother made her a drink and put her to bed, and then went out, clicking the door softly shut behind her.

Then and only then did she allow herself to cry...

CHAPTER TEN

JED pulled up at the end of the drive and sat for a moment, looking at the house. Big, built of stone, it looked
a real family home—the sort of place you could retreat
to, where your family would close ranks around you.

He switched off the ignition and picked up his mobile
phone, keying in her number. A woman answered,
sounding like her and yet not.

Her mother?

'Mrs Andrews?' he hazarded a guess.

'Yes.'

'Could I speak to Gabrielle, please? It's Jed Daniels.'

There was silence for a second, and then her mother
said, 'She's not here.'

'Oh.' Disappointment and relief fought inside him,
and disappointment won. 'Can you tell me when she'll
be back?'

'Well, she is here and she's not. She's in one of the
cottages, but she's not on the phone yet. Can I get her
to call you? I'll see her later.'

'Um…' He hesitated, then said, 'I'm at the end of the
drive. Perhaps I could just call and see her.'

There was another pause. 'Well, I suppose so—come
up to the house. I'll give you directions.'

He pulled up outside the front of the house and Mrs
Andrews came down the steps to meet him, wiping her
hands on an apron. She'd been baking, he imagined from
the smudge of flour on her nose. It made her look more
approachable.

She stopped at the bottom of the steps and he got out

of the car. They stood there for a moment, weighing each other up.

'The cottage is over there,' she said without preamble, pointing across a field. 'You have to go back down the drive and take the track off it. She's probably in the garden—go round the back.'

'Are you sure she won't mind?' he asked, suddenly doubtful about the wisdom of this.

'No, I'm not sure of anything except I think it's about high time you came to see her. She's had a lot to cope with, and she could have done with some support.'

He ducked his head. 'I'm sorry. I've been away again—back to Pulau Panjang. It's not very easy to pop in from there.'

'Well, you're here now, that's all that matters. Just don't upset her.'

He scuffed the ground, feeling like a teenager. 'Is she OK? The baby?'

'They're fine. She'll tell you.'

He nodded and got back into the car, turned it around and headed down the drive. She was still standing there on the steps, watching him.

He found the grassy track, followed it and pulled up outside a pretty little cottage, with flowers blooming in colourful disarray all around the front. He cut the engine and got out, closing the door softly.

Crazy. His palms were sweating, his legs felt like jelly and his mouth was dry. For two pins he'd have got back in the car and driven away, but that wouldn't help at all. He retrieved the parcel from the back seat and knocked on the front door, but there was no reply. Taking Gabby's mother's advice, he went round the back to the garden.

She was there, standing with her back to him bending over a rose, and he stood there riveted to the spot and just drank in the sight of her. She was wearing the sarong Jamal's daughter had given her, and it looked soft and faded and well loved.

He thought she was probably naked under it, and desire raked through him just as she straightened and turned, and he realised with a shock that she was still pregnant.

Pain stabbed him, taking his breath, and then common sense resurrected itself and he dragged in a lungful of sultry summer air.

'Hello, Gabrielle,' he said softly, and she looked up and froze.

'Jed,' she whispered, the roses she had just picked falling unheeded at her feet.

He bent and picked them up, handing them back to her with trembling fingers. 'How are you?' he asked gruffly, and cleared his throat. God, how could he behave normally when all he wanted to do was drag her into his arms and tell her how much he'd missed her?

'All right. What brings you here? Run out of research material?'

She turned and went back towards the cottage and he followed her into the kitchen. 'I've finished. I've brought some photos to show you—of Hari and the babies, and all the others.'

'How are they?' she asked with a smile.

'Fine. Gorgeous. You're a legend over there, you know—the woman that bullied the *dukun*.'

She laughed. 'Someone had to force the issue. She was dying.'

'Yes.' He put down the bag he'd brought from the car and propped his hips against the worktop, looking at her. She'd filled the kettle and was getting mugs down out of a cupboard.

'Tea?' she asked.

'Anything.' He looked at her swollen body and felt a great surge of protective instinct. 'I thought you would have had the baby by now,' he said, struggling for small talk.

'No—it's not due for another fortnight.'

'Oh.' Funny, he'd thought— Oh, well, never mind. He hadn't been thinking clearly then. 'You—um—you haven't got married?'

'Married?' She dropped two teabags into a pot and looked at him. 'No, I haven't got married. Should I have done?'

'I thought—maybe the father—?'

Something happened in her eyes, something sad that made him want to take her in his arms. Anger flickered inside him at the unknown man.

'The father isn't interested,' she told him bluntly.

'Oh.' How could he not be? How could any man turn away from her and her child? Hell, he couldn't, and it was nothing to do with him!

'Is there—um—you know—any—ah—other man—?'

She eyed him straight. 'No, Jed, there's no other man.' She turned to pour the water on the teabags. 'No one at all.'

Hope dawned in him, but he suppressed it. She wasn't interested. She'd said so, at the top of her voice on Monkey Skull Island.

His next words came unbidden, without permission.

'I've missed you.'

She looked up at him sharply and looked away. 'Have you?'

'Yes. Every day.' He looked down at his fingers. 'Funny, I never knew you were missing from my life until I met you, and since then nothing's felt the same.' He gave a short laugh. 'Crazy, isn't it?'

'Jed, what are you trying to say?'

He looked up at her but he couldn't read her expression. She was good at hiding her feelings—all those years of nursing, he supposed.

'I don't know. Only that I want you in my life, and—well, I know it's different these days and loads of women have babies on their own, but if you didn't want to—well, I'm around—'

'Are you offering to be there for the birth?' she asked somewhat incredulously.

'Well—not exactly. Yes, if you wanted me to, but I had in mind perhaps the next fifty-odd years, really.' He swallowed. Hell, this was difficult. He'd never proposed to anyone in his life and he was floundering like a beached whale. 'I think I'm asking you to marry me.'

She gave him a suspicious look. 'Have you got malaria?'

He laughed, a little nervously. 'No, of course not.'

'I just wondered. So, why would you want to marry me?'

He stared at her. 'Because I love you.' He waved a hand. 'I know you don't necessarily love me, but I promise I'd look after you and the baby, and treat it as if it were my own, and perhaps later we could have others, if you wanted…' He trailed to a halt and stopped.

'Forget it. I can see it doesn't appeal. I'm sorry.'

'Oh, you're wrong,' she said softly. 'It does appeal—it appeals enormously. I just wondered what changed your mind about me.'

His brows pleated together. 'Changed my mind? When?'

'When we came home. Well, before, really, but you were very preoccupied and you'd been ill so I could forgive that, but when that doctor told us all I was pregnant you just said goodbye and went, in seconds. I thought you hated me.'

'Hated you? I loved you. I was going to get you better and finish my research, and when everything had settled down again I was going to ask you out, but then I realised that there must be someone else and I felt a fool. You'd told me, after all, that there wasn't anyone so it came as a bit of a surprise.'

'There wasn't.'

'So when—if the baby's not due yet,' he said, going back to the thing that was nagging in his mind, 'when did you—? Was it after we came back?'

She shook her head.

'So there had been someone.'

'No. It happened in Indonesia. I met someone and fell in love.'

Pain stabbed him again. 'Oh. I see.' He cast his mind back through the time they'd been together, and drew a blank. 'Who?' he asked. 'Not your cousin, surely, or Derek?'

'No.'

'Bill.' He said it flatly, as if it left a bad taste in his mouth.

'No. Not Bill.'

'One of the Indonesians, then? Luther?'

She shook her head. 'You've forgotten someone, Jed.'

He thought of the young man who'd lusted after her. He'd seen them coming out of the jungle, laughing, the day before they'd been released. Had they started a relationship while he'd had malaria?

'Who?' he asked hoarsely.

'You.'

The word didn't register for a moment, and when it did he felt the blood drain from his face. 'Me?' he said soundlessly.

His eyes dropped to the swollen abdomen under the sarong, and a great lump formed in his throat. 'Me?' he said again, and emotion rose up and choked him. He turned his head, fighting the foolish tears that prickled at the back of his eyes.

'But—I'd remember—'

'You had malaria.'

He looked back at her, seeing the truth in her eyes, and the tears spilt over and splashed onto his shirt. 'Why didn't you tell me—'

He scrubbed a hand through his hair and fought for composure. 'Damn it, all this time you've needed me here to look after you and you didn't tell me—Gabby, I missed you so much—'

His voice cracked and he scooped her into his arms, hugging her fiercely to his chest. He could hardly reach her for the baby between them so he hooked out a chair with his foot and sat down, pulling her onto his lap and burying his face in her soft breasts.

Wave after wave of emotion washed him—relief, shock, love, hope for the future—swamping him so that he could hardly think.

'I ought to be able to remember,' he said eventually. 'Imagine doing something so fundamental as making a baby and not remembering it afterwards.'

'You were very ill. It was right at the beginning—straight after we operated on Hari. We stayed up till dawn, then went to bed and—well, it just happened.'

He tipped his head back and looked into her eyes, striving for a memory. 'Was it all right? I didn't hurt you or anything? If I was delirious I might not have been very communicative—'

'You were wonderful,' she said softly and, bending her head, she kissed him, then slipped off his lap and took his hand. 'Come to bed,' she murmured.

'But—the baby—'

'The baby's fine. I'm not. I've missed you so much.'

Her façade crumbled and tears welled in her eyes. 'I thought you didn't love me. I thought you just wanted me out of your life. I thought you thought the baby was just the excuse you needed—'

'Sounds like you thought much too much,' he said gently.

'I've had nothing else to do for eight months.'

'Oh, darling.' He wrapped an arm round her shoulders and squeezed. 'Where's the bedroom?'

'Here.' She pushed open a door and they went into a pretty, airy little room with white bedlinen and soft, floaty curtains.

It made him smile, but only until they reached the bed. Then she freed the top of the sarong and it fell to her feet, and his breath jammed in his throat.

Reaching out trembling hands, he laid them on the warm skin of her abdomen, over his child, and tears welled in his eyes again. 'Oh, angel,' he murmured brokenly. 'I love you so much.'

She undid his shirt buttons and pushed the garment off his shoulders, then freed his belt. His fingers came back to life and he stripped off the rest of his things and lifted her, setting her down gently in the middle of the bed.

'Are you sure this is all right?' he asked.

'It's fine. It might be a little complicated, but it's possible, I'm told.'

He laughed softly, then sobered. 'Just stop me if I hurt you or it's uncomfortable.'

She didn't stop him. She just held him, and cried out, and he lost himself in the magic of her body. She was right, it was complicated, but it was beautiful to hold her, to feel the child kick against his abdomen and know that it was his.

It reduced him to tears again but it didn't matter because Gabby was crying too, and he just shifted so he was lying on his back and she was on her side, one leg draped over him, and he held her tight until their hearts slowed and their tears dried on their cheeks.

'OK?' he asked her, and she nodded, her hair like a halo around her head. He stroked it, loving the feel of it—the feel of her.

'I feel as if I've come home,' he said softly, and she lifted her head and stared at him.

'You said that before.'

'Did I? I've never felt like this with anyone else. It just seems so right to be here with you like this.'

'Good. It needs to because it's where you're going to be for a jolly long time, Professor Daniels.'

He felt his skin colour. 'Don't call me that, I hate it.'

She laughed softly at him. 'I thought they were joking at first. I didn't realise you were a real professor. It was only then that I realised your research might actually be valid and genuine, you know.'

'I kept telling you.'

'I know. I just didn't listen. I'm sorry.'

He hugged her. 'Don't be. It's all right—now.' He shifted his head so he could see her. 'Perhaps you'd want to tell your mother you're OK. She was a bit wary about me.'

'Of course she was. She knows you're the father of her grandchild, and she thinks you dumped me.'

'I had malaria! Anyway, you didn't seem to want to know. I didn't want to push myself in where I wasn't welcome.'

'I'll speak to her. I suppose she'll want to start planning a wedding. It'll have to be September or October now, of course—'

'What?' He sat bolt upright and looked down at her. 'Sorry, darling. I'm an old-fashioned man. This baby's going to be born in wedlock if it kills me—just resign yourself to getting married in about three days. If you want a big palaver with lots of relatives, we can have a church wedding later with all the pomp and circumstance you could dream of, but we're getting married just as soon as the registrar can do the paperwork.'

To his relief she smiled. 'Good. I agree. I just didn't want to hassle you. I don't want a big wedding at all, just a few friends and family.'

Women had a gift for hyperbole, Jed discovered three days later. 'A few friends and family' turned out to be over fifty people, a hastily erected marquee and a catered finger buffet.

'Thank God you didn't want a big wedding,' he said laughingly to her as they stood side by side, preparing to cut the cake.

'What?' She looked round and chuckled. 'This is Mum. I had nothing to do with it. I was busy trying to find a dress that didn't look like another marquee or a set of net curtains in a stiff breeze.'

He hugged her, laughing till the tears ran down his face, and then held her at arm's length. 'You look beautiful,' he assured her proudly. 'I can't wait to get you away from here.'

'Where are we going?' she asked for the hundredth time, but he just smiled and refused to tell her. 'You'll find out,' he promised. 'Now, smile for the birdie, the cameraman wants our attention again.'

'Open your eyes.'

She looked around at the elegant façade of the familiar and very exclusive hotel and smiled. 'It's lovely. It's always been one of my dreams to come here. How on earth did you find a hotel like this so close to home with a vacancy at this time of year?'

He grinned, obviously pleased with himself. 'Easy. Friends run it. They were able to jiggle it, but only for three days.' He slid out from behind the wheel and came round to open her door. 'We've got a little private lodge on the edge of the woods, with its own hot tub and maid service and telephone, and we can either have room service or eat in the main building, depending on what you want.'

'Room service,' she said instantly, making him laugh. She grinned. 'I do. I don't want to get up at all the whole time we're here. I can't think of anything more wonderful than lying about in a hot tub and relaxing. They can send the food over and you can feed me.'

'You'll come out like a prune.'

'I don't care. I just want to be pampered.'

His eyes darkened. 'Good, because I have lots of that in mind for you.'

'I said pampered, not seduced.'

He laughed again and helped her out of the car, then, offering her his arm, he led her inside. It was cool, the interior lofty and quietly elegant. It must be costing a fortune, she thought, and then put it out of her mind. It was once in their lives, and she was going to love every second of it.

'Mr and Mrs Daniels,' he said to the girl behind the reception desk.

'Ah, yes. You've got the honeymoon lodge. I'll get Nick to take you over.'

A young man in livery appeared and showed them down a tree-lined path to the little lodge, nestling in the trees at the edge of the park. 'I'll bring your car round with your luggage, sir,' he said to Jed, and disappeared, leaving them to look round.

Gabby sat on the comfy sofa and bounced. 'Oh, it's lovely—soft but firm. I wonder what the bed's like?'

He opened a door and whistled, and she got up and went and peered round him. 'Oh, my. A four-poster.'

'And French doors out to the private patio with hot tub.'

'Mmm.'

'Just hang on. He'll be back in a minute with the car and you can do what you like.'

Jed's BMW slid to a halt outside, and Nick came in with the keys and the cases. 'There's champagne on ice on the house, and the hot tub's full and ready to go. Will there be anything else, sir?' he asked.

'No, thank you, that's fine.' He handed him a folded note, took the keys and turned to Gabby. 'Right, my darling, about this tub.'

They played in it for ages, sipping champagne, then moved to the bed and made love slowly and languorously. Room service brought a light supper of cold smoked salmon and salad with fresh crusty rolls, and they curled up on the sofa and watched a soppy old film on the television, before going to bed early.

The next day was more of the same, and by the evening she was feeling totally relaxed.

The next day, though, she woke with dull backache. 'I thought the bed was a bit soft,' she said ruefully. 'That's the price you pay for comfort.'

'Turn over,' Jed ordered gently, and rubbed her back, then nibbled her neck.

She laughed and swatted him away. 'I'll have breakfast in the hot tub,' she told him, and slid her feet over the side of the bed and vanished into the bathroom. By the time she came out he'd uncovered the tub, called room service and their coffee and croissants were on the way.

He fed her in the tub, little bites of croissant with rich strawberry conserve, and trailed little nibbly kisses over her neck and throat as she swallowed.

She giggled and swatted him away again. 'Stop it, you're tickling me.'

'Sorry.' He put down the plate, took her into his arms and kissed her thoroughly. 'Is that better?'

Would she never tire of looking into those beautiful blue eyes?

'Much better,' she said with a smile.

His hand ran lightly over her abdomen and left a shivery trail in its wake. 'How can I be so pregnant and you still want me?' she asked, faintly amazed. 'Come to that, how can I still want you?'

His mouth quirked in a smile. 'We always did have something pretty explosive in the way of chemistry,' he reminded her. 'Hopefully, Mrs Daniels, we always will.'

She ran her finger over his jaw, feeling the stubble and remembering Pulau Panjang. 'Mmm, we did. Call me Mrs Daniels again, I like the sound of it.'

'Mrs Daniels. Mrs John Daniels.'

She swivelled her head. 'Why *are* you Jed and not John?'

'Because my father's John, and the alternative was Jack. I didn't fancy being called after a whiskey so I opted for my initials—John Edward Daniels. Simple.'

'It doesn't sound like a professor.'

He grimaced. 'I hate being a professor. It sounds so erudite and formal.'

'Or mad. I shall have to watch you as you grow older. Only five years to go and you're forty. Maybe you'll go off the rails then.'

'I thought, according to you, I already was.'

'Ah, but you had the good taste to marry me.'

He grinned. 'So I did.' He bent his head and blew the

bubbles away from the slope of her breasts, then trailed a finger across the pale skin. 'I don't suppose you want to finish this off in bed?' he asked softly.

She smiled and held out her hand, and he stood up and pulled her to her feet. As he did so she felt a massive tightening in her abdomen, a hugely powerful gathering of forces. Her eyes widened. 'Jed?'

'What is it?'

'I think we're going to have to put off finishing this for a while,' she said, struggling to breathe normally.

'What's wrong?'

The cramp eased and she smiled uncertainly at him. 'I think I'm in labour.'

His jaw dropped, and then he scooped her up and carried her through to the bedroom, setting her down gently on the bed. 'I'll call for a doctor.'

She laughed. 'You are a doctor. Just give me a minute and I'll get dressed and we can go to the hospital. It's only a few minutes away.'

He sat down, and a moment later she had another contraction, this one even more powerful. She tried to relax, but it was just too strong and she had to push—

'Aagh!'

Jed ran for the phone and called Reception, and told them to get a doctor to them quickly. Then he ran back.

'Just stay with me,' she panted. 'You can deliver it— you delivered Hari's by Caesarean section in candlelight with a kitchen knife and they all survived—I'm sure we'll be all right.'

He took her hands and held them tight. 'I love you,' he told her fervently. 'Just remember that when you end up hating me because I got you pregnant.'

She laughed. 'I won't hate you. I love you much too much—oh!'

Ten minutes later, when the door opened to admit the

doctor and the receptionist, Jed was sitting on the side of the bed with his daughter in his arms and a rather thunderstruck smile on his face.

'Good job I hurried,' the doctor said drily.

Gabby just smiled. She was glad the doctor had been too late because nothing on earth could compare with being alone with Jed and seeing his face when he lifted their baby in his hands...

EPILOGUE

HE LOOKED like something out of an old B-movie.

Faded khaki shirt and shorts, feet propped up on the veranda, hat tipped over his face, chair tilted onto its back legs—and he was in the shade. Gabby should have disliked him on sight.

His shirtsleeves were rolled up to expose deeply tanned and hair-strewn forearms, rippling with lean muscle, and long, rangy legs strewn with more of the same gold-tinged wiry hair stuck out of the bottoms of crumpled shorts. His feet were bare and bony, with strong, high arches and little tufts of hair on the toes. They were at her eye level as she approached the steps to the veranda, and a little imp inside her nearly tickled them.

She couldn't see his face because of the battered Panama hat tipped over his eyes, but his fingers were curled loosely around a long, tall glass of something that looked suspiciously like gin and tonic. The side of the glass was beaded with tiny droplets of water, and in the unrelenting tropical heat it drew her eyes like a magnet.

She reached for the glass.

'Don't even think about it.'

She blinked at the deep growl that emerged from under the hat. She thought she saw the gleam of an eye, but she wasn't sure. He hadn't moved so much as a single well-honed muscle.

'I'm thirsty.'

'So get your own. I need this, I've been busy.'

She poked her tongue out and his arm snaked out and grabbed her leg, hooking her closer. His hand slid up the inside of her thigh and curled possessively around it, his palm icy from the glass. 'Go and put on something with long sleeves, and some sensible shoes and trousers. I've got a surprise for you.'

Long sleeves? She'd been about to head for one of the resort's many pools. 'What about Bethany?'

'She's all ready. We're waiting for you.'

'You've got shorts on.'

'I'll change.'

The chair crashed to the floor and he unfolded himself, tipped back his hat and grinned at her, clearly pleased with himself.

'Where are we going?'

He tapped the side of his nose. 'Just go and change.'

She did, wondering what on earth he had in mind. A trip to Monkey Skull Island? Hardly a surprise—they'd done it once. The power-station site? Ditto.

It was too far to the village, the only other place she really wanted to go, and not even Jed was mad enough to have hired a helicopter.

He scooped Bethany out of her playpen and blew raspberries on her tummy while Gabby changed, then fastened her securely into the baby seat of Sue's and Derek's Jeep that mysteriously seemed to appear just around the corner in the shade.

They headed up the hill out of the resort, past Telok Panjang and the bungalows where Jon and Penny and their children and Sue and Derek and their little boy lived, and up towards the power station. The road was vastly improved—but she knew that, just as she knew that the grave trees and their surroundings were now protected by an enclosure, with a sign that explained what they were and asked people to treat the area with respect.

'This,' she said drily, 'is not a surprise. We've been here.'

He just smiled and turned into a clearing in front of the resited power station, and there, sitting on the ground, was a gleaming white helicopter with *Freeman* written on the side in red.

She looked at Jed. 'Where *are* we going?' she asked, excitement catching her for the first time. 'Tell me, dammit. We're going to the village, aren't we?'

He just grinned, lifted the baby out of her seat in the back and straightened her sun hat, then headed towards the helicopter.

'Hi, Bill. All ready?'

The developer grinned down at Gabby from the cockpit. 'Morning, Gabby. Happy anniversary.'

She climbed up beside him. 'Morning. Thank you. Jed, where are we going? Is it the village?'

But Bill fired up the engine and the rotors started to turn, drowning out his reply. The door slammed, they were strapped in and then they were off, swooping low over the canopy and following the line of the river up into the hills.

Suddenly a tiny clearing appeared ahead, not much more than a gap in the trees, and Bill was setting them down on the familiar patch of bare earth in the centre of the village.

He cut the engine and opened the door so that they could climb out, and as they stepped out into the sunshine the wide-eyed children started to seep back out of the fringe of trees.

'Gabby?'

She turned at the voice, and saw a graceful young woman with two gorgeous little children clutching her legs standing in the shade of a hut.

'Hari? It *is* you!' She ran towards her and hugged her,

tears clogging her throat. Then she crouched down and looked at the babies, twin boys with bright, curious eyes and chubby cheeks. 'They're beautiful,' she said softly, and had to swallow hard. They could so easily have died. She stroked their shoulders and they turned their heads away and clung to their mother, clearly overawed.

Gabby straightened with a smile, just as Hari patted her on the shoulder and looked towards Jed. He was coming towards them with the baby, and she took Bethany from him and handed her to Hari. The little one beamed, a great gap-toothed smile with sparkling blue eyes inherited from her father, and Hari laughed when the baby pulled her hair and explored her face with chubby little hands.

'There's somebody else to see you,' Jed said softly, and she turned just as the crowd parted and a wizened old man limped towards her.

'The *dukun*—oh, yes!' And, without any thought for cultural differences and social standing, she ran over to him and hugged him, then stood back and looked at him. 'Oh, I've wanted to see you so much,' she said, choked, and to her surprise Jed translated.

The old man's face lit up in a beaming smile that almost matched Bethany's, and he patted her shoulder and drew her into the shade under his hut. Jed, the chief and Bill followed, and the children were whisked away by the older girls and the women.

Hari brought them coffee and little cakes, and then sat and joined them, and Jed and Bill managed to act as translators. They talked about the resort, and the trees, and little Bethany, and the *dukun* took Gabby's hand in his and looked searchingly at her, then said something to Jed.

He looked puzzled, then something dawned in his

eyes. The *dukun* handed her a piece of wizened root, and she smiled in understanding and put it in her pocket.

Then it was time to go, and they bade their friends an emotional farewell. It was only later, after they were alone again and the baby was asleep, that Jed turned her in his arms.

'Was he right?'

She smiled. 'The old man? Of course.'

'We're having a boy.'

'Are we?'

'So he said. Do you need the ginger root?'

She patted her pocket. 'I'll keep it for insurance—just in case. Sue says it works better than the commercial variety. I wonder what Bethany will make of a little brother?'

Jed laughed. 'Mincemeat, if she's as bossy as you are with me. Poor lad, I feel sorry for him already.' He rested his forehead against hers. 'How about slipping out of those things and putting on something cool and refreshing?'

'Like what?'

'A *mandi*?'

She leant back in his arms and smiled. 'With you?'

He grinned wickedly. 'Of course. That's the best thing about this resort of Bill's—he's taken the best bits of everything and put them together. After we've played around in the water we can come back into the air-conditioned cabin and—well, play some more.'

She laughed softly. 'Again?'

'It is our wedding anniversary.'

'So what's your excuse every other day of the last year?'

He chuckled. 'How can it be my fault if you drive me crazy?'

She smiled and pulled off her clothes. 'Last one in the *mandi*'s a rotten egg,' she laughed over her shoulder, and ran...

Modern Romance™
...seduction and
passion guaranteed

Tender Romance™
...love affairs that
last a lifetime

Sensual Romance™
...sassy, sexy and
seductive

Blaze™
...sultry days and
steamy nights

Medical Romance™
...medical drama on
the pulse

Historical Romance™
...rich, vivid and
passionate

29 new titles every month.

*With all kinds of Romance for
every kind of mood...*

MILLS & BOON®

Makes any time special™

MAT4

Treat yourself this Mother's Day to the ultimate indulgence

3 brand new romance novels and a box of chocolates

= *only £7.99*

Available from 15th February

MIRANDA LEE

Secrets & Sins revealed

SEDUCED BY HER BODYGUARD AND STALKED BY A STRANGER...

Available from 15th March 2002

*Available at most branches of WH Smith,
Tesco, Martins, Borders, Eason, Sainsbury's
and most good paperback bookshops.*

0402/35/MB34

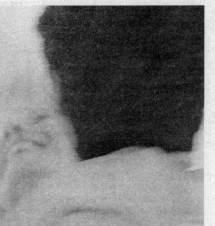

SANDRA MARTON

raising the stakes

When passion is a gamble...

Available from 19th April 2002

Available at most branches of WH Smith,
Tesco, Martins, Borders, Eason, Sainsbury's
and most good paperback bookshops.

0502/135/MB35